12/19

WITHDRAWN

D0088440

THE FIRST PROTECTOR

EARTH: FINAL CONFLICT
Books from Tor Books

The Arrival
by Fred Saberhagen

The First Protector
by James White

Requiem for Boone
by Debra Doyle and James D. Macdonald
(forthcoming)

GENE RODDENBERRY'S

EARTH
FINAL CONFLICT™

THE FIRST
PROTECTOR

JAMES WHITE

TOR®

A TOM DOHERTY ASSOCIATES BOOK
NEW YORK

GENE RODDENBERRY'S EARTH: FINAL CONFLICT—THE FIRST PROTECTOR

Copyright © 2000 The Norway Corp.

© 1999 Tribune Entertainment Company and Alliance Atlantis Communications Inc.

Edited by James Frenkel

A Tor Book
Published by Tom Doherty Associates, LLC
175 Fifth Avenue
New York, NY 10010

www.tor.com

Tor® is a registered trademark of Tom Doherty Associates, LLC.

Design by Lisa Pifher

ISBN 0-312-84890-0 (hc)
ISBN 0-312-87409-X (pbk)

First Edition: February 2000

Printed in the United States of America

0 9 8 7 6 5 4 3 2 1

THE FIRST PROTECTOR

ONE

Excerpt from the Journal and Report on Sapient Earth Peoples, Cultures and Levels of Technology by Investigator Ma'el on Day 112,537, in the local calendar reckoning 308 years since the Birth of the Christus, subsequent to my arrival . . .

T he barbarity and senseless cruelty that pervades this beautiful land is a disappointment and constant irritation to me. My sensors reveal two nearby sources of danger involving the use of the solid weapons that these people call swords. No physical harm can befall any Taelon on this world but my new servant, who has a lively if traumatized mind and for whom I have developed a feeling of sympathy over the past few years, will certainly die if I do not eliminate the threat by revealing the full extent of my advanced technology.

"Following the terrible mistake of Days 432 to 461 I have forbidden myself to interfere in the affairs of these Earth people or to display my powers to them other than with a few simple tricks. My ability to see future events on this planet has become uncertain. Unless there is a favorable combination of the laws of chance, the working of which these people call good luck, I fear that I shall lose my latest, most psychologically intriguing and affectionate servant. . . ."

On Declan's right the winter sun was dying a bloody, spectacular death behind the distant Mountains of Arne to the west and shedding a deep orange light that colored the heather and trees around him a deeper and more intense green, while the peak of Slieve Devilsipit to the northeast still remained in bright sunlight. In the near twilight to his right a full moon was rising in a clear sky that promised another night of biting frost. But Declan had no eyes for the beauties of the sunset, the moon, or the scenery around him because the stiffness of fatigue in his limbs, which would not be improved by the mists rising from the damp ground all around him, and the resounding flatulence of hunger in his belly was so loud at times that he thought surely his intended victims would hear it.

He had attention only for the two people in the driving seat of the tented wagon he had been following since it had left the settlement at Menagh three hours to the north.

One of them was a tall old man wrapped in a heavy cloak whose cowl had slipped briefly to reveal a shining and utterly hairless head. The other was a boy, shorter, thin, and still too young to have hair on his chin. Their features were shaded by the awning that sheltered them from the weather. They were probably itinerant tinkers with nothing of great value in their wheeled dwelling. Declan had never before killed an old man or a boy, but he was so cold and hungry and angry that if they did not give him food, no matter how little they had for themselves, he might do just that.

Trying to still the chattering of his teeth and angry with impatience, Declan pulled his ragged cloak more tightly about him and began gradually closing the distance to the wagon, but keeping among the trees and undergrowth that bordered the rutted track the tinkers were using. He would wait until they had stopped for the night, probably in the wooded region a few leagues ahead, and were preparing their evening meal before making his attack. He checked that his long-axe was moving freely in its shoulders harness and at his waist the gladius, which had failed to protect the life of its former Roman owner, was also easy in its scabbard.

The sunset had died to a red smudge in the sky behind him

and the trees ahead were showing black and silver rather than green in the strengthening light of the full moon when the wagon turned off the track into a small clearing and stopped. The old man climbed to the ground slowly while the boy jumped down and began unharnessing their horse. A few minutes later he tethered it under a tree and fetched blankets which he draped and fastened around its neck, back, and haunches to protect it from the night chill before shaking out some hay for it to eat. Obviously a considerate as well as a practical boy where horses were concerned, Declan thought, as the other began building a fire which the old man kindled with surprising speed.

Warmth and food was all he wanted, and Declan was telling himself again that there was no need for anyone to die, when suddenly he froze.

Voices. There were three, no four of them coming from the undergrowth midway between Declan's position and the tinkers' campfire. They were talking quietly, but his ears were good and he could hear every word they spoke. One voice sounded older, deep with authority and a hint of breathlessness that suggested that the speaker was large in girth. This speaker was making it plain that they, too, were waiting for the campfire to be fully alight so that the eyes of their victims would be too dazzled to see the attack out of the darkness until it was too late. Unlike Declan, the man was making it plain that he was greedy for loot rather than hungry for food because his orders were to kill the tinkers first and then plunder their possessions. The wagon and beast would fetch a good price, he said quietly, his voice beginning to wheeze with excitement, because only the rich or highborn could afford horses. From the talk they had heard in surrounding villages and farms, it seemed that these two tinkers were strange and secretive people who did not really need to ply their trade. It was said that their wagon might even be carrying a small hoard of silver or gold.

Some people had the minds of credulous children, Declan thought angrily, and these four had the minds of cruel, greedy, and uncaring children.

But his anger, he told himself truthfully, was due more to disappointment and the fear of unassuaged hunger than any strong feeling of sympathy for the tinkers. He did not want to have to share the available food with four other robbers, always supposing that they, with their greater strength in numbers, would agree to a sharing and not try to kill him outright for his impertinence and presumption in asking for a share. If he was to go on living through this night and perhaps the day or days that would follow with cold and hunger, Declan could see only one solution to his problem.

He left them talking quietly about all the wonderful, exciting, and depraved things they could do with the tinkers' hoard, but not quietly enough for them to be able to hear the sound of his light, swift footfalls as he turned and ran under the trees in a wide semicircle that would bring him out at the other side of the tinkers' camp.

Declan's approach to the two people at the cooking fire was hidden by the wagon, but he allowed his feet to fall heavily because his intention was to warn the tinkers of his approach rather than frighten and harm them. But by the time he appeared, the thin youth had heard him coming and had run back to the vehicle where he was trying to pull a sword from beneath the driving bench. The weapon was longer than the gladius at his waist, heavy and with its bronze edges blunted so that it was more of a club than a sword. Declan shook his head and strode quickly to the cloaked figure beside the fire.

"Old man," he said quickly, pointing across the fire toward the darkness under the trees, "listen carefully and do as I say. There is a band of four robbers out there who are going to attack you and the boy within the next few moments. Their purpose is to slay and rob you. Both of you must go to the wagon, place your backs against the lowest and most strongly built part so that they will not be able to take you from the rear while I guard against a frontal or flanking attack. . . . What are *you* doing, boy?"

The youth was running at him, his too-heavy sword upraised to strike. Declan stepped back quickly to avoid the wild, unbalanced swing while drawing the axe from its shoulder harness, and at the next swing he knocked the tip of the boy's sword to the ground. He used the flat of the axeblade so as not to nick the iron cutting edges because those he tried to keep as finely honed as a shaving knife.

"If you want to fight," he said in a tone that mixed exasperation and admiration at the other's bravery, "you should try to defend your . . ."

He had been about to say father or grandfather, but hesitated. At close quarters he could see that the old man's face was completely hairless and totally without expression. Not only was his skull as shining and featureless as an ocean-washed stone, there was not the slightest trace of hair around his mouth and chin or even where his lashes and eyebrows should have been. This, Declan thought, was a person who had suffered some strange malady or, perhaps, he had travelled from a far country where everyone looked like that. When compared with the thick, black hair and delicate and animated features of the boy, it was obvious that there was no family relationship.

". . . your master," he corrected himself, and went on, "Stand before him, guard him from attack and don't try to swing that pig-sticker around your head or try to slash with it. It's blunt, too heavy for you and it would swing you off balance and leave you open to a counterattack. The only advantage it has is its length. You are young and fast on your feet, so duck under your enemy's slash then step forward and stab with it, straight-armed. . . ."

"Like this?" said the boy, jabbing the point of the blade viciously at his chest. Surprised at the the other's strength, Declan danced backward out of range.

"Behave yourself, boy!" he said angrily. "Do you want me to take the flat of my hand to your skinny rump? I am not your enemy."

"So you pretend," said the boy, showing no sign of fear as he moved back, his sword still raised. "We are not gullible fools and we don't believe your generous offer of help. You wear the rags of a beggar but carry a large, bright long-axe. You, too, are a robber like the others, if there are any others."

Ignoring him, Declan turned to the old man and said, "Control this cheeky young cub's tongue, and both of you move back to the wagon, now, and do as I say. I've no time to waste on stupid arguing because . . ." He heard the quiet thump and swishing of feet in the undergrowth and, looking away from the fire to avoid losing his night vision, he swung around to face the sound before ending, ". . . they are here!"

There were four of them as he had guessed, advancing at a confident, unhurried run in close line abreast, their cloaks thrown back to free their arms for fighting. Two of them carried short swords and knives while another, who was armed with only a pikestaff, broke away without a word being spoken, to begin running in the direction of the wagon and the old man and boy. The fourth man, who was a little in front of the others and plainly their leader, was swinging an axe that was in length and weight the equal of Declan's own.

The other's belly, as he had suspected it would be from hearing the man's wheezing voice earlier, was larger than his chest but not by much, and the arms that bulged out of the short-sleeved tunic looked as if they had been grown on a tree. The hair and beard showed streaks of reddish-white in the firelight which also glittered on teeth that were bared in a wide, snarl of anticipation.

The big man was the principal danger and, if the other two made a simultaneous flanking attack, he would be unbeatable and Declan would not have to worry about feeling cold or hungry or anything else for much longer. This would have to be a short fight, he decided, because he would certainly lose a long one and it was plain that they were confident of being able to kill him. Somehow he had to try to make them overconfident so that they would not worry about attacking him one at a time so that he would be able to spring his surprise. He lowered his weapon and made a low, frightened, pleading sound, the cry of an arrant cow-ard who has no wish to do battle, then he turned and ran around the fire and toward the trees.

But not nearly as fast as he was able.

One of the his attackers stopped and gave a low, scornful laugh while the second one's run slowed to a walk. It was plain that they did not wish to spoil their leader's fun by sharing in the kill. Declan ran slowly and waited until the sound of the big man's pounding feet and his loud, labored breathing were close behind him, then he sprang his surprise. Instead of running faster he checked his pace and turned, swinging his axe transversely at chest level.

The other was a large man but slow he was not. His axe was already raised for a vertical blow that would have split his victim's head in two, but Declan was able to alter the direction of his own attack so as to knock the other's swinging blade down and away from his body while raising his own weapon to aim another blow. But Declan did not check his swing to defend himself as the other would have expected. Instead he pivoted on both feet, increased the speed of his swing, rotated full circle and, ignoring the blade coming down at him, jumped forward. He heard the thick leather of the other's tunic and underlying clothing rip apart and felt a slower pull against his wrists as a protruding tip of his axe met the stronger and softer resistance of flesh before pulling free. Frantically he dodged aside to avoid the other's two-handed vertical swing as the big man gave a high-pitched grunt.

The other's axeblade thudded harmlessly into the ground beside Declan, then he took one hand away from the handle to press it tightly against his middle. He backed away then, dragging the axe along the ground while blood that looked black in the firelight trickled between his fingers. Plainly the big man was no longer a threat, but the fight was not yet over. The heat of the nearby fire was warming his body, but hunger and his recent exertions were making him so weak that the axe felt like a heavy wooden log in his hands.

The man who had held back earlier to allow his leader to

slay Declan was running at him from one side while the other
one was rounding the fire to attack from the opposite flank. The
wagon and tinkers were out of sight behind him and he couldn't
risk looking back to see what the pikeman was doing to them.
He ran at the nearest of the two attackers swinging the axe
around his head but, he realized at once, not to good effect. The
other was able to fend off the blow with his shorter weapon,
duck forward and under and slash at his lower body with the
knife that he also carried. Frantically, Declan bent forward at the
waist so that the blade tore a long rent in his already-torn garments but not in him. He jumped back and swung around to see
what the other attacker was doing.

At first it seemed that the man was standing still at about ten
paces distant and doing nothing at all. Then he saw that the other
had dropped his short sword to the ground and was holding, not
a knife but a vicious looking gae bolga, a throwing weapon with
forward-angled spikes along both sides of its short blade behind
and below his waist, and with his arm stretched back to hurl it at
Declan. Without a stout shield to deflect the thrown blade, there
was only one defense possible and that was another attack.

He changed quickly to a one-handed grip on the thick shaft
of his axe and with a great effort raised the blade to the level of
the other's face. He began to run toward the man sideways so as
to present the thinnest possible target against the dark background of the trees but, he felt sure, awkwardly and far too
slowly. His hope, a truly desperate one, was that the sharp,
advancing point of his axehead would worry the other enough to
put him off his aim.

But it was something else that did that.

The clearing and surrounding trees were lit suddenly as if by
a flash of lightning that had come to ground close behind him.
So bright was the light that for a moment the flames of the
cooking fire were bleached out to show only the gray of char-
ring logs. He was so surprised that he scarcely felt the points of
the thrown gae bolga as they ripped across his cheek.

His two attackers backed away, blinking, their faces contorted by fear, and were turning and running for the trees when a sharp cry from behind him made Declan swing around.

The old man was holding something in his hands that shone brightly, although the light seemed to be fading from white to yellow as he watched. Beside him the boy was holding his sword at full extension as he had been instructed and the pikeman, his weapon already dropping to the ground, was backing away, clutching at his shoulder and whimpering with pain. The robber turned quickly and, still dazzled by the old man's strange light, he too stumbled toward the shelter of the trees. The battle, it seemed, was over and won.

Declan replaced his axe in its harness and tried to keep from staggering with weakness as he strode back to the wagon. Relief made his voice harsher than he had intended.

"Pleased I am to see that you fared well, old man," he said. "But you, boy, you should have aimed and stuck that pikeman in the chest or belly. He wanted to take your life, and you gave him another chance to do it someday. . . ."

"I do not take life," the boy interrupted, his voice almost strident with anger. "I am a healer."

"Even a stupid apprentice healer," said Declan scornfully, "must continue to live if he hopes to practice the high art."

"Enough," the boy replied, glaring up at him. "Your cheek is opened, the blood is flowing and the edges of the wound will need to be pulled together. I promise you, our ragged and uncouth guardian, that the work will be neater and you will feel less pain if you curb your unmannerly tongue."

TWO

The old man held up a hand for silence with a gesture that was graceful and almost fluid, then looked at Declan with large, soft eyes that were set in a face that bore no lines or wrinkles either of age or character. In a gentle voice that was low and clear like a woman's, he spoke for the first time.

"We owe you a great debt, young man," he said. "How may we repay it?"

Declan had expected to be stealing from the two of them rather than being offered a reward. He shivered and a sudden yawn stretched his jaw and caused more blood to trickle down his cheek. "You may pay me with warmth, and rest, and food."

The old man pointed to the fire. "Warm yourself," he said, "Light and heat are needed to mend your face, and to cook our food. In a short time you may eat your fill and later, before you leave us, as much more as you wish to carry."

"Thank you," he replied, grateful that he did not have to steal. "My name is Declan."

"And I am Ma'el," said the old man.

"There is no need," said the boy, "for one such as you to know my name."

"May-ell?" said Declan. He looked at the stiff, angry face of the boy for a moment, then went on, "A name can be a proud or a shameful thing. If you do not give it I will not know which."

"Ma'el," the old man corrected him gently, and quickly before the boy could respond he went on, "and this one calls himself Sean. My hand light is nigh to expiring and I must wait for it to renew its life. Let us move to the fire."

A few minutes later Declan was seated crosslegged and as close to the light and heat of the fire as he could bear while the boy busied himself with boiling a pan of water in which lay strips of torn cloth, a small, bone needle and what looked like a length of fine catgut already threaded onto it. An apprentice healer he might be, Declan thought, but the boy had been taught the habits of cleanliness. Ma'el brought two sharpened, divided branches from the wagon which he pushed into the ground on opposite sides of the fire, and within a few minutes there was a large wood fowl, already plucked and gutted, rotating on a spit between them. The smell of the roasting bird was causing his stomach to remind him noisily that it was empty. His mouth was still watering when the boy tipped the boiling water from the pan onto the ground to allow the needle and dressing to cool, then held the top of Declan's head and chin between his small hands to look closely at the torn cheek.

"The cuts have bled themselves clean," said the boy in a strangely mature and self-assured voice, glancing across briefly at Ma'el. "No poultices or ointments will be needed to draw dirt or poisons from the wound and slow the healing. Seven, maybe eight stitches will suffice. . . . You, hold still!"

Declan held his head still, teeth pressed tightly together and neck muscles tensed against the expected pain. But it was not as bad as he had expected. Although Sean was young and could not therefore be a fully tutored apprentice healer, the boy's hands were deft and sure and even gentle in their touch. Declan felt scarcely any pain at all and he began to relax. The work ended with a soft, sharp-smelling pad which, the boy said, contained herbs that would speed the healing, being applied to cover the closed wounds. A long strip of clean cloth was wound vertically around his head and chin to hold the covering firmly in position.

For the first time he was beginning to feel grateful and well-disposed towards young Sean, but the feeling lasted only until the boy spoke.

"You may eat now," Sean said, putting aside his materials. "Do not wolf the food or you will loosen the dressings and open the wound again. I'm presuming that an unmannerly ruffian like you is capable of eating in small mouthfuls?"

"Guard your own mouth, boy," said Declan sharply, "or I'll loosen a few of its teeth."

"Be at peace," said Ma'el, "and use your mouths for eating."

The old man's tone was chiding, gentle and soft but, Declan thought with a small shiver, it also carried within it the quality of quiet confidence and authority found only in a commander of men. With persons such as this the habit of command, and of obedience to those commands, was instinctive. Declan stopped speaking. So, apart from the few words needed during the carving and separation of the wood fowl, did the boy.

"Declan," said Ma'el, breaking a long silence, "we shall return to my wagon now. Sean takes his rest under the awning over the driving bench, which is wide and softly padded. He will bring you blankets so that you may sleep by the warmth of the dying fire. . . ."

"I shall not sleep," Declan broke in. "There is little danger of the robbers coming back this night. Sean wounded one and I cut another, very deeply I think, and they did not have the look of nor did they act like the bravest of men. The small chance of them returning troubles me not, and I feel sure that both of you can sleep in safety."

"You have a listening look, Declan," said Ma'el. "Is there something else that is troubling you?"

He nodded, and began, "There is a sound among the trees. . . ."

"I hear it, too," Sean broke in. "It's like the low, uneven

whining of a wounded animal. Perhaps it is the prey of a wolf or fox who escaped its attacker, but perhaps not with its life."

"It is not an animal," said Declan.

He climbed to his feet, pleased that the fire's warmth had taken the stiffness out of his limbs, and checked the free movement of the shortsword in its scabbard. He stepped around the fire and strode toward the trees, saying over his shoulder, "Stay here. I will look to it."

At once he heard the light sound of Sean's footsteps behind him. He turned to speak sharply to the boy only to find that Ma'el was following him as well. *One word from me*, he thought irritably, *and they do as they like.*

He followed the sound until they came to the base of a tall tree whose gnarled branches had been left blackened and leafless by a lightning strike so that bright moonlight shone down on the white face and figure of the leader of the robbers whose back was to the thick trunk. There was no sight or sound of his men who, as Declan had guessed they would, had deserted him. Thick, drying blood covered the sides of the other's mouth and darkened the gray streaks that had been in his beard, and the ground under and around him was also saturated by a dark and widening stain. His axe lay in the grass several paces away and both of his hands and forearms were pressed tightly against his middle. Declan stepped closer.

The man must have heard him because the moaning ceased. He opened his eyes, looked up at Declan and started to speak but coughed blood instead. A moment passed and he tried again.

"Please," he said. "End it."

Before Declan could reply, Sean moved forward, quickly went down on one knee beside the man, and said gently, "Ease your mind, I am a healer."

The boy lifted the man's arms and hands clear of his belly and placed them at his sides, then peeled back the blood-soaked clothing to bare the chest and stomach. It was a long, deep, transverse wound that gaped open to reveal the man's entrails, many of which had been severed and were sliding wetly onto the ground. There was a strong smell of excrement. Declan heard the boy's sharp intake of breath before he looked up at him and said angrily, "You made a bloody mess of this one."

Declan wanted to tell him that the man had tried to make a bloody mess of him, and had nearly succeeded, but he held his tongue because he knew that this was not the time for logical argument. Sean had turned away to look at Ma'el.

"You are a great wizard, master," he said in a pleading voice. "I have seen you work wonders, near miracles with your magic and charms. Can you . . . ?"

Sean's words trailed away into silence because Ma'el was shaking his head.

"Both of you withdraw to the wagon," Declan said firmly. "This will not be a pleasant sight for the eyes of the young or the old."

While their footfalls faded with distance he stared down at the leader of the robbers, a cruel and violent man laid low. His intention had been to slay the tinkers and Declan did not like him for that, but neither did he hate him enough to let the man suffer for hours or days of continuing agony from such a terrible belly wound that he could have no hope of surviving. Declan's eyes moved upward to the other's face as he grasped the hilt of his gladius in both hands with the point hovering above the man's body.

"Are you certain in your mind about this?" he said.

The man nodded slowly.

"Are there last words you would speak?" said Declan quietly.

The man opened his mouth, coughed blood again for a moment then shook his head. Declan raised his sword high and drove the sharp, broad point into the middle of the other's bared chest.

He caught up with the other two just before they reached the wagon. Ma'el's face was impassive as usual, Sean's showed anger, and neither of them spoke to him.

"If you carry a pick and shovel," said Declan, pointing at the wagon. "I would borrow them."

The old man climbed to the driving seat, ducked below the awning, and as he moved between the heavy curtain of animal skins behind it, a light much brighter than that of the moon shone briefly from inside the wagon. A moment later he emerged with the implements Declan had requested and with them two unequal lengths of yellow, planed wood. He gave Declan the pick and shovel, but before passing down the pieces of wood he held the shorter one transversely across the longer, closed his large, soft eyes for a moment and then handed them to him joined together as one single, crossed shape.

"How did you *do* that, master?" said Sean, excitedly asking the question that Declan was about to ask. "My family have always followed the Druidic teachings, but I've heard tell of that symbol. They say that it is reverenced and used on their grave markers by a religious sect that is gaining support in the Mediterranean nations and there are a few even in Hibernia. They call themselves the Followers of the Christus. Are you also a . . . ?"

"I am not . . ." Ma'el began gently.

"Nor I," Declan broke in, shaking the joined wood. "What means this?"

"They are the followers of a Jewish lawgiver and prophet," Sean replied in the voice of one who is anxious to impress others with his knowledge. "He was gentle and taught the ways of meekness and love and respect between all men." He pointed to the wooden cross in Declan's hand. "For teaching that dreadful heresy, three centuries ago the Romans nailed him to a tree."

". . . but I was interested in his teachings," Ma'el went on as if the others had not spoken, "because among other things he taught that there was a life after this one. I regretted his shameful and unjust death and that I was prevented from meeting and talking with him, but . . ."

"Do you think," said Declan in a disbelieving voice as he gestured with with the cross toward the trees, "that the leader of the robbers was one of these followers? Considering his violent and bloody plans for you, surely that is most unlikely?"

". . . the Christus preached of the existence of a supreme being who knew all things because he himself had made all things," Ma'el continued gently, "and who was all-powerful and, withal, was understanding and compassionate with all of his creatures. My feeling is that the dead robber may have need of such a benign and forgiving being."

Without another word Declan walked slowly toward the trees, the pick and shovel handles gripped in one hand and the wooden cross in the other. He was no longer feeling cold but twice he gave a small shiver of wonder.

The first time was when he took a very close look at the grave marker. The join between the vertical and and horizontal pieces was smooth and without a hairline crack showing, and it was work of a degree of excellence that would make a master carpenter proud. But Ma'el had used no tools, instead he had merely closed his eyes and pressed the two pieces of wood together. Many times Declan had watched so-called wizards and magicians practicing their craft at country markets or for the amusement of the highborn, where the onlookers had gasped or shouted with wonder at their tricks and tossed coins or bought the magic potions that were on sale afterward. But this simple joining of wood was a quieter and much more wondrous form of magic because he was holding it in his own hands and there was no trickery involved.

The second shiver was when he remembered the old man's words about the Christus who had died over three centuries ago. Ma'el had not said that the holy man had died before he was born or when he was too young to travel to meet him. Instead he had said that he regretted that something had prevented them from meeting and talking together as Ma'el had wanted. Surely that meant that old man and the Christus had been alive at the same time.

Just how old, Declan wondered, was this old man supposed to be?

When the work of burying the robber leader was done, he returned to the others to find that all was silent. Ma'el was inside the wagon and Sean was stretched along the driving bench and breathing evenly underneath his blankets. Declan laid down the pick and shovel silently and moved back to the dying fire.

For a long time he sat crosslegged with Ma'el's blankets draped around his shoulders, warm and tired and comfortable but with his mind too busy for any thought of sleep. It was not the thought of the robbers coming back that disturbed his mind; they were a craven bunch who would prefer to rob less danger-ous victims, but thoughts about the strange people he had met and saved: the old, old magician of power, and his young appren-tice healer and servant who seemed to know many more things than a boy of his age should be able to comprehend.

Declan did not know whether he stopped thinking about them before or after he fell asleep. But suddenly he was looking at the gray and white ashes of the dead fire, the sun was rising in a cloudless sky above the trees in whose branches birds were singing, and an ungentle foot was kicking him in the back.

"For someone who was supposed to remain wakeful all night," said Sean, looking down at him with an expression of dis-favor, "you make the most horrendous sounds while you are not sleeping."

THREE

Excerpt from Ma'el Report, Day 112,538 . . .

. . . It had gone much better than I thought it would, and my feeling of pleasure is only slightly diluted by the knowledge that my recent choice of inaction, apart from the use of a nonviolent hand light which helped save my servant's life and that of the new one if he chooses to join me. But it is becoming increasingly difficult, even for the most respected scientist member of the Synod, to remain unfeeling where the subjects of his report are concerned.

"Until my assignment to this planet I could not have believed that a species with so many handicaps could exist, much less continue to survive and develop a rudimentary technology as well as a wide range of variant social systems. They have no ability to view their own future, either as individuals or racial groups, unlike the gifted among the Taelon who can see hours or days or, in flashes, even years ahead if they themselves should be personally involved in the events to come. The people of Earth have knowledge only of the past and present while the future remains a dark curtain through which they stumble blindly from second to second, although a few of the more intelligent specimens are able to use the experience and information gathered from their past to predict, very inaccurately, their future.

"By Taelon standards they are pitifully underdeveloped both socially and scientifically, and a scientist of my standing must not become emotionally involved with specimens under examination.

"I allowed that to happen during the second century of my visit, and many specimens died needlessly and the continued survival of the whole species had been placed at risk until my peripheral experiment with mind-altering substances was corrected. I do not want to repeat such mistakes.

"But today's decision is a minor one, merely whether or not I should reveal my advanced technology behind my chart, and perhaps risk frightening both of them into flight, or to hide it from them by telling only a small part of the truth.

"Moral cowardice dictates that I choose the latter course. . . ."

As soon as Declan climbed to his feet he saw that another fire had been kindled several paces away, probably at Ma'el's insistence so that Sean's preparations for the morning meal would not interrupt his rest. A kindly and considerate old man, he thought as he sat down across from the two of them, and one he had decided that he would not willingly offend in either word or deed.

Ma'el pointed at a bowl and platters that were close to Declan's hand and then at the pot of gruel that was bubbling over the fire. In his gentle voice he asked, "You are hungry?"

"Always," said Declan, smiling.

He ladled hot gruel into his bowl and spooned it carefully into his mouth, feeling its heat warming his body right down to his toes. The platter contained a few pieces of heavy, pleasantly spiced bread which, despite their small size, seemed to fill him to such repletion that his belly had scarcely room for the large, yellow apple with the blush of pink on it that followed.

No apple should look and taste so fresh and crisp and juicy this late in the year, he knew, when most of the autumn fruit in store was expected to be either drying up or rotten, yet this one tasted as if it had been picked that morning. He finished it slowly and without speaking a word, thinking this was another small but very real piece of magic to add to the old man's strange hand light and his seamless wooden cross. Finally he gave a contented sigh and looked up at Ma'el.

"My thanks for your hospitality," he said. "Should I take my leave of you now?"

"Yes," said Sean firmly.

Ma'el ignored the boy and his large, soft eyes rested on Declan for a moment, then he said, "Without the food I promised you, do you wish to leave us now?"

It was Declan's turn to be silent as he remembered his original plan to rob this old man and boy of their food and possessions, and the strange change of mind that had caused him to defend them instead, and the even stranger things that had happened as a result of his doing that. He shook his head violently, but it was partly in an effort to still this confusion and shake some sense into his mind. Ma'el waited silently for him to speak.

"I would be grateful for the food you promised," he replied finally, "but it is not of great importance. I think it is knowledge that I now seek. Who are you, Ma'el? What are you?"

"Declan," said Ma'el gently, "if I was to give you the knowledge you seek, which I may never do, you would first have to earn my trust over many years as my servant and protector. . . ."

"*No!*" Sean broke in sharply. In a quieter voice the boy went on, "You already have a protector in me. I lack the height and thick-muscled arms and the bloody long-axe of this one, but I can advise you about the country and its often coarse and ill-tempered people and, with the help of your magic and my skills, keep you safe. You have no need of another. This one is of a kind with the people against whom you promised me protection. I have the feeling that he, too, is a robber, but one who changed his mind because he thought there would be more profit in defending than in attacking us. But he could change his mind again, and kill us at a time of his own choosing. Give him the promised food and send him hence!"

Declan remained silent. It would do him no good to make a

denial when the others would disbelieve every word he would
say, especially when the accusation was partly true.

"Peace, child," said Ma'el quietly. "Your recent past has
made you untrusting of others, and with good reason. But allow
me to judge the worth of this stranger as, you will remember, I
judged you when first we met. As well as a healer and trusted
advisor like yourself, I have need of a man of stature and formi-
dable aspect who has proficiency in the warlike arts and who will
discourage, hopefully before violence occurs, the cruder-natured
people we may chance to meet. There have been many such as
Declan who served me in my past and there may be more in my
future. Do you follow my reasoning, young Sean?"

The boy glared at Declan, but remained mute.

"As my protector," Ma'el went on, turning back to Declan,
"there would be times when you would be called on to face many
strange and unusual dangers, among people in even stranger
places far across the seas. Have you ever traveled beyond this
land and, if you have not, would you prefer not to do so?"

He could have asked if Declan was afraid to do so, but had
used the word "prefer" instead. This was a considerate man who
did not want to shame him in front of the boy into making a
hasty, braggart's reply that he might later regret.

"I have sailed thrice to the western isles of Scotia," he replied,
"once to the island kingdom of Man and once again to a coastal
fishing village in Gaul. High wind and the heaving waters make
me sick for a time, but I am not afraid of the sea. I swim
strongly."

Ma'el dipped his head. "Then I will offer you employment in
my service." he said. "But please think long and well before you
accept it."

Declan thought long and well while ignoring the restive
movements and disapproving looks of Sean. He had no fear of
unknown dangers in strange and far-off lands although, until he
met them face-to-face, he could not say in truth whether or not
he would feel afraid of them. He had heard many tales about
strange and terrible beasts, mostly from seafarers whose minds

had been addled by too much ale at the time, and had discounted them as tales of pure embroidery. He had no ties to hold him to Hibernia because his family had long since disowned him, but that was a painful part of his life that he did not like to think about for too long. Finally he looked straight at Ma'el and nodded.

"I accept," he said.

"But your face and manner tell me that you have questions," the old man said. "What are they?"

Declan nodded again and said, "Firstly, what reward can I expect for my long service to you . . . ?"

The boy made a loud, disgusted sound but did not speak.

". . . And you said that Sean and myself are not your first servants," he went on, ignoring the interruption. "My expectation is that this will be interesting, exciting but not particularly safe employment. What happened to your other servants?"

"The majority of them died in my service," Ma'el replied without hesitation. "Others accepted their reward in gold or other riches and some of them also died as a result of various excesses and lack of care about their personal safety. There were others more fortunate. One in particular, a giant of a man called Severus, was of low education but great good sense, wanted only enough to buy a farm in Tuscany where he later found happiness and died peacefully of old age among his large family and friends. Have you another question for me?"

Declan thought for a moment, then said, "No."

There was another silence while the boy Sean continued to regard him with a look of disfavor and the old man gazed into his eyes with no expression at all. It felt as if Ma'el was looking into his very mind. It was not a pleasant feeling and one that Declan wished to end as quickly as possible. Deliberately, he looked aside at the boy and spoke again.

"Now that we are both in your service," he said, "what dire and dangerous commissions would you have us do for you, and what will be the order of their doing?"

"The first one is not onerous," said Ma'el, his smooth, expressionless features looking as if they might be close to a smile. "You will sit in the sunshine of this pleasant morning and talk with me while we make and agree our future plans. Come closer and observe."

From a recess within his cloak Ma'el produced a thick square of material, no more than the size of the palm of his hand, that had the dull grey sheen of metal. He placed it on the ground beside him before tapping it sharply with his index finger. As they gathered around it the card opened up into four squares joined at their edges then continued to unfold it until it was an arm's length in width and depth. In a moment it lay flat and stiff on the ground as a picture without any marks of folding or wrinkling on it.

"I've never seen you do that spell before!" Sean burst out, pointing excitedly at the outlines of the picture it showed. "It is a chart, a map of Hibernia with the Isle of Man in the Celtic Sea and the coasts of Scotia, Cymri, and Gaul showing. But it is not well-drawn. The penmanship of the artist is careless, smeared, and lacking in detail. The outlines of the mountains and loughs are there, but the names of the cities and settlements have not been inked in. Their positions are represented only by small, gray smudges. A careless and untidy mapmaker did this."

"Perhaps it was the work of another apprentice," said Declan, lending weight to the last word while deliberately not looking at the boy.

Ma'el raised an admonishing finger at him. "Make your tongue behave itself, Declan, and both of you cease this constant skirmishing with words," he said, then to Sean, "You might consider instead that it is not a map but a picture, a painting in dull colors of a scene which the artist imagines is being viewed from a great height. The outlines are true, but are they clear enough for you to chart a course by them?"

"They are," Sean replied, flashing an angry look at Declan and immediately changing tack so that he was complimenting rather than criticizing the artist. Pointing, he went on, "Here, centered in the northern Kingdom of Dalriada, is plainly the outline of Lough Neagh. To the south and west is a smudge showing the position of Eman Macha and on the coast to the east is the Lough of BealFeirste, which our thick-tongued Saxon cousins call Armagh and Belfast. Further down the east coast are these very large smudges which appear blue rather than gray. They must be the heather-clad slopes of the great mountains in the Kingdom of Mourne. . . ."

Declan moved closer to the map and bent over it for a better view. He was surprised by the boy's breadth of knowledge which seemed to be greater than his own, even though he himself knew just enough to be sure that the other's information was accurate. He could have admired and even respected a boy who possessed such wide knowledge, if the other had not been so self-assured and arrogant in his display of it.

". . . Further down the east coast," Sean went on, ignoring the movement, "you can see the promontory of Howth, and below it the smudge that is the city of Baele Atha Cliath and its harbor, the Black Pool Dubh Linn. The next smudge of importance is Cork on the south coast, inland of the harbor of Cobh in the Kingdom of Munster. . . ."

"Do you know," Declan broke in quietly, "where we are now?"

Sean glared at him for a moment, then tapped a finger on the map. "Plainly our new protector grows impatient with the acquisition of knowledge that has naught to do with killing and the arts of war," he said. Deliberately omitting place names, he added, "We are here."

Declan looked at Ma'el. "And from here, where do we go?"

The old man pointed to the lower edge of the chart. "We will travel to Gaul," he replied quietly, "and thence to Rome. . . ."

"*Rome!*" Sean broke in, his voice going high and womanish with excitement. "The center of the world, at least of its imperial power and the commerce from countless lands. But such a journey will be fraught with many dangers, not just those offered by the robbers and Roman soldiery we will meet on the way, but from the natural obstacles of wide rivers and the high mountains that protect the Eternal City's northern approaches. Master, have you considered well the hazards of this journey?"

"We two are with you," said Declan quickly, looking at Sean and feeling excitement and wonder, but worst of all, if the boy's warning should be heeded by the old man, was the possibility of the greatest adventure of his life being denied him. He went on, "To show you that I do not speak idle promises, may I say that I myself have dreamed of climbing the icy heights of the mountains of Helvetica, and of walking the streets amid the palaces and amphitheaters of Imperial Rome itself and of . . ."

The old man, Declan had noticed long since, possessed the ability of gently ignoring interruptions rather than losing his temper and chiding the interrupters. He continued as though neither of them had spoken.

". . . From Rome," said Ma'el quietly, "we travel onward to Far Cathay."

FOUR

T he boy's mouth opened in astonishment but no words came out of it, and for several moments Declan's tongue and mind were in the same state of paralysis. Not wishing to give Sean the impression that their ultimate destination had in any way discomfited him, Declan cleared his throat noisily, looked at Ma'el and spoke as though the news was of no particular consequence.

"The first stage of the journey," he said quietly, "will be to reach Gaul. There are short and dangerous paths we can take to that destination, and other ways that are longer, less risky and, as well as traveling through the familiar lands of Hibernia itself, they will require shorter and less-dangerous sea voyages. Is the time taken for this journey an important consideration?"

Ma'el looked at him steadily for a moment, then made a gesture that could have signified yes or no.

"Even in Hibernia," Declan went on, "if you are a stranger journeying through unfamiliar territory, that alone could involve us in lengthy negotiations and the levying of taxes by the tuaths we encounter on the way. These will be small clan or family kingdoms for the most part, comprising a few towns and a score or two of fortified farms, but the smaller they are the greedier they will be to exact payment for freedom of passage. If you agree to these demands, and especially if you haggle over the payment to show that you are not overly rich, we should be allowed to pass in safety. Or you might prefer to hire and provision a force of local warriors, if they appear trustworthy, who will escort you on foot for as long as you can pay them."

Sean was staring at his sword and axe. He said softly, "Much about you is becoming clearer."

Declan ignored the gibe and went on, "If we go north through the mountain Kingdom of Mourne, where a few angry men can halt an army much less a tinker's wagon, and into the Kingdom of Dalriada we could arrange the short sea passage to Scotia, where the people are wild but well-disposed toward us. The navy of Dalriada is respected by the Norsemen and feared by all others including the ungainly vessels of Rome. They are captained and manned by dark-featured, dour but on the whole honest men of Ulster who drive hard bargains and honor them. From Scotia we would have to travel down the length of Roman Britain, through mountains, forests, and cities that are not known to me, and which may be governed by imperial representatives more greedy and rapacious than the worst of robbers, until we reach the south coast at the point nearest to Gaul where we can arrange for a second, shorter, and more risky sea crossing. The risks lie in us not knowing anything about the ships or seafarers who will be carrying us."

As Declan paused for a moment to draw breath, Sean said softly, "And you acted as though I was being long-winded."

For a moment the old man looked steadily at the boy, who averted his eyes, then he said, "Declan, please continue."

"There is the short and safer land journey to Dubh Linn," he went on, and then across the Celtic Sea to the coasts of Gwynedd or Ceredigion. The journey through mountainous Cymri and the southern reaches of Britain would be much shorter than travelling north to Dalriada, across to Scotia and then down to the South Britain coast."

"Much shorter," said the boy, his eyes on the map, "if we were hungering for suicides' graves."

Declan held his temper with an effort. "I am advising on possible journeys," he said, looking at Ma'el, "not advocating one that we should take."

Ma'el nodded slowly. "Are there other possibilities?"

"Only two," Declan replied, tracing a new path with his forefinger. "The first involves a short and fairly safe land journey followed by one by sea that is long and fraught with many dangers that are due to the elements rather than the designs of greedy men. It would involve traveling west to Drumshambo and northwest to Callooney and on to the harbor at Sligo in the Kingdom of Connaught, and there taking one of the Dalriada ships to our destination. . . ."

"We have come from there," the boy interrupted. "Ma'el was visiting the tomb marker of the Warrior Queen Maeve on Knocknarea, and the burial places of the Kings on the Hill above the Strand. He says that he gains much power from that legendary place."

"It would be unwise," Declan continued quickly before the boy could speak further, "to sail directly southward along the west coast, which is broken and rocky and has seen the death of many ships in the sudden winter gales that blow up. Instead we could go north and then eastward past the shores of Tirconnel and the peninsula of Innishowen, then south into the more sheltered Celtic Sea passing, or if the need arose, calling at BaelFeirste, the island Kingdom of Man, or Dubh Linn, for supplies before continuing southward to the shores of Gaul."

"You are ragged, uncouth, and unshaven," Sean broke in, suspicion is his voice. "But for a robber or a beggar or whatever you are, your knowledge of these matters worries me."

Ma'el held up a hand and, turning his eyes on the boy, he said, "Please."

". . . But if we were to bide our time," Declan went on, "and seek the counsel of local persons of substance, we might find a trustworthy captain who would have the knowledge to advise us further regarding the conditions we would encounter in Gaul. . . ."

"No!" the boy broke in again. To the old man he said, "Don't listen to, to this witless amadan. His brains must have been addled by an old head wound or his mind destroyed by drunkenness for him to suggest such a dangerous course. . . ."

"As I have already stated plainly," said Declan loudly, beginning to lose control of his anger, "these are suggestions only and not recommendations. Shall I go on?"

Tracing a new path with his forefinger and without waiting for the old man's reply, he continued in a quieter voice, "In the second possibility, the initial part of the journey would be safe, or as safe as it is possible to be in these disorderly times, but the second would be fraught with many dangers from both hostile elements and treacherous men. We would travel to Cashel, where sits the King of Leinster, skirting the Comeragh and Monavullagh Mountains, into the Kingdom of Munster and thence to the city of Cork and its harbor, Cobh. It is a large seaport that has commerce with many nations. There we might find a ship that would convey us on a longer sea journey to Gaul. I have no knowledge of the seaports and townships of Roman Gaul, but . . ."

Deliberately he did not complete the sentence.

The old man lowered his head to stare at the map for a long time, but it seemed to Declan that he was looking far beyond the shapes it displayed to places and times that he saw in his mind alone. Sean watched him closely, not speaking and seeming scarcely to breathe. Finally Ma'el looked up.

"I agree," he said gently, "that for this journey great care and patience must be exercised in the choice of a ship, and in the weighing of the characters of its captain and crew, and in taking all of the precautions that it is possible for us to foresee before the decision to embark is made. Protector Declan, I favor your last suggestion. We will travel to Cobh."

Ma'el rose slowly to his feet and returned to the wagon. Sean maintained an angry silence while he smothered the fire, replaced the cooking utensils, untethered the horse and harnessed it to the wagon. Several times Declan offered to help him with these tasks, but on each occasion he was either refused with discourteous words or ignored.

The sun had climbed high above the trees when they resumed their journey. Declan was seated on the wide driving bench beside the boy, all of whose attention was concentrated on guiding the wagon out of their clearing and onto the rutted forest track. Ma'el was inside the tented section, quiet and presumably resting. Declan decided that whether their journey together was to be long or short, he would rather that the boy would use civil words to him rather than continually nagging like an old shrew. He tried again.

"All directions are dangerous and it was not my decision that we take this one," he said, nodding his head toward the rear of the wagon, "it was our master's."

Sean did not reply. Declan summoned up patience and went on, "He has the manner of a kindly and considerate man, and I do not believe that he would willingly place a boy like you in danger. Before we reach Cork, I'm sure he would understand if you were unwilling to leave the land of your birth, perhaps forever, and asked to be released from his service."

The boy shook his head. "There is nothing left for me in this land except the darkest of memories," he said, then in a quiet but very firm voice, "I shall not leave him because I owe him too much."

It was Declan's turn to remain silent, for he had the feeling that Sean wanted to talk now and, with a little more patience on his part, the boy's answers would come without need of him asking the questions.

"When I was little more than a grown child . . ." he began, and broke off to glare for a moment at him as if expecting a derisive comment before going on, ". . . when I was a youth of less than twelve summers, he found me alone, cold, hungry, hunted by the hired assassins of my murdered family and in danger of losing my own life. He helped me, showed me how to hide from them in plain sight, cared for me and, in time, he gradually banished my fears of the day and the worse ones of night that constantly plagued my dreams, first by speaking gentle words to me and then by encouraging me to practice and improve on the healing skills taught to me by my father. He did much else besides.

"I will not leave him even if he should order me away."

Some of the reasons for Sean's unfriendliness and suspicion toward him had become plain, Declan thought, and he was even beginning to feel a certain admiration for the boy, especially for his loyalty toward the old man.

"If enemies are or were wanting you dead," Declan observed, "it is likely that Sean is not your true name."

The boy's lips pressed tightly together and Declan felt the old hostility return. He went on quickly, "I have no wish to know your family or clan name, lest in a moment's lack of thought I let it slip in the wrong company. But curiosity eats at my belly like a nest of worms, and there is one thing I would like to know if you are at liberty to divulge it. You say that the old man did much else for you. Did he, perchance, instruct you in the use of his spells and magical arts?"

"No," Sean replied, a shadow that might have been of disappointment passing briefly across his face. His manner began to thaw once more as he went on, "He always makes sure that I am warm and sheltered by day and night, and at times he spoke counseling words that were valuable beyond price . . ." he gave a small, backward jerk of his head, ". . . but I have never been allowed to see inside his wagon. I doubt if any living soul other than himself will ever do so."

Declan smiled. "Then I, too, shall not ask to see his secret lair," he said, "so that I, too, will be spared the embarrassment of his refusal. . . . Damn it to hell, this accursed wagon likes me not!"

Their horse was pulling them forward without complaint at a steady walking pace, its hooves thumping quietly into the patches of grass and soft earth that made up the uneven track they were following. But they had come on a stretch that was so deeply rutted that their thick, solid wheels sank almost to the axles before being pulled free. Several times Declan had to grip the edge of the driving bench with both hands while pressing one foot tightly against the handle of his axe, which he had laid on the timber floor within easy reach in case of a sudden attack, to avoid the weapon and himself being thrown sideways to the ground. Sean, who was half-standing and swaying easily from side to side as if on the deck of a sea-tossed ship, was not discomfited. When the track became even it was the boy who spoke first.

"Ma'el is a strange man," said Sean as if their conversation had not been interrupted, "very strange, subtle, and mysterious, but good. Declan, promise me that you won't lay plans against him."

"If he has you on his side," he replied, smiling, "I wouldn't dare."

Sean frowned, looking anxious and disappointed. Declan stopped smiling.

"For what my word is worth to you," he said seriously, "I swear that I will harm neither of you so long as I am in Ma'el's service. But I am vastly curious about him. How does such a mild-mannered person live and gain sustenance in this uncaring country? What protection other than ourselves does he have? Who are his patrons? What advantage does he provide for them?"

"I don't know," Sean replied. "At least, I don't know enough to speak with full knowledge and I prefer, therefore, to remain silent rather than indulge in conjecture. But enough about our master and myself, what of yourself? Are you tied to Hibernia by family, friends, or loved ones? Is Declan your true name?"

"It is one of my true names," he replied, and suddenly he felt himself wanting to speak to the boy as he had done to no other person in his memory, but caution put a brake on his tongue as he went on, "But it is the only name you will ever know. I will not speak the names of my family or clan because to learn those, if your curiosity was to persist and you sought further information about them, you would also learn of my shameful and at times unruly past."

When Sean's eyes were not on the horse or the track ahead they were on him. Obviously the boy was waiting for more.

"Unlike you." he went on, "my father is still alive. My mother died at my birthing, which may explain but not excuse my father's unalterable lack of affection for me, or for the hostility toward me of his second, and very comely wife and her children. In anger I disowned him with harsh words before he could disown me and . . . But enough, I begin to whine like a whipped cur."

Sean looked for a moment at his tattered cloak and disheveled aspect but did not speak, knowing that the further questions that were on the tip of his tongue would not be answered.

Declan climbed to his feet and stood on top of the driving bench, which he had done at regular intervals since they had set off that morning, to see if possible enemies were following or flanking or lying in wait ahead of them, but they seemed to have the sunlit winter countryside all to themselves. He resumed his seat and resolved to change the subject.

"Before we reach Cashel," he said, "I will ask Ma'el for a few coins of silver or gold. There is something I would like to do there."

"I have no doubt of it," said Sean angrily. A dark, disapproving cloud settled on his features. In the face of a look like that, Declan thought, it would be a waste of time and breath for him to try to explain further. They rode in silence for the remainder of the afternoon.

The sun was touching the treetops behind them before he spoke again. This time the subject was a safe one, Declan knew from observation, and one that was close to the boy's heart.

"That is a fine horse," he said, "very strong but no longer young. No danger threatens for as far as I can see. Don't you think it deserves a rest after pulling this heavy wagon for most of the day?"

They rode for several minutes in silence before Sean replied.

"The wagon is only as heavy," he said, "as Ma'el allows it to be."

FIVE

This day I made tentative plans for the visit to Rome and amused my mind by deploying the sensors so that I could overhear and witness my two servants trying not to fight with each other. . . ."

Cashel was a small, orderly, and usually busy town which, because it was winter and business was seasonably quiet, was hungry for any form of trade that happened to be passing by. Its buildings showed a few examples of pillared and decorated Roman stonework, but the majority of its places of business and dwellings were of native construction: rounded, wickerwork buildings reinforced with clay and with some of them additionally thatched against the elements. In spite of the earliness of the hour, from one of the larger houses came the sounds of drinking and loud conversations where the king's warriors were taking their off-duty ease. This, Declan knew, was another reason for the peacefulness of the town because it was a matter of honor that if any disorderliness was to occur, it would be they rather than unruly passing strangers who caused it.

It was midmorning when their wagon passed the great Rock

of Cashel and the royal castle at its top and entered the town itself. The mud of the streets was still solid from the previous night's heavy frost as they stopped in the empty market square. They did not put out an awning and trading stall, so any chance passerby would know that the tinkers were not there to do business and continue to pass them by. Ma'el tossed Declan a purse that was small but not particularly light, then wrapped himself tightly in his cloak and sat on the driving bench while Sean, who had been fighting a senseless war of words with Declan since the second day of their journey, saw to the comfort of the horse.

"Have you visited Cashel before now?" he said when the boy had finished his task. "Would you like to walk with me?"

"No, and no," Sean replied. "Ma'el has promised to give me instruction in the furtherance of my art among other things." He inclined his head toward the drinking house they had passed and in a sour voice added, "I will know where you are when the time comes to help you find your way back to us."

Declan looked up at Ma'el, who gently shook his head, then he turned and showed his anger by striding away.

The building, which he had already noticed while on their way to the market square, was set back a few paces from the road, solidly built with walls which had been washed in lime to make them almost white. A large wooden awning with thatch on top ran the full width of the building. It gave deep shelter to the entrance which was flanked on both sides with low benches and round-headed wall spikes displaying sheepskins, bolts of homespun cloth and leather harnesses shaped for man-carried weapons as well as the shoulders of beasts of burden. In a thicket-enclosed yard behind the house there was another, less well-kept building which comprised a stable, a tannery from which drifted the pungent smell of curing leather, and a lean-to washing house from whose partly curtained door smoke and steam were leaking out to cloud the winter air. It was an establishment, he decided, which could supply all of his present needs.

As he entered, Declan tried to make his gait and manner neither furtive like a beggar nor threatening as one come to kill and rob, although he well knew that the fresh, healing, and uncovered scar on his cheek would not be a reassuring sight to those inside.

There was a long workbench scattered with items of clothing dividing the room, with a bent, old man and, Declan presumed, his slightly younger wife behind it. The man was unrolling a bolt of homespun tweed and the woman had a needle in her hand and a garment of some kind spread across her knees. Both of them looked frightened and about to run for the door which he could see a short distance behind them.

Without speaking, Declan unbuckled his sword belt and the long-axe harness and leaned both the weapons and their scabbards against the nearest wall. He unfastened the torn and ragged cloak and let it fall to the floor before walking across to the bench where, without looking at it, let the purse Ma'el had given him fall onto it with a muffled clinking.

The old man did not look at the purse, either, but he appeared vastly relieved as he said, "How may I serve you, good sir?"

Declan smiled. "As you can see," he said, "in my travels I have fallen among thieves and robbers. My needs are for new apparel, a bath, and barbering."

For an instant the other's gaze rested on the weapons leaning against the wall, then he too smiled and said, "One wonders how many of the thieves and robbers are also fallen. My name is Padriag, good sir, and I can fill all of your needs, although I would respectfully suggest not in the order you have expressed. If the bathing and barbering were to be done first, we could use the time to ready your garments. What manner and quality of apparel is your pleasure?"

"I require a warm cloak and thick, woollen garments," Declan replied, seeing no good reason to give his own name, "that are suited to a long journey by sea and land. And high, tight boots, and oiled skins to keep the water out and the warmth in. If you have other advice that would be helpful in this matter, please speak it."

Slowly and with much protesting of age-stiffened joints, the old man ducked under the bench and came forward with measuring cords and a writing slate in his hands. The seamstress pushed aside her present work in readiness for this new commission that was plainly of greater urgency. While the other plied his cords and called out dimensions to his wife, Declan remained silent, not because of deliberate discourtesy but due to the fact that the man was so pleased and excited by the advent of this unexpected patron that he left no spaces between his words for anyone else to speak more than a single syllable.

It was more than likely, Declan thought, that the tailor would also be a barber. In the event it came as no surprise that he had guessed aright.

Padriag continued to talk as he trimmed the overgrown hair but fell silent in concentration while he was scraping the tufts from Declan's chin and face, particularly when he was working around the fresh and older scars. This furnished the opportunity for Declan to ask a few questions rather than politely refusing to answer the other's.

The place in Cashel in which to relax in convivial company was further down the street, the drinking house owned by his younger brother, Prontius, who would bid him a warm welcome if Padriag's name was mentioned. Declan had expected to spend time there collecting information that might be helpful on their journey. He had not concealed from the other that his destination was Cobh because, considering the type of clothing he had ordered, there was no other place he was likely to be going. But now it seemed that he would have to spend very little time in the brother's drinking house because the old tailor was a very knowledgeable man where the safest tracks and passes were concerned and when, if unforeseen circumstances should arise with people on the way, the mention of the name Padriag of Cashel might well ease matters.

"And now for your bathing," the old man went on when the barbering was complete. "We can offer a cleansing block of the soap we import from Gaul. There is cold, clear water taken from a stream or that which is warm, but more odorous, drawn from the tannery. . . ."

"Let it be warm and soapy," said Declan firmly. "The smell of tanning leather will not inconvenience me."

He was led out to a small bath house that had a stone-flagged floor and a sunken, man-sized tub tiled in closer-fitting stones. While it was filling, Padriag offered him a large, coarse towel and an apology.

"I will leave you to bathe without company or conversation," he said, "because I needs must help my wife with the cutting and stitching. Most of the garments we have in stock but a few will require alteration. This will be done while you soak yourself."

Declan nodded and the old man hurried away.

The trickle of heated water entering and leaving the bath had kept it comfortably warm and he was relaxed and half sleeping with all but his head and knees submerged for he knew not how long, when he heard approaching voices. Both were familiar, one for a longer time than the other. The old man entered closely followed by Sean.

"This boy was seeking you in the drinking house," said Padriag. "My brother sent him here. Is his company welcome?"

"Yes," said Declan, the water splashing about as he sat up quickly. "Sean, is aught amiss?"

"No," the boy replied, shaking his head. "I, we, wanted to know if you fared well, or needed help to . . ." He shook his head again, this time in perplexity. "This place is not where I expected to find you. And, and I see that you have many scars. The wounds are not neatly mended, at least not as neatly as I would have done the work. But ease your mind, Declan, we are not required back with any urgency."

"Good," he said, standing up. "The water is pleasantly warm and still fairly clean, and it will help ease the sores and stiffness of travel. Would you like to disrobe and . . . ?"

"No," said Sean with unnecessary loudness, turning away. In a quieter voice he added, "I shall await you outside."

Declan smiled at his departing back and to Padriag he said,

"The boy is serious in his study of the arts of healing according to the Druidic tradition which, I believe, includes bathing only in icy mountain pools while reciting interminable tribal lays, with a view to concentrating the mind."

Padriag gave a small shudder. "At my age," he said, "that would not be my preferred method of cleansing myself. You may remain soaking if you wish, the garments are not yet ready for you."

"My thanks," said Declan, dropping to his haunches and sliding under the water again. "But the boy. He, too, needs to be fitted for the same journey as mine, with warm garments, a cloak, high sea boots and oiled skins . . ." he hesitated, ". . . if there is enough to recompense you."

As he turned to leave, the old man waved a dismissive hand. "More than sufficient," he said. "But the boy is slight of build and looks not to be strong. Would smaller, less weighty weapons be required? My youngest brother is a smithy and armorer and would willingly . . ."

"No," Declan broke in. "You will remember that he studies the healing arts and for this reason, he tells me, has forsworn the use of all weapons."

Slowly the water grew cool and lost its warm temptation. Declan climbed out and toweled himself vigorously until it felt as if the coarse material was removing his skin as well as the moisture by the time he had finished. Padriag entered then carrying a tray containing a flagon of mulled wine and pieces of spiced bread still hot from the oven which he placed on a nearby bench with apologies for the delay, which would not now be of long duration, in providing Declan's clothing.

"The boy?" he asked.

"Your healer," said Padriag, inclining his head and giving a small smile, "was served as you have been, although the hot wine was scarcely touched, and has also been appareled as you directed. We talked of many things, of concerns for the future as well as the secret things that the young sometimes reveal to those who are older and, presumably, wiser, and which, you will understand, I shall not pass to you. But as a result of our talk and the healer's advice I have been given, I have taken the liberty of adding protective enhancements of my own which should prove useful for both of you in your future journeying together. . . ."

"Rest your mind, Padriag," Declan broke in, "I have no wish to pry into the small secrets of a boy. We appreciate your concern for us, but I have not the wherewithal to pay for enhancements."

". . . It is a helmet of thick, layered leather," Padriag went on, his old eyes shining with enthusiasm for this latest work of his mind and hands, "with a strong fore peak. Strips of thinly hammered metal give it strength without too much weight, and it is padded within for comfort and to deaden the force of heavy blows. The fore peak shelters the eyes, and a square of oiled cloth placed on the head before donning it will give protection to the face and neck in inclement weather or, should you travel to hotter climes, a square of lighter material will guard you against the burning of the sun."

He tried to speak again, but the old man gave a gentle smile that was not unlike Ma'el's and raised a hand. "Please," he said. "Consider the headpieces as my gift to you both. If they give useful service, you may want to mention the name of Padriag of Cashel among those you chance to meet."

By the angle of the sun shining into the street outside, Declan judged that six hours had passed before the work was done and he was again fully dressed and accoutred. His undergarments were warm and easy, the long leather tunic fell halfway to his knees, the boots were long and tightly fastened and the peaked helm of which Padriag was so proud sat firmly but with comfort on his head. His cloak, which was the rich, dark color of a ripened plum, was warm and long, but not so long that it would sweep the ground and muddy its hem. And the leather of his scabbard and the long-axe harness had been cleaned and oiled until they shone.

The work had been well done, he was greatly pleased and felt comfortable with it, and he told the old man warmly of his feelings. Then he made a small bow to Padriag's wife and seamstress, who looked up at him and smiled a secret smile. Declan wondered if she was remembering another young man and, perhaps, times and people and opportunities long past, and walked out to join the waiting Sean.

The boy stared at him for what seemed like a long time without speaking, then said, "Of a certainty, Declan, you do not now look like a beggar. In truth, you look very well."

He eyed the boy up and down. "We both look well," he said.

Sean gave a long sigh. "But now you will visit the drinking house," he said, "and I must wait close by to help you find your way back to the wagon?"

Declan drew out Ma'el's purse and shook it gently. From the light, quiet sound it seemed that there were very few coins remaining in it.

"Not this day," he replied. "The information and guidance I would have sought in the drinking house has already been given to me by Padriag. I have a mind to return Ma'el's purse to him while it is not quite empty, and surprise him."

The boy smiled for the first time in many days.

"Do that," he said, "and you will certainly surprise me."

SIX

On this exercise in foretelling I shall risk no gratuitous displays of Taelon technology, but shall use instead the combination of knowledge, past experience, and observation that these people refer to as common sense. . . ."

Without further let or hindrance they followed the southwestern path that took them past the Galty Mountains and under the frowning mass of Galty Mor toward Fermoy where they stopped to eat and sleep. This was because Ma'el, rather than proceeding due south to Cork, wished to make preparations for the coming voyage. He did not specify their nature other than to say that they involved materials and spells brought with him from his recent visit to the Hill above the Strand in distant Sligo.

Declan knew that hill well, having been taken there by his father. It was a beautiful if disquieting place whose gentle, seaward facing slopes bore the burial stones of the past Kings of Connaught, and far above them on the dark mountain of Knocknarea, the burial chamber of the famed and infamous warrior Queen Maeve herself. Thinking of those markers, their westward facing stone surfaces weathered by the Atlantic storms, Declan shivered without knowing why.

"What reason," he said to Ma'el, "had you, who are plainly not a native of this land, for visiting that place of our heroic dead?"

"As I have already said," the old man replied in his usual inscrutable fashion, "it is a place of power for me where I renew myself and my magic before setting off on any journey."

Declan looked at the other, thinking about his own unhappy and unruly past, then he shrugged angrily and said, "It is not a place where I shall ever lie."

Ma'el stared at him for a moment and seemed about to speak, then shook his head before returning to the wagon.

For much of the following night, while Sean slept on the canopied driving bench and Declan by the fire, a low, half-humming and half-singing sound came from inside the wagon, and there seemed to be more of the pale blue light than usual squeezing out between the folds of the heavy skins hiding its interior.

The streets and buildings of Cork were similar to those in Cashel, but writ large and with much more noise and movement of people, beasts of burden, and the drays and wagons they pulled. In spite of several days of cold, dry weather, there were so many comings and goings that the ground had no chance to remain frozen and it formed a deep, uneven layer of mud under their wheels. But the noises were of commerce rather than conflict because here the community had learned the lesson well that there was more profit and longlasting pleasure to be gained from honest, or more often dishonest, trading than in the more customary forms of robbery.

They drove to a market square that was but a short distance from the busy establishments of the shipwrights and boatbuilders, and the even busier drinking and gaming houses along the waterfront, which Ma'el said they would have to visit at a later time. This square was busy with the owners of many stalls and benches displaying their different wares. They paid the usual tithes to the two very large Cork City Gardai, who were on duty at the entrance to discourage the activities of thieves, pickpockets, and others whose crimes were not cloaked by commercial dealings, and were fortunate to find a place large enough to accommodate their wagon with space all around it.

Sean, who was no longer wearing his helmet, cloak, and sea boots because they were apparel not appropriate for a lowly servant boy, unharnessed the horse and led it to a nearby stable, which looked to be well-ordered and clean. There he made payment for its comfort, feeding, and safety from thieves before returning to assist Declan in setting up the old man's stall and displaying his amulets, potions, and the other arcane wares of a magician and fortuneteller against one side of the wagon.

Ma'el took up his position on a padded stool behind the stall, his cloak and cowl arranged so that his hairless features were in shadow, and gave quiet directions.

"Sean," he said. "You will move about among the other stalls seeking to buy the freshest food they have to offer. My tastes are simple with no strong preferences, so choose the varieties Declan and yourself prefer. While you have done that, move about in the crowd and speak of me in a loud but confidential voice, as if you were excited and imparting great secrets, about the accomplishments of the great magician and soothsayer who has come among them. You already know well what to do, so please do it once again.

"Declan," he went on, "your hearing is keen and your movements fast. You I would like to stand at a distance, but ready in case one of the visitors to my stall offers me violence. Make it appear that you are adjusting items of your equipment or some such ruse so that it will it seem that your attention is elsewhere. This is because some of the people who will come to me may wish to discuss matters that are confidential, and it would save them embarrassment if you did not appear to be listening."

"I understand," said Declan, turning to take up the position assigned. "I will view each of them briefly on their approach, in case one appears ready to make a sudden attack on you, otherwise

I shall listen only for what I judge to be threats against you, then act accordingly."

Without further speech, Ma'el began to arrange the collection of charms, small carvings, and strangely shaped roots on top of his bench.

The first to take an interest in the stall were two youths, clean and fresh of feature, who were a few inches taller than Sean, deeper-voiced and with the look of brothers born within a year of each other, or they might even have been twins. Their clothing was plain, well-fashioned, clean and bore no signs of the stains and wear of recent toil so it was likely, Declan thought, that it was rich parents who had toiled to provide the garments for them. They paused at a distance that they must have considered was beyond earshot to talk together when they were not trying to push each other forward or breaking off to giggle nervously like a pair of immature colleens.

"A good day to you, young men," said Ma'el in a voice just loud enough to carry the distance to them. "In what manner may I assist you?"

The one who seemed to be older, by a year or perhaps only a few moments, came closer with his brother a pace behind him.

"You are a wizard?" he said. "A purveyor of charms and potions that . . . that would cause others to change their feelings toward me?"

"Of course," said Ma'el, dipping his head. His next words were a statement rather than a question. "You desire of me a love potion."

The timid brother edged forward. "It, it must be a true love potion," he said in a nervous voice. "There must be enough for both of us to use. We will recompense you, but it must not be a phial of colored water."

Ma'el ignored the insult. "Let me comprehend your situation correctly," he said. "Have you each a single object of desire or . . ." he hesitated in what might have been mild disapproval, ". . . do both of you desire no specific object in particular?"

The brothers looked at each other for a moment, then the second one stammered, "We each . . . They are sisters, but they won't even . . ."

". . . talk to us . . ." the other joined in, "at least, not for more than a few moments. They say that we're unmannerly, impetuous gossoons who . . ."

"Good," Ma'el broke in. "Whenever possible I prefer not to cater to persons who want to shake a tree for whatever fruit chances to fall out. A potion that will bring you true love, that I can provide."

He had their complete attention as he went on, "But for the greatest efficacy it must be supported and sustained by your own actions and words, and the manner in which you converse when next you meet them. Remember that you are young men, not impatient and impetuous and unmannerly boys, and you should not act or speak as if you were. My words are for each of you. Be slow and gentle in your approach, listen rather than trying constantly to impress with a braggart's speech, and instead try to relate interesting rather than boastful things about yourself, and invite her to do the same about her family, friends, life, and future hopes. Above all be unselfish and patient but very persistent. The potion will make her see that you are a serious, responsible, and thoughtful young man who knows what he wants in life and who may already have found it and, if such be the case, one who will work with patience and consideration to achieve his goal. Follow these instructions with care and perseverance, young men, for this is how the potion of true love will work for you."

He reached down to a small wicker basket at his feet, opened it and withdrew two small flasks containing a deep purple liquid with traces of a black sediment at the bottom, which he shook vigorously before he placed them on top of his bench. The brothers stared at them, silent and serious. The first brother cleared his throat.

"The liquid is a strange color," he said. "In water will it show? Has it a taste? How and when should it be given to them?"

"Regrettably, the taste is truly vile, and lingering," Ma'el replied, "and it is not to be given to them. Instead, you will each take it as soon as is convenient before your next meeting with these young women. Place a few drops on your tongues and allow them to remain there for as long as possible without swallowing. The lingering taste will serve to remind you of my other words to you, which are an important and continuing part of the very powerful spell that accompanies this potion."

Ma'el gave a small nod to indicate that the consultation was over and watched as the first brother placed a coin on the bench before him. He continued to look at it without expression until the other had added three more coins before he gave another small nod, this time of dismissal.

As they were leaving, Sean returned carrying a large sack in each hand. He was still looking at their departing backs when Declan joined him to help put away the foodstuffs.

"Those two looked as if they were having deep and serious thoughts," he said. "I wonder what Ma'el told them. And Declan, you look angry. What has happened? What's wrong with you?"

Declan knew that he looked angry, but his anger was not directed at the old man or the boy or even at himself. It was simply that for the first time in many years he was thinking of what his life might have been like if his father had talked to him with the same sympathy and consideration and good sense as Ma'el had shown to those two young men, and he was angry because his only parent had never at any time done so. He shook his head.

"Nothing," he said, pulling his lips into something like a smile, "nothing but an unpleasing childhood memory."

When they had transferred the food into the wagon's exterior storage boxes and draped them in wet cloths to keep the contents fresh, Declan and the boy withdrew to the position and distance stipulated by Ma'el. There they kept watch on the stall while making a pretence of talking together. But a passing listener, if there had been one, would have heard no words pass between them because they had nothing to say to each other not, that was, until the fat, capless, red-haired man with a deeply freckled face appeared.

"I like not his manner," said Sean in a quiet voice. "He moves toward Ma'el, but his eyes twitch about among the other wagons and stalls."

"Nor do I," Declan agreed, reaching back and sliding out his axe. "Your eyes are sharp, boy. That cape he wears is too short to conceal a sword, but there could be knives or cudgels in his belt. Slowly and quietly, let us move closer."

"You're not going to *use* that frightful thing!" Sean protested, looking around him. "Not in the middle of a marketplace. Why is there never a Gardai about when you need one?"

Having already looked all around him and seen that nobody was paying him any attention, the red-haired man now had eyes only for Ma'el. He advanced toward the stall, smiling and loosening his cape. There was a moment's view of the knife and short-handled stone hammer that he carried.

"How may I serve you, good sir?" said Ma'el.

"I heard a boy in the crowd telling everyone that you were a great magician who can foretell the future," he said in a quiet but threatening voice, "and I want to foretell your future. The credulous men and women among us say that great magicians can turn stones into gold, but I have always doubted that. Instead I believe that they have a hoard of gold or silver coins hidden about their persons or possessions. You may serve me by yielding them up now. And your future, old man, if you do not give them to me without delay, will be to die with your scrawny chest and bald egg of a skull stove in."

Declan moved closer, to a position five paces from both the red-haired man and the stall, and changed to a one-handed grip on his long-axe at its center of balance and began to spin it in vertical circles. It was a difficult trick to do with such heavy, thick-shafted weapon, and he knew that more than a few moments of it would pain his wrist, but it impressed and often discouraged a would-be attacker. In this case it had the effect of making the other's freckles look black in his suddenly pale face.

"Master," said Declan, giving the man a look of disdain, "would you have me open this one's stupid head?"

"No . . . !" Sean began, before Declan silenced him with his upraised, unencumbered hand.

"The boy is a healer and soft-hearted," he said to the man. "He would feel shamed if I did something to you that he, with his limited experience of the healing arts, could not mend. I myself care little what I do to one who threatens the life of our aged and frail master. . . ."

"No, no, I beg you," the other broke in, beginning to back away. "Have pity. I am impoverished, weak with hunger and needing only a few coins to support my ailing wife and children. I drew no weapon and no bodily harm was done to your master. Please, I meant to threaten his life only with words. . . ."

The last few of his words were lost as he suddenly turned and ran with remarkable speed, Declan thought, for a fat and starving man.

Declan watched as the would-be robber dodged out of sight between the other stalls and wagons, and sighed. "I'm going soft," he said, "talking like that instead of doing physical violence to him. I suppose it comes of spending so much of my time with a healer."

Before Sean could reply, Ma'el raised a finger to point into the crowd behind them and said quietly, "My thanks to you, Declan. But now this frail and aging body of mine is no longer at risk and I would like both of you to withdraw as before and remain watchful. We have another caller."

SEVEN

T his time it was an old man, a merchant wide of girth and halting and feeble in his movements, who said that he wanted not so much to know his own future during the few short years remaining to him as whether or not his three sons would agree to his proposed division of his property between them. When Ma'el asked what manner of young men they were, the other spoke without hesitation and at length about their virtues and vices large and small. But soon his talking moved to other subjects, his business concerns and those people who lived and wrought in the town and who envied him his success. He said that he welcomed this chance to talk to and be advised by a traveler who knew nothing about the people he spoke of and whose advice, therefore, would be more balanced than that of self-seeking friends who might seek advantage from the words he spoke. But it was evident to the listening Declan that the old merchant wanted to talk, and even gossip and relate shameful or humorous facts about others to what he considered to be a safe pair of ears. In time he left pleased and with his own ears filled with Ma'el's good advice, which included the suggestion that his future might not be as short as he expected.

There followed two colleens, bright, fair, open of face, and scarcely mature who, like the young men who had called earlier, pushed each other forward in their shyness. They, too, wanted to know the future but as yet had no clear idea of what they wanted their futures to be. Ma'el talked to them kindly and sent them away with good advice and vague promises that satisfied them. They were followed by another caller who apart from being female, Declan could see at once, was in no other respect the same.

She was a young woman, small, strongly built and with a confident and competent look about her that was at odds with the hesitancy of her approach. Her bare feet and the hem of her well-worn dress were splattered with the mud of the soft ground, but the shawl around her shoulders was new or at least freshly washed, and her long, dark hair was held in a comb that was worn with an air that suggested that it might be her most valued decoration. Her face was broad and plain with eyes that were dark and lively and, Declan thought, in spite of the hands worn rough by toil and her lowly circumstances, she had a mouth that was no stranger to a smile. It was Ma'el who spoke first.

"Come forward, young woman, and speak of yourself," he said quietly. "Doubtless I look old and strange to you, but I am not a demon, and the passage of years and the kind of life I must lead have robbed me of all my hair. Is there a service you would ask of me?"

The other's face deepened in color and she spent more than a little time in thought before she nodded her head with firmness before giving answer.

"If you please, venerable one," she said, "I—I would know the future."

"Of course you would," said Ma'el. He spent a long moment of his own looking at her without movement of feature or even the blink of an eye, then went on gently, "But would you know what the future holds for you yourself, or for another, or for both of you?"

Her color deepened again. She glanced sideways at Declan

and Sean who were standing some thirty paces distant, then she said in a firm but quiet voice, "It is for both of us. I would know if we, in our bodies as well as our futures, will lie together. But how did you know this? Is it because you are a great magician as that boy over there proclaimed?"

Ma'el continued to regard her with steady eyes but gave no answer.

While pretending to be interested in some other person or event in the marketplace, Declan nodded knowingly to himself. Most of the young women like this one who sought the services of a fortuneteller were curious about what the future held for herself and her young man. A magician though the old man might claim to be, he was honest in laying no claims to the possession of wizardly powers while he was simply making a guess that was almost sure to be the correct one. As Ma'el spoke on it pleased Declan greatly for some strange reason that in the simpler trickeries of his craft the other was being honest.

"Child," said Ma'el, "from the look of your eyes and face, it is clear to see that you are deeply in love with a young man. But if I am to look into your future lives, whether they are to be lived together or apart, I must know something of your pasts. First you will tell me of your own past life, and then of his."

She bobbed her head, smiled and without further hesitation began, "My name is Maeve, a spinster, the youngest and least comely of four sisters, two of whom are wedded, and their husbands and the children to come will share in my father's farm, which is not large enough for all of us. . . ."

It was a common situation and a continuing tragedy throughout the land, Declan knew, that a family's unsupported young had to find their own livelihoods elsewhere than on the homelands they had known. But it became clear, as Ma'el drew out the words from her and gave his gentle reassurances in return, that this was an uncommon young woman who had a great warmth of feeling and a bright and lively mind that contained no sorrow for herself.

". . . He is older by a few years than I," she was saying, having moved the subject of conversation to her perhaps not so young man. "He is a seafarer, tall and strong but . . ."

"That is profession," Ma'el broke in gently, "fraught with many dangers. And temptations. Would not another young man who remains closer to home be a better choice for your future life?"

"No!" said the other with quiet but respectful vehemence. "He will remain true to me, as I will to him, for as long as we shall live."

Ma'el made no reply and she went on, "He is not well-favored in his face, and in manner he is uncouth and even harsh to those around him when his master bids it so. But to me he has always shown gentleness and consideration, even when we are . . ."

She stopped speaking as Ma'el raised his hand, then opened and closed it several times as if to relieve a stiffness of age in his fingers before returning it to rest on the bench top. He said, "Please continue."

Declan felt Sean's hand lightly gripping his upper arm. "That was Ma'el's signal for us to move away," said the boy, "and a sign that matters of a personal and intimate nature may be discussed. Perhaps the young woman's deepest and most private feelings will be revealed, and matters which he thinks are no concern of ours."

"I think he is right," said Declan, with feeling. They walked away slowly until the distance from the stall had more than doubled. Their movements were seemingly aimless but they were always able to keep the wagon in sight. They walked together slowly for what seemed to be a very long time before Ma'el gave another hand signal which, Sean informed him, meant that they should return.

The woman was about to leave by the time they were close enough to see the smile that was on her face and in her eyes, and to hear her words of profuse thanks. She drew a small purse from under her shawl and emptied the few coins it contained onto the bench in front of Ma'el. The old man gathered them up, returned all of them to the purse, then gave it back to her.

"Go," he said gently, "and may good fortune attend both of you."

When she had gone, Sean said, "Master, you spoke with her for a very long time and made no charge whatsoever for your services. With respect, this is not the way to gain a comfortable livelihood."

"Fear not, child," Ma'el replied, "I shall not make it a habit. In truth, I should have paid that young woman for the valuable knowledge she imparted on many subject of interest to me, but doing that would have given rise to much talk and general speculation about the health of my mind, so all I gave her was the best advice that I could give.

"Besides," he went on, in a voice that made it difficult for Declan to decide whether or not the old man was being serious, "a few coins are of little matter to me. You are forgetting the hoard of gold and silver that I am reputed to keep hidden in my wagon."

Sean made a irritated by respectful sound and said, "It grows dark. Shall I light the cooking fire?"

Ma'el shook his head. "No, child," he said. "Tonight we eat, and perhaps drink a little, with a roof over our heads before returning here to sleep. Both of you will dress in your new apparel so that all who meet us will think that you master is a person of substance."

With the approach of darkness the vehicles, stalls, and goods belonging to the other merchants were covered and secured before their owners, too, left to spend the evening elsewhere. Ma'el's bench and stall were dismantled and stowed away and the old man, without going into details, let it be known that a spell was in place which would ensure the safety of their wagon from thieves or the merely curious. Such interference was an unlikely possibility because the two Gardai on duty would patrol throughout the night and any person who did not have business in the marketplace would, without exception, have his head cracked open. It was a point of honor with the Garda authorities in Cork, whose continuing livelihood depended on its merchants both resident and passing through, that they be able to conduct their business with as much peace of mind as was possible.

As one who knows precisely where he was bound, Ma'el led them to the waterfront and a wide, low building which had the warm, yellow light of innumerable lamps and the subdued roar of many voices pouring from its entrance and window openings, in company with the smells of cooking food and ale. The old man led the way into a wide room whose smoke-blackened ceiling beams were supported by pillars of carved and decorated wood. A log fire crackled in a raised, centrally placed stone hearth which had cooking spits and long-handled pans laid across it, and most of the smoke was finding its way out through a square hole in the roof that could be covered by a hinged flap in case of heavy rain. It being still early in the evening, the place was not yet crowded. Declan pointed to a table close to a nearby wall with the softspoken advice that, as first-time visitors, they should place themselves where they could not be surprised from the rear.

A young bar servant appeared and quickly brought three empty stools to the table and recited the list of food and drink that was available before asking what was their pleasure.

"Please bring two more seats," said Ma'el. "I am expecting others to join us presently, and our needs can await their arrival."

"But surely we are strangers in this city," said Sean. "Who can you be expecting?"

The old man answered the question by pointing toward the entrance. "They are here," he said. "Sean, please approach them with politeness and speak respectfully to them thus. . . ."

Declan watched as the boy went across to the two men quickly but not in a manner that might constitute a threat. They were both experienced seafarers, judging by their dress and by way they stood on wide-braced feet as if expecting the sanded clay floor beneath them to pitch and roll at any moment. Perhaps, he thought, if they partook of enough ale throughout the evening to come, the floor might indeed do that.

One of them was tall, with white hair cut short and square

features that were burned dark by wind and spray. His chin was
shaven clean and he had gray eyes that, once fixed on an object,
seemed never to look away. He had shoulders so broad and powerful that they made it seem as if he had no neck, and his arms
and legs were fashioned in the same muscular mold. So far as
Declan could see, he wore no weapons, but with a build like that
it was doubtful if he needed any.

His companion, whose position half a pace behind the older
man made it plain which of them had the rank, was equally tall
but of slighter build and with black hair untouched with gray.
Thick brows shaded his eyes and the ink-dark and probably self-
barbered beard began high on his cheekbones and partially concealed the unusual width of his large mouth before coming to a
point under his chin. But the mass of black facial hair served only
to accentuate the long, crooked nose that that split his face vertically like a yellowed and blue-veined mountain range. Declan
thought that it came close to being the ugliest face he had ever
laid eyes upon.

They followed Sean to the table where the white-haired one
stopped to regard them in turn, beginning and ending with Ma'el
before he spoke.

"I am Seosadn Ui Nuallain, or Joseph Nolan if you are a
Saxon, and this," he said, indicating his companion, "is my ship's
Ionadacht who is known, for obvious reasons, as Seamus Dubh.
The boy said that you wished urgent words with us."

"I am Ma'el," said the old man, "a traveler from a far land
whose family name and clan would mean nothing to you and
should therefore remain nameless. The boy is Sean and the large
one is Declan." He pointed to the vacant seats and went on, "You
are welcome at our table because your name, Captain Nolan and
that of Seamus the Black, your first lieutenant, are known to us
and your reputations go before you. I have a commission of
importance to offer you which . . . Ah, here is the bar servant. We
can discuss the matter before, during, or after eating and drinking as you prefer."

The servant was once again reciting the house's offerings

when Ma'el held up on a hand for silence. "As men of the sea," he said, "you are perhaps overly familiar with the taste of fish. Please feel free to order beef or lamb or fowl should one of those be to your preference. And, of course, something to wash it down."

The large and dreadfully uneven teeth of Seamus flashed white and his superior also smiled because, out of consideration for the unknown depth of Ma'el's purse, they had been ordering what they knew to be the least-costly food. They set about changing their selections without delay.

"Ma'el, the extent of your hospitality pleases and honors us," said Captain Nolan with the smallest of smiles. "But I have long learned that there is no such thing as a free feast. This being so, you will understand why we shall not drink with you until your commission of importance has been fully discussed and agreed upon. An agreement between us, if there should be one, ought not to be the uncertain product of ale-befuddled brains. So we will wait instead until we can drink in friendship to a successful conclusion to our business, if we can find one. Is there agreement on this?"

Without hesitation it was agreed.

As time passed and Nolan and Ma'el ate and talked and at times argued but, progress was being made because the two sea-farers were looking more and more at ease and had begun to drink with them. Seamus made a pretence of ignoring his master's words and instead asked questions of the other two servants at the table, Sean and Declan. His manner was direct, forthright and at times verged on the uncouth as he said whatever it was that came into his mind. Declan spoke less and less until finally he had to keep his lips pressed firmly together because he was so furious with Seamus that that was the only way he could hold onto his temper.

". . . And your master treats you well," Seamus was saying, looking them up and down, his eyes moving from Declan to Sean and back again, "and your clothing is useful, but pretty. . . ." His gaze went to the long-axe that was propped against the wall behind their table ". . . Can you use that thing think?"

When it was plain that Declan was not going to reply, Sean made an angry sound and said, "He can."

"I wasn't talking to you, boy," said Seamus. "You should not break in without permission when grown men are speaking. What frets you?"

Declan joined in before Sean could lose a temper that was much shorter than his own. "I would not want to make empty boasts about my battles," he said in a voice that had quietness forced upon it, "but the boy has seen the results of some of them. He is a healer, young but skilled in the art as you can see . . ." he touched his recently scarred cheek ". . . and it angers him that some of my opponents he has been unable to mend."

Seamus nodded and showed his uneven teeth again. "Now that is a useful accomplishment," he said, his tone changing suddenly from the critical to the complimentary. "Hurts, large and small, are always being sustained on board ship even when there are no sea battles to cause them, as well as poxes and fevers and blains from the cold. And the long-axe is a weapon favored by Norse sea raiders in close ship engagements. It would discommode them to find it being used against as well as by them. Can you take an oar?"

"Yes," said Declan.

"Also useful in a sea chase . . ." the other began, and stopped because Captain Nolan had raised his voice.

". . . Three passengers and the wagon I can accommodate," he was saying in a voice that was loud but not yet angry, "but not the horse. If the seas were rough it would suffer great hardship. Maddened with fear it might kick a hole in our thin-walled craft that was built for speed. If the drinking water should run short on a long voyage, its ration would be many times that of a seaman, and if it were to break a limb we would have to end up by killing and eating it. Taking it with us would be a needless cruelty. No horse."

Ma'el inclined his head gently and said, "No horse."

In a soft, sad voice, Sean looked at Ma'el and said, "I really loved that old horse. Are you sure we can't take him?"

The old man did not reply because Captain Nolan was tapping the table top for attention as he began speaking again.

"Besides," he said, "there is a circumstance not yet mentioned. I already have a prior commission, for which payment in advance has been made, to take a passenger of great importance, Brian of the Clan O'Rahailley, who is about to embark on a very long voyage indeed, a voyage whose expenses are shared by the kingdoms of both Tirconnel and Dalriada, so that your own needs would be secondary to his. He is the principal advisor on commercial and military matters to the King of Tirconnel. Brian is a far-traveled scholar and philosopher of great renown who has been honored by many kingdoms near and far. . . ."

"Brian O'Rahailley," said Black Seamus suddenly in a loud voice, taking a large swallow from his flagon, "is a spy."

EIGHT

Ma'el Report, Day 112,548 . . .

The officers and other passenger on this ship are cultured and intelligent by their standards, and the crew are strong-willed and sensible so that they will dismiss my magic for what they think it is when they see or hear about it.

"Nothing more of Taelon technology will be revealed other than that already shown to my servants. . . ."

The ship that lay alongside the jetty projecting from the west shore of the harbor of Cobh was a strange vessel, completely without grace of line and seemingly built by shipwrights who had changed their minds several times in the course of its building. In some ways it was like the ships of the Norsemen, except that it was longer and somewhat broader in the beam and mounted two masts and booms to carry a large square sail, and the shield-lined rowing and fighting positions amidships were higher above the waterline, and as an additional defense there were five posts that projected upward at equal intervals along each side to support the nets used to inconvenience would-be boarders. There was an additional mast and slanting boom forward that resembled drawings Declan had once seen of an eastern Mediterranean felucca and, just barely visible in the water under the bow, there was the dark shape of a long, sharp ram that belonged on one of the old Greek war galleys. The stern section, as well as mounting a heavy tiller for the rudder, was raised to give a view forward in the manner of a Roman fighting galley. Concealed by its weather covers amidships was an object that looked like a large arbalest. Altogether the vessel had such an odd look that Ma'el's skin-covered wagon, which was already secured to the deck and with two low shelters rigged under it for Sean and himself, seemed almost normal amid these other strangenesses.

It was plain from the captain's manner that the vessel was his pride and joy, an object held in greater esteem than his wife and family if he had one. As they were going on board Declan was careful not to mention any part or aspect of the sea-going monstrosity for fear of giving offense, but not so the captain.

"Your silent forbearance does you credit," he said, and gave a wry smile as he gestured toward the weapons Declan carried. "In many ways we are all robbers in that we steal many of the things that have been used against us over the years by enemies, and improve on them and use those same weapons to fight back. You have a Norseman's long-axe, specially weighted and improved to your needs, your sword is a well-tried Roman gladius and the shield we found for you, only that is Hibernian because there are few known to us that better it in lightness and strength."

He paused for a moment to watch Ma'el enter the wagon, the tenting of which had been firmly lashed down, and Sean climb onto the driving bench that no longer had its canopy in case a strong wind should blow it away. The boy stood on the bench, holding onto the nearby rigging and staring all around him with the bright-eyed, fearful, yet excited look of one who is viewing such surroundings for the first time.

"This is why honest men like myself become robbers, too," Captain Nolan went on. "We steal not just the goods and weapons of attacking seafarers but their sailing and ship-handling methods as well. This . . ." He gestured all around and above him

". . . is a vessel completely lacking in beauty of line or proportion. It is a mis-shapen mongrel of a ship. But it has qualities that a stranger and land-dweller like yourself might not see. She has a very shallow draft, almost flat-bottomed, and with a narrow keel and rudder that enables her to move close inshore into waters where other vessels would run onto reefs or beach themselves. She has many other useful qualities, but suffice it to say that in a favoring wind *Orla* can outrun any other ship that I have met or learned of by hearsay. If there is an adverse wind she can even . . ."

The captain looked away and fell into the uncomfortable silence of one who thinks he has talked too much. There was an enthusiasm and a softness about this Captain Nolan, Declan realized, that did not show on the craggy surface. He laughed quietly.

"I begin to feel great affection and trust for your mis-shapen mongrel," he said, and quickly raised a placating hand. "Remember, Captain, those were your words for her, not mine."

"True, but you will not at any time use them in anyone else's hearing," said the captain, then briskly, "We leave at once. Seamus! Raise the main sail. Stand by to cast off."

"B-but," Declan stammered, "without your other passenger?"

Captain Nolan shook his head. "He came on board last night, preferring that as few as possible of the local authorities in Cork know of his presence or business here. You will meet him this evening. But now, Declan, there is much work for the crew to do and you would oblige me by not allowing your large body to interfere with it. Go join your friends at the wagon and remain close to it."

The wind off the land was light, bringing with it the smells of a city preparing for a new day, so that the slow, regular creaking and splashing of the oars and the occasional shouted command were the only sounds until they were clear of the jetties and wharves of the city and had turned southward past Cobh into the wide, land-sheltered expanse of greater Cork Harbor. There the strengthening northerly caught their sail and made further row-

ing unnecessary, except when the wind brought them close to the
shoreline of the south passage and they had to row themselves
clear. But when they passed south of Ballinuska, almost hidden
by frosty mist and the wood smoke of its fires, the oars were
shipped because ahead lay the open sea and to the west the even-
more–open ocean of legendary Atlantis.

Very soon the long, smooth-topped Atlantic waves were
striking the vessel amidships and making it roll alarmingly,
except that no other person on board, with the exception of the
boy beside him, showed any signs of alarm. Declan wanted
badly to talk, about anything to anyone, so as to have something
to think about other than a belly that wanted to empty itself
when there was nothing in it to throw up. But the pallid-faced
and sweating boy was not disposed to talk, and there seemed to
be an invisible but very real barrier between the busy sailors he
approached and idle passengers like himself, which would not
allow anything through it but a few impatient, grunted words.
He clenched his teeth and when he felt particularly bad he
looked through slitted eyes at the sun, which was the only object
he could find that was moving slowly enough not to make him
feel sick. Several hours later when it was touching the horizon
and throwing wide, orange reflections off the larger waves, a
member of the crew came to offer the boy and himself a ban-
nock of wheaten bread and something in a stoppered flask
which both of them refused.

After sunset, Declan transferred his attention to the bright,
still shape of the rising moon. He was feeling much better
although not yet well enough to eat, but by the time the moon
had climbed high and a crew member came to say that Ma'el and
his servants should come at once to the captain's cabin for the
evening meal, his stomach was complaining of hunger rather
than seasickness.

It was plain from the navigational instruments and rolled-up
charts on the shelves behind it that during his working day the
captain's table was used for purposes other than eating. Presently
it was set for with six places with Captain Nolan at its head, his

lieutenant Seamus at his right and the other passenger, Brian O'Rahailley, seated on his left.

"My name is Brian," he said, smiling as he looked up at Ma'el. "Please, sit by me. I have been told that you are a wizard and a seer of future events, and this is the first opportunity I have had to discuss the subject with one who may be truly versed in the magical arts."

The manner and appearance of the other passenger came as a complete surprise, Declan thought as Ma'el took the proffered place while Sean sat facing the captain and he seated himself between the boy and Seamus. He had expected that a court advisor, a well-traveled philosopher and scholar and, according to Seamus the Black, a spy, should be old and wizened with hands gnarled by the twisting stiffness of age and a face marked deeply by long and varied experience. But Brian O'Rahailley showed none of those signs. Instead he could not have been more than a decade older than Declan, shorter and more widely built and with a round and open countenance that smiled readily and gave no appearance of his possession of high rank. It was only his eyes that looked old.

Brian talked freely and in a manner that was friendly, amusing, and interesting, so much so that even Sean looked at ease in his company and was sparing more attention to him than to the wine he was drinking. But Declan noticed that the other was somehow able to talk continuously while saying nothing of great importance, particularly about himself. Instead he was trying, with words that were subtle questions, to draw information from Ma'el. Only gradually did Declan realize that the old man was doing precisely the same thing to the other passenger and that he seemed to be winning the contest.

It was Brian who was first to lose his patience as well as his politeness.

"Come, come, Ma'el," he said quietly, but with an angry edge to his voice. "Shyness sits ill on a magician who is, or at least should be, an entertainer. Perform for us, if you will, a few of your tricks. Tell us of the success that will attend our endeavors . . ." he looked aside and smiled knowingly at Captain Nolan and Black Seamus, ". . . for I doubt that you would spoil our evening by foretelling death and destruction. Perhaps you will tell me of the next lady I shall meet, and whether or not she will bestow her favors or even, after many unsuccessful endeavors throughout my life, if I will find true love with her?"

Ma'el looked at the other for a moment, his smooth features seemingly as impassive to insults as they were to all other acts of threatened verbal or physical violence. "I do not perform tricks," he said, placing his hands palm downward before them in one of his fluid and almost ritualistic gestures. "But by using my mind and my eyes and my experience of the past and present, I can often see how future events will transpire." His gaze moved slowly from Brian to rest in turn on the captain and lastly on Black Seamus. "There is one here who will not find true love in his lifetime, and one who needs not the love of a woman because he loves only the sea, and another who has already found the true and undying love he hungers for, but is as yet afraid to admit even to himself that this great good fortune is already his."

Brian began to laugh, softly at first and then more loudly before his face became serious again and he said, "Ma'el, you are indeed a trickster, but with words, and for a frail old man you placed yourself at great risk." He smiled, waved a dismissive hand and went on, "No, not from me, because your telling the company that I would never find true love was, I suspect, but an angry and well-deserved response to my earlier bad manners toward you for which, Ma'el, I now beg your pardon. And telling us that Captain Nolan's greatest love is the sea was a safe forecast, because there is not a man who serves in the fleets of Dalriada who would not use the same words about him. But telling the ugliest . . . My apologies, Seamus, you are a good man in a fight but we both know the description is regrettable but true . . . telling the ugliest man in that same fleet that he has found the true and undying love of a woman is . . . If you had been a younger man, Ma'el, I think by now you would have felt the fist of Black Seamus in your face."

Everyone including his captain was looking at the ship's Ion-adacht whose eyes were regarding Ma'el from beneath lowered brows. All other expression was concealed by the thick blackness of his beard. But to Declan's surprise his mouth was closed and remained so for he neither moved nor spoke a word. Around them the quiet and almost unnoticed sounds of a ship at sea began to seem loud.

"You are a pleasant, educated, and interesting table companion, Ma'el," said Brian, breaking the long silence, "who will doubtless help us shorten the monotony of this long voyage but, alas, a wizard and magician you are not."

The bottom of Sean's drinking beaker slapped loudly onto the tabletop, without spilling any wine because there was none remaining in it. Speaking with the careful clarity of one whose mind is befuddled and his tongue reluctant to do his bidding, he said, "Ma'el *is* a wizard. He is not a trickster. I—I have seen him do great works of magic."

"In vino veritas," said Brian, using a phrase of scholar's Latin, a language he would not expect servants to understand. He smiled again as he looked from the boy to the old man and went on, "My compliments, Ma'el, you have a loyal servant who has complete belief in you."

Declan cleared his throat and, looking steadily at Brian, said in a quiet voice, "He has two."

"Enough!" said the captain, slapping his open hand on the table. When the eating utensils had stopped rattling he went on, "This voyage will be a long one, and with enough dangers as it is without them being worsened by ill feeling among this company. I have no wish for, nor will I tolerate for a moment, fighting among my passengers regardless of whether their stations in life are highborn or lowly or, indeed . . ." he gave a small nod toward Brian, ". . . the part one of you played in providing the excellent food and wine we have all enjoyed this evening. Verbal warfare only will I allow, provided it is polite and, above all, entertaining, and it does not extend beyond this table. As the captain of a vessel at sea may I remind you that I am the sole and ultimate authority on board, the dispenser of high, middle, and low justice. This must be understood by everyone here present. Is it?"

He looked around the table until all had either spoken or nodded their heads in assent, then he smiled.

"Good," he said. "Providing the wind and weather favor us, and no other agency real or magical deems otherwise, we will dine here tomorrow evening.

"You have my permission to withdraw."

NINE

By the following evening all of the diners seemed to be in a particularly good humor. This, Declan decided, was because the sun had risen and set in a sky totally without cloud, the wind had continued light but steady from the north and the Atlantic swell was smooth and regular enough not to inconvenience the stomachs of any of the passengers. His last view of Hibernia before the sunset mists rising from the sea had covered it had been as a gray line too thin for the southern mountains to show, while as yet too indistinct to be seen by moonlight. The tip of the long peninsula that the Britons called Land's End lay fine off the port bow. Under a favoring nor-noreasterly wind stiff enough to make the use of oars unnecessary, the end of the third day saw them passing the tip of the great peninsula of Gaul that projected westward into the Atlantic.

That evening the meal went well. Again there was much verbal thrusting and parrying between Brian and Ma'el, but it was too good-humored and friendly for anyone to feel insulted or angry, and not once did the captain remind them to behave themselves as he had had to do on the first evening of their voyage. It was plain that Brian was still trying to draw out and, if possible, discredit Ma'el, but he had changed his strategy.

Instead of asking questions he was volunteering information about himself, usually in the form of amusing anecdotes in which he did not always come off best, in the hope or expectation of Ma'el returning the favor. Many times he had the company hanging on his every word, with Sean in particular paying close attention and, respectfully, asking questions at every opportunity. Occasionally the boy could not help letting slip past incidents involving Ma'el's past.

Brian was a subtle and persistent man, Declan thought, who would elicit the knowledge he desired from lesser sources if the greater was closed to him. Unfortunately, the stratagem did not work where Declan was concerned because he had not known Ma'el long enough to let anything slip.

Unlike the first evening, which had given the boy a sick stomach and a very sore head for the rest of the following day, Sean had been merely sipping at his wine. But he was bright-eyed and excited and the convivial company seemed to be all the intoxication needed to loosen his tongue, as now, when it threatened to stray beyond the limits of good manners into matters personal.

"With respect, sir," he said, "you have recounted many of your adventures in far places, among strange people whose customs are even stranger, and have brought back knowledge of them that must be beyond price to the learned of our homeland. I truly envy you the things you have done and the life you live. As a person you are gifted and resourceful and daring, although modestly you try to discount you own bravery. . . ."

"You are well versed in the art of flattery, young Sean," said Brian, smiling, "as well as that of healing. Your words go around my heart like a warm blanket. Pray continue."

The boy continued, and it was clear that he was choosing his words with care as he said, "You are easy and gentle of manner, regardless of the lowliness of the company you keep, such as a servant like me, and it is certain that you do not look the part.

But I have a curiosity that will not let my mind rest. . . ." Sean did not so much as glance toward Seamus, who Declan knew to have been the recent sayer, ". . . . But I have heard it said of you that . . . Why are you called a spy?"

They were all staring at the boy: Ma'el with his customary lack of expression; Seamus with his expression hidden behind his hairy mask; and the captain, his face deepening in color while he slowly filled his lungs for a shout of anger that would have carried the length of the ship. Brian's features were still and pale for a moment, then they relaxed into another smile as he gazed intently into the boy's eyes, nodded, then spoke.

"It is because I am a spy," he said.

The heads around the table turned as one toward this new center of attention, but it was Captain Nolan, the earlier anger toward Sean fading from his face, who spoke first.

"Have a care, Brian," he said quietly. "Seamus and I know well what you do and this is not the first time we have helped you do it. But with respect, this is a stupid and dangerous admission for you to make in public. I advise you to say no more on the subject."

"Rest your mind, Captain," Brian said with a reassuring gesture of one hand while he used the other to take a long draught from his goblet. He smiled again and went on, "This is scarcely a public place and I trust the discretion of all those here, including the trusted and loyal servants of our magician, not to add substance to the few rumors that may be circulating about some of my activities."

Ma'el looked slowly from Sean to Declan and nodded his head, signifying that in this matter their lips were to remain sealed.

"Spying is generally thought to be a profession practiced by avaricious and unprincipled men and women who are without honor or morals," Brian went on, looking only at Sean, "and dangerous to those who do the work badly by revealing either themselves or their intentions. Without false modesty, I can say that I do my work very well, by appearing to reveal everything about myself and thus disarming all suspicion.

"As the captain knows," he went on, "this will be my second voyage to Rome and Athens and Alexandria, and wherever else in the Mediterranean that present knowledge of local political, commercial, and military matters was or is of interest to my employers. But the interest I show while visiting those great cities is open and unfeigned, the natural curiosity of a far-traveling scholar and seeker after truth who is impractical with respect to the realities of the world, who appears to be without guile and who has a reputation for revealing all kinds of interesting information when the wine flows freely. . . ."

. . . In Egypt under the Pharaohs, he went on, it had been the custom to provide important visitors—and Brian admitted to being neither reticent nor completely factual while describing his own importance—with accommodation, servants, and a pension suited to their station in life together with invitations to the court functions and entertainments. Since the time of the Caesar, Julius, when Egypt's power and influence waned and it had become a mere province of Rome, the quality of the entertainments had diminished, but they were still lavish indeed by Hibernian standards.

On these occasions the usual diplomatic games would be played, with the visitor being wined and dined and encouraged to talk about his homeland, its concerns and ambitions, as well as the the lands and cities he had visited and the dress, customs, and achievements of the people he had met on his epic journey from Hibernia. The majority of his listeners would have no interest in the matters he described, but his lightest word would be examined for content of a commercial or military nature by the merchant princes and the generals who were present, while at the same time he would be trying to extract the same kind of information from his hosts. In this game neither party was expected to tell the truth, but due allowances were made for the obvious fabrications and misdirections, just as a high level of exaggeration in the related exploits was accepted for no other reason than that it made the tales more entertaining.

As a visitor Brian was popular as a teller of tales but disappointing as a source of commercial and military intelligence. Whenever he had imbibed too freely of the dark and deceptively potent wines of Egypt and Gaul, which was nearly every evening, he would relate shocking and highly scandalous gossip concerning the unrecorded activities of the rulers and the other highborn of the courts and palaces he had visited—tales of a kind which, had they been told of the person or family of the local ruler, would have cost the teller his head.

But from Brian they never seemed to learn anything useful, anything that was not already known, because he did not seem to know or display other than the polite curiosity that was required by good manners about matters that they themselves considered important. And the reason given for this large area of ignorance in an otherwise intelligent and cultured person was that Brian professed himself to be a seeker after knowledge for its own sake who had no interest in the coarser pursuits of martial conquest and the acquisition of wealth. Although there had been many occasions when the ladies of a court would have been pleased to broaden his education, he seems to have only three abiding interests: the sampling to excess of the local wines; consorting with others of a similar turn of mind to his own; and browsing in the greatest libraries of the known world where he was most likely to find these intelligent and impractical people, people who unknowingly had much practical knowledge that they were unaware of giving away. . . .

". . . As you will already have observed," Brian went on, raising a deprecating eyebrow at Sean, "I am such a simple, friendly, outgoing man that not one of the jaded sophisticates of the many courts I have visited ever suspected that I was better at playing their games than they were themselves."

A long silence fell around the table. It was plain from the stillness in the faces and bodies that the captain and his lieutenant had received further confirmation of something they had long known. Sean's mouth was open and his eyes shining with excitement at the revelations, and Ma'el was as inscrutable as ever. But Brian was beginning to show his impatience again.

"We are alike in many ways, old man," he said, turning to Ma'el. "You collect knowledge of the past and present to chart a course into the future, and if your charting is accurate this can be valuable in many ways. But I think you have other talents besides and it is these which interest me. There is a strangeness, a feeling of certainty about you, and an even stranger lack of fear in you that does not go with your frailty of age. I have an odd feeling about you, old man, and my feelings are rarely wrong.

"You are in possession of knowledge of great importance," he went on, "and secrets greater and more valuable, I feel sure, than any of those I glean in the course of my travels. Come, Ma'el, play the game with fairness. I have told you everything of importance about me, it is now for you to oblige us with the same information regarding yourself."

Ma'el inclined his head for a moment, but he was looking at the captain when he spoke. "There is a small but very important secret, a piece of knowledge I had intended to impart," he said quietly, "when an opening in Brain's very interesting account of his work allowed it. . . ."

"I know I talk too much, old man," Brain broke in, an irritated edge to his voice. "But we don't want your small secrets, we want matters of substance, and especially not the paltry little secret of whose existence we already know. The captain and Black Seamus saw through it at once, but of course said nothing about it, at their first meeting with you. I myself learned of it during the first evening's meal. It is a small matter, and of no real interest or importance to us, that you employ a female servant who pretends to be and dresses as a boy. . . ."

"*What!*" Declan broke in, his voice rising almost to a shout. "Brian, the wine has rotted your brain. That is a stupid thing to say. I have traveled with Ma'el and the boy since . . ."

"Even your other servant, it seems, was unaware of this small secret," said Brian, ignoring Declan and keeping his eyes on

Ma'el. "Strange. But the personal perversions of an old man are of no interest to me, it is your other . . ."

"No!" said Sean, his face turning deep pink with anger and embarrassment. "I was little more than a defenseless child. He rescued me, hid and protected me, and saved my life. But at no time did he try to . . ."

The words were cut short as Declan jumped angrily to his feet, or at least tried to until the cabin's low overhead deck timbers cracked against his skull and further added to his mental confusion. Ma'el held up both hands palms outwards for silence, one directed at Sean and the other at Declan.

"This is a matter of small importance," said Ma'el, "which we will discuss fully at a later time, if there is a later time for all of you." He turned to divide his attention between the captain and Brian and went on, "I wish to perform a necessary act of magic or, to be precise, an accurate foretelling of the future stretching over the next three days. . . ."

"Mere fortunetelling," Brian scoffed. "No magic, just trickery with words. I want more than that from you, old man."

". . . To you it will be magic," Ma'el went on in his high, gentle voice that was somehow able to silence all others, and he regarded everyone in turn before his eyes came to rest on Captain Nolan, "which requires that you follow my instructions exactly. You must guide your ship southeastward so as to round the point of Finisterre and then run for the nearest bay that will give shelter from a high wind. It is best that you do this without argument or delay.

"I am using a form of magic that will save all your lives."

TEN

In spite of Ma'el's advice to the contrary, there was delay and argument that threatened to rage without end. Declan took no part in it because the words of a seemingly untutored servant would be ignored and he was, withal, feeling too angry and confused to speak. Sean remained silent also, staring at him with the color deepening on his or, as he had now learned, her face.

There had been many signs, he now realized, that he had been too trusting and stupid to see. The lack of physical strength and slim build that had been so at variance with the surprising breadth of knowledge accompanied by the confidence of manner shown by a boy so young should have made him suspect it, because the minds of females matured earlier than those of boys, as should the sure and gentle touch of the hands when the wound to his face was being treated. There had been the knowing smile of Padriag of Cashel after he had fitted both of them with new apparel and, from the first night after the incident with the robbers, Ma'el had made it clear that they should sleep apart in spite of the fact that their shared body warmth would have been a comfort in the frigid nights of late winter. On the land journey as well as in the individual shelters rigged on the ship, the old man had seen to it that they were separated. He made his voice low but clear so that it would carry though the louder arguments raging around them, and tried to keep the anger he felt from showing in it.

"So you are a girl, or perhaps a young woman," he said. "You should have told me this. What is your name, or are you still hiding that? How old are you?"

She shook her head and replied in the same, low-pitched, clear tone, "I am Sinead and, and old enough for what you are thinking."

"You know not what I am thinking!" Declan replied in a furious undertone. "I promised to guard both of you from all harm. What kind of man do you think I am?"

"The kind of man I thought you were," she replied, the trace of an apology creeping into her voice, "was a ragged, starving, sword and axe-bearing robber. Since then I have changed my opinion for the better, but I felt a certain embarrassment about revealing my secret to you, and Ma'el would not tell me if or when I should do so."

Before Declan could reply, Brian broke off his argument with Ma'el to say angrily, "Please order your servants to stop muttering among themselves, it is an irritating distraction. Better still, let us use Latin so that they will have nothing to mutter about. Or am I wrong in thinking that a magician of your apparent standing is schooled in Latin?"

"I will understand you," said Ma'el, touching a small ornament suspended from his right ear, "in whichever language you care to speak."

"One of the qualities you do not lack," said Brian dryly, "is modesty. Then let us proceed. . . ."

Few indeed were the people who could converse in other than their own native tongues, but Latin was spoken throughout the Roman Empire as the language of commerce and diplomacy and used only by the well-educated and highborn families, the far-traveled scholars, seafarers, and traders who needed to converse with philosophers and merchants in distant lands. Declan looked at Sinead and for an instant he allowed one of his eyelids to drop, and she responded with a small nod. That meant they both understood Latin and could follow the conversation as respectfully silent but understanding servants.

". . . And I prefer to trust the lengthy, sea-going experience of Captain Nolan and Black Seamus here," Brian was saying with great vehemence, "than the mouthing of a smooth-tongued fortuneteller. You seem to be ordering, in your soft voice and self-effacing manner, the captain of this ship to change course and head for shelter east of Cape Finisterre. You, who are not a seafarer and cannot even see the sky from this cabin, say that the wind is turning westerly and strengthening and is pushing the Atlantic swell higher as we speak. . . ."

"It is," said the captain quietly, "because the motion of the vessel and the wind in the rigging tells us of this change in the weather. . . ." Beside him Seamus gave a nod of agreement, ". . . but I do not believe that anyone, regardless of their profession or sea-going experience or lack of it, can predict with such accuracy the wind direction and strength of a coming storm. At best weather forecasting is guesswork based on past experience. You could be right in what you say or, more likely, completely wrong. With respect, I will not lose my self-respect as a captain, and the faith of my crew, by making an arbitrary and senseless alteration in course at the behest of a magician."

Brian's mouth shaped a smile that had no amusement or friendship in it and said, "What game do you play with us, Ma'el? Does making others do your will against their better judgment give you satisfaction? Is it a matter of self-aggrandizement pure and simple? I ask again, what is the reason behind this stupid game of words you play?"

The old man's gaze moved slowly around the table, coming to rest on Captain Nolan. "I wish to save the lives of my friends," he said, "as well as the officers and crew of this ship."

"You make no mention of saving your own life," said Brian. "That is most unselfish of you."

"My life," said Ma'el, "is not at risk."

"So now you tell us that the ship and its complement are in dire peril," said Brian in an incredulous voice, "but you are not? Ridiculous! Ma'el, you wriggle like a many-times–severed worm. In desperation your words move in different directions seeking escape. Unless you consider us all to be gullible and superstitious fools, which we most decidedly are not, nothing you have yet said warrants making a change of course." He shook his head in angry impatience. "You tell us that you have true and accurate knowledge of an impending great storm, but you cannot tell us how you can know of it."

Ma'el's face remained impassive and it did not seem that he would ever reply. The long silence was broken by Sinead.

"We also know of it," she said, anger making her come to her master's defense. With a side glance at Declan she went on, "I cannot be certain whether or not he consulted it earlier this evening, but he has an enchanted map which I know shows things as they are now and, perhaps, as they will be in the future."

Brian looked surprised. With his eyes still on Ma'el he said, "Well, well, it seems that even your lowly but plainly well-tutored servants comprehend the language of Rome." He looked at Sinead. "My thanks to you, young woman, for speaking out in defense of your master. Please continue."

She hesitated and waited for a slow nod from Ma'el before going on, "The chart appeared not to be the work of a mapmaker's pen but that of an artist, a painter who used dull, smudged colors to depict a scene viewed from a tremendous height. It showed the entire land of Hibernia, its mountains, loughs, inlets, towns, and the surrounding islands as well as part of the Celtic Sea, Scotia, Cymri, southwest Britain and a small stretch of the coast of Gaul. Small areas of the picture were obscured by soft-edged masses of gray. I did not mention it at the time because other matters concerned us but, knowing our position on the map at the time, when I looked in the direction where one of these gray areas should have been, I saw only wisps and bubblings of high cloud."

Her face took on the expression of one who does not fully

believe her own words as she ended, "I formed the opinion that the map was a picture seen from a great height, from a very great height indeed, above those clouds."

"My thanks again," said Brian. "You speak clearly of what you saw, or perhaps thought you saw but, with respect, you may have been willingly misguided by one you trust. . . ." He turned his attention to Ma'el. "Old man, we would know more about this enchanted chart of yours, but not described in words. We would see it for ourselves."

"I would have preferred that none but my close friends be privy to this secret," said Ma'el, drawing the flat, gray square that Declan had seen him use at the beginning of their journey. "But it seems that Brian and the officers of this ship have much in common with Thomas, the doubting apostle of the Christus, and will not believe my words without physical proof."

While he was speaking, Sinead leaned across the table to move aside the platters, eating utensils, and goblets so that the middle was clear when Ma'el placed the small gray square at its precise center and gave it three sharp taps with one finger. There was a muttered exclamation from Brian, then nothing but ship sounds as the map slowly unfolded itself.

"But, but Hibernia is smaller," Declan burst out, leaning across the table, "and the upper half is covered by that white stuff. It shows Scotia, Cymri, and all of Britain as well as parts of the nearby coast of Gaul, and much more of the Atlantic. This is a different map."

"Be silent," said the captain in a voice that needed no volume to gain instant obedience. "Ma'el, this is a strange map indeed, the like of which I have never seen before. From my own seafaring experience, which you may believe is considerable, the outlines and contours of the land masses appear to be both indistinct yet accurate. But this, and this . . ." his finger pointed at two areas of ocean, ". . . What is it that I see here? Please do not try to confuse me with words. Let your description be detailed and precise."

Ma'el held the captain's eyes for a long moment before he

replied, "Very well, Captain, if that is how you wish it. You are seeing a picture of events that are taking place as we speak, viewed from a space satellite in geo-stationary orbit high above this world's atmosphere. The image has been enhanced because of the reduced level of light from the moon and it is blurred because of distance, atmospheric haze, and clouds associated with a rapidly developing low-pressure cyclonic weather system that you see just here. . . ."

He pointed to the area of ocean west of Gaul where it seemed that the ghostly figures of two fat, bulbous worms were frozen into stillness in the act of curling around each other and chasing each other's tails. His hand moved down the picture and opened in a more inclusive gesture.

". . . The large, cloudless area you see," he went on, "is the anticyclonic or high-pressure system which has given us clear skies over the past few days and which, regrettably, is filling and decaying toward the northeast. But it is the deepening cyclone that most concerns us. . . ."

"Wait, wait!" said Brian loudly. "These are nonsense words, the language of Babel. This is more trickery. Captain, ignore the babblings of this old fool."

"You asked for a full and precise explanation, Captain," Ma'el said, "and that is what I am giving you. Even though I am speaking them clearly, many of my words are without meaning to you, but that is because it will be many, many of your years before you and your people will learn how to use them, and the events and objects to which they will one day apply. . . ."

"Captain," Brian broke in again. "I see you weakening. Consider your reputation and ignore this charlatan. These are the ravings of a mind rotted with poppy juice or worse. I strongly advise that you land him and his party in Gaul and be rid of him before he can . . ."

Ma'el raised his other hand and made a slow, complicated gesture in the air before him. Brian continued speaking, but it was as if he had been surrounded by a wall of silence, because none of his words were being heard, although it was obvious from his expression that he could still hear the others around him. The captain and Seamus stared at the old man, surprise, uncertainty, and a growing respect in their eyes. But whether they were respecting him as a magician for silencing his interrupter or as a foreteller of storms, Declan could not say. Sean, or Sinead, he corrected himself, had the wide-eyed and trusting look of a child.

"I cannot foretell the exact path of the storm," Ma'el resumed, "only that it will travel quickly through southern Britain and Gaul causing much havoc in its path. The effect on us will be an increasing northwesterly wind that will veer north, gaining further strength and pushing up mountainous waves as it moves until it blows us straight onto the coast of northern Iberia where your ship will certainly founder. That is why you must make all possible speed to seek the sheltering coastline south of Finisterre."

Captain Nolan stared down at the map for a long moment, his brows drawn down and lower lip trapped under his teeth in indecision. Seamus was staring at his superior, also awaiting that decision. Brian, no longer trying to talk, was growing redder of face as if he was forcing himself to a great effort of strength, but it seemed that the wall of silence around him was also restricting his physical movements. Finally the captain spoke.

"I have experience of how sudden and with what violence these winter storms can strike," he said doubtfully, "but never before have I seen their workings explained and shown thus. That is, if it is a true explanation . . . But wait. Those twisting clouds, the object you called a low-pressure system, has altered. I could swear that the image has changed in subtle details from the one you first showed us. It, it seems to be *moving!*"

"It is indeed moving," said Ma'el, "because it is a picture of events that are happening as we speak. Please observe. We will look at the area more closely."

He tapped the corner of the map several times in a measured but irregular fashion with one finger. Everyone at the table drew in their breaths sharply, although, where Brian was concerned the sound he made remained inaudible, as the spiral of clouds expanded to fill the the entire map. Plainly they could see the great northwestern peninsula of Gaul far astern and a fat finger of cloud curling down to obscure it. The captain swore, but too softly for any of them to hear the name of the god he invoked.

"I don't know what you're doing or how you are doing it," he said, raising his eyes from the map to Ma'el's face, "and I do not comprehend your strange words. In the future stories may be told about my gullibility, and of how I was led into stupidity by a smooth-tongued trickster, but no matter. Against all sense and reason I shall act on your advice. . . . Seamus!"

"Captain?"

"Change course to west by southwest," said the captain, his eyes still on the map. "From what I see here it is clear that we must round Cape Finisterre by mid-day tomorrow. Set all sail commensurate with the strengthening wind and have the oars manned in relays throughout the night. At once, Seamus, if you please. The rest of you may go."

"Wait, Captain," said Brian, making himself heard for the first time since the old man's spell had silenced him, "and be careful. This man is a powerful wizard, I freely admit that now, with my apologies for earlier disbelieving him. He held me motionless while my loudest words fell silently from my lips. But this moving map is an impossibility! He is ensorceling our minds, making us imagine and see moving pictures which are not there. We saw him take the map from an inner pocket of his cloak and, by some trick of the hand, make it unfold itself, so it must be made from the thinnest of vellum. Look here. . . ."

He grasped the edge of the map, lifted it from the table and tried to refold it before letting it fall again.

". . . It, it won't bend," he went on in a disbelieving voice as he stared at his fingers, one of which was showing traces of blood. "It's as stiff and hard as a plank of wood and, and the edges are *sharp.*"

He broke off to give the old man a confused look. Ma'el tapped the map, put it back inside his cloak when it had refolded itself, then nodded to the captain before he turned to follow Seamus out of the cabin. Sinead leaned across the table to take Brian's unresisting hand in her own.

"The cut is clean-edged and shallow," she said in the impersonal healer's voice that Declan knew so well, "and nothing for you to concern yourself about. Wrap it in a firm, washed binding and by tomorrow it will have knitted together and healed."

She released the hand and followed Ma'el from the cabin.

Before he did the same, Declan heard Captain Nolan laugh quietly and say to Brian, "By tomorrow, old friend, I fear you will have more to worry about than a cut finger."

ELEVEN

By first light next day the Atlantic rollers were marching across their beam like a procession of round-topped mountain ranges, their dark gray valleys filled with increasing frequency by spray blown by a wind that made the rigging sing and struck soft, muffled blows against the upperworks and deck cargo. The ship's rolling and pitching was continuous, but over the past three days Declan had become enough of a seafarer for the motion to make him feel worried but not sick. When one of the squalls blew past, briefly hiding the rising sun, the thunderous rattling of rain or hail on the decks made it difficult to talk or, at times, even to think.

Sinead and Declan were crouched in the lee of Ma'el's wagon, rather than spending the time in their dark and leaking deck shelters, while the worst of the weather blew over and past them. She was wearing, as was he, the long, thick, cloak, high boots, helmet, and oiled skins supplied by the venerable Padraig of Cashel a scant two weeks earlier and, apart from her rain-streaked face she, too, seemed to be warm and dry in them. But in spite of the fact that Ma'el was inside his wagon, Brian sheltering in the ship's only passenger accommodation, and its officers and men were too busy working the ship to spend time on the idle chatter of nonseafarers, she did not seem disposed to help pass the stormy monotony of the day ahead by talking to him.

It was not that Declan wanted to talk to her. He was still angry over the way she had concealed the fact that she was a female from him, and particularly for the deep, personal insult implied in the reason she had given for concealing it. He looked at the thin, serious, rain-beaded face and wondered if there were dark thoughts going through her mind, thoughts, perhaps, that she would prefer not to be thinking so that she might welcome a change of subject. He waited until the latest rain cloud had cleared the sun and the turbulent ocean shone dark green rather than gray, and tried again.

"It is close," Declan shouted as he raised a hand to point out past the port bow where the dark, frowning outlines of Finisterre rose from the sea, "but it looks to be coming no closer."

When she did not reply at once, he began to wonder if he had sounded too angry. The truth was that he was angry, and it was difficult to hide the feeling when one was shouting at the object of one's anger. But when she did shout her reply, Sinead's words were banal and voiced only in tones of loud disinterest.

"A watched pot," she said, "never boils."

Another squall covered and then cleared the sun, sweeping the ship with rain that was more than half snow and leaving the windward edges of the masts and rigging outlined in white. Declan maintained an angry silence and neither looked at nor spoke to her, but when Seamus was passing them on his way aft to the captain, he grasped the lieutenant's arm.

"What is it?" the other said, his voice loud and harsh with impatience. "I have no time to stop for idle talk."

"And I have nothing to do," Declan shouted back. He pointed again at the dark mass of the land ahead with the waves breaking at its base like churning milk. "Suddenly it is coming very close. Can you use another oar?"

Seamus showed his crooked white teeth. "It is and we can," he said. "Follow me."

The ship's Ionadacht moved along the heaving deck as

quickly and surely as if it had been a Roman paved road, while Declan grabbed at the bulwarks on one side and any other piece of rigging or structure inboard that looked strong enough to steady him. When he caught up to the other, Seamus had untied and was holding up a section of the weather shelter that had been rigged along the vessel's waist amidships, while he shouted to someone. One of the nearby oars swept upward until it was well clear of the sea and remained in that position while a small, wiry sailor with gray hair emerged and moved quickly in the direction of the crew accommodation forward. Impatiently Seamus waved Declan inside the shelter, squeezed in after him, and quickly secured its fastenings before the wind could get under it and blow it away.

He felt as if he was in a long, dark, and heaving tent that smelled of sweating bodies, wet clothing, and other smells that he could not identify. The only light was coming from the vertical slits through which projected the oars and it revealed dimly the indistinct shapes of the line of oarsmen ranged in front of him. They did not seem to have breath enough for conversation, but as they bent forward from the waist and pulled back on their oar handles, many of them were grunting in unison. Seamus pointed to the space lately vacated by the old sailor.

"Sit on the deck, there," he shouted above the sound of the rain and spray that was rattling against the shelter. "Bunch your cloak under you if you have a bony rump or are afraid of getting a deck splinter in it. Place both feet against the blocks in front of you and brace your legs as you pull. Try not to kick a hole or get a foot entangled in that roll of defense netting running along the side. It will take enough damage from a would-be boarding party without adding to it ourselves. But first, free your oar by removing that retaining loop around its handle which is holding it clear of the water. . . ."

Apart from the notched base of the rowing slit which was the point of leverage, the entire weight of the oar was pulling the handle against the heavy leather strap. Declan struggled briefly with it and succeeded in sliding it free.

". . . When you've done that," Seamus went on loudly in his ear, "the oar will drop to the water of its own accord. That mark that faces you on the handle tells when the blade of your oar is in the vertical position. Keep it so at all times, for if you let your wrists rotate it will simply slide through the water to no effect. And don't waste strength by lifting the oar at the end of a stroke. In these weather conditions, when we roll to starboard it will be lifted naturally from the sea, when you will move it forward against nothing but air in readiness for the next stroke when the roll to port returns it to the water. Take the timing from the hortator's drum, and the length of your stroke from the oarsmen in front of you. If you pull too slowly you will contribute little and be a drag on their efforts, too fast and you will be trying to move the weight of the entire ship on your own with a similar lack of result. Do you understand me?"

Rather than make a shouted reply, Declan decided to do what he had been told and give his answer in actions rather than words. Seamus watched him for a few moments, nodded, then left him to his work.

It had been three years since he had used an oar. On that occasion it had been while his vessel was being chased by a lumbering Roman trireme over a placid sea, but never before had he rowed during the prelude to an Atlantic storm of this severity. He had almost forgotten what unceasing, back-breaking work it was, but gradually he began to settle to it and to take his mind off protesting muscles by watching his severely limited view of the world outside.

When the ship rolled to port he saw a sky filled with wind-tattered clouds, and to starboard only the churning, gray sea, but during the moment when the view was moving from one to the other he had a glimpse of Cape Finisterre and the sea bursting in a continuous high, white curtain of spray over the rocks at its base. It was close, he thought, but was it coming any closer? The answer came when the ship veered toward it so that his field of view moved aft taking it out of his sight. They were in danger of being blown farther out to sea.

He swore loudly and long, knowing that the squall of hail that was beating against the shelter would prevent the other oarsmen from hearing him and, if they did, they would probably consider his language mild in the extreme.

Captain Nolan's intention was to round Finisterre and run south to find a bay or inlet where the enclosing land mass would diminish the force of the northerly storm. The proximity of a coastline would also ensure that the waves would not be able to build up to a height that would swamp and wreck them. But if they were to be blown past the sheltering inlets, they would certainly be lost and the promising and very interesting life he had found in the service of Ma'el would come to a premature end.

For some odd reason the thought made him feel more angry than afraid. He swore again and transferred his anger into the steady and regular pulling on his oar until the growing ache in his arm and back muscles pushed fear and anger alike to the back of his mind.

But Declan was becoming very tired, tireder than he could ever remember being in his whole life and, with the sun obscured by hurrying storm clouds, he had no way of knowing for how long he had been pulling with his blistering hands on this stupid oar other than that it felt like a goodly fraction of eternity. By now Seamus should have ordered someone to relieve him, but more time passed with no sign of that being done. He thought of shipping his oar so that the other would see it pointing skyward and know that Declan was exhausted and in need of a relief, but everyone else on deck would also see it and know of his weakness and he did not think that he could bear the shame of that. Even so, he was about to surrender to his fatigue by sliding the oar handle into its retaining loop when the bottom edge of the weather shelter lifted to admit a blast of spray-filled wind and the roaring voice of Seamus. Declan laughed aloud, thinking that his back-breaking term on the oars had ended just before he had to embarrass himself by calling quits, but that was not to be.

It was the oarsman directly in from of him who was relieved and his position taken by Brian, who received the same shouted advice that Declan had been given what seemed like an eternity earlier. Only then did Seamus turn to him with a white-fanged snarl of approval.

"You have rowed strongly and well, Declan," he shouted, "and you will be relieved shortly. But before them Brian wanted a few words with you."

"For which opportunity," Brian called loudly over his shoulder, "I had to volunteer to become an accursed galley slave even though, Seamus tells me, we have rowed to the lee of land and are no longer in imminent peril of being blown out to sea, so that my sacrifice was an unnecessary one." He nodded toward the line of oarsmen in front of them. "My words to you are private. May we converse in Latin?"

Declan returned happily to stroking his oar now that he knew his rest would not be long delayed, and shouted back, "I speak and comprehend a little, but have no fluency in it."

"Then tell me when my meaning is unclear," Brian replied, interrupting his speech and twisting his head backward at the end of every pull to resume it, "and I shall use simpler words . . . I am curious and would learn more about Ma'el, your master."

When Declan remained silent, the other went on. "In my time I have met many charlatans and so-called wizards. . . . But now I believe that I have at last met a true magician . . . and in my stupidity have grievously insulted and angered him. . . . I would like to make my peace with this Ma'el the Magician. . . . But if I am to give my apology proper form and substance . . . I must learn more of his ways and his thoughts as well as of the full extent of his wizardry. . . ."

"I am in his service but two weeks," Declan interrupted. "In that time he said nothing about himself . . . so in truth I, too, know nothing about him."

"But you must know *something* about him," Brian said, then stopped speaking to make a few strokes. He was sounding breathless as well as impatient when he went on, "Something he did or said, perhaps . . . that seemed of no importance to you at the time. . . . The workings of that enchanted map of his . . .

would be of enormous value to the rulers of any seafaring nation in the world . . . and those who obtained its secrets could find themselves wealthy and powerful indeed. . . . The wage paid to a servant, no matter how generous, would be as nothing. . . . And what of the other magic devices his wagon contains?"

Brian was talking so much as he pulled on his oar that he was almost gasping for breath. Declan would have laughed if he had not been so tired, both of rowing and of the other trying so obviously to subvert him. He pressed his teeth together and remained silent.

"I find subtlety of speech difficult," the other went on, "while playing the part of a dammed galley slave. . . . I do not suggest that you betray your new master. . . . I only want to know what you know . . . and think about him. . . . Speak to me, Declan. . . . Surely you must have wanted to delve into Ma'el's secrets when his wagon was unattended . . . ? Your pardon, I did not mean to suggest . . . that a trusted servant like you would steal . . . only that you would want to satisfy your curiosity. . . . Have you been inside his wagon. . . . and what did you see?"

"No," Declan replied, "and nothing. Ma'el forbids entry to Sinead and myself."

He took a deep breath and went on without pause, "Once when I tried to look inside, there was an outer screen of animal hide that moved aside easily, and an inner one that looked to be the same but was as solid and immovable as a wall of stone. When I persisted, strange and frightening pictures came into my mind and so I moved back quickly."

Brian was silent for several strokes, then he said, "With respect, Declan, there was no stone wall. . . . It, and the fearful phantasms you imagined . . . were but an enchantment of Ma'el's given substance by your own imaginings. . . . I have heard of magicians and sorcerers from the East who could work such a spell. . . . What if by accident you had tripped and fallen against that imaginary wall . . . or thrown a stone at it . . . ?"

"Enough!" said Declan, making no attempt to hide his anger as he shouted above the din of wind-driven hail rattling off the weather shelter, the slow beating of the hortator, and the other noises made by the ship and the sea. "These are questions you should ask of Ma'el himself. To his servants he seems to be a gentle old man who is slow to anger. After your recent unmannerly behavior toward him, if he had wanted to change you into a toad he would have done so last night."

Brian said nothing after that and he did not look around when Seamus returned with the relief oarsman and beckoned Declan outside. He was surprised to find that many hours had passed, that daylight was fading into a stormy twilight, and that the high, sheltering cliffs looming on their port bow were checking the wind and reducing the height of the waves around them. Seamus followed him to the lee of the wagon where Sinead was sheltering and seeming not to have moved since he had last seen her.

"Your Declan has done well this day," Seamus said, showing his teeth, "but he is unused to hard work. Would you be so kind, healer, as to attend to his blistered hands?"

TWELVE

The meal in the captain's cabin that evening was a hurried one for two reasons; the ship was rolling and pitching so violently that their platters and the food on them were continually threatening to slide onto the deck, and the captain was mentioning with increasing impatience his need to consult Ma'el's enchanted map again. Declan and Brian ate awkwardly because of the soothing ointment Sinead had smeared on their hands and the tight bindings that held it against the blisters. They did not look at or speak to each other or anyone else, and it was plain that the other was uneasy regarding the things Declan might have told the old man about their conversation while they had been on the oars together. It was Brian who spoke first in an obvious attempt to reduce the verbal damage he might have done to himself.

"Ma'el, you are a unique person in my experience," he began smoothly, "and earlier today I was trying to satisfy my curiosity by asking Declan about your powers, your thoughts and your magical devices, and no doubt he has already told you about our conversation. I trust you will forgive the liberty . . ." he laughed quietly, ". . . and that you will not think that I was trying to wrest your deepest secrets from a servant. . . ."

"My servants," the old man broke in gently, "know nothing of my deepest secrets, nor are they required to report to me everything they see, hear, do, or think. I reward them for the work they do for me, but I do not own their minds. Declan did not mention the conversation to me so it is obvious that he did not think it important. You were curious about my map?"

Before Brian could find his tongue, Captain Nolan slapped the top of the table. "And I, too, am curious about your map," he said. "Not about the magical how and why it came into your possession but simply to consult it as an aid to saving your lives and my ship. . . ."

"Not necessarily in that order of importance," Seamus murmured.

". . . Please, Ma'el," the captain ended, ignoring his first lieutenant, "tell me that you have it on your person now."

Ma'el inclined his head in affirmation, produced the map, and tapped it until it had unfolded to cover the table.

"This is a different map!" the captain burst out, excitement raising the tone of his usually deep voice. "We see only the coastline around Finisterre and nothing of Britain or Gaul. . . ."

"It is a closer and enlarged view of the scene you saw yesterday . . ." the old man began when the captain interrupted him.

"Indeed it is closer," he said. "And there is a narrow, uneven ribbon of whiteness that follows the coastline that must be, although I can scarcely believe it, the sea breaking against the cliffs. But beyond the white line there are patches and points of a pale grayness that shades into black in deeper waters. What means that? Where are we on this chart, and why do we see none of your great, slow-spinning storm clouds?"

"The pale grayness shows the position of rocks close to the surface," Ma'el replied, "which you will want to avoid. At the center of the map there is a small point of gray that is our position. The storm clouds cover us but the picture uses a special light which enables us to look through them."

The captain's eyes began to shine with the wonder of a small child. He said, "If what you tell me is true, and I have no reason to doubt that, with this I can navigate past the most dangerous of reefs, in the darkness of a starless and moonless night, with complete safety. But what of the storm? Does your magic tell us if or when it will abate?"

Sharply Ma'el tapped an area of the map again. Around the table there were grunts of surprise as the image began to shrink rapidly until the coasts of Iberia and Gaul crawled into view followed quickly by the land outlines of the whole of western Europe. The fat double spiral of their storm was again visible. It was Ma'el who spoke first.

"As I have already told you," he said, "the forecasting of weather changes depends on many things and can never be wholly accurate. I have been told that the movement of air displaced by a bird's wing on the other side of the world can, in time, contribute to major changes in the weather an untold distance away. The storm whose lower edge is covering us will, I feel sure, move northward and thence into the Arctic wastes. Two or perhaps three days will elapse before this happens. The storm will be replaced by a high-pressure continental air mass, that is a large area of dry and calmer weather, which will produce gentler but very cold winds from the northeast. This wind direction will favor you. . . ."

"Yes, yes, it will," the captain broke in. "I still don't understand some of the strange words you use, old man, even though I believe them. But . . ." he pointed to the tiny coastline east of Finisterre, ". . . I can't use this to navigate safely among inshore rocks."

Ma'el tapped the map gently and the original image returned. The captain gave a huge, relieved sigh. Brian, who had never taken his eyes off the map since Ma'el had begun speaking, licked his lips.

"Ma'el," he said, nodding toward the chart, "as I mentioned to Declan earlier, my principals in the Kingdoms of Tirconnel and Dalriada and, indeed, the ruler of any other seafaring nation, would reward you handsomely if you were to provide them with such maps. This is a secret more valuable than any I have ever uncovered in my years of spying. If you were to reveal the secret of the workings of such maps, you could have wealth beyond your wildest dreams."

"Regrettably," Ma'el replied with a gentle shake of his head, "there is but one map and only I know how to use it."

Captain Nolan exchanged looks with his lieutenant, then they both stared hard at Brian. "In that case," said the captain, "we must ensure that no harm of any kind comes to our magician navigator, either to his person or his property, for the remainder of this voyage. Do you take my meaning, Brian, old friend?"

For a moment Brian looked uncomfortable, then he nodded but made no other reply. Seamus showed all of his crooked teeth in a wide smile.

"Of course he does, Captain," he said, then went on in a sardonic voice, "Like us he knows nothing about our magician navigator who, for all we know, may already be rich beyond the dreams of avarice."

Captain Nolan smiled and in a moment their heads and that of Ma'el were again bent over the map. Brian watched the three of them without a word or an expression of any kind on his face until the conference was over and the captain was wishing his passengers a comfortable night. He also asked if he could retain the map overnight so as to help him steer a safe course among the reefs that stretched out from the base of the passing cliffs, and Ma'el surprised everyone by giving his permission.

While Declan was swaying and rolling about in his hammock and listening to the rain beating against the tightly stretched skins of the shelter, the expressions and conversation he had seen and heard around the captain's table came back to him. Brian, he thought, was easy talking, slippery, and untrustworthy and should be watched closely but not, he was sure, the other two. It was a very strange thought indeed, but just as the fatigue of stroking oar all day drew him into sleep, he wondered if in the dour captain and his ugly, straight-talking first officer Ma'el had found himself two new servants.

By the next morning the rain had stopped and the sun

showed from time to time between scudding clouds. With the aid of Ma'el's chart, the captain guided the ship among the sunken rocks in safety under the high cliffs that sheltered them from a wind that howled far overhead and left them to contend with little more than a stiff breeze. They followed the twisting coastline, using relays of oarsmen or sails when their course made the wind direction favorable, towards a bay that they expected to reach before nightfall and where they would be able to anchor and rest their tiring seamen. Declan was greatly relieved when Seamus, showing his teeth in a particularly wide, snarling smile, said that their situation was neither dangerous nor urgent so that the passengers need not volunteer to row.

Ma'el spent most of the day aft in with the captain, where he was instructing the other in the use of the magic chart to navigate the shallows. Sinead remained outside her shelter and seemed disposed to talk to Declan, until he made the mistake of calling her "boy" which made her angry. When he explained in a low voice that lacked all semblance of an apology that there were sea-men within hearing and did she want everyone on the ship to know that she was a young woman, she became even angrier and stopped speaking to him altogether. When Brian appeared and began talking to her in his easy, amusing fashion and making her laugh from time to time, Declan spent the rest of the day feeling even angrier without knowing why.

They were rounding a tall headland whose upper slopes were still lit by the setting sun when he saw movement and called to Seamus, who came to stand behind him so as to follow the direction of his pointing finger.

"Two, no, three men," said the Ionadacht. "You have good eyes, Declan. I must tell the captain about this without delay. But the light is fading. Keep watching them for as long as you can."

"That should be easy," he replied, shading his eyes and squinting at them through half-closed lids. "I think they're building a fire."

Already on the move, Seamus turned his head around to shout, "I was afraid of that."

He continued to watch the figures around the tiny, flickering point of orange light that grew brighter in the deepening twilight while the ship rounded the headland to drop anchor in a small bay whose narrow beach showed dark gray against the blackness inland. Another and larger fire was being kindled on the sand as he watched. One of the seamen came to ask that Sinead, Brian, and himself go to the captain's cabin at once. Ma'el and the captain were waiting for them there, but as soon as Declan entered he knew that tonight they were not being invited to dine.

"While we have the opportunity to talk undisturbed," the captain began without preamble, "I intend to discuss and assign your fighting positions and duties . . ." he glanced at Sinead ". . . or lack of them during the coming attack. Declan, Seamus tells me you have good eyes. Did you see anyone around or close to the large fire on the beach?"

"Yes, Captain," he replied. "At first I saw upward of fifteen, maybe twenty men carrying fuel and heaping it onto the fire, then all of them withdrew into the surrounding darkness. I thought that strange but . . ."

"Your pardon, Captain," Ma'el broke in gently. "I am inexperienced in these matters as you know, but is it not possible that the fires on the headland and beach were lit as acts of friendship to guide us into a safe anchorage?"

Seamus gave a scornful laugh that was silenced with a look from his superior officer.

"That is possible, Ma'el," the captain went on, striving to put patience into his voice and failing, "but it is much more likely that they are wreckers and robbers, or worse. Having failed to lure us onto the submerged rocks around the entrance to the bay, thanks to your magic map, they will now try to capture the ship instead of pillaging the wreckage that would have washed ashore of its valuables, including any survivors who could be sold as slaves. . . ."

Ma'el held up a hand and broke in gently. "You said that they might be wreckers and robbers, or worse. What is your meaning of worse?"

The captain nodded. "That unnecessarily large and unattended fire on the beach," he said, "and the speed with which it was built and kindled after the first signal fire on the headland was lit, suggests a situation where many persons are acting rapidly and in concert. It is, I feel sure, a tactic aimed at attracting our eyes to the flames and thereby reducing our night vision while an attack takes place out of the darkness on our flanks. If I am right, and I usually am in these matters, rather than a rabble of badly armed robbers and wreckers we will be facing an attack by well-disciplined Roman soldiery. Seamus."

"Captain."

"We may have little time to prepare," he went on quickly, "so many things must be done at once. Ship the oars all but for two on each side. Man these with two men each and use them with blades level to sweep the air at head height above an attacking craft, or to jab a hole in its hull if it is small and skin-covered. Raise the nets and make them loose enough to hamper rather than aid attacking boarders. Ready the arbalest, but warn that it must not be used until an enemy craft can be clearly seen close by, and certainly not if one of our own crew is standing in the way. If a target becomes visible and it should be a skin-covered coracle or curragh, aim for the waterline. It is better to sink the craft and force the weaker swimmers to discard their weapons than to waste such a heavy bolt to spear one man.

"The wind and sea are making noise enough to hide ordinary conversation," he continued, "but during the fighting warn everyone to speak softly and continuously to each other in Gaelic. This will aid the identification of friend from foe in the darkness. The Roman soldiers are recruited mostly from peasant stock and speak nothing but their native language, so anyone who talks Latin will be an enemy and should be killed without hesitation. No lights are to be shown by us at any time or for any reason. In case some of the attacking craft lose sight of us, we don't want to show them our position."

Seamus nodded and was turning to leave when the captain raised a restraining hand.

"Wait," he said, then looking straight at Ma'el he went on, "Can we expect any magical assistance during this endeavor?"

Ma'el shook his head slowly. "I can provide you with a few moments of bright light," he said, "but that would be unhelpful because you say that darkness is necessary to your defense. Regrettably, I am forbidden from killing or using violence on any other person. . . ."

"Who by?" Brian interrupted sharply, a mixture of impatience and fear coloring his voice. "A magician greater than you are?"

Ma'el's features were without expression but there seemed to be a hurt in his large eyes as he said, "Once in the past I interfered and the result was many, many deaths of innocent people. I will not do so again."

Declan cleared his throat and said quietly, "There was the leader of the robbers who attacked your wagon, and he died. With respect, the situation here is fraught with much greater risk."

"It was you, not I, who killed him," said Ma'el quietly.

The captain shook his head angrily. "This is not the time for a religious or philosophical debate," he said, "and after all that Ma'el has already done for us I cannot insist that he perform miracles. Seamus, you know what has to be done. Do it. The rest of you, apart from Ma'el and the healer, will do as I say. . . ."

THIRTEEN

I am faced with a decision that is also a serious temptation. My two servants, the complement of this ship, and the vessel itself will perish in the attack to come if I do not use my advanced technology, or as they would see it, a blatant display of wizardry, to save them. But again I remind myself of my self-imposed promise never to bring about the deaths of any of these subjects under investigation, and must refrain from interfering when groups of them are, as now, trying to kill each other.

"But the thought of losing two promising servants causes me feelings of irritation and with it a minor level of grief because, although they are little more than laboratory subjects, they are beings for whom I have developed a liking.

"I have decided not to vacate the ship with my traveling habitat and equipment until the last possible moment, in case a miracle not of my making should occur to save them. . . ."

Ma'el had moved inside his wagon where he had insisted to everyone that he would be safe; Sinead had been placed in the lee of the vehicle and wrapped loosely in oiled skins to resemble an untidy piece of deck cargo with instructions to be still and silent, and Brian and Declan had been assigned to guard the stern with whomever could be spared to help them when the attack would develop.

It required a great effort of will for Declan to look only to seaward and into the darkness that hid the projecting reefs growing like rocky horns from each side of the bay. To add to his difficulty, their ship was swinging at anchor so that there were times when the fire and the illuminated area of beach began creeping into the corner of his eye and threatening to dazzle him. Beside him neither the man on the tiller nor Brian reported seeing anything, and he wondered if the beach fire was giving enough light for the attacking craft, which would also contain men with sharp eyes, to see them.

All around him there was total darkness that was broken only by the sounds of the sea, the high wind, the ship and the soft, occasional voices of the seamen as they spoke their names to each other. Beside him Brian was speaking softly and continuously as he recited an endless, bawdy poem that he had learned somewhere on his travels. The helmsman was appreciating it but Declan felt sure that it was not one that Sinead should hear.

He continued to stare into the darkness but seeing only a mental image of her lying on the deck under the wagon like a forgotten sack of foodstuffs, cold, uncomfortable, but safe, unless this coming engagement were to go the wrong way, whereupon the mind pictures of what would happen to her became much worse. He was so busy trying to push those pictures out of his mind that he almost missed hearing the new sound, the thump and scraping noises of a boat making intermittent contact with the stern.

Quickly he felt for Brian in the darkness beside him, found his arm, and them moved his fingers down until he found the other's wrist.

"Brian," he said quickly. "Grip my belt at the back and hold it firmly. I'm going to lean far over the rail."

He was already raising his axe high in the air and leaning forward into the blackness while Brian fumbled and took a tight hold on his belt. Before he let the weapon fall in a wide, circular, two-handed sweep he remembered to twist the shaft so that the heavy blade would not strike edge-on. Captain Nolan would not be pleased with him if he was to damage the ship's rudder post. But he hit someone. There was a grunt of pain followed by the heavy splash of a body going into the water. He allowed the weight of the axe head to sweep upward and then down into another swing.

This time the blade glanced off something but otherwise raised only a great splash of water.

"Quickly," he called over his shoulder, "let me go further out."

He heard Brian's drop to the deck and felt the other's two-handed grip around his belt and continued to swing with the axe blade forward. This time it met more than water. There was a grunt of pain, the sound of splintering wickerwork and the tearing of covering skins followed by the sound of splashing and cries of alarm.

"Pull me back," he shouted. When this was done he laughed and added, "I hit one of them, and I think I knocked in the side of their boat."

"Good," said Brian. There was a fumbling and scraping against the deck as he retrieved his pike in the darkness.

"Not good," said the helmsman in a low, disapproving voice. "If you've sunk their craft they will be angry, and will have nowhere to go except onto this one. Guard yourselves and speak your names. Tomas, Tomas, Tomas."

Brian and Declan did so as they both moved few paces to each side of him, and he heard their pikes tap sharply against the stern rail as they sought in the darkness for an aiming level for the blind thrusts they would shortly be making against the boarders. Declan did the same with the shaft of his long-axe. He had decided to use it like a heavy spear and jab rather than swing with it. That would render it less effective as a weapon but it would also reduce the risk of him accidentally killing his two companions. Every few seconds he spoke his name and jabbed into the darkness above the rail, without striking anything but the empty air.

From what seemed like one or two paces to his right there came the betraying sounds of leather scraping against against wood and the scuffling of a heavy body scrambling over the rail. He was drawing back his axe for a jabbing thrust at the sounds when there was a sudden scream of pain, the splash of someone falling into the sea, and a burst of swearing in Brian's voice.

"Are you wounded?" said Declan, continuing his thrust into empty darkness and drawing back to make another. "Where, and how badly?"

"No," said Brian, swearing again. He went on quickly, "I stuck one of them, in the face or arm, I think, because I felt no armor. But he grabbed my pike and took it when he went over the side. What the hell do I do now I've lost my bloody weapon?"

"Reach out your arm to me," said Declan, changing to a one-handed grip on his axe shaft and reaching out toward the voice until he encountered Brian's arm. He gripped it loosely, slid his hand down to the wrist of the other's hand then moved it to the handle of his gladius.

"Use that," he said. "Jab, don't swing it. You'll have to fight closer, it's shorter than a pike but does more damage. If you lose it over the side I'll kill you myself."

"*Go ro mait agat . . .*" the other began, but his thanks in Gaelic were interrupted by the sound of heavy feet jumping onto the deck all around them, and suddenly Brian was speaking Latin.

"Careful, fool!" he growled in an angry undertone. "Strike to your left, soldier, you all but killed your own officer!"

"I'm sorry, sir," another voice began in Latin, but it ended with the soft, soggy thump of a blade driving into flesh, a high-pitched grunt of pain and the sound of a body falling to the deck followed by the voice of Brian again speaking in Gaelic.

"I'm sorry," he muttered in a voice devoid of sorrow, "that pretence was most dishonorable. But then, I'm a diplomat, not a warrior. My tongue is supposed to be my strongest weapon."

"Utterly dishonorable, and effective," said Declan, laughing softly. "But be careful in its use lest you be mistakenly slain as a Roman. . . ."

He broke off because more feet were landing on the deck in front and to one side of him. Brian and the helmsman were still softly speaking their names out of the darkness. He moved backward a pace to a distance where he could swing rather than jab with his long-axe without endangering his friends. He went down on one knee, the better to avoid the attackers' body-level stabs and slashes, as he made the first wide, circular swing.

Declan felt a double shock run up the handle to his wrists and heard a scream as the heavy blade took someone's legs from under them, but the next swing met only empty air. Still keeping low, he moved forward and swung again. This time the handle was nearly jarred loose in his grasp as the outer point of the blade tore through leather and underlying flesh and bone of a head or chest, and that man crashed to the deck without making a sound. He was twisting the axehead free, a small part of his mind trying not to think about the terrible wound it had made, when suddenly he was able to see everything that was happening.

The wind had cleared a small area of sky that contained a few stars and a thin sliver of crescent moon. There was just enough light to show Brian desperately waving his gladius two-handed at an attacker while he tried desperately to fend off the thrusts of the other's spear, while beyond them the helmsman, Tomas, who was limping and at times hopping on one leg, was engaging another Roman with a shortened pike the first few inches of whose point had presumably been left in someone else. Declan shifted his grip and raised his weapon high before swinging it down to strike with the flat of the blade like a massive club onto the top of the first Roman's helmet. The man dropped to the deck as if he had no bones in his legs. Brian laughed his thanks and turned to attack the helmsman's opponent in the flank, and a moment later the Roman went down.

Declan saw a movement out of the corner of his eye and turned to see two heads, separated from each other by about three paces, appearing above the stern rail. He swung the axe in a wide circle and struck hard at the first one. There was the sound of a body splashing into the sea, although he could not be sure if the head was still attached to it. When the second boarder saw what had happened to his companion, he threw his sword awkwardly at Declan and pushed himself backward to fall into his boat. For the moment the deck was clear of attackers, at least living ones. Tomas pointed at the fallen bodies.

"Over the side," he said. "We don't want to trip over them in the dark. I can't help you. A leg wound."

Quickly Brian retrieved the attackers' weapons, passed a spear to Tomas and returned Declan's gladius because he now had one of his own. Together they lifted the bodies by their legs and shoulders and swung them high over the rail, hearing two splashes and then a splintering sound of one of them crashing down onto a boat. As he paused a moment to look around, from amidships came the loud twang and thump of the arbalest which now had moonlit targets at which to aim.

Too many targets by far.

Declan swore as he glimpsed upward of twenty craft, three of them large and loaded down with men and the rest small dugouts or skin-covered curraghs bearing three or four each. Now that they could see their quarry, the men in the boats were cheering, and those in the bows where whirling grappling hooks on long hemp lines around their heads to launch them slingshot-fashion at the ship. A few of the hooks clattered on board and found purchase on deck projections, but most them became entangled in the antiboarding nets, tearing and pulling them down as the lines were pulled in. The boarders from the few craft that had been able to find them in the dark must have been repelled, although a few of them still hung from the nets like fat, black flies caught in a spider web. Suddenly the commanding voice of Captain Nolan rose above the enemy shouting, speaking aloud the very thought that were in Declan's mind.

"Seamus," he called, "they are too many for us and we'll be over-run within moments. Raise the anchor and set the foresail.

All portside oarsmen who can get blades in the water, pull and bring her around. Helmsman, head for the open sea and let the wind take her. . . ."

His words were interrupted by the twang of another arbalest bolt being fired, followed by a small outcry from the target boat as it struck, and the rest of his words were spoken to someone close by him and too quietly for Declan to hear them. Not so the words of Tomas.

"Something is fouling the bloody rudder," he said. "Declan, see if you can clear it. Brian, help me here."

While Tomas and Brian put their shoulder to the tiller and pushed with no effect, Declan moved quickly to bend double over the rail where he looked along the length of the rudder. The dim moonlight was shadowed by the stern overhang so that he could sense movement but saw only a large, indistinct mass that was probably a boat, and a thin line of lighter material joining the rudder with the ship's stern timbers. He jabbed at it with the head of his axe and heard the clink of metal. It might be a short sword with the hilt removed, he thought, that was being used to wedge the rudder immobile. He gripped the shaft of his axe in both hands and jabbed downward even harder and felt the metal obstruction bend and fall away. The rudder was moving freely again.

Declan was about to straighten up when he felt two things happening in the same moment, hands grasping at the shaft of his axe and a sudden, glancing blow striking the side of his leather helmet, delivered by what felt like a spear or sword point and all but knocking it from his head. He jerked the long-axe free, the only clear thought in his mind the saving of his best weapon, and staggered back with lights that were in his mind rather than in front of his eyes bursting all around him. Still dazed, he leaned against the tiller to steady himself.

"There's no need to do that, Declan," said Tomas, "it's working well again. But standing out to sea in this storm beyond the shelter of the bay is risky. Perhaps the captain is hoping that the small craft trailing astern will founder in the high waves before we do, but I very much doubt that."

"I do like an optimist," said Brian dryly, then, "Declan, are you all right?"

He shook his head vigorously in an attempt to clear it rather than as an answer, and said, "Yes."

The combination of oars and rudder were bringing the ship around so that the wind was striking the foresail edge-on, making it flap loudly and ripple like a flag in a gale, then suddenly it began to fill. Underfoot the deck motion was changing as the vessel began to surge forward, but slowly because of the cluster of smaller craft that had attached or were still attaching themselves to her with thrown grappling hooks. With their shallow draft the high wind behind the foresail should have been taking them over the waves at speed, but instead they were moving as sluggishly as an overloaded barge. Suddenly, above the ringing in his ears he heard the high, clear voice of Sinead and the quieter and some-how clearer one of Ma'el calling out to the captain, but the wind shredded the words of their meaning.

A grappling hook clattered onto the deck at Declan's feet. Before it could find a hold on the deck structure he stooped quickly and threw it back into the sea. The effort made him so dizzy that he had to use the shaft of his axe to steady himself. On the rail to his right two pairs of hands were visible, then they dis-appeared into total darkness as a cloud blew across the sickle moon. Through the persistent buzzing in his ears he heard the sound of feet landing on the deck. Tomas and Brian began saying their names again to give their positions and identities in the blackness.

Declan did the same as he moved a safe distance away from them and took a double grip on the lower end of his axe shaft. Then slowly at first but picking up speed he began spinning around on his heels and toes with the long-axe held at full exten-sion. He still felt dizzy but in the darkness he could not know if or when he was falling, and somehow he was able to remain erect. His idea was that if he could see nothing then he would try to hit everything that came within range, and hit it hard. Three times he felt the axehead catch and tear against something, probably clothing or leather armor, and move on. He judged them to be wounding rather than lethal blows.

Brian and Tomas were still alive because he could hear them saying their names, but suddenly two things happened at once. Declan overbalanced and fell heavily onto his side and the other two's voices were drowned out by the stentorian tones of the captain.

"Men, hear and believe my words!" he shouted. "One of our passengers is a great wizard. He is about to conjure up a creature monstrous and terrible beyond belief to aid us in our time of need. But fear not, for he promises you that it will do no harm to any member of our crew. . . ."

Behind Declan a light like that of a great, blue sun had come into being, a light that he had seen once before during the robber attack in the clearing. So Ma'el had broken the solemn promise he had made to himself and had decided to help slay their attackers. Declan was too relieved to feel disappointment, but he doubted that the old man's terrible and magical beast would come soon enough to save his own life.

There were five or six Romans around him, none of them further than three paces distant, and two with weapons raised to strike. Declan tried to bring up his heavy axe, knowing that he could not do so in time. But the expected blows did not come. Instead the men were looking past him, their mouths wide open. One of them dropped his weapon to the deck, cried out in fear, turned and jumped over the stern into the sea. The others followed, including those who had been attacking Brian and Tomas. He heard them shouting to the other craft as they jumped back into their own boats or the water alongside. By the time he had climbed to his feet, Ma'el's bright blue light had died, but the darkness was not complete because the moon had cleared the clouds again.

It gave enough light for him to see that the ship was clear of boarders, the ropes attached to the grappling hooks had been released so that they trailed loose in the water, and the attacking craft were being rowed hurriedly back toward the beach while their frightened crews shouted fearfully to each other.

"What the . . ." said Declan, searching his aching brain for an oath colorful enough to suit the occasion without finding it, "What happened?"

"Like you," said Brian, laughing, "we were too busy looking aft to see. . . ."

"That was well done, men, all of you," the voice of the captain broke in. "It was a close-fought thing even with the magical intervention. Seamus! Lower the foresail. All men able to row, man the oars. Helmsman, steer us back to the weather shelter of the bay and drop anchor."

He broke off to laugh loudly and long before going on, "Set a double watch to keep an eye on the Romans, but I very much doubt that they will trouble us again this night."

FOURTEEN

... **I**t was not necessary to slay any Earth person. On the ship their survival was due to the intervention of minor and nonviolent Taelon science in conjunction with human ingenuity. It begins to concern me that such a high level of intuitive intelligence is available to a species with only the rudiments of technical education or support.

"This incident illustrates my difficulty in continuing to treat these people merely as subjects for investigation. . . ."

By first light the storm had abated to a stiff breeze and they had resumed the voyage because Ma'el, in his clear if partly incomprehensible words, had informed the captain that the troublesome low had moved north into Skandia and was being replaced by a high-pressure system that was deepening over the continental land mass, and that this would ensure favorable winds and weather over the ensuing four or five days. But the emotional weather in and around the shelters of Declan and Sinead continued rough, and its far from calm storm center was the healer.

Sinead had been tending the previous night's wounded without pause during the hours of daylight, so that she was both tired and short-tempered. She insisted, and her words were backed up gently by Ma'el, that Declan remain in his shelter instead of stumbling about the deck like a drunken man and perhaps falling over the side, that he rest as much as possible but not fall asleep in case he went into a coma and did not wake again, and that the compress she had given him for the enormous lump on his head must be kept wetted even if the cold water did run down his neck.

When he objected she said that last night's blow to the head might have permanently addled his brain, and that rest and the reduction of the swelling was the only treatment she knew short of opening his head, a procedure which she had never attempted before. She asked Brian to relieve Declan's boredom and to ensure that he remained awake.

But Brian wanted only to talk about the fearsome monster conjured by Ma'el. He was being eaten alive by his own curiosity, he said, but the healer and everyone he had asked about the magical beast would not talk about it. With the crew numbers reduced by wounded, they had said that they were too busy with other duties and that Seamus would have hard words or even harder fists for them if they stopped for idle chatter. Declan had replied truthfully that he, too, had seen nothing. In the end Brian changed the subject to that of Ma'el himself, seeking out scraps of information about the old man which, because of Declan's possibly addled wits, he might be able to pry loose. In the event he was unsuccessful because Declan had no new information to give him. But Brian at least made the hours pass quickly until Sinead arrived to say that it was time to join the captain.

It was a quiet and hurried meal because there was only one subject that Captain Nolan and Seamus wanted to discuss, but good manners forbade them from bringing it up over food. When the platters were cleared away, the captain said, "Healer, what of our wounded?"

"Apart from general bruising and scrapes that are of little consequence," Sinead replied in a voice self-assured beyond her tender years, "there are seven of which I shall speak in the reverse order of their severity. First there is Declan, who sustained a heavy blow to his head which could well have led to a coma and death or at least to seriously addled wits. Fortunately he is able to converse, has not fallen asleep and his wits do not seem to be addled, at least . . ." she smiled ". . . no more than is usual with him. If or when required, he is able to take an oar. . . ."

"Thank you, healer," said Declan in an angry undertone.

". . . There are four others, each of whom have taken two or three shallow cuts or stabs," she went on, ignoring him. "All of the wounds are clean and, if the men are rested, should heal in a few days. The injury to the sixth one, Tomas the helmsman, is more serious."

"He took a deep stab wound to the calf muscle of the left leg," she went on, "which is not clean. In spite of applying a poultice to draw out impure substances, by the end of the day the lower leg and foot had become swollen and inflamed. Until now I've never seen a wound turn bad so quickly."

"I have," said the captain, his voice quiet but very, very angry. "It is caused by the weapon of a cowardly and vindictive enemy who has dipped the point in cow or pig dung so that the smallest of wounds will lead to poisoning and death. What are you doing for Tomas, and can you save him?"

"A very tight cord has been tied just above the knee," she replied, "which should cut off the flow of poisoned blood into his upper leg and body for a time. This has also stopped the flow of blood to the lower leg, so that the early stages of corruption are already taking place. The affected limb will have to be removed as soon as possible from about a hand's width above the knee. I have no experience of cutting. My healing is concerned mostly with the use of medicines and poultices, but I watched when my father had to cut off a limb. . . ."

The captain held up a hand. "Then you know more about it than we do," he said. "What instruments will you need?"

Declan watched Sinead hesitate for a moment before visibly coming to a decision. She tapped the table with a small fist and said, "I'll need this table, at least two more lanterns to light it, enough rope, and the help of three strong men. They should

include you, Captain, as his superior officer to help him steady
his mind, and Brian and Declan to hold him motionless and help
me when needed. For the patient's sake he should be rendered as
insensible as possible while we are working."

"That means two or three flagons of my best wine," said
Brian softly. "Don't worry, healer, he'll have them. But I'm not
sure I can help you. I abhor the sight of blood and may sicken."

"For the wine, thank you," she said, then went on impatiently, "but it will not be your blood that is flowing so try to control your feelings. I will need many jugs of water. They must be
clean salt water taken from the sea rather than the drinking casks
which sometimes have mites swimming in them. Also tools from
the ship's carpenter, a few of his keenest knives and a handsaw
that is sharp. The blades, and our hands, must be thoroughly
cleansed with water and then alcohol that is stronger than wine if
we have it. . . ."

Brian nodded and said, "There goes my poteen."

". . . Our hands must be shaken dry," she went on, with a grateful nod in his direction, "rather than being dried with a cloth that
might contain harmful impurities. There is more than enough poison in that leg as it is and its removal should be done speedily.
That's why I need the lamps now rather than waiting for daylight."

The captain looked at Seamus, who nodded and left quickly
to begin making the necessary arrangements, then turned his
eyes on Sinead again.

"What of the seventh man?" he said.

She paused for a moment, her face clouding over and plainly
seeking for inner composure, then went on, "He is the young
man, Liam, and the worst of them all. He took a deep thrust in
his lower belly that opened his bowel, so it did not matter
whether or not the blade was poisoned because his own wastes
escaped into his body with the same effect. He has a high fever
and is in great and continuing pain, and moans softly and constantly when many another man would be screaming in agony,
but he tells me that doing such a thing would make him feel
unmanly and ashamed of himself. There is no way that I can save

his life, which will end in four or five days' time. The potion I administered, which is itself a slow poison, deadens his pain a little but does not remove it.

"In greater strength the potion would kill him within a few moments," she ended, "with no pain at all."

"Healer," said the captain gravely, "is that the action you yourself would take?"

"It is," she said, looking at his face for a long moment without either blinking or looking away. "But the final decision must be yours because you are his captain."

"I am much more than his captain," said the other in a low voice that was filled with pain, "I am also a good friend of his family who has known him since he was a babe in arms. Neither I nor they would disagree with your proposed action, so your recommendation is approved. But before you put him into the endless sleep, I shall say my last words to him and, when you are administering the potion I would like you, too, to speak to him, not as another boy but with gentleness as the last woman he will ever meet."

"I will do that," she replied softly as the captain was leaving.

Ma'el looked at Sinead, picked up his folded map and rose to leave. "I hear the captain and Seamus outside with your patient," he said. "Regrettably, I can be of no help in what you have to do. I wish steady hands and calmness of mind to all of you, and to Tomas the best of good fortune. . . ."

"Please, before you go," Brian broke in. "Declan and I were too busy last night to see the magical beast that frightened off the Romans. What did you do, what was it, and what did it look like?"

"I merely shone a light onto the foresail," said the old man gently, inclining his head toward Sinead. "It was the healer who conjured up the terrifying beast."

"Sinead," said Brian, "you're a healer, not a magician. What does he mean and what did you *do?*"

The captain and Seamus arrived carrying Tomas at that point and Sinead, looking uncomfortable, told him that she had done very little and she had too many instructions for them to waste time answering unimportant questions. But suddenly the subject and the question arose again and from a source she could not very well refuse to answer.

They were ready to begin work and the medical situation and their plans for remedying it had been explained in detail to Tomas. He had already downed almost two flagons of wine so that, he told them with a wide and completely relaxed smile, if he had not been roped tightly to the table he would have been floating close to the ceiling. But before the work began he, too, wanted to know all about the terrible monster that had been conjured up to protect their ship, and which he had not been able to see for himself.

He said that if he was to die this night it should not be from curiosity.

"The magician lit up the foresail," Sinead said, her face coloring with embarrassment, "and I produced the monster. Are you quite sure that you want me to do it again?"

"No," Tomas mumbled, then immediately contradicted himself, "I mean, yes. Captain, you told us that it wouldn't hurt any member of the crew. If it is too fearful, I'll tell myself that the wine is affecting my mind and I will simply disbelieve in its existence."

The captain laughed quietly and said, "It will not hurt you, drunk or sober. But your mind is working clearly and with the logic of a philosopher, so it may be that you are still too sober. Have some more of Brian's wine, look at the monster and then, Tomas my friend, we must take off your leg. Healer?"

Sinead nodded and reached up to the lanterns hanging from the low roof beams, turning down the wicks of all but one which she lowered on its chain to chest height before closing all except one of its windows. A single square of yellow light shone on the cabin's aft wall in clear sight of everyone. She placed her hands between the light and the wall.

"When I was very young," she said. "My father showed me how to make shadow pictures . . ." her hands clasped together in different ways as she demonstrated, ". . . of a dog, like this, or a duck or my favorite, a butterfly that moved its wings. Later I became more imaginative and made pictures of fearful demons and flying monsters including this one, of which, to humor me, my father pretended to be afraid. Last night this same one appeared briefly in giant size, filling the entire expanse of the foresail which rippled and bellied in a wind which made the monster's body move with great realism. The boarders glimpsed it for the few moments that Ma'el's light was shining and thought that we had conjured up a terrible, winged demon. Unlike my father they were not pretending to be afraid of it and so they ran back to their boats."

For a moment Tomas stared wide-eyed at the dark picture and the illuminated hands that were making it, then he swore and began to laugh. "It frightens me, a little, even when I know what it is," he said, and looked into her face for a moment before he went on, "Thank you, healer, for the most hilarious and outrageous joke I have ever heard, as well as for everything else you are trying to do for me. I am ready."

Declan was to remember the sights and sounds of that night for the remainder of his life, and they were to trouble his sleep for many weeks to come. Tomas had screamed throughout, stopping only to breathe, and Declan had not blamed him because in the same position he would have been doing the same.

Despite the padded cord that had been twist-tightened around the upper leg to reduce the flow of blood, after the first deep, circular cut was made to the depth of the bone there was a frightening amount of it oozing and pumping sluggishly onto the captain's table. It was even worse when Sinead, her words calm but her face the palest he had ever seen on a living person, made two more deep vertical cuts at the edge of the original one and asked him to hold the resulting flaps of muscle and bleeding flesh backward and away from the bone while she used the saw. The job had fallen to him because, in spite of the tight ropes encircling his body, both the captain and Brian had been needed to hold the struggling Tomas still. As she worked Sinead had explained that the bone had to be cut short so that a flap of muscle and flesh could be folded over the end of it to form, if the work was successful, a fleshy pad that would support a wooden leg.

But then she had asked him to hold tightly a slippery, pulsing artery between two tightly pressed fingertips and a thumb while she tied off the end with a length of poteen-soaked catgut while explaining, as if he had been some kind of high druid examiner of healers, or perhaps her dead father, that the ends of the knot were being left long so that they would project beyond the wound and be withdrawn when healing was complete.

She had done many other intricate and bloody things before he had been asked to hold the edges of the fleshy flaps together while she joined them together with more cleansed catgut except for a small slit containing a short length of quill which, she had said, would allow bad blood and pus to flow away so that the wound, if the fates willed it, would not go bad on the inside. By the time that had been done and the stump bound firmly in washed rags, Tomas was quiet again. She had given Declan a small, serious smile, then thanked everyone and told them that their faces were paler than the patient's and that they should all sit down for a while.

Lastly she had bent over Tomas, raised his head slowly in one hand while holding a small cup to his lips with the other.

"Tomas," she said gently, "this night your body has worked harder than it has ever done in a month of labor, and endured more pain than most men are called on to suffer in a lifetime. It is all that hard work and pain, more than the mind-dulling potion I have administered, or the soft, warm hammock that awaits you, that will put you to sleep.

"So rest easy, Tomas," she said, laying her hand gently on his forehead, "you have done very well."

FIFTEEN

... **T**he weather remained fair and the winds favorable until we passed through the Pillars of Hercules and turned eastward into the Mediterranean, whereafter the wind continued westerly and mild. In spite of explaining that this good fortune was due simply to the operation of the meteorological laws of chance, the crew believed me responsible and thanked me many times for it.

"I am deliberately curtailing the use of my 'magic map' because it would be an unkindness to make the captain too dependent on it before I leave his ship.

"On the second day after repelling the Roman boarding craft off Finisterre there was a ceremonial disposal of the form of flesh that had recently housed the young man Liam. The rite involved the officers and some of the crew speaking words of praise and admiration about his short life and I, although present, did not take part because the philosophical reasoning behind it was unclear to me as there is nothing with any resemblance to this ceremony among the Taelon.

"The damaged helmsman, Tomas, is progressing well after giving the healer initial cause for concern when his stump became inflamed for a few days and required constant poulticing.

Now, when the sea is calm, he moves about the deck on two crutches made for him by the ship's carpenter, who has also promised to make him a thick, wooden peg and attachment straps so that he will be able to balance his weight naturally and discard the crutches. The healer insists that this should not be done for several weeks so as to enable the fleshy pad at the end of the leg stump to heal and harden to the point where it will support the helmsman's weight without pain. By now all of the crew know that the healer is female, but they maintain the pretense and use only her title rather than her name, and from conversations I have overheard on my sound sensor it is clear that they would be willing to die rather than allow any harm to befall her.

"I am particularly impressed by the way the helmsman, Tomas, has been able to overcome his disability. The idea of a physically crippled Taelon is inconceivable and repugnant to me.

"Apart from my servants, who are still not entirely at ease with each other, the psychological behavior of the humans on board is very good, a condition which Captain Nolan describes as being in good spirits. When they are not otherwise engaged and the sun is out, they have taken to projecting hand pictures on the deck or superstructure and compete with each other to see who can make the most realistic subjects. As the person who saved them by showing the first picture, the healer is called on to judge the competitions. At times they have a tendency to behave like children, which is strange because their life spans are too ephemeral to waste on activities that are nonessential. But from time to time they do this, and in spite of the desirability of remaining emotionally detached from the specimens under evaluation, I am aware of a strange feeling for these ridiculously short-lived beings that is analogous to the affection felt by them for their even more transient and nonsapient work animals and pets.

"It was this strange feeling, as well as the inconvenience of losing and having to replace servants, which caused me once again to intervene secretly so that their lives could be saved. . . ."

·   ·   ·

They were passing between the southern extremities of Sardinia and the north coast of Africa and turning northeast with a light following wind onto the heading that would take them to Rome, when the triangular sails of two ships were sighted astern. Within moments Seamus joined them beside the wagon.

"Healer, Declan," he said, his voice unnecessarily loud because it was plain that he wanted Ma'el, who was resting in the wagon, to overhear him as well. "They are pirate craft out of Carthage by the look of them, with about the same spread of sail as ourselves but with the advantage of rested oarsmen or, more likely, galley slaves who can be whipped half to death to give them the speed they need. A stern chase is usually a long chase, but the captain estimates that they will catch us by midafternoon unless . . ."

He left the word hanging.

"You want Brian and I to take an oar . . . ?" Declan began.

"No," Seamus broke in, glancing at his long-axe and gladius. "We need you rested if you are to fight well."

Sinead looked at Declan and made an obvious attempt to force calmness into her voice as she said, "If they catch us as early as that, there can be no fearsome beast to threaten them from the sails. Or were you suggesting something else?"

"I don't know what I'm suggesting," said Seamus grimly as he was turning to leave. "These pirates are worse, much worse, believe me, than the Romans we fought off Finisterre. But Ma'el has withdrawn from us. Even though he remains friendly he will not even show us his magic map. I was hoping that you would ask your master to help us."

When he had gone, Declan looked up at the wagon and said, "We'd better tell Ma'el about this."

Sinead shook her head. "There's no need," she said, "I have the feeling that he hears and knows everything that is happening on this ship. Whether he will do anything about it is another matter."

They watched without speaking as the pursuing ships crept closer and the climbing sun began to warm the deck timbers around them, the silence broken only by the steady creaking and splashing of the oars, and the drum that gave them their timing. But something incredible was happening, and the suddenly excited voices of the captain and Seamus aft showed that they, too, had seen it. Gradually, and in spite of their filled sails and the sunlight flashing off their oars, the pirate ships were falling behind.

Seamus returned when the ships were shrunken with distance, his teeth making an uneven white line across his bearded face. "The captain says that we must have encountered a strong, northeasterly current," he said jubilantly, "one that our enemies have not been able to find. It is aiding both sails and oarsmen and if we can stay in it the pirates will be out of sight by sunset. . . ." He paused to glance at the wagon ". . . . So if you haven't done so already, there is no need to worry the old man about this matter."

When he had gone, Declan grasped one of the ropes, many of which the crew had considered unnecessary, that anchored Ma'el's wagon to the vessel's structure, and felt it thrumming in his hand like the string of a silent lute before he looked at Sinead.

"It is not a fortuitous current that is helping us," he said quietly. "I think we both know that it is . . ."

She raised a warning finger to her lips and said, "He will hear you."

"Yes," said Declan, "but on our first night out of Cobh he told Brian that he did not want to control our minds or how we used them. But I would not want Ma'el to think that my mind was a stupid one."

She didn't speak and he went on quietly, "Look at the ropes holding Ma'el's wagon. They encircle or are tightly attached to the strongest and best-supported cross-members of the hull. When the ship pitches and rolls and the vehicle's weight moves off center, the ropes on one side should tighten and on the other loosen, yet they all remain the same and as tight as . . ." He groped for a suitable word without finding it and went on, "You are not stupid, either, and must know what is happening because

I remember you telling me that Ma'el used to lighten his wagon for the horse's sake."

Still she did not speak. Declan struck the nearest rope with the edge of his hand and watched it vibrate for a moment before he continued, "There is no favoring current. He and his wagon are lifting us so high in the water that there must only be a fraction of the ship's bottom immersed, so that means the light wind is pushing us with greater speed and the oarsmen are assisting it because they have a lesser weight to pull against. There is no doubt in my mind now. Ma'el is a truly great and powerful magician, but he doesn't want anyone to know about it except, for some reason, we two."

Sinead stared for a long moment at the side of the wagon. "I don't believe that Ma'el would hurt anyone for talking about him," she said, "but let us keep this knowledge to ourselves."

In the captain's cabin that evening, the only subject of conversation between the old man, Brian, and the ship's officers concerned the plans for off loading Ma'el's wagon and party at Ostia in two day's time, and the discussion became even more intense when Brian advocated a complete change of plan at the last moment.

"My onward trip to Alexandria is not all that urgent," he said, "and I will enjoy a short stay in Rome while Ma'el is doing whatever it is that a magician does there. It will mean that he can safely leave his wagon on board and away from prying eyes while we use local conveyances for travelling to and from the city. Ma'el, I know my way about Rome and will gladly serve as a guide, as well as gaining you entry to libraries, establishments, and homes of the Patrician families that you might otherwise find difficult of access."

Ma'el smiled the gentle thanks of one who has been offered a service that he might not need.

"After all," Brian added disarmingly, "with you as a close companion it is likely, nay, certain, that I will be able to discover more secrets of value than any obtained during my lifetime of spying."

And so it was that they threaded their way through the constantly arriving and departing grain ships that filled the bellies of the citizen of the Eternal City, to tie up at a dock assigned by the harbormaster while the sights and sounds and smells common to any busy seaport, as well as those peculiar to this one, filled the morning air. Brian, as good as his word, busied himself arranging transportation, Sinead was so bursting with quiet excitement, as was Declan himself, at the thought of visiting Rome itself that they paid little attention to the organization of the affairs of a docked ship and its crew.

With the quietly listening Ma'el beside them, Captain Nolan and Seamus had been discussing the pay of the off-watch crew members whose turn it was to go ashore, and the advisability of doling it out in small, daily, or nightly amounts so that they would be able to spend it piecemeal on the more substantial pleasures rather than squandering it all away on a few hours of excitement in a gaming house, to return to their ship as poor as they had been when the voyage had begun.

The captain had smiled then and added that these monetary restrictions would not, of course, apply to the more generous pay of his Ionadacht who was free to spend as much of it and as many nights away from the ship as he desired, or as long as his considerable bodily strength could sustain him, and who well deserved a few of the pleasures of the flesh. Seamus had shown his teeth and agreed with enthusiasm that his captain's advice was good and he would most certainly take it.

"Seamus," Ma'el broke in at that point, "the advice is well-meant but it is not good. With respect to your captain, I advise you not to take it."

They joined Sinead and Declan in staring at the old man with their mouths open. It was Seamus who found his voice first.

"You and your servants have done very well by us and we are grateful," he said angrily, "but guard your tongue, old man. This matter is of no concern of yours."

Ma'el shook his head in gentle disagreement. "Without your knowledge or permission I have made it my concern. In a marketplace in Cork I spoke with a young woman who gave me valuable information about your captain and yourself, knowledge which was the direct cause of me travelling in your ship . . ."

"You, you spoke with *Maeve?*" Seamus broke in. "What business had she talking to a . . ."

". . . In return for this intelligence," he continued gently as if the other had not spoken, "I foretold the joined futures of Maeve and yourself, as well as promising her that I would try to guard you from harm. But I cannot fend off harm, either physical or that caused by the pangs of mental guilt that a wrongdoing would later cause you to inflict on yourself. Maeve would not, I believe, want her man to do this weak and foolish thing."

The small area of Seamus's face that was not hidden under his thick beard had turned deep red, so much so that the captain, looking concerned, put a restraining hand to his arm. But the high color died and in a moment he shook his head and sighed.

"That she would not," he said in a very serious voice. "For a strong man I can be as soft and weak in some ways as a child. Thank you, Ma'el, for your timely reminder. Captain."

"Yes, Seamus?"

"It seems that I will not be spending my evenings carousing in the fleshpots of Ostia after all," he said, "so if you feel like doing so, or visiting your beloved chart room in the museum of shipping, or swapping tall tales or the latest lore of your profession with the other visiting sea captains, I shall stand the shipboard night watches and be reluctantly virtuous."

"Until I return," the captain said, laughing as he clapped Seamus on the shoulder, "bearing a flagon or three of Italy's best red wine with which to toast your distant Maeve."

Before the sun had reached its zenith Sinead and Declan were seated, as befitted a servant and a guard, above and in front of their master with the driver between them, in the extravagantly decorated wagon that Brian had provided, traveling the most famous road in the world, the Appian Way into Rome.

SIXTEEN

In spite of the fact that I am in pos-
. . . session of more information on
Rome and the other Imperial cities and centers of power on this
planet as well as its places of learning, art, and culture, the Earth
beings from whom I gathered the data firsthand have lived out
their short lives or have added little to their stock of knowledge,
so that a person like Brian is required to perform the necessary
introductions that will bring me abreast of current developments.
I have learned over the centuries to control my irritation when
people of this kind assume that they know more and are therefore
more intelligent than I am.

"Although considered a scholar and philosopher of repute
among the learned of his own people, his interests in law, art and
drama are a pretense designed to serve his covert profession, and
his first concern is the acquisition of knowledge and the second is
the worldly riches it would bring. This is regrettable because
otherwise he would have made another valuable servant and
adviser in that which lies ahead.

"Instead I can foresee him taking many stupid risks which
could make his short human life even shorter.

"But why does the healer, Sinead and the protector Declan,

although their loyalty is unquestioned and their mental powers are potentially greater than any others of their kind that I have met, indulge in verbal violence at every opportunity . . . ?"

While crossing the bridge over the Tiber and on the wide road into the center of the city the wheeled, mounted, and pedestrian traffic increased to the stage where their conveyance either stopped or moved forward at a slow walking pace. Their horse seemed to appreciate the chance to rest and the driver, in the manner of his profession, used the time to point out with pride the many architectural wonders of a city filled with the classic beauty of the forum, temples of gods both current and almost forgotten, the theaters, the coliseum, and the whitely gleaming mass of the recently completed Arch of Constantine of which he was justly and extravagantly proud, all of which would no doubt be of interest to visitors of importance. But he spoke with enthusiasm of other places as well, establishments managed by relatives of his which would offer more varied and amusing if less-learned diversions to servants such as themselves who were obviously visiting this wonderful and wicked city for the first time.

Declan was reminded of Padraig of distant Cashel, the friendly old tailor whose relatives had a finger in every commercial enterprise in the town, and laughed aloud. But the sound had an embarrassed edge to it because the driver was becoming specific about the entertainments that were on offer and did not suspect that the person on his other flank was female.

". . . A well-built and mature man like yourself would have no difficulty in finding a beauteous companion, or companions," the driver went on, nudging Declan knowingly in the side. "But with gentle intuition a boy can grow into a man very quickly in this most sinful of cities. For example, there are the young female slaves who serve in the Baths of Appolyon in the Street of the Silk Vendors, fair-haired Teutons, sloe-eyed Orientals, and dusky Nubians who are particularly adept at . . ."

Sinead's lips were pressed tightly together and her face was deepening in color. When Declan pointed at and asked about a particularly ornate, two-horse chariot that was crossing their path, she gave him a grateful look, but the driver said that it was one of the charioteers that they could see racing in the Coliseum on the morrow, and resumed giving her the benefit of his experience.

". . . You look uncomfortable and red in the face, boy," he went on releasing the reins to clap a large, hairy hand on her knee, "as I was the first time. But there is no need, you will be experiencing the greatest of all delights for a man young or old. Naturally you will be eager, but be gentle also and curb your natural inclinations because then the rewards will be greater. In your case it might be better if you confessed that it is your first time because some of the young women, although they will appear and may truly be younger than you are, may feel like mothering you and will . . ."

"If you please, enough," Sinead broke in, her face flaming into the redness of a setting sun. "I thank you for your advice, driver, but it does not interest me in the slightest. The physical attraction that you describe and that you think I am feeling would, if it was present, be directed at a handsome young man."

For the first time since they had boarded his vehicle the driver was silent for a few moments. Then he looked from one to the other several times, but before he could open his mouth to speak, Declan forestalled him.

"He speaks the truth," he said, fighting hard to keep a straight face, "although I am a little too old to arouse such feelings in him."

The quiet, choking sounds that Sinead was making were covered by the driver's hasty words of apology.

"Please believe me," he said quickly, "I meant no insult to either of you. The city caters for all tastes. Should you wish an introduction to others of your kind, young man, there is an establishment on the Street of the Green Arches that . . ."

Declan cut him off with a raised hand. "To avoid giving further offense," he said, "perhaps you should confine yourself to describing your city's beauties of stone and marble."

"Yes, please," said Sinead with quiet fervor.

The traffic thinned and they continued in silence until the driver halted at an arched entrance to a many-pillared villa that was built from delicately veined marble. The impressive figure that advanced to meet them wore polished, dark brown leather armor that was several shades lighter than his skin, matching boots and a helmet the dazzling whiteness of whose plume was repeated in an ankle-length cloak whose folds did not quite conceal the presence of a dagger and a gladius, both of which looked bright, clean, and very sharp. He towered over Declan even though he was on the raised driving seat and the other's feet were on the paved roadway, but his attention was on Ma'el and Brian.

"Your pardon, citizens," he said politely in a thick and strangely accented form of Latin that Declan had never heard before. "Who are you and what is your business at the home of the noble Marcus Grappilius Medina?"

Brian's manner was equally polite but with a trace of condescension as he replied, "I am Brian O'Rahailley, traveler and scholar and known to your master these many years, and this is my traveling companion, Ma'el the Magician, for whose good behavior I can also vouch. We are recently arrived from Hibernia and crave the boon of an audience, as well as surcease from the dust and smells of the city and a little light refreshment. Kindly inform your master of our presence."

There was a sound of hurrying, sandaled feet from somewhere behind him as the other bowed, stepped to one side and gestured toward the villa entrance as he said, "News of your arrival is already being conveyed to my master, who will doubtless wish to welcome a friend and far traveler without delay. Please step down and enter, citizens, a slave will conduct you to his presence.

"Regrettably," he added with a glance at the driving seat, "in these unsettled times I am required to search and disarm your slaves."

"Of course," said Brian, and added quickly in Gaelic, "Easy,

Declan. Slave and servant are the same word here, so do not take offense and allow the search without argument."

Declan laughed and jumped to the ground. Speaking in Latin so that the enormous guard would hear and understand him, he said, "Ease your mind, Brian. I take no insult nor would I dream of starting an argument with this polite black mountain of a man. Will Ma'el and yourself be safe without us?"

"In the home of the foremost lawgiver, advocate, and magistrate in Rome," Brian replied, smiling as he also returned to speaking in Latin, "your master could be in no place safer."

At the guard's polite direction, Declan unbuckled his long-axe harness and sword belt and placed them on the ground before dropping his cloak and helmet on top of them. Quickly and thoroughly every pocket and fold of the cloak was searched, then the enormous black hands with their pink palms moved to cover the surface of his clothed body before the guard stood up and turned to Sinead.

"That one is a healer," said Declan quickly, hoping to save her physical embarrassment, "and bears no weapons."

"An admirable calling," said the other. His smile was as broad and white as that of Seamus, Declan thought, except that this one's face was black rather than just the beard. In an apologetic voice he went on, "If you were discovered to be bearing concealed weapons inside the house, regardless of the one committing the offense and whether or not you were using them at the time, both of you would be instantly slain, and I would be severely chastised with whips for dereliction of my duty."

He paused several times while his hands were patting Sinead's clothing, but when he stepped back he made no comment other than to say, "Please follow me. Your weapons, cloaks, and helmets will be returned on your departure. Until then you may eat, bathe, and rest as you wish in the slaves' quarters. My name is Klum'bgaa, and I have questions which I hope you will be kind enough to answer. You are the first Hibernians I have seen. . . ."

"And you the first Nubian we have seen," Declan broke in, smiling, "so it is likely that the questions will be many and come from both directions. I am called Declan by friends and this is Sinead. If I may presume on your kindness by asking the first question . . ." he stared at the man walking beside him from head to toe, ". . . why is there not a Nubian empire to rival that of Rome? You have the body and the bearing of a soldier, a commander of men and a person of rank rather than a slave. . . ."

He broke off as for a moment Klum'bgaa's dark features became as still and hard as polished obsidian. When he spoke his voice was so quiet that it carried no farther than to Sinead and himself.

"Have a care, Declan," he said. "In this city, slaves do not speak in this manner to each other even, and especially, if the words they speak are the truth. But I will tell you that in my lands there are stories told of a great civilization of my people called the Nok that covered much of central Africa long before the Pharaohs held sway. . . ."

The other's voice remained quiet but the hurt and anger in it could not be concealed as he went on. ". . . It was broken up, as so many cultures are, and the pieces were conquered by invaders until they lost everything but the memories of past glories. I was the defeated chief of one of the largest pieces, and then I became the greatest and most valuable gladiator in all Rome, until I succumbed to the malady called Christianity which teaches that might is not always right and that the greatest wrong of all is to kill another man.

"When the most feared gladiator in Rome," he went on, the anger fading from his voice, "began refusing to kill or even seriously injure an opponent in the circus, my former owner sold me for a handful of coins to the present one, who is not a Christian but is sympathetic to them, and I became the fearsome gate ornament that you see."

"I'm sorry," said Declan. "The answer to my question has caused you pain. I shall ask no more. If you would ask any of me I will be happy to . . ."

"I have a question," said Sinead, looking up at the enormous figure beside her. In a quiet but very serious voice she went on, "If Declan had decided to attack you, as a Christian would you have, well, turned the other cheek?"

Klum'bgaa looked uncomfortable for a moment, and Declan decided that if his face had not already been as black as ink he would have been blushing as he said, "Perhaps. But I confess to not being a very good Christian."

Sinead and Declan laughed quietly and, after a moment of uncertainty, Klum'bgaa relaxed and joined them. They were still smiling together as they arrived in the surprisingly large and comfortable slaves' quarters, and Declan was answering one of the guard's questions to the effect that it was only certain deranged Britons rather than the Hibernians who painted their skins with blue woad before going into battle when the other held up a hand for silence.

"That is fortunate," he said, still smiling, "because otherwise you would have been asked to scrape your skins clean and wash yourselves from basins in the yard before entering the baths, lest a foreign dye should permanently stain the master's decorated tiling which is of exceptionally beautiful craftsmanship. The baths are in that direction, you can see the steps leading down to the pool, and there is an antechamber where you both may disrobe and leave your travel-stained clothing to be freshened, after which you should follow that corridor; your noses will give you the direction as well as your eyes. In the kitchens you may rest and eat and talk about yourselves, bearing in mind that the more you satisfy the slaves' curiosity, the more generous will the refreshments be. . . . Is there something amiss?"

Sinead was shaking her head firmly and slowing to a stop while she looked in the direction of the kitchens. "I—I would prefer to eat and rest now," she said, changing to Gaelic speech and staring at Declan. "You bathe first."

He shook his head and made a sound that had too much impatience in it to be a laugh. "Brian tells me that in Rome the baths are public places, whether large and maintained by the city or those within homes that are privately owned. It is the custom here. Do you want these people to think that you have unclean habits? You can hear the voices of others who are already bathing. . . ."

"That," she replied in a quiet, angry voice, "is not what concerns me, and well you know it."

"Don't be an amadan entirely!" he said angrily. "You are not a fool and should not talk like one, and I am not a rampant animal in heat who would lose control of myself at the sight of the wet, scrawny body of a near child. . . ."

"Scrawny!" she broke in angrily. "You have the decorum of a, a . . . And you should talk. That time I saw you in Cashel, I thought your body had more stitches than a patchwork quilt. . . ."

The angry words raged between them until Klum'bgaa raised a hand and cleared his throat loudly.

"Normally it would be considered unmannerly for you to speak in my presence a tongue that I do not understand," he said when they fell silent, "so I assume that you are having a personal dispute of some kind that is no concern of mine. From the heat of your faces and anger in your voices it is fortunate that neither of you are armed. When the disagreement is settled you know where you are to go and what is expected of you.

"I must now return to my post."

In the event it was Sinead who bathed first while Declan talked to the kitchen and household slaves. It was plain from the beginning that the limbs revealed by their short, sleeveless clothing bore no marks of the whip and that their love for their master far outweighed any fear of him. They ranged in age from mature adults to young children and it was obvious that some of them had been given permission, which they told him was unusual for a slave, to marry. Declan was hoping that he would get a chance to meet the strange pagan saint who was their master when Sinead reappeared muffled in a white, togalike garment, and it was his turn to bathe.

He found that Sinead had elected to await his return before eating, and so had the others. It became a very pleasant evening among people who behaved as if they were the friends and family he had never known, but it was cut short by the arrival of Klum'b-gaa who no longer looked like a gate ornament.

The sharp, bright weapons were still at his belt but the white plumed helmet and matching cloak had been replaced by darker and less decorative wear and with boots that did not shine and trod the floor without sound.

"Your master, Ma'el, has expressed the desire to visit the cat-acombs under the Via Latinum at a time before dawn when few citizens will be about to see you, and my master has acceded to his wish. The noble Marcus Grappilius and the other Hibernian visitor, Brian, are engaged in conversation and feasting that will doubtless last the night, and I have been instructed to serve as a guide and guard to your master and yourselves during this excursion.

"Your weapons will be returned to you at the gate," he added, looking at Declan. "You are advised to wear them."

SEVENTEEN

Ma'el Report, recall and review for sociological comparison purposes of Days 36,511 to 36,549 in the local calen-
der year 67 Anno Domine . . .

...**E**ven though the peoples of this world are merely subjects for investigation and evaluation, I am finding it increasingly difficult to remain emotionally indifferent to individual members of a species that is capable of such extremes of nobility and depravity. In spite of the fact that they have conceived and formulated a structure of Roman law that will be the standard of judiciary practice for many centuries to come and their arts, culture, and philosophical breadth of mind is wholly admirable, I must continually remind myself that they are nothing more than a potential Taelon resource and I am here to observe them.

"Without feeling.

"Today I watched a bloody naval engagement that was not fought at sea but inside the shallow, land-locked confines of the Circus Maximus. Four vessels took part, two war galleys on each side, and their masts were bare because they did not need the wind to move them in the restricted space, and sails would have obscured the view of the battle for the occupants of the higher terraces. Instead they carried armed galley slaves who were expected to fight when they were no longer required to row.

"My understanding of these events is due to the knowledgeable freedman, Severus, who I have employed to guard my person. He was himself a renowned gladiator who fought so fiercely and well, and earned so much gold as a result of his master's gambling on him over the years that, his owner out of gratitude first appointed him as instructor of the gladiatorial team and later gave him his freedom. According to Severus, no long-range weapons such as slingshots, bows or ship-mounted catapults were being carried in case one or more of the gladiators, the majority of whom were expecting to die anyway, should in a fit of vexation aim his weapon at the august person of their Emperor and self-declared God who had decreed that this battle should take place for the entertainment of his beloved but unruly citizens of Rome. Severus added that the tunics of the contenders, white on one side and yellow on the other, had been chosen the better to display the flow of blood from the combatants' wounds.

"The tactic favored by both sides was to overcome the initial inertia of their vessels and to build up as much speed as quickly as possible with the oars so that they would be able to pierce the hull of an opposing craft with the submerged, pointed ram in the bow and sink it to the bottom. Since the engagement was taking place in the muddied waters of a flooded arena rather than at sea, the stricken vessel did not sink very far and simply became immobilized with its decks awash. This meant that its crew had to fight either clinging one-handed to the upperworks or while stumbling and splashing waist-deep over an unseen deck. When one of the vessels suffered this fate a few of the spectators were amused by the incongruity of the sight of gladiators behaving like the most unsubtle of clowns, but the majority seemed to be bored by it and shouted loudly for more blood.

"More blood was forthcoming.

"But the tactic of ramming the opposing vessel broadside on was effective only once because the commanders of the defending craft immediately began countering it by turning their rams and strengthened forward hulls in a bow-to-bow collision. This was a difficult maneuver to perform with accuracy inside the restricted space of the arena and a misjudgment meant that the two vessels concerned either bumped and scraped heavily past each other, breaking off the oars on those sides and transfixing or grievously injuring the rowers with the splintering wood, or the rams tore open the length of their hulls with the same result for the oarsmen. For a short time the screams of the dying and drowning men could be heard over the noise of the crowd, and the muddy water around them was not dark enough to hide the spreading stains of red.

"Only one vessel was able to avoid damage and it turned, positioned itself and rowed forward to ram amidships an opposing vessel that was already listing and beginning to sink. Due either to overenthusiasm or misjudgment, its ram completely transfixed the other craft and, unable to reverse the oars in time to pull clear, the sinking victim pulled its attacker down with it until the other's bow was submerged and it, too, flooded and sank.

"None of the four vessels remained afloat, but they were joined by their rams or otherwise tumbled together into an untidy mass of partially sunken wreckage. Their fighters could still move, in spite of having to climb and wade chest-deep, or swim with their heavy weapons, from one ship's deck to another, and so the battle continued slowly and awkwardly and without any clear indication of which side was winning it.

"Their Emperor, Severus had previously explained to me, had promised the crowd a unique and costly spectacle against which all others of the past would pale into insignificance, a bloody sea battle fought before their very eyes inside the arena rather than on the distant secrecy of an ocean. He had promised them that he would awe, amaze, and stir them to heights of excitement far beyond anything in their previous experience, and to ensure that the combatants would give of their best during individual and ship conflicts he was introducing a new measure.

"For the greater glory of their Emperor and the entertainment of his beloved citizens of Rome, and to avoid tiresome pauses in the action while he was asked who among the fallen should or should not die, they had been instructed to fight each other to the death without exception. But on this occasion they had been given an even greater incentive to wage bloody battle. The survivors on the winning side would be rewarded and decorated by their Emperor, while those who had fought but did not die on the losing side would be killed in full view of the crowd. The fighting would, therefore, be all the more fiercer and completely without mercy.

"But the great spectacle that Nero had promised was fast becoming the greatest of all anticlimaxes. Hampered by the depth of the water covering the decks, the gladiators had to feel their way with their feet across the timbers and fight slowly and carefully while those who lost their footing and fell overboard into deeper water had to discard their weapons if they were to remain afloat. Watching slow and awkward swordfights or men trying to save themselves from drowning was not what the crowd had expected to see. They began booing and hooting in disdain, and many of them were looking up at the Emperor's enclosure as they did so.

"It was plain from the color of Nero's already red and angry face that he did not like this mass show of disrespect to his august person, but there were not enough Praetorian Guards ranged around him, or even among the reserves in the palace barracks, to chastise the ungrateful crowd as it deserved. Instead he spoke sharply to one of the personages standing close to him, the man wearing the bright orange toga and diagonal red sash of the Master of the Arena, who quickly disappeared. For a long time the slow, waterlogged conflict and the angry, derisive shouting of the crowd continued while nothing else seemed to be happening except that the Emperor was standing beside his purple-draped divan, smiling broadly and pointing at the sunken ships. A few moments elapsed before the shouting from the crowd died away into a surprised silence as it was borne in on them that the sunken vessels were rising slowly out of the water and a new sound was heard, the loud splashing and gurgling of fast-flowing water.

"The arena was being emptied.

"When the fighting men realized what was happening they

leapt down from the canted and slippery decks to continue the battle on what they thought would be the steadier arena floor, but in this they were wrong. The last of the water was slow to drain away and it covered the normally hard-packed ground in a layer of thick, wet mud. But they fought bravely and fiercely, singly or in groups that charged and countercharged between the canted, broken hulls of their vessels and over the splintered oars and the still and muddy bodies of those who had been killed or had drowned earlier.

"The crowd howled with laughter as they cut, thrust, slipped and fell to rise again so muddy that it was no longer possible to tell the team colors apart. But moments later they were shaking their fists and screaming in frustration when the fighters regrouped and began using the shelter of the spaces between the hulks of their ships as strong points, which meant that they all but disappeared from the view of the audience. The battle became a long, bloody, muddy shambles, with few of the fighters knowing who were friends and who enemies, that continued until the sun dipped behind the high, banked terraces on the western rim of the circus. The clash of weapons could still be heard, but all that could be seen were a few glimpses of muddy figures fighting on a similarly muddy ground in the lengthening shadows of the vessels' hulls.

"It was not the spectacle to end all spectacles that the Emperor had promised, and he was screaming in exasperation and waving his fists as loudly and angrily as any of the crowd. Then Nero gestured for the senior officer of his Praetorian Guard to come forward, spoke to him briefly before the man disappeared on what seemed to be an urgent errand. Moments later a guard detachment armed with long body shields and spears emerged from the gateway under the Imperial enclosure, formed into a single line abreast to march slowly across the muddy ground toward the ships. Ex-gladiators all, they had gained their positions to Caesar's elite guards regiment by being the best or, more accurately, the very worst and most heartless members of that pitiless profession.

"Stronger and rested and better armed than the weakened or wounded fighters, they moved through the small groups of sur-

viving combatants and unhurriedly and with a complete lack of
drama or even effort, began spearing them to death regardless of
whether their tunics showed traces of yellow or white under the
mud. As they reformed and matched back the crowd went wild
again, but not all of them.

"In a few places there were people who had stopped watching
and cheering the Praetorians as they dispensed Caesar's reward
for disappointing and embarrassing him before his people.
Instead they were looking at the portly figure of Nero himself as
he smiled and acknowledged the applause of the crowd. One of
those who stared at the Emperor was Severus.

" 'Those men should not have been put to death like that,' "
he had said, a scar on his forehead showing dark against a face
white with anger. 'A gladiator expects to die, but there is always
the small chance of life and a fighting man's reward. A few of
them should have been given that chance, and not slain by those
Praetorian butchers just because the Emperor's idea for a sea battle was a stupid mistake from the beginning.

" 'Nero is the one who deserves to die.' "

"Severus is not a thinking man. I did not tell him that a Caesar who was so profligate and uncaring about the lives of his gladiators would give rise to unease among his own guards who had,
after all, been recruited from gladiatorial schools. It was not one
of my increasingly rare timesightings but a simple calculation of
present cause and future effect.

"The pictures forming behind my closed eyelids at the time
were of a Circus Maximus increased to planetary dimensions, and
a sapient species of primitive technology waging hopeless, defen-
sive war against an enemy who would make the monstrous Nero
seem gentle and kind by comparison,

"The Jarridians . . ."

Forward to Day 36,549 . . .

". . . The arena has not dried out sufficiently after the abortive
sea battle of Day 36,511 for the scheduled chariot race to take

place, so that it was replaced by another and always popular event, a mass execution of the Christians who, rumor had it, had been responsible for the fire that had razed a large part of the city to the ground. The Christians ranged in age from very young children to the most senile of adults, and included many family groupings. On this occasion Nero, rather than filling the arena with crosses, the symbol of their dead and supposedly resurrected Redeemer, having the victims tied them to them and then drenching them with oil before putting them to the torch, had decided to give the crowd the sight and smell of raw rather than cooked flesh. The Christians would be armed with sharpened stakes, and lions that had been starved of food for many days would be sent against them.

"For the further amusement of the crowd, Nero had arranged that the pile of crude, wooden weapons for the Christians' use would be too small in number to arm all of their adults so that they would fight among each other for possession of them while the lions were being released. But perversely they did the unexpected.

"Instead of fighting barehanded among themselves for one of the weapons, the old ones moved forward into the path of the lions to slow their approach with their own bodies while the younger, who had armed themselves, formed a wide, protective circle around their young, with the unarmed ones standing close by to seize the weapons of the fallen. Strangely there were few screams of fear or agony, except from the children who could be forgiven their weakness, as the jungle cats began ripping their victims into bloody shreds.

"Severus had turned his head away from the arena, saying that he was accustomed to the sight of blood but had never liked looking at it, and this was like watching cattle being killed in a particularly inefficient slaughterhouse. He spent the remainder of the show trying to attract the attention of a young female several tiers behind him. I merely closed my eyes and my ears to the bestiality taking place because there was much I had to think about.

"I thought about this most powerful and populous of empires and of the strange cult of gentleness and extraordinary bravery growing here in its heart, of the sentient and sapient yet bestial crowd around me who venerated the deranged human monstrosity that was their leader, and of the defenseless people in the arena that he hated simply because they had been taught and believed, no, they *knew*, that there was eternal life on the other side of their individual deaths. I would have liked to meet this teacher of theirs, because this is not a concept that sits comfortably on the mind of an already long-lived Taelon.

"In spite of my ability to isolate mentation from external sensory input, the cries of fear and the dying sounds made by the children in the arena intruded and affected the quality of my thinking. They are like terrified puppies: normally playful, harmless, innocent, affectionate, and with the unconscious ability to attract the affection of others. It must be a hitherto unsuspected weakness in me, a scientist who should remain emotionally aloof to any problem, but I feel that I will not be able to continue thinking constructively until something has been done, no matter how small that thing may be, to reduce the number of unnecessary deaths among such innocent beings. . . ."

EIGHTEEN

The return to Rome three Earth centuries after my previous visit has proved to be both a comfort and a disappointment. The violence and excesses are reduced in volume and their practice has become less overt, but the subsequent events including the death of Nero, last of the once proud family of Caesar to hold the position of Emperor, did not come about exactly as I had foreseen. There can be little doubt that my precognitive faculty has become untrustworthy and, considering my complete misreading of the outcome of the sea raid off Finisterre among other incidents, the possibility exists that I may be regressing toward the avatus state and losing it entirely. I dread being like these creatures around me who can see ahead only in the dimensions of space but not through time.

"In an effort to discover the reason for this I have subjected my entire sensorium and memory network to a full empathic inventory and feel sure that I have uncovered the problem. Regrettably the solution, if adopted, will destroy the objective worth of this investigation, and there is a strong probability that it could bring about the premature termination of my own life as well as those of my servants, who are becoming much more to me than two subjects for study out of this worlds' many billions.

"The lives of Sinead and Declan are short enough as they are. . . ."

Talking incessantly in a respectful near-whisper, and with his enormous body bent almost double, Klum'bgaa led the way through a seemingly endless system of low-ceilinged tunnels. He was being, closely followed in silence by Ma'el, with Sinead and Declan, who were each weighed down with a large bundle of torches, bringing up the rear. In spite of its softness the Nubian's voice came back clearly to Declan.

They passed the last resting places of countless martyrs. The majority of them were narrow, horizontal niches in the rock walls containing the dusty, cloth-wrapped bones of their nameless occupants while a few were beautifully and elaborately decorated. Klum'bgaa said very little about them because, he insisted, there were too many here who were now wearing martyrs' crowns in Heaven for a few to be given preferment. Instead he kept trying to discover, in a respectful and roundabout fashion that the diplomat spy Brian would have admired, why a foreigner was wanting so badly to visit this hallowed ground. When they paused briefly to rekindle a fresh torch from the dying flame of an old one, Ma'el answered him.

"I am interested in the beliefs of others," he said, "and especially those who fear the pains of dying, as all of you do, but not death itself because they believe it to be but a curtain through which they will pass to a better life. I am not Christian and believe nothing. But I am interested in hearing the reason why so many of you believe in such a strange and illogical thing. Can you explain the thinking and proofs on which it is based?"

Klum'bgaa shook his head. "My master can introduce you to men more learned than I who will explain or debate these matters with you. He might even arrange an audience with Constantine,

who is a firm and just man who has a mind, my master says, that
has no closed doors. It is expected, or perhaps it is only a hope,
that he will become the first Christian Emperor. But I myself can
tell you only of stories and sacred writings that have been handed
down to us for three centuries, and others that come from even
further in the past. But I have no proof of their truth, only a
strong belief that they are true.

"But three centuries ago," he went on, "there was only one
Christian and many who became merely interested. Now there
are many Christians. Perhaps in time you will become one of
them."

In the light of the newly lit torch Ma'el's expression was as
unreadable as ever. He said, "As a foreteller of the future I cannot
see such an extraordinary event ever taking place where one of
my people is concerned. This part of the tunnel is familiar to me.
Please turn into the opening on the right."

"Please reconsider, Master," said Klum'bgaa in a worried
voice. "That is a steeply descending tunnel which has not been
used in living memory and perhaps for centuries. It has sustained many rock falls, there are noxious odors and the water
seepage is . . ."

"There is no danger," Ma'el broke in gently, making a complicated, fluid gesture with one hand. "The noxious vapors are
gone and the sound of dripping water is silent. You may pass the
torch to Declan and await our return while we investigate. . . ."

"I am not afraid!" the Nubian broke in. "At least not for
myself. I was charged to guide you in safety, but if you insist on
taking risks then I must take them also."

Ma'el inclined his head and a moment later they were following Klum'bgaa into the descending tunnel.

Declan had never been happy in confined spaces and the time
that followed was a waking nightmare for him. Not only was he
choked and blinded by the smoke from the torch, the tunnel
floor was covered by fallen rock so deep in places that they were
forced to scramble over it on hands and knees. The smoke could
not disguise the stale smell of the air around them and the torch

flame was reflected in glistening red patches of wetness from the uneven ceiling. He thought of turning back, but the second thought of what Sinead, who was less than two paces ahead of him, would say about that made him go on.

She was climbing over a loose pile of rocks and had put up a hand to the ceiling to steady herself when she made a sudden, surprised sound.

"What's wrong?" said Declan. "Did you cut yourself?"

"No," she replied in a perplexed voice. "This area of rock above me. It's shining and looks wet but it is completely dry to the touch. The whole ceiling ahead seems to be the same. Feel it for yourself as you move past."

Declan did so and and found that the surface was dry, hard, smooth and with no flaking or traces of rock dust around it. Suddenly a childhood memory, one of the few pleasant ones, came back to him.

"I remember being shown a very small rock like this," he said excitedly, "by a visitor to my father. He told me it was a piece of melted stone from a volcano. But there are no volcanoes under Rome. . . ."

He broke off because suddenly the the tunnel had opened into a chamber that was just high enough for them to stand upright and so large that the torchlight did not reach to its farther walls. The floor was clear of rubble and the ceiling reflected back the torchlight as if from the black ripples on a pool that had been frozen into immobility. The quiet voice of Ma'el seemed to fill the chamber.

"Stay together and move around the walls until you have located all of the torch supports," he said. "Sinead, Declan, place one of the spare torches in position after Klum'bgaa lights them. Look around for signs of cracking or subsidence in the ceiling or walls of the main chamber and those opening off it, and if you find any report them to me at once."

With torches burning at intervals around its walls and reflecting bright, uneven highlights from the rippled ceiling, the size of the chamber became clearly apparent as did the fact that there was no supporting structure other than at its bordering walls. No wonder, Declan thought, Ma'el wanted them to look for evidence of a ceiling collapse.

There were a few long and very low tables in the middle of the room with even lower stools grouped around them, and small platters and cups crudely fashioned from clay and wooden utensils to the same diminutive scale were scattered across the top surfaces. Some of them still contained scraps of food that had been rendered rock hard by the passage of time. Scattered across the tables and on the floor around them were small blocks of wood in the shapes of cubes, triangles, rectangles, and long pegs, with a few pieces that had been roughly carved into human shape. When Sinead lifted one of them, a piece of cloth encircling its waist fell away in scraps of dusty fiber.

"Master, I see no signs of rock falls here," she said, waving her free hand around her. "But this furniture: a few pieces are adult-sized, and all these small tables and stools and the childrens' playthings scattered about. What kind of catacomb was this?"

Before Ma'el could answer her, a low, moaning cry came from one of the side chambers. Quickly they followed the sound to its source. The voice was barely recognisable as that of Klum'bgaa. He was standing before a wall painting that was partially hidden by his body, but as soon as they entered he dropped to his knees before Ma'el.

"Master, Lord," he said, bowing his head almost to the ground, "or are you an angel? Should I have recognized you? I am but a sinner and unworthy of a visitation from from on high, but you have only to command me and I shall . . ."

"Please stand before me, Klum'bgaa," Ma'el broke in gently, "and do not distress yourself. I am not an angel and I am certainly not your Lord, nor are you mine to command."

The Nubian climbed to his feet, doubt showing on every line of his dark face as he turned and moved his torch closer to light the picture that covered most of the wall behind him. Faded with age because it had been executed in charcoal and a few coloured

pigments, it showed upward of thirty very young children standing, sitting or playing around a tall figure in a dark cloak, the
cowl of which had fallen backward to reveal a shining, hairless
head and a caste of features that were unmistakable. Sketched
faintly in the background were a few adult women who appeared
to be caring for the children. The artist had given the tall man a
halo.

"There are stories told of secret places like this," said
Klum'bgaa, looking as if he wanted to go down on his knees
again, "that date back to Nero's persecution of the Christians.
Few remember the stories that were passed down to us, and
nowadays fewer believe them, of a place cut out of the living rock
by an angel sent by God. It was a sanctuary for little children
whose parents were martyred in the arena. They were hidden
here until they could be moved to foster homes in the city or
country. But that . . ." he pointed unsteadily with the torch at the
tall, cloaked figure, ". . . Master, that is *you*."

They were all staring silently at Ma'el and waiting for a reply
that did not come. Declan began a shiver that turned into an irritated shake of his shoulders, and spoke quickly so that he would
not have time to think.

"It is *not* him!" he said harshly to the Nubian. "Think, man,
and stop trying to frighten us. The event shown in the picture
happened three centuries ago. Ma'el is frail and bald and ancient
in years, but he cannot possibly be as old as that. We are seeing a
person skilled in the magical arts as is our master, one of his
countrymen, no doubt, who was . . ."

"Who was as kind and gentle as our master himself is,"
Sinead joined in. "Well do I know of his aversion to needless suffering and death, particularly where a helpless and deeply troubled near-child like myself was concerned. It may well be that his
people are also magicians and as kindly as he, but he is not your
God."

Glad of her support for reasons that he did not himself
understand, Declan gave Sinead a grateful look and returned his
attention to the old man. But Ma'el merely looked back at them

for a moment, inclined his head and, as was his way when he did not wish to answer questions, ignored the subject.

"This chamber remains structurally intact," he said, "and may be used for my present purpose. If you are willing, friend Klum'bgaa, there is an important task that you may be able to do for me. You will have to talk widely but with discretion among all those who know and trust you. I have an urgent need for young women to be enticed into coming here. Many young women."

The Nubian looked as surprised as Declan was feeling, but it was clear that the other was still not sure who or what Ma'el was and he might be thinking that his faith was being tested.

"It will be done, master," he replied without hesitation, "but how many young women and how much time can you give me?"

"I can give you five, perhaps six weeks," Ma'el replied, "before I have to leave Rome. In the beginning I realize that it will be difficult, perhaps personally embarrassing for you, to convince the early ones to come. But with your perseverance, more and more of them will come until this place will be filled to capacity, after which there will be a gradual diminishing of numbers before my departure. Without telling them what it is, you must interest them in what I am doing while not making extravagant claims about me or what you think I will be doing for them. I am not starting a new religion, nor will I try to change or influence any beliefs they may already hold.

"The females should be young, married, or of marriageable age," he went on, "and include as many non-Italian races as possible. I want representatives from all of the European races, those from as far south as Nubia and, if any are presently visiting the city, young women from the Orient.

"Assure them that they need not fear for the welfare of their bodies or their souls," he continued. "They will not have to do anything but listen to me and perform simple, mental exercises while I perform a laying-on of hands. All they will be asked to do is to accept a gift from me which they and a few of their children, and a few of their childrens' children to the end of time, may be able to use to avoid future harm."

Ma'el lowered his eyes to look at the floor, and for a long moment the silence was so complete that the sputtering of their torches seemed loud. Then he raised them again to look directly at Sinead.

"This gift," he said quietly, "is also for you."

NINETEEN

The project has had a measure of success but is a personal disappointment to me because of the continued lack of effect where the female Sinead is concerned. It is possible that there is a genetic defect, or that the emotional and physical trauma suffered in her early years has inhibited or destroyed the latent faculty she carries. I shall in future reduce the frequency of the stimulation lest overexposure cause long-term damage to her mind.

"My work took longer than anticipated because the initial attendances were small, and by the time the numbers reached capacity, the meetings were stopped without violence and I was placed, at Brian's request and with the agreement of the magistrate himself, under house arrest in the home of Marcus Grappilius Medina pending interrogation by the Emperor. . . ."

Their sandaled feet sounded loudly on the marble floor as a Nubian servant, decked out even more richly than Klum'bgaa had been and with a haughty cast of countenance that suggested that they rather than he were the slaves, conducted them into the audience chamber. It was not overly large but beautifully proportioned and rendered bright and spacious by arches and pillars in marble that was almost white. Occupying the spaces between the pillars on three sides of the chamber were many fine, life-sized sculptures while the opposite wall was hidden by purple and gold drapes that set off the dais that contained the throne. Six guards, three on each side, were ranged beside and slightly behind it. Their helmets and armor, which were of polished bronze rather than leather, shone brightly as did the blades of their short swords and the grounded spears revealed by the white cloaks that were thrown back from their shoulders. They, too, stood absolutely still, but unlike the statuary they would have come violently to life at the first sign of danger to their Emperor.

The man seated on the cushioned, marble throne wore a simple white toga with a cloak of imperial purple thrown around his narrow shoulders and falling to and partly covering his thin, aging legs. A small crown of laurels, looking as if it had been placed there without thought and then forgotten, encircled his graying head. His features were stern and showed the impatience of one who was too old to waste time on unimportant matters and who had the authority not to suffer fools gladly. The eyes that looked out at them were old and wise and the mouth below the thin, hooked nose bore deep lines of asceticism, or perhaps they were the sign of one who suffered from a troublesome digestion.

He did not look like the most powerful man in the known world, Declan thought, but it was said that out of all the emperors who had preceded him, Constantine was the one who had earned and truly deserved the title Great.

"Do not grovel or flatter or lie to me," said the great man, with a tired gesture of one hand. "As the Emperor I know or am quickly told everything that is happening in my city whether it is good, bad, scandalous, seditious, or merely interesting. Your recent activities I find curious. As you must already have learned, I am liberal in the matter of personal beliefs, but some of the new faiths that are springing up try my patience and credulity. The minds of my citizens are free if not, for the most part, particularly gifted with intelligence, and I will not allow the gullible among them to be exploited by a religious charlatan. Ma'el, who are you, and why are you starting a new religion when the people already have a surfeit of them to choose from? Speak."

Ma'el did not abase himself but he did give a very small bow, a gesture of respect that Declan had never seen him accord anyone in the past. Sinead and Declan gave deeper bows, and the physical deference shown by Brian was deep indeed. He spoke quickly before Ma'el could reply.

"Great Imperator," he said, "I can vouch for this man's good conduct while in the city. He is a learned traveler and seeker of knowledge who, some say, is a magician but not a charlatan. On the voyage here I have had direct experience of his powers. But he has been at all times gentle and fair in his dealings and does not deserve to be . . ."

"Your name is not Ma'el," said Constantine in a quiet voice that nevertheless sent a shiver along Declan's spine. Without taking his eyes off Ma'el, the Emperor went on, "I have no time to watch trickery, no matter how well it is performed, nor have I a need for character references because this is simply an interrogation and a search for truth. If or when it becomes a trial then I, as the First Magistrate of the City and the Empire, will decide on what this man deserves. Well, magician, waste not my time. If you are able to speak for yourself you have my permission to do so."

"My thanks, Imperator," said Ma'el promptly, and went on, "I am a Taelon, one of a race that dwells in a strange land far beyond the borders of your empire, and a scholar who is anxious to travel, to learn, and occasionally to teach. Our people have great knowledge and many talents, one of which I was trying to impart to some of the young women of your city. My teaching does not place their bodies or their souls in jeopardy, nor does it influence their present beliefs in their different gods. I am not a god, the messenger of a god or even a prophet. At present I believe in no deity because I have learned of so many of them that I am confused and unable to make a choice."

"In that you are not alone," said the Emperor dryly. "But in

this nonreligion that you teach, are your students invited to contribute, voluntarily of course, to cover the cost of providing
tapers, candles, food, wine, and such to maintain an agreeable
level of worldly comfort for their teacher?"

Ma'el's reply was quiet, deferential and the words well-chosen
as befitted one who was telling the most powerful man in the
world that he was wrong.

"Imperator," he said, "no collections are taken up. The
young women who come to me are required to bring nothing
with them but their minds. If any of them should try to make
such a contribution, they are thanked and instructed to give or
spend their coins elsewhere. I have no need of wealth or property
beyond that which I already possess, and feel no desire to compli-
cate my life by making additions to it."

"If what you say is true," said the other, a skeptical edge in his
tone, "then you are indeed a wealthy and contented man. But
what exactly do you teach, and why is it taught only to young
women?"

Ma'el did not answer at once and the Emperor said impatiently, "Come, come, learned magician. Do not waste my time
on verbal invention. Be truthful or at least let your lies be consis-
tent with the truth I already know, because certain young and
nubile slaves of my household attended your meetings and
reported the proceedings back to me. It surprised me when they
said that you taught without asking anything for yourself, not
even the payment in carnal pleasure that a young woman can give
to an old and loveless man. Speak without delay."

"My apologies, Imperator," said Ma'el. "I paused but to
order my thoughts and fit the right words to them. . . ."

As he listened, Declan was reminded of the time the old man
had explained the workings of his magic chart to Captain Nolan
when he had been warning him of the impending storm. Then
his words had been strange, precise but confusing. Constantine
was an intelligent man, but it would not be wise for Ma'el to risk
confusing him to the point where he might feel stupid in front of
strangers. An angry Emperor and judge was not what they

needed just now. Fervently he hoped that the old man would think about their situation and use words that were simple and reassuring rather than precise and confusing.

Sinead had refused to tell him anything about those meetings, either out of sheer perversity or because there was nothing to tell, and he and Klum'bgaa had been unable to see or hear anything because they had been standing guard at the mouth of the access tunnel to ensure that it was only females of the specified ages who gained entry. He already knew how the deep underground chamber looked when it was empty, but now Ma'el's clear, simple words were painting bright pictures in his mind of what had been happening there.

He saw the big chamber lit by a hundred long candles each of which was being held in the joined hands of young, bareheaded women dressed in white robes. They had not been required to wear this form of dress, Ma'el said, but all of them had elected to do so because they sensed the importance of the occasion and wanted to be fittingly attired. Each candle was being held so that its flame was at eye level to the bearer, who stared at it without word or movement. The only sound was the soft, clear and continuous voice of Ma'el as he moved among them to stand briefly behind each one in turn while he placed his hands lightly on the top of every head.

". . . The laying on of hands and the focusing of attention on the candle flames," Ma'el was saying, "have no religious significance. They are simply a means of concentrating the recipient's mind on what I am saying to them, for it is they who must do the real work. They use my words to travel and explore the inner paths of their own minds so that they can find and, of more importance, recognize a gift that is already in the possession of all women. Alas, many of their minds will not be responsive enough to be able to find, recognize, or use this gift that is already theirs. . . ."

"Magician," the Emperor broke in impatiently, "your words are clear but their meaning is not. You must now make the meaning of your words clear to me. Describe this gift, how is it used, and why it is that only women possess it?"

Please, Ma'el, Declan pleaded silently, *no living charts, no weather systems and no geostationary orbits, whatever they are. Keep it simple*. But when the old man resumed it was as if he had overheard the unspoken thoughts.

"Imperator," Ma'el replied, "the last part of your question is the most important and bears on the rest, so with your leave I shall answer it first.

"Women are your childbearers," he went on, "and on them depends the future of mankind. Men play an important part also, by combining and passing on the inheritance of health, strength, and beauty that they receive from both their male and female parents. But unlike the man, it is the woman who has a direct connection through her own body and those of her mother and her mother's mother before her into the distant past. The connection that exists between this succession of females bodies also extends into the far future.

"If I have succeeded in awakening it, which is by no means certain, the ability will make it possible for these women to see into the futures of their female descendants and to view the important events that will affect their lives."

Constantine looked as if he wanted to speak but could not find the words, and his features were beginning to darken with anger.

Ma'el went on quickly, "In the past that is distant beyond the memory of memories or the writings of our earliest ancestors, when the world was young and savage beasts ruled the earth, the ability would have been used to warn the fighting men of dangers that would threaten the unborn young and the future of their tribe. But in these times of civilization and culture and the rule of law, there is less danger and the ability has fallen into disuse and been lost.

"But occasionally, when dire events impend, the ability is awakened and future events are seen, perhaps imperfectly, in the form of visions or dreams. An instance could have been the warning dream of Calpurnia before the assassination of Julius Caesar, her husband, which caused a great upheaval in the Empire. Another might have been the . . ."

"Enough," said Constantine, an angry edge in his voice, "of your metaphysical babblings. It might be amusing to debate this strange theory with you if matters of state left me time for amusement. Your idea is ridiculous. You are saying that men, who in the past have carved empires out of the wilderness and raised great cities and temples that are eternal works of art, live only because of their womenfolk and are blind to their future. Magician, this is demonstrable nonsense."

"With respect, Imperator," said Ma'el gently, "your men are the builders and defenders and fathers of their people, but the women are the lifegivers and preservers. I wish to help them to warn and preserve your people from the many grave dangers that are to come."

The Emperor was silent for a long moment while Declan joined Sinead and Brian in holding their breath. When Constantine spoke again his tone was still angry, but judicial.

"Ma'el," he said, "I find no evidence of criminal intent in your activities, and you furnish the proof yet again that an intelligent man can be a fool and misguided in the thinking of which he is capable. Your contention that women are equal if not superior to men is untenable. Women are both a necessity and a pleasure for the continuance of life, just as is the grain and the cattle we eat to sustain us and the beasts of burden that work for us or carry us into battle. Like those beasts we feed and treat them with fairness and consideration or, if the circumstances warrant it, by applying the whip. Often, like beautiful and docile beasts, we come to love some of them deeply. But they are not and never will be the equals of men."

He fixed his gaze sternly on Ma'el and went on, "My verdict and decision is that you are fool rather than a criminal, and that you have been preaching a harmless sedition that has already caused embarrassment to a few of your converts who tried to set

themselves up as soothsayers while the others, plainly not wanting to be held up to similar ridicule, maintain a sensible silence.
The harm you have done is minor as will be the punishment.

"You have two days," he continued, "in which to employ, at
your own expense, artisans who will collapse the entry tunnel and
seal off your secret chamber so that it can never be used again. By
the end of the third day I will expect to hear that the magician,
Ma'el, and his Hibernian slaves will have left Rome never to
return."

"You have my permission to leave," he ended. "Do so at
once."

As they returned through the audience antechamber,
watched curiously by the richly garbed and obviously powerful
persons who were waiting there and asking each other loudly
why these four should have had the ear of the Emperor before
themselves, they neither looked aside nor spoke. But it was plain
from the heightened color of Sinead's face that she had angry
words that were waiting to burst forth. But it was not until
Declan's weapons had been returned to him and they were clear
of the palace and its listening ears that she was able to speak.

"A beast of burden," she said in a tone of quiet fury. "A
necessity for the continuance of mankind, of *man* kind, and an
object for their pleasure. Constantine is said to be a cultured and
liberal Emperor, but personally I do not think that he deserves
the title Great."

TWENTY

I decided to omit the visit to Athens and have proceeded without delay to Alexandria for two reasons. One is that in Greece my work among the young women would be hampered as it was in Rome, while in Egypt I would have more freedom of action due to the respect gained during a previous visit of three centuries ago when my physical similarity to one of their deities was used to good effect. The second is that I am increasingly troubled by a sense of personal urgency, the cause of which I am no longer able to foresee and cannot, with the information available to me at the present time, explain.

"For a Taelon who is virtually indestructible on this world and with half of a very long lifetime stretching ahead, I should not be subject to feeling of urgency about anything. I can only conclude that my diminishing precognitive faculty is the reason and that my psychological difficulties shall remain until I again find a means of seeing into the future, even if it has to be through the sensorium of an Earth person that I trust.

"But the young woman Sinead still shows no indications of acquiring the timesight faculty. The possibility exists that she is genetically as well as emotionally flawed.

"Brian ordered Captain Nolan to take us to Alexandria because, he openly admits, he still wishes to acquire my magical knowledge. If I was to give it to him, fully and with complete truth, it would frighten his primitive Earthly mind into complete dysfunction. Instead I asked him to arrange and supervise the outfitting of Sinead and Declan with garments and equipment suitable for our onward journey into India and Cathay because, unlike the Taelon, this species has no natural environmental protection other than a few wisps of body hair. But the purse I offered Brian to defray the cost was graciously refused with a hint that he would prefer to have my knowledge rather than my gold. He is a most persistent man.

"With covert assistance from my Taelon technology, the voyage to Alexandria was made without interference from marauding sea raiders. On the way to our berth in the west quay, the ship passed under the famed lighthouse on the island of Pharos, a structure that is generally acclaimed to be one of the seven wonders of this world, except by the native Alexandrians who scarcely look at it. . . ."

It was a city of great interest and beauty in spite of being a bustling seaport and with an atmosphere entirely different from Rome because, Brian told them as he sniffed the air delicately, of the preponderance of camels that were being used as beasts of burden. He pointed out the Temples of Serapis and Poseidon and the Soma, the mausoleum that contained the remains of the great Alexander who had given his name to the city, as well as the museums that he would visit later because they were said to contain a few of the half million books, some of them scrolls measuring thirty paces in length, that had been rescued from the great Alexandria Library before it had burned down.

Whenever they came to a street of merchants containing displays of goods such as brightly woven carpets, costly and exotic viands or, on one occasion, a platform and enclosure for the sale of slaves that was attracting a large crowd of onlookers, he

warned them to keep a tight hold on their valuables. The pickpockets here were reputed to be among the most light-fingered
in the world because those who proved themselves inept suffered
the summary amputation of a hand.

At all times Brian was entertaining and gracious, particularly
to Sinead, and he treated them as equals rather than servants, but
in a roundabout fashion he was always asking questions about
Ma'el. The only information they could give him was that their
master planned to continue the journey by land as soon as possible, but it was plain that that knowledge disappointed him.

"This is a good place," Brian said suddenly. "I remember it
from my last visit."

He had stopped them at the entrance to a merchant's establishment that was flanked by displays of clothing and attractively
displayed materials, and looked so familiar to Declan that he half
expected Padriag of Cashel to emerge smiling with his measuring
cords. Without realizing it he must have been thinking aloud.

"In Cashel old Padraig asks a fair price," said Brian, laughing, "and he is such a gentle old man that you would feel
ashamed if you paid him less. Here it is a little different. Let me
warn you . . ." his voice became apologetic, ". . . that you are
about to see the nasty side of my nature. . . ."

The clothing they needed was produced and fitted quickly
inside curtained alcoves by smiling slaves, servants, or perhaps
they were members of the proprietor's family. By the time
Declan's long woolen cloak and warm under garments worn during the voyage and in colder Rome had been stowed in his pack
with the new purchases Ma'el had suggested, they had been
replaced by an equally long but much less warm white cloak that
concealed his sword and axe, a large, matching square of cotton
worn under his helmet to protect his neck and ears from the sun,
and open sandals for use for walking rather than riding. Apart
from the weapons, Sinead was similarly dressed. The fact that
one of the foreigners was a young female who wanted to dress as
a boy aroused no comment because foreigners were wont to do
strange things and foreign gold was as good as any other kind.

But it seemed that the actual amount of gold that was expected to change hands was a matter for serious dispute which, while it stopped short of physical violence, involved the exchange of a great many insults concerning the persons and ancestors of both the proprietor and Brian as well as their improper sexual behavior with various beasts. Incredibly, the dispute ended amicably with bows and smiles and urgings for Brian to patronize the establishment again when next he visited the city.

"Your mouths are open," he said, laughing, as they returned to the street, "so allow me to answer your questions before you ask them. This is not Hibernia. Here we must haggle, or rather I will haggle for you until you learn the way of it, over everything you buy. There are two reasons for this. The first and most important one is that not to do so would mark us at once as rich, stupid, and ignorant foreigners, and soon we would be pestered by many unscrupulous people trying to take advantage of our ignorance so as to relieve us of our riches. This is not a reputation that would help you here."

"I see," said Declan. "And the second reason?"

"It would have been unkind of me to spoil the transaction's entertainment value for the proprietor. But a good argument makes me hungry. Please be my guests. Further down street there is a place that serves very good food. There you can put down those heavy bags, eat, shelter from the midday heat and, of course, have a pleasant conversation."

About Ma'el, Declan added with silent certainty. At home it was the custom for bards to sing for their supper or, indeed, for any other meal. Not for the first time Brian was expecting them to talk for it.

They were replete with a variety of exotic, highly spiced dishes that criminally assaulted the tongue but still compared favorably with shipboard fare when Brian began to exact payment.

Pleasantly he said, "I suggest we use the Gaelic, an uncommon language here, to foil would-be eavesdroppers. Your master's explanation to Constantine of what he was trying to do for those young women in the catacombs intrigues me, but there is a question at the back of my mind, or perhaps it is an inconsistency, that I cannot tease out into the light. As one who took part in many of these initiations, perhaps you could help me to clarify it, my lady."

Giving an impressionable near-child like Sinead such a grown-up title was an unecessary and inaccurate form of respect, Declan thought cynically, but then words were Brian's most potent and subtle weapon. He watched the impatience that had begun to cloud her face clear into a smile at the compliment.

"Of course," she said. "But I have already described the rituals to you many times and told you everything I know about them. My apologies, but I know and can tell you no more."

"Is it possible," said Brian, "that you know or have seen or felt something that you have forgotten or thought too unimportant to be mentioned? Would you indulge me again, my lady, and describe all you saw, heard, felt, or thought about the ritual?"

Sinead nodded, closed her eyes to shut out external distractions and began to speak. She described Ma'el's opening instructions when he had told everyone to keep their eyes on the flame of the candle they each held so that they would see nothing else, and listen to his words and hear nothing else, and feel only the touch of his hands on their heads and any other sensation that might come to them because of his words and touch. His words had been gentle and encouraging and about the gift of future sight that they would pass on to their children and children's children who would pass what they saw or learned back to them, the possessors of the original gift. As women, he had told them, those who survived past the period of birthing carried within themselves an unbroken line of life and a gradually diminishing awareness stretching forward to the ultimate end of their kind. They should concentrate their minds so as to learn and feel and know the truth of what he was saying to them.

". . . When he laid his hands on me," she went on with an edge of self-reproach in her voice, "they felt as light and fragile as a bird's wings. Many of the others tried to describe the strange visions that came to them of events and people they knew or did not know and which frightened and confused some of them. If they spoke about them in public I could understand why they were not accepted as soothsayers. I wanted it to happen to me for Ma'el's sake, but I myself did not see or feel anything except for an itching inside my head. I fear that I am a grave disappointment to Ma'el, and to you.

"Perhaps," she added with a laugh that had no humor in it, "the gift is not for a woman who dresses as a man."

Brian hesitated for a moment, and when he spoke his tone was sympathetic and with an apology in it as if for a hurt to come. "I speak truth rather than flattery," he said very seriously. "You are, or are soon to become, a comely young woman, fair of face and lively of wit, and one who in time any man would count himself fortunate indeed to win. But your master has said many times that his gift of future sight comes back to you through your descendants. I am truly sorry, my lady, but the reason you have not received the gift may be that never in your lifetime will bear children."

"I have no intention of bearing . . . !" Sinead began angrily, then she moderated her tone and went on, "There were events, and injuries, in my past that may have rendered me barren. This I have accepted. My anger is not directed at you, Brian, because in your way you are a kindly and thoughtful man. I know that your words can be subtle and deadly weapons, but there are also times, as now, when you try to use them as instruments of healing. I thank you for that, but let us return to a less painful subject."

Brian gave her a sympathetic smile but remained silent. Declan said, "We could talk about you, Brian. Or Ma'el, a man who is . . ."

There was the sound of dishes and eating utensils rattling as Brian slapped the tabletop. "That," he burst out, "is the inconsistency that has been nibbling at my brain. The ability to see into the future, Ma'el tells us, is the prerogative of a direct succession of women. But he is a man who has, but should not have, the gift.

"Are we sure," he added after a pause, "that he is in fact a man?"

Declan stared at him, feeling his jaw drop in surprise, and Sinead's mouth was open, too. But before either of them could speak, Brian went on, "With respect, my lady, you have already said that Ma'el treated you with kindness, protected you, and did not, well, take advantage of you as some old and dishonorable men would have done. He may be a kindly old man, but his actions where you are concerned, if he is in truth a he, are more befitting those of a kindly woman and mother. Would you agree?"

They both stared at him, too astonished to speak. Brian looked at Sinead and gave an uncomfortable laugh.

"My lady," he said, "I know the idea is completely ridiculous, so let us change to a subject less hurtful to you. How best I can help you spend the rest of this day?"

When Sinead did not reply, Declan said, "We are strangers here to whom everything is new. Go where you will and we will be pleased to follow wherever you lead."

"You speak too hastily, Declan," he replied, but his eyes were looking an apology at Sinead. "My lead would not take you to places of scenic interest or entertainment but to a museum, an establishment filled with scrolls, drawings, and relics of the past that is said to contain material salvaged from the great Alexandria Library before the fire had totally destroyed it. You would not, I think, find my search among the dusty chambers and stacks particularly interesting."

Sinead was making a determined attempt to lighten her mood. She smiled and said, "The degree of interest would depend on the object of your search. What are you searching for?"

Looking relieved and pleased, Brian returned her smile. "Knowledge," he said, "I am a seeker after knowledge but, unlike your master, I have never been averse to making a profit from whatever I learn."

An almost boyish enthusiasm crept into his voice as he went on, "This time I am searching for the drawings, calculations, and perhaps a model of the device called an aelophile that was

invented by Hero of Alexandria, a mathematician of the time of
the Sixth Ptolemy. It was said to be comprised of a spherical
bronze kettle mounted on and free to rotate horizontally around
two metal supports. The kettle was pierced at diametrically
opposed sides of its circumference by two small, short lengths of
pipe that were angled in opposite directions. When it was partly
filled with water and a fire lit under it, steam puffed from the two
small, angled pipes and this caused the spherical kettle to spin on
its supports, quite rapidly, it was said.

"Hero himself did not think much of his device at first,"
Brian went on, "which he insisted had been built solely to prove
to himself that heat could be converted into rotary movement,
but later he suggested that a larger device might be capable of
pumping water or perhaps moving the wheels of chariots. When
his Pharaoh witnessed a demonstration, his response was that it
hissed like a nest of vipers and filled the room with steam, and
that slaves and beasts could fetch water and pull vehicles much
more cleanly and cheaply and that Hero should forget the idea,
which he did.

"Myself I think the idea has possibilities," Brian ended defen-
sively, "which is why I want to find the drawings and make copies
of them in case my principals in Hibernia would be interested in
trying out the device for use as a . . ."

Sinead held up a hand and looked at Declan for agreement as
she said, "Now that we know what it looks like, we would be
pleased to help you find it."

But in the event they did not find it, even though Brian was
known to the museum curator and was given every assistance. On
the way back to the harbor he seemed much less disappointed
than they were, and explained that a search of that kind was time-
consuming and could take many weeks or months without any
certainty of a successful outcome, and added that they should not
concern themselves because he did not expect them to help him
search every day.

The sun had set, dusk was falling rapidly and they were about
twenty paces from the ship's berth when Sinead broke a long

silence. There was not enough light to show her expression clearly, but her voice sounded strangely adult and very serious when she spoke.

"Brian," she said, "I hope you don't think me impertinent or needlessly inquisitive about your personal affairs, but are you a wealthy man? Do you really need to travel the world doing this very dangerous work? Would it not be more sensible and safer for you if you returned to Hibernia and enjoyed your wealth and reputation in comfort instead of continually risking your life?"

"It would indeed be sensible and safer," he replied, his teeth showing dimly in a smile. "But I would soon grow bored with that life and tire of endlessly recounting my adventures, and my friends would soon tire of listening to me. This style of life is unsafe, but interesting, and if . . ."

He stopped suddenly in his tracks so that Sinead and Declan had to turn back to him. In a troubled voice he said, "Have you found Ma'el gift at last? Can you see into *my* future, and are you warning me?"

"No. Yes. Perhaps," Sinead replied in confusion. After a moment she went on, "With respect, Brian, I have come to know you as a likable and learned rogue who lives and avoids death by your wits. I do not foresee the time and manner of your death, whether it be due to drowning at sea, the violence of enemies, or a foreign plague, but I strongly advise that when next you return to Hibernia you should stay there.

"It may not be a prediction," she ended in an embarrassed voice, "but a simple feeling of concern for a wayward friend in need of good advice."

"I rarely take good advice," said Brian, sounding relieved. "But for your concern, my lady, I thank you."

TWENTY-ONE

It is now sixty-three days since we unshipped my vehicle and left Alexandria to join a caravan bound for the Orient along the dusty, unpaved, and often sand-obliterated track that the natives, who are wont to use poetic license rather than accuracy in their descriptions of the local environment, so lyrically refer to as the Golden Road to Samarkand. Because of the heat, windblown sand, and insects I remain in the wagon, telling my servants that I need time to think and I am not to be disturbed unless an emergency arises. Since Sinead and Declan have been given custody of the chart with basic instructions in its use, such interruptions are few. But the thinking that I am free do is neither positive nor constructive, and the process is being worsened by an increasing physical debility that I suspect may have a psychological basis.

"I am becoming increasingly prey to self-doubts regarding my mental and physical ability to complete this investigation. My insistence that I be served from all but the most tenuous contact with the Commonality—ostensibly so that I could concentrate on my work without interruption but in reality, as they must already have realized, to avoid my every decision being scrutinized and debated endlessly by a Synodal committee—was perhaps too academically arrogant and overconfident on my part. I am not yet ready to discontinue this investigation, but I did not realize that complete isolation from our people would adversely affect my Taelon faculties to this extent.

"My timesight becomes less trustworthy with each passing day, yet I urgently need a view into near-future events. That is why the decision was taken to induce this faculty in the Earth species so that they, however imperfectly, will be able to provide me with the operating data and foresightings that I need. This is an action that will certainly draw censure from the Synod, and regrettably the result has been a failure where success was most needed.

"Following repeated cranial stimulation the female Sinead, who as my servant would have been the ideal local access window to the future, has proved to be an unsuitable candidate for pre-cognition. Reluctant as I am to do so, for I have formed a liking for this servant, if I am not to remain completely blind to future events on this world it is imperative that I acquire another female who can be given the timesight. . . ."

Because they were driving the only horse-drawn vehicle in a caravan of forty-three heavily laden camels and were expected to be the slowest of the company, they had been assigned the position at the end of the line. There the plodding feet of the beasts and the small contingent of foot guards ahead of them stirred up a constant cloud of dust that settled in thick layers on their clothing and tried to penetrate the narrow openings of the voluminous head wrappings to get into their eyes. When the wind was in the wrong quarter, as it was now, the smell of the camels was horrendous.

"You've a horse and are free to go where you like," said Sinead in a sarcastic voice from the driving bench. "Why don't you ride out bravely, cloak streaming out behind you in the wind, and scout the surrounding desert so as to warn us of a possible attack?"

Before setting out, Ma'el had provided Declan with a handsome white Arabian stallion who was smaller and perhaps half the age of the gray mare who was pulling the wagon. Once he had learned how to mount and ride it he had found that it was surefooted and could move like the wind. Right now the temptation to exercise his lovely mount was great, but in spite of Sinead's words he knew that that was not what she really wanted him to do.

Declan had discovered long since that she liked company in her misery.

"Does the chart show any signs of us being followed?" he asked. "Or of an ambush being laid between here and the caravanserai, or an attack developing on our flanks?"

"In order," she replied, "no, no, and I'm not sure."

"Let me see it," said Declan. He dismounted quickly, tied the reins loosely to one of the wagon shafts, and jumped up beside her.

The chart showed the land surface that lay within a day's march in every direction, and the morning sun was still close enough to the horizon for it to reveal the shadows between hills, dunes, and major surface irregularities around them. It also showed the long finger of windblown dust that was their caravan, and far to the north of the line of hills that lay ahead of them, a smaller and rounder cloud.

Declan pointed to it. "What's that?"

"That," she replied, "is what I'm not sure about."

"Let's have a closer look," he said, and tapped at the group of small and almost invisible circles on the lower corner of the chart. Immediately the picture slipped away to one side and shrank until the eastern edge of the Mediterranean and the Red Sea came into view. Declan swore in self-irritation.

"I'm a ham-fisted amadan," he said.

"That you are," she replied. Her tapping fingers, thinner and almost as delicate as Ma'el's, quickly brought the picture back to the area they wanted.

"That round cloud could be due to wind eddies among the

dunes," she went on, "if it wasn't for the fact that whatever is causing it is not moving in the direction of the wind. Do you want a closer view?"

"Please," said Declan.

Suddenly the dust cloud, looking tenuous and in places almost transparent at close range, was almost filling the chart. On the windward side it was seeded with the tiny points of darker gray made by small groups of men on foot and with larger and longer shadows that indicated the presence of camels or horses. He estimated their strength at between sixty to seventy men, ten horses, and four camels. As he watched two of the long shadows moved ahead of the main group and separated to form tiny dust clouds of their own.

"Can you expand the picture to show individuals," he asked, "and the weapons they are carrying?"

"No," Sinead replied. "If I magnify it too much everything begins to wobble like stones under running water."

"Then pull back to the original size," Declan said, disappointed, "and call Ma'el at once. He must be told about this."

Sinead hesitated. "I'm not being contrary just because it's you who's giving me orders," she said, "but I'd rather not. Ma'el told me not to rouse him unless it was an emergency, and these people are still a long way off. Can we handle this matter ourselves?"

Rather than give a short answer that would be sure to cause an argument, Declan decided to explain the situation as he saw it and let it speak for itself. His index finger moved about the chart as he spoke.

"I believe this to be a large party of desert raiders who will intersect the caravan track just here, where we would be hemmed-in between this broken ground to the south and the hills to the north, which would also hide the attack from the lookouts in the caravanserai. Unless there is a traitor among the merchants' servants, the raiders cannot know that we are so close to them and are probably intending to ambush the first caravan that comes along. I don't know if their number is enough for them to capture the entire caravan, so they may be content with cutting out the tail, which will probably be the last thirty or forty camels and, of course, our wagon, while the forward section flees for the safety of the caravanserai. We can't drive off the raiders unaided. . . ."

"No?" she said impishly, looking at his long-axe.

"No," he said firmly, "not even if they lined up and came at me one at a time. Be serious. I can't ask the caravan merchants to divert to the south to try to avoid the ambush because only a few of them speak Latin, and I would have trouble making them obey me or even believe how I learned of the danger. So the only course is for the wagon to slow down and detach itself from the caravan while I head for the caravanserai. If the raider scouts should see you they will think that the wagon has broken down and leave it to rob at their leisure, and by that time I will be back with the caravanserai soldiers to drive off the . . ."

"Quite apart from them not understanding a word you say," said Sinead, checking him with an upraised hand, "do you really think that the soldiers, or the few who know Latin, will do such a thing just because you ask them?"

Declan shook his head and said, "Yes, they will. The merchants pay the officers of the garrison a fee, but only for the camels that pass through the area in safety and with their loads intact, not those that have been robbed. Besides, I will offer gold to ensure the safety of this wagon first, and then more for their help in turning back the raiders. I don't know how or where Ma'el gets it, but he never seems to be short of gold, and I believe that he would honor any promise of payment I made.

"I think you should call him as soon as you can," he ended firmly. "This *is* an emergency."

Before she could reply, the curtain of skins behind the driving bench twitched aside and Ma'el said, "I agree."

The old man's voice sounded weak and tired and carried in it the impatient tone of one whose thinking on another subject has been interrupted. And again he used words the meaning of which they could only guess at.

"Your viewpoint alterations in the chart were repeated on my monitor screen," he said, "and your conversation regarding them was overheard so that there is no need to repeat yourselves. The strategy and tactics suggested by Declan are approved. However, while my timesight is untrustworthy at present, I have an unsupported feeling that there will be a greater chance of success if the communications difficulties that Sinead has already mentioned are removed."

While he was speaking, Ma'el drew two ear decorations from an inner fold in his cloak, followed by two wide collars. They were finely worked in bright metal and identical to the earpiece and collar he himself was wearing.

"These are valuable charms," he went on quickly, placing them on top of the chart, "devices whose use is normally restricted to members of my own race, and which to others will appear only as body decorations. Wear them as I am wearing mine. The earpieces will enable you to hear any words said to you, in whatever language or dialect that is in local use, as if they were in your own native tongue. The collars will convert the words you speak into the languages of those around you. Both of you, follow these instructions without delay."

Sinead nodded and pulled back her burnoose. "Like the chart," she said in an awed voice, "this is very powerful magic."

"It is magic," said Ma'el impatiently, "because as yet you do not understand how or why it works."

"Wait, please," Declan said as the old man turned to re-enter the wagon. "I understand your instructions, but not why you wear these ornaments when we already know that you speak perfect Gaelic, Latin, and who knows how many other tongues besides. Surely you don't need them."

Ma'el paused to touch his collar before he replied, "Think before you ask a question, Declan, and you may find that you do not need to ask it or that it has already been answered. I do not now, have not and have no wish to speak and understand Gaelic, Latin, or any other of your languages for the reason that there are too many of them to learn even in my long lifetime. I speak, through this collar only in my native Taelon language. It is you, and everyone else who listens to me, who hears it in the words of their own language."

As Ma'el was turning to re-enter the wagon's interior he paused for a moment. His voice had lost its impatience and sounded gentle and almost sad when he spoke.

"You embark on a difficult task, Declan," he said, "and the lives of Sinead and yourself will depend on its successful outcome. Regrettably my timesight is untrustworthy and I am unable to forecast what this outcome will be. So use your mind, and your skills, and act in calmness and not when you are in the grip of strong emotion. Remember that you know more about the situation we face than any others that you will meet, and act with the confidence this knowledge gives you. And if you have a personal god who might provide you with an invisible means of support, ask this entity to grant you good fortune."

Sinead watched Declan intently, her eyes being the only feature visible through the narrow opening in her burnoose, but neither of them spoke as he remounted and she slowed the wagon. The caravan master would probably send someone back to ask why she was doing such a stupid thing, and with the help of her new ear ornament and collar she would be able to tell him a credible story. Quickly he removed his cumbersome burnoose, rolled it up tightly, and tossed it to Sinead. For the rest of the day he would be moving fast and leaving his dust behind him rather than riding into that stirred up by others, and his helmet, sun cloth, and cloak were all the protection he needed. Still without speaking he raised his hand in farewell and gave his beautiful Arab stallion its head.

With the lovely, surefooted beast moving smooth and fast like a wind blowing over the sand, and air that was free of the smell of camel dung cooling his face, Declan felt happier than he ever been for as long as he could remember. The thinking and planning for the future he would push aside until he reached the caravanserai and learned of the situation there. He would enjoy the next few hours, the hot, bright desert that was so different from Hibernia that he almost felt that he was dreaming it, and the smooth, regular movement of his splendid animal that seemed to be an extension of himself. But suddenly, and in spite of the sun that was blazing down on the desert all around him, he shivered.

He was remembering Ma'el's final words to Sinead and himself. The old man had spoken as if he might never see them alive again.

TWENTY-TWO

The sun was setting when he reached the caravanserai just as the heavy, double gates were about to be closed for the night. As he dismounted, the soldier in charge of the guard detail that was standing easy nearby looked admiringly at Declan's horse, glanced with interest at his gladius and long-axe, and smiled before he spoke.

"You are just in time, friend," he said, "to avoid having to spend the night in the desert. But you must give me your name and business here before I can allow you to pass within."

Declan did nor know what language the other was speaking, but the words that came through his ear ornament were in clear and unambiguous Gaelic. He hoped the collar Ma'el had given him would work as well in the other direction.

"I am Declan," he replied, remembering what Ma'el had told him about knowing more than these people and trying to project the easy assurance of command, "a warrior lately from Hibernia and the personal guardian of a rich merchant who travels with the caravan that is a day's journey from here, and which is shortly to come under attack from brigands. It is about this matter that I wish to speak urgently to your commanding officer."

Abruptly the man stood up very straight, snapped his fingers at one of the guards in the casual manner that marked him at once as an officer, and pointed at the horse before turning on his heel. "Your mount will be watered and fed," he said over his shoulder. "Please follow me."

He had heard much talk about this establishment from the camel drivers and merchants who had been sharing their journey. Set in one of the most dangerous stretches of the camel route to India, and manned and maintained by a local sheik who extracted a tithe from every man and beast for the services provided, it was said to be the most well-appointed and defended caravanserai that they were likely to encounter. Without appearing to be openly curious, Declan's eyes took in every detail of the structure as he followed the man.

It was a large, open rectangle of cleared ground enclosed by a stockade of wooden logs that was more than the height of two tall men. Four higher guard towers stood at each corner with two more on each side of the entrance gate he had just left. Additional defense was provided by a continuous raised walkway mounted on the inner walls that was served at frequent intervals by stairs or ladders. Built against the two shorter walls were a forge, smithy, the open, slatted structure of a food store, and the garrison barracks that seemed small for the number of men lounging about or cleaning weapons and equipment outside it. Running the full length of the wall facing the gates was a structure comprised of stables at ground level and another walkway giving access to the living quarters above, probably for the use of officers and the richer merchants who would pay not to sleep on the ground beside their camels. The enclosure had a well and drinking troughs and was just large enough to accommodate all the beasts of the caravan he had left, although there would be little space to spare and the smell would be horrendous.

As he followed the man up steep, uneven stairs to the officers' quarters, Declan had to throw his long, white cloak back over his shoulders to avoid tripping on it. The action revealed his studded leather tunic, high boots, and the weapons he was carrying. He kept his hands well away from them as he was led into the commanding officer's quarters, a long, low-ceilinged room that was divided by rich, hanging drapery into a spartan work area and the more luxuriously appointed living and sleeping space.

While his escort spoke the words of identification that had already been used at the gates, Declan watched the man who bore the ultimate power in this place and who, if Ma'el's magic collar and his own Hibernian wits would guide his tongue in the right direction, would use that authority as and where it was needed.

He was an enormous man both in height and girth even while he was seated, as now, on a padded stool behind a trestle table on which lay papyrus charts, measuring sticks, a beaker filled with an aromatic liquid, a large, curved sword, and two weighted throwing knives. On the front of his turban there was an ornament that looked costly but which might have been a symbol of rank. But the steady, blue eyes that were regarding Declan from the peak of his leather helmet to the toes of his high boots, and the long, hooked nose and full black beard with streaks of gray in it were not the features of a person who would be easily convinced about anything. Declan was thinking that he was being faced with the Arabian equivalent of Black Seamus when the resemblance was increased by the other showing his uneven white teeth in a smile.

"You look to be rich, Hibernian," he said, "and your apparel is pretty for a soldier. You are well-tutored in our tongue." A sour edge entered his voice. "Were I a young woman I would be greatly impressed by the sight of you. Are the weapons you carry additional ornaments or do you know how to use them?"

Declan took a deep breath, then said calmly, "Sir, I am omitting the courtesy of addressing you by your name, rank, and title because, as a traveler and stranger in this land, I am unsure of what they are. It is my master who is rich, not I. Among other things, he provided me with clothing and the ability to converse in many tongues, but the weapons are my own and I have long favored the axe. It is not the company of women that I seek but immediate military assistance."

Beside him Declan's escort seemed to be having difficulty with his breathing. In an outraged voice he burst out, "Know, stranger, that you are addressing the noble Achmed ben Imaubim, Prince of the Sheikdom of Khasant and the lands of . . ."

"Enough," said Achmed, raising one large, fat hand. " 'Sir' is a strange title, short and seemingly respectful but free of the verbally unnecessary compliments with which I am usually addressed. You may continue to call me 'Sir' as long as you are here. But I find you a strange man, Hibernian. You are not easily stung to anger by personal insults, you do not boast of your prowess with the weapons you carry, and you appear to place duty before pleasure. There is a calmness and certainty about you more befitting to a master than a servant. Intriguing. If you are indeed a servant, Declan, you must have the complete trust of your master, and be very well paid. Am I correct?"

Declan inclined his head without speaking or changing his expression, only then realizing that it was a gesture he had learned from Ma'el.

"You are right," said Achmed, "those matters are unimportant and do not concern me." His tone became friendlier but at the same time more brisk as he went on, "You have had a long and tiring ride, Declan. May I offer food, rest, and refreshment before we discuss your master's needs and, of course, the sum he will have to pay me to provide them. . . . But I see you looking at my wall map and growing restive. What troubles you?"

"My thanks, sir," said Declan, "for I am indeed hungry and thirsty. But if it pleases you, the matter is urgent. May we talk before I eat?"

"Before that," said Achmed, glancing at Declan's escort, "you will divest yourself of your cloak, helmet, and weapons and give them to my lieutenant, Bashir, who will place them in a safe place until you need them again. You will understand and forgive my apparent distrust, but these are unquiet times and I must be constantly on guard against assassination. Bashir will also return to us without delay so that he, too, can hear what you have to say to me."

Declan moved to the large intricately woven tapestry that almost filled the wall on Achmed's right. In spite of the garishly colored areas that marked the ground contours, the bright, contrasting tufts of yarn that marked the peaks and other special ground features, and the lines of beading showing the main camel routes, he was surprised to find that it was every bit as accurate as Ma'el's chart. When he heard Bashir re-enter the room he remained facing the tapestry and began talking quickly, describing all that had appeared on Ma'el's chart but pretending that he had seen it with his own eyes. He was allowed to finish without interruption, but when he turned again to face them, Bashir was looking grim and Achmed's features were suffused with anger.

Uncertainly, Declan said, "That was the position and deployment of the raiders as I saw them early this morning, and what I consider to be their intentions regarding the caravan. I think I know what should be done about them, but . . . I'm sorry, sir, I seem to have said something to anger you."

It was a moment before Achmed found his voice. "The tale you tell angers me, Hibernian," he said, "not the teller. Are you quite certain of the number of men and beasts that you saw? Do you perhaps add drama to the tale with a storyteller's exaggeration?"

Declan shook his head. "I told of those I could see clearly enough to count. There may have been more of them concealed by their dust cloud. Are a few more raiders an important consideration?"

It was obvious from his expression that Achmed was too angry for an exchange of conversation. Instead he snapped at his lieutenant, "Explain it to him. Tell him everything."

Bashir nodded, took a deep breath and said, "There have been rumors that something like this was being planned against us. They are not desert raiders but a force sent by a neighboring sheik who is our enemy but not yet ready or brave enough to declare open war. The caravanserai is too well-defended for them to risk an attack on it, so instead they must intend to rob the caravan while killing everyone who might link them to the crime. No right-thinking person would suppose that we had anything to do with it, but our good reputation for ensuring a safe passage through our lands would come into question, the merchants would seek an alternative and probably riskier path for their caravans, and we would lose an important source of revenue. In time this would force us to abandon and destroy the caravanserai to forbid its use by our enemies. . . ."

Prince Achmed silenced his lieutenant with an upraised hand. He used the same hand to indicate the map and said, "How would a Hibernian warrior solve this problem?"

"With a surprise attack from the eastern flank, here," Declan replied. Trying to keep the eagerness out of his voice he went on, "You have many men here who are rested and, perhaps, bored with inaction. If they were to . . ."

The hand was raised again. "We would be fighting a pitched battle against an enemy with superior numbers," Achmed said. "If we were to lose it, the camel train and the caravanserai would be captured and I, if I survived, would no longer be my father's favorite son. Half my force must remain here to defend and maintain my establishment and the other half, if I was to do as you suggest, would be outnumbered three to one. The casualties would be heavy indeed, and we might save only a few camel loads and even fewer of my men. You are a young hothead and your solution is too costly in blood."

"With respect you are wrong, sir," said Declan, ignoring Bashir's shocked expression at a stranger suggesting that his prince was something less than omniscient. He turned back to the wall map and went on, "My intention would be to set an ambush for them, here, here and here, by allowing them to move southward past our positions, and wait until they have taken their places in the hills along the camel track where they will wait until the entire caravan is in view. Depending on the lie of the land

and the speed with which we can get into position, we will either surprise them from behind or make a flanking attack from the east out of the rising sun. If our movements are fast and precise, that is, if they are guided into place by someone who knows the area, and if I am allowed to instruct them in methods of fighting unfamiliar here, and if they can remain steady of mind rather than going into a frenzy of rage in the face of a close enemy, and they do exactly as they have been told, half of your men should be enough and there will be a successful outcome with few losses."

Bashir cleared his throat noisily and said, "You must not tell wildly optimistic stories to the prince . . ." he made a small bow toward Achmed, ". . . who depends on me for military advice. Describe to us in full, if you can, the arcane forms of combat they use in Hibernia that enable you to fight a battle without a butcher's bill of dead and dying? Declan, the idea is preposterous."

Declan sighed in relief, glad that the other had stopped short of calling him a liar and thus avoided the complications of offended honor that the accusation would have caused, and said, "Time is short. With your permission, sir, I would like to explain everything to the men as well as yourselves before they set out on their night march. . . ."

"A night march!" Bashir broke in. "You have already ridden all day and now you're going to spend the night . . ."

"Sleeping," said Declan. "At least, for the next few hours, then I will catch up on the men before sunrise. But someone with a good knowledge of the ground will have to accompany them and place them in the attack positions."

Achmed gave his lieutenant a long, questioning look, the significance of which was lost on Declan, and received a nod and a smile in return. As Bashir was turning to go he said, "I will be pleased to do that service for you. But now I will pick and assemble the best men for our purpose and you must come with me to explain your tactics and to exhort them to deeds of wild Hibernian bravery."

"Before you go," said Achmed, standing up and revealing his true girth and height, "I wish you to carry my own weapon for the day. . . ." from the wall behind him he took down a long, curved sword whose broad blade was wider at the tip than at the jeweled hilt and held it out to Declan in the palms of both hands, ". . . because your gladius is unsuitable for fighting on horseback. Bear it with honor and success. Much as I would like to accompany you, there is not a horse that could carry me and even the legs of a camel would buckle under my weight. You have no time to waste on further conversation with me before you set out, so speak loudly to the men so that I will overhear and learn your plan. After which you will take the rest you need. Go, now."

"Thank you, sir," said Declan, accepting the weapon and stepping back so that he could swing the hilt up to his face in salute. "I shall wear and use it with honor."

The sword was hanging from his belt, his other weapons had been returned to him, and they were descending the stairs to the enclosure before the lieutenant spoke again. Considering the surprising nature of his words, Bashir's tone was completely without rancor.

"You wear it it," he said, "because in this enterprise I know where I'm going but, unlike you, I do not know what to do when we get there. You wear the personal weapon of my master for all to see because you, Declan, have been placed in joint command of this operation."

The eastern sky was showing a dark hazy stripe of gray and there was no slightest breath of wind when Declan reached the place where he should have overtaken the men on foot, but there was no trace of them until a man's low voice called out to him.

"Effendi? The Hibernian warrior?"

"Yes," said Declan, moving his mount closer to a slightly darker patch of darkness. "Who are you and where are the others?"

"I am the favored bowman, Mareth," the other replied softly. "The riders were making such good time that Bashir said they could afford to slow their progress by allowing my bowmen to share the mounts. I was left behind to continue on foot so as to guide you in case you became lost."

Declan knew a hint when he heard one. Freeing a stirrup so that the other could climb on he reached down with one hand into the darkness. "Ride behind me and hold on tight."

"My thanks, effendi," said Mareth.

The man was thin and wiry under his burnoose so that the horse accepted the extra load without complaint. He barely spoke except to give occasional directions, and when Declan tried to start a conversation to relieve the tedium of the ride, the other reminded him respectfully that on a still night voices carried a long way in the desert.

By the time they arrived the sky had lightened enough to show clearly the ground features around them, the line of men lying prone under the rim of the hill ahead and the the horses, hungry after their long night ride, cropping contentedly on the patches of sparse grass further down the slope. Declan tethered his mount beside them while the other man pointed ahead toward one of the figures lying huddled under his cloak.

"That is Bashir," said Mareth quietly. "We will approach him from behind, the last few paces on our bellies so as not to show ourselves above the skyline to the enemy."

"Lead the way," Declan murmured.

Keeping flat against the rising ground they drew level with Bashir, who nodded to Declan and said, "I know that you have keen eyes, but most of the area is still shadowed. Take an instant's look, show as little of your head as possible, and tell me what you can see and what you think it means."

Declan did so, but when he lowered his head to the sand again he closed his eyes before he spoke, the better to fix the picture of what he had seen in his mind while he was describing it.

"There are two groups spread out and hiding in the rocks above the camel road," he said, "in an uneven line stretching east to west. They are already in ambush positions, so during the night they must have sent a scout westward along the track and know that the caravan is due soon and are ready for it. The first and smaller group, numbering no more than fifteen to twenty men, is just below us and very close while the larger one, which has about twice the strength of the first is farther and strung out in an uneven line to the westward. In a depression behind the larger group are their animals, about four camels and horses whose number is uncertain because there may be more concealed behind those I could see. . . ."

"You *have* good eyes," said Mareth softly.

Bashir nodded and said quickly, "What else did you see, and think?"

Declan hesitated. "The light was uncertain but it is strengthening," he said. "May I take another look?"

The other nodded impatiently, and when he lowered his head again Bashir he said, "Well?"

"This may not be important," Declan replied, "but their camels are piled high and hung about with stores while their horses carry double saddles. It also seems to me that all of the enemy I can see are wearing broad belts and diagonal sashes with headgear of the same color which looks black in this light but may be dark green or red."

Beside him the silent Mareth seemed to grow even more quiet while Bashir cursed softly and said, "This is worse than I expected. They wear the markings of our enemy sheik's personal guard, men who have been born without pity or had it scourged out of them. The reason they make no attempt to cover their military dress is, of course, that they will slay everyone in the caravan without exception who might link them to the bloody massacre they intend."

He paused, looked at Declan very seriously and said, "If you do not wish to share the fate of your master, which is certain, you should ride at once to the caravanserai with the news of what has happened here so that my sheik will learn of this crime, and then go wherever you desire. . . . But your body wriggles in silent argument. Speak it in words, brave and probably stupid though the words may be."

"My master has another servant," said Declan awkwardly, "who is little more than a child. I would not want to abandon them."

"Do as you wish," said Bashir impatiently. "Now I must engage the enemy. . . . But I sense another argument coming from you. What is it?"

"I am a stranger here," said Declan carefully, "and although I bear the prince's swords, I should not presume to give you advice. But I think there might be a small chance of us winning this battle."

Mareth was nearly strangling himself in an effort to laugh silently while Bashir's voice was scornful as he said, "Are you about to suggest some wild, Hibernian tactic that will triple our strength? You do presume, Declan, but give your advice. It is my decision whether or not I take it."

"Of course," said Declan. He raised his head for an instant to look down on the closest enemy position, then he went on quickly, "Am I right in thinking that the enemy is so confident of holding the element of surprise that they haven't bothered to post any outlying lookouts? If that is so then we are in an ideal position to make the surprise attack you plan. But I think the surprise would be more effective if we waited until the sun has risen a little above the horizon and is behind us and dazzling the eyes of the men below.

"Waiting would give us three advantages," he went on, unable to keep the enthusiasm from his voice. "The imminent arrival of the caravan should attract all of the enemy's attention to the leading camels in the train, and the trouble developing here on their eastern flank would not be clearly seen because of the low sun. That will make them uncertain, especially if you choose the same moment to attack their main body from the rear. While these things are happening, and to further confuse the enemy, later I would like two of your horsemen to ride with me from the front to the rear of the caravan. On that first pass we would not stop to fight. Instead we would ride like the wind, shouting loudly to the camel drivers as we went by that more help was coming. That would not be strictly true but it would further confuse the enemy. . . ."

"It would be a barefaced lie," said Bashir, his teeth showing brightly in a face that was still gray with the growing light of dawn, "but an allowable stratagem in times of war. You have more advice?"

"Yes," said Declan, looking at Mareth, "for the bowmen."

"Go on," said Bashir.

Declan's eyes were on Mareth as he said, "The group below us are all lying prone, most of them with their backs to us as they watch for the caravan. They will make easy targets. At my signal, have your bowmen rise from cover and take careful aim, for the sun will be in the enemies' eyes and there will be plenty of time to aim and shoot the first flight of arrows as one and making each one of them find its mark. They will then advance down the slope on the enemy shooting at will, but I suggest they stop and kneel to steady themselves because an arrow loosed by a running bowman rarely finds its mark. By this time the survivors of the group will have organized themselves and will be shooting back, they will still be dazzled by the sun behind you and will squint and hesitate while taking aim. When an enemy bowman has drawn back his bowstring and is about to loose an arrow, drop flat so as to give him the smallest possible target, the top of your head and shoulders, at which to aim and, hopefully, miss. When he is notching another arrow, either shoot back at him or advance closer. Soon you will be too close for an exchange of arrows and you will use your swords to press home the attack. While you are doing this, I shall be drawing some of their attention with a flanking attack to further unsettle them. My horse is fast enough to make me a difficult target.

"But remember," he went on, "your men must remain calm and level-headed at all times. There must be no death or glory charges, no stupid heroics, and no heaps of brave, dead soldiers. We have a saying before battle that nobody lives forever, but in this case I want your men to try. This may not be your customary manner of warfare, but we are seriously outnumbered and must therefore fight in this cowardly fashion. Do you understand?"

Before the other could reply, Bashir said, "Declan, your advice is good and I'm taking it, all of it. Mareth, instruct your men accordingly and do not attack until Declan gives the word. When I see you go into action we also will attack. I have orders of my own to give. . . ."

Bashir was moving down the slope toward the horses and Mareth was crawling with instructions toward the closest of his bowmen.

It was a time for patience, Declan thought, as the rising sun turned from red to orange as it cleared the hills behind them and the caravan had not yet come into sight. Mareth's bowmen were spread out in an open line under the brow of the hill, watching him silently. Deliberately he did not raise his head too often, but the next time he looked the first of the camels were coming into sight and the eyes of the enemy would be on them. He gave Mareth the signal and bent low as he ran for his horse.

He watched from their flank as the bowmen rose into sight only enough to loose the first flight of arrows in unison at their unsuspecting targets, then more sporadically a second and a third flight before the enemy realized where the attack was coming from and began to shoot back. As expected, with the sun in their eyes their aim was hopelessly inaccurate. When Mareth's men rose to their feet and charged down the hill, Declan urged his horse forward and did the same, but instead of charging down on them in a straight line he rode in a semicircle so as to come at their position from the flank.

From that angle the sun was not in their eyes so that they had a clear view of him. He was attracting many arrows, but his original intention was to take the enemy bowmen's attention from the men who were attacking more slowly on foot, and it seemed to be working. Deliberately he guided his mount from side to side as he came rather than riding down on the position in a straight line. So many arrows flew his way that he wondered if the enemy bowmen would soon run short of them. Only two came close to him, however, one that tugged sharply as it went through his cloak and another that whispered past his ear. But their number and frequency was diminishing and suddenly he realized why.

More than half of the enemy lay still or writhing on the ground with arrows sprouting from their bodies, most of them the victims of the first few moments of the attack. Mareth was following instructions, but not quite to the letter because he had added an improvement that Declan had not considered. Most of the men had drawn their scimitars and were closing rapidly but erratically on the enemy as they tried to make more difficult targets of themselves, but not all of them. A few of Mareth's bowmen, probably his best marksmen, were holding back and continuing to kneel on the ground while they shot at any opposing bowman who was threatening their companions' advance. Declan dropped his reins so as to free both hands, drew the long-axe, and used his knees to urge his horse forward.

He was almost on top of them when the barb of an arrow scraped past his horse's neck, leaving a short, deep scratch and causing it to rear and shy to the side so violently that he almost lost his seat. The axe swing he had been aiming at the enemy bowman tore away the other's burnoose without touching the head inside. By the time he had regained control of his mount and returned to the attack, the fight was over.

Declan derived no pleasure from seeing wounded and already dying enemies being hacked unnecessarily to death, so he looked away in the direction of the other battle where Bashir's men had also surprised the enemy, although not as completely as had happened here. As he watched, Bashir detached himself from the fighting and began galloping towards Declan a few moments before Mareth joined him.

"You must have been a popular commander, Hibernian," he said, smiling broadly and waving his bloody scimitar. "We didn't lose a single man. . . ."

He broke off as Bashir arrived, looked around and nodded approval.

"This was well done," he said. "Now they outnumber us by only two to one. Mareth, retrieve as many arrows as you can, theirs as well as yours, because you will need them. Then gather your men and follow Declan and me on foot as we ride along the caravan shouting about the relief force that is coming to help them. That is you although they and the opposition will not know that at the time. Do not climb the high ground to attack. Use the shelter provided by the loaded camels to shoot up the slopes at the enemy, support the caravan bowmen, stay alive for as long as you can, and try to make every one of your arrows, and your lives, count. Declan, when you're ready."

To make the enemy think that they were the vanguard of a new force rather than a remnant of the old one, they took advantage of the high ground to the east to circle back and join the camel track. It was not until Mareth's men were out of earshot behind them that Bashir spoke again.

"Declan," he said quietly, "you have done well, and if any of us were to survive this battle, which we certainly will not, many stories about you would have been told. That is why, after we have ridden the length of the caravan, I want you to continue on as fast as you can to rejoin your master's wagon that you've said lies far behind. The enemy may ignore it because they have many richly laden camels that are closer by to rob, so your master, the other servant, and yourself may survive. Your presence here would make no difference to our ultimate fate except that you would die with us."

"But if the enemy thinks that a relief force is coming," Declan began, "will they not withdraw from what they believe is a stronger enemy?"

"They would not refuse battle," said Bashir quietly, "no more than we did when faced with them. Declan, you must try to save yourself."

TWENTY-THREE

Ma'el Report, Day 112,889 . . .

...**F**or the first time Sinead is going against my wishes as well as all the dictates of good sense. Yesterday at Declan's urging I had agreed to allow the wagon to fall behind the rest of the caravan in the hope that the robbers would either not see us or dismiss our single vehicle as unimportant, but later she insisted on rejoining the caravan as quickly as possible.

"During the night drive to do so, and between short periods of sleep, she continually studied what she still calls the magic chart and became increasingly agitated. She asserts that unless we catch up on the caravan by sunrise, Declan will die; and unless I use a greater magic than any she has seen me use before, he will die. The concern she displayed for his welfare appeared to be more personal than that previously shown, and I wondered if she might be manifesting the emotional responses that could lead to the inception of a rudimentary form of timesight.

"To test this theory I asked her what kind of magic she thought I could use. She replied that she did not know, but that on the few occasions she had been sleeping she had seen something terrible in her dreams, something falling from the sky that had screamed and thundered and resembled a monstrous insect with great, shining red eyes. She said that it looked worse than the worst nightmares of her childhood but that, strangely, it did not frighten her. Then she said that I should not listen to her bizarre dreams and apologized for wasting my time.

"Shortly afterward I decided to place my thundering and screaming monster on low orbital standby. . . ."

The fast gallop along the length of the camel train that Declan had been expecting was reduced to a gentle trot because Bashir found difficulty, in spite of the blasphemously colorful language he was using, making the camel drivers and their few unmounted guards flee as he wanted. The result of their slow progress was that the relief force he was telling them about, Mareth's bowmen, were already coming into sight at a slow, steady run. Bashir and he were about halfway along the camel train when the first arrows began falling around them.

"Don't concern yourself," said Bashir, breaking off his shouted directions to the nearest camel driver. "The remainder of my men are trying to keep them occupied up there so as to give some of the criminal train a chance to escape, but those bowmen are at extreme range and they are shooting in hope rather than with the expectation of hitting anything. It is a criminal waste of arrows. If Mareth was in charge of them he would leave them speaking in women's voices and incapable of fathering children."

Declan laughed and they trotted past three more heavily laden beasts while Bashir shouted to the drivers that they should urge their mounts to all possible speed and scatter across the open land approaches to the caravanserai so as to make it more difficult for nay robbers who might chase them. During the next interval between camels, Bashir spoke to him again.

"It was a pleasure and an education fighting beside you, Declan," he said, pointing toward the other end of the camel train. "There is nothing more you can do here, so leave before a chance arrow finds you. Ride back to your master's wagon and . . . What's wrong?"

Declan had looked in the direction of Bashir's pointing finger, and the sight had made him swear long and luridly. He did not know what Ma'el's translation charm around his neck was making of the Gaelic words, but Bashir was looking impressed.

"My master is what's wrong," he replied furiously, "or rather he and the other servant have done a stupid thing. After I advised them and they agreed, to stay far behind the caravan, they have rejoined the end of it. How can a great and wise magician be so utterly dim-witted at times?"

"Then ride ahead and join him at once," said Bashir. He swiveled in his saddle and called back, "Mareth, take your bowmen to that wagon at the end and help defend it." In a quieter voice he went on, "We will have to make a stand somewhere, so whatever force remains to me will help you for as long as we are able. That much, at least, we owe you. And if your master is a great magician . . ." his tone became skeptical, ". . . he may have a spell that will save us. Ride now."

As he galloped closer to the wagon Declan could see Ma'el and Sinead on the driving bench and that the horse, like the majority of the camels he had passed, was unharmed in spite of the arrows flying around them. It seemed that in this land the lives of heavy pack animals were of much more value than those of the servants who drove them so that a camel or a horse would not be deliberately killed. But the thought of Sinead and Ma'el lying riddled with arrows or their bodies hacked to pieces with scimitars did nothing to improve his temper.

"Whose stupidity was this?" he shouted as he pulled his horse to a standstill level with them. "We agreed that you would stay well behind the caravan, out of sight of the robbers, where I might have joined you later. That way we all would have been safe. . . ."

"You would not have been safe!" Sinead broke in. "On the chart we saw the absurdly small party that set out from the caravanserai to rescue us, with your white horse and your cloak showing bravely as you rode to join them. Stupid yourself. I asked

Ma'el to rejoin the caravan to try and save your stupid life, and he said that for my sake he would try. . . ."

"Then my thanks to you both," he broke in. With an edge of anger still in his voice he looked at Ma'el and went on, "but your nobility is going to get all of us killed. Master, we are fighting, or rather defending ourselves against hopeless odds and . . ."

An arrow thudded into the driving bench a few inches from Ma'el's hip. He looked up at the high ground from whence it had come and his expression was that of a general calmly studying the tactical situation on a battlefield. Then he rose unhurriedly to his feet and inclined his head gently as he moved aside the curtain behind him.

"I must leave you now," he said, "because there are small course and distance adjustments I must make. Pass the word that I am about to produce a work of great and terrifying magic. They will better understand you if you use their own words and refer to it as a djinn, but that, appearances to the contrary, it will not harm the men of the camel train or our defenders in any way. . . ."

"What kind of djinn?" Declan broke in. "There isn't time for magical tricks. . . ."

". . . Some little time will elapse before it arrives," he went on as if Declan had not spoken, "so Sinead and yourself must try to stay alive lest my considerable efforts on your behalf are wasted."

Another arrow hit the curtain of skins he had just pulled shut behind him. It bounced away and fell as if it had struck a rock. Declan pointed at the curtain and said, "I don't suppose . . . ?"

Sinead shook her head. "Ma'el allows nobody to see inside. Nobody."

"Then hide under the wagon," he said. "You should be safe from the arrows there."

"What about you?" she asked.

"It would not be fitting," Declan replied as he unlimbered his long-axe, "for me to hide under a wagon."

Before she could reply, Bashir rode up with Mareth's bowmen running close behind him. He waved his scimitar at the groups of the enemy soldiers moving down the slopes towards them.

"They must have believed our lie that more men are coming to our aid," he said, "because their intention now seems to be to attack and cut out this end of the caravan before our imaginary reinforcements arrive, so this is where the battle will end. We need all the fighters we can get, skilled or otherwise . . ." he glanced at Sinead, ". . . so give the boy a weapon."

"She is a healer," said Declan, stressing the first word, "and has forsworn all acts of violence."

"A female healer," said Bashir, showing his teeth briefly. "That explains your anxiety to rejoin your master and, of course, his other servant. But no matter. Give her a sword anyway. If nothing else she may want to fall on it rather than let this bunch of two-legged jackals take her."

He wheeled his horse and went galloping toward the nearest group of the enemy who were charging down on them. Unsheathing his gladius, Declan grasped it carefully by the tip and extended the hilt toward Sinead. She looked very seriously at him as she took it, but before she could speak he fastened the retaining strap of the long-axe tightly around his wrist because he would need to use it one-handed. Without another word he urged his mount forward to follow and draw level with Bashir.

Of the horsemen who had set out from the caravanserai, only Bashir and Declan remained mounted and those on foot, including Mareth's bowmen, numbered less than twenty with the number diminishing with every moment that passed. Because they were the only two mounted targets on their side, the opposing bowmen were giving them most of their attention so that the arrows were whispering past them thick and fast. Declan waved at Bashir and pointed at the largest and closest group of the enemy, three mounted men surrounded by a handful of others keeping pace with them on foot, and propelled the horse forward with a slap on its rump. Bashir nodded, showing his teeth again in a ferocious smile as he took the new direction.

He could not speak for Bashir, Declan told himself, but his

action was not especially brave nor stupid. It was simply that with the number of arrows being aimed in his direction, he thought that a safer place to be was in the middle of the enemy group where the bowmen would be hampered by their unwillingness to risk hitting their friends. Bashir might have had the same thought, but the likelihood was that the other was braver than he was and less thoughtful.

As the enemy group came charging down the slope Bashir, being careful to stay out of range of his swinging axe, and Declan rode up to meet them. Used one-handed, the long-axe was not a precise weapon, so he had decided to swing it as wide and fast as he could in a continuous figure-of-eight while he leaned as far as he could to each side and straightening up between swings so that the shaft would not hit his mount's head. Two very brave and unthinking swordsmen tried to attack simultaneously from both flanks. One of them had his scimitar raised to make a jabbing strike upward at Declan's stomach when the twin points of the axe caught and ran down the other's blade to shatter the hilt and make a bloody ruin of the hand holding it. The man screamed and staggered backward out of range. When the swing continued on the other side, that enemy tried to drop below the level of the axehead, no doubt intending to slash upward at Declan's legs or body when it had gone safely past. But he did not duck low enough and his burnoose was suddenly a blood-soaked rag.

While Declan was still extricating the weapon to begin another swing, one of the opposing horsemen was suddenly on top of him, raising his scimitar so high that he must have intended to cut the Hibernian vertically in two. For an instant he thought of letting go of the axe handle and rolling off the horse, then swore as he remembered that the weapon was fastened securely to his wrist. He raised his free hand in a desperate attempt to push the descending blade sideways and away from him.

Then suddenly the heavy blade was falling, not on Declan but tumbling to the ground, and there was an arrow protruding from the swordsman's right eye. The man rolled off his horse, beating at the sides of his head with both fists. As Declan straightened himself in the saddle and began swinging his axe again, another arrow tugged at his cloak. He wondered briefly whether it had been the marksmanship of one of Mareth's men or the bad aim of an enemy that had saved him.

The remaining three swordsmen on foot had withdrawn out of range of his axe while the others nearby, two of whom carried bows, were running closer. Bashir was engaging one of the two remaining horsemen, their swords clashing together with a sound reminiscent of a busy smithy. The other horseman, who was also staying out of range, was trotting around Declan in a wide circle. Suddenly he stopped, beckoned to one of the running bowmen and shouted for the other to mount behind him. Declan thought quickly, decided that a mounted bowman would be a greater threat than the other one and the swordsmen on the ground.

He urged his mount forward, attempting to time his arrival when the horseman would be helping the bowmen into the second saddle behind him and for a moment both would be preoccupied. With his long-axe blade making a wide, glittering circle around his head, he had almost reached them when the second bowman who, either because his aim was poor or he wasn't an animal lover, sent an arrow deep into his horse's throat. The animal gave an almost human squeal of pain as it reared suddenly and twisted to one side, unseating him. He managed to swing the axe groundward and used it to break his fall. Even so he landed heavily on his side and for a moment he was too shaken to move. The cautious swordsmen were again closing on him, weapons raised, when he struggled onto his knees and began swinging the long-axe again. The axehead caught the wrist of one of them and knocked the legs from under another before they withdrew.

Suddenly he felt a sharp blow and a burning pain in the back of his leg just above the top of his thigh boot and stared disbelievingly at the arrow that was sticking in him. Still swinging the axe around his head, Declan followed its direction of flight back to the bowman on the ground who was also kneeling and notching another arrow. Just before he judged the other was about to loose it, he flung himself sideways so that the arrow caught him in the shoulder instead of the middle of his chest. But at the same time another arrow, loosed by the newly-mounted bowman who was closer and shooting down from saddle height, took him in the side, then the stabbing pain as another two in quick sucession struck his buttock and just below his hip. He swore because for some reason he could neither push himself upright nor grip the handle of his axe. More swordsmen were closing in, weapons raised to finish him off.

But they remained upraised because suddenly there was a peal of thunder from directly overhead, followed by a bloodcurdling sound that was something between a continuous shriek and the hissing of a thousand serpents, and everyone was looking up at the nightmarish thing that was dropping on them out of the sky.

For a moment they remained paralyzed with fear, then they dropped their weapons and ran back up the slope screaming to each other that a terrible djinn was coming to eat them all.

The monster looked like a gigantic, fat-bellied insect with large holes in its body that showed the sky above and behind it. A mass of thin, spidery legs, some with strange, glittering objects at their ends, sprouted from the body in all directions, but the most frightful feature of all, because the screaming and hissing sounds seemed to be coming from them, were the two enormous, blazing eyes. The thing dropped lower and lower until it was drowning out the cries of the fleeing enemy, then it rose quickly and there was another crack of thunder as it disappeared into a widening circle of blue light in a sky that to Declan seemed to be growing dimmer by the moment.

His wounds were no longer hurting and he was sure that his eyes were open even though he wasn't seeing anything, but he could still hear. Sinead was bending close over him, calling him stupid and using swear words ill-becoming to a young woman, and Ma'el was speaking quietly to Bashir.

He said, "The djinn will not return if our attackers do not do so, and that is unlikely. I suggest that you gather your surviving force and use it to escort the camel train to the caravanserai while we remain here with my wagon, for there are many matters to which I must attend. Please do that now."

"At once, Magi," said Bashir, his voice soft and heavy with feeling. "But first there is the matter of payment for our services. Declan said you would agree to pay whatever the cost might be. But I can assure you, on behalf of my master, that after all that has transpired here you have incurred no debt. In fact, we are indebted to you. I shall return the sword, which Declan bore with honor and courage, to my master, but there is a favor that I would ask for myself. It is that I be allowed to take his ferocious long-axe, not to be use because I have not the ability, but to place it in a position of honor in memory of a great warrior who . . ."

"No!" Sinead broke in sharply. "It is his favorite weapon and he might want to use it again."

Bashir was silent for a moment, then in a gentle voice he said, "I think I understand. I suspect that you have strong feelings for him, as I think he does for you, and you do not want to believe that you will lose him. But, young woman, if you can wrestle Death Himself for this man and win, then you are indeed a healer."

Declan felt himself being moved back to the wagon on a litter that felt as if it was floating on air, then hearing as well as sight left him. The last thing he remembered feeling was a sudden explosion of intense cold.

TWENTY-FOUR

Ma'el Report, Day 113,062 . . .

   I am increasingly concerned about the way I continue to reveal more and more Taelon technology to beings whose presently low levels of intelligence and culture might be seriously affected, if not destroyed, by it. As a planetary investigator my behavior in this matter will be considered reprehensible by the Synod. My only defense, which is a scientifically unsatisfactory one even to me, is that up to now both of them have demonstrated a flexibility of mind which suggests that they will be able to adapt to the new situation without mental damage. Nor, I feel sure, will they pass on the knowledge they have discovered to others of their species if I request otherwise, so that a complete obliteration of their memories can be avoided.

"I am at a loss to understand my growing emotional attachment where these two subjects are concerned. It is a recent development because, during the Finisterre incident, I was willing to sacrifice their lives and those of the others on board *Orla* to the attacking Romans. But it was the quick and original thinking of Sinead, with minimal assistance from me, that saved everyone's lives.

"There have been other instances of unusual and even intuitive thinking from both of my servants and it is these abilities of which I will be able to make use. My lengthy separation from the main body of the Commonality has caused my timesight to diminish, and I shall be forced to abandon my investigation if I cannot develop a local source of accurate precognition. That is the primary reason why so much of our technology is being revealed and used in order to keep Sinead and Declan alive. I still have hopes of her acquiring a dependable timesight faculty.

"If they prove to be forlorn hopes then I will be forced reluctantly to wipe their minds clean and look elsewhere."

He felt cold, colder than he had ever felt before or would have believed it possible to feel. With his teeth chattering uncontrollably he pushed himself up onto one elbow and opened his eyes to look around.

The awning of a tent was shading him from a sun that was reflecting off the rippled surface of a large, clear pool that lay a dozen paces away, and shining down on the thin, uneven carpet of short grass between the water's edge and the strange, pale gray litter on which he was lying. A hot but gentle breeze was warming his face and bringing with it the scent of the few desert flowers that were pushing up through the short grass. For a moment Declan wondered if he had died and had awakened in Paradise, but he quickly discounted that idea for three reasons; he had never believed in any kind of heaven; his wounds were still hurting; and Sinead was on her knees beside him observing unnecessarily that he was awake at last.

"I'm c-cold," he said, still looking around him. He saw that they were in a narrow ravine with an uneven, grassy floor. The horse and wagon were about twenty paces behind him and Ma'el was looking down at them from the driving bench. "What happened? How did I get here?"

"Your body is still thawing out," she replied, "and Ma'el says you will be warm again very soon. So ease your mind, save your strength, and don't tire yourself asking questions that I'm about to answer. Lie down again, onto the same side because that's the only part of you that wasn't punctured with arrows. I cut the shafts away as close as possible to the entry wounds, but the heads are still in you. They were barbed and will have to be cut out carefully rather than being pulled out so as to avoid causing even more damage. Do you think you can hold still without fidgeting while I'm doing that?"

Declan stifled a groan as he lowered his raised shoulder back to the litter, discovering that his body was covered by one thin and impossibly white sheet and nothing else. At least he wouldn't have to suffer her pulling off his tunic and boots because that had already been done.

"Yes," he said.

"Good," she replied, folding back the sheet. "And it would make you feel more comfortable if you don't try to look at what I'll be doing to you. We'll start with the easy ones, the hip and buttock wounds. . . ."

He fixed his eyes on what from his position was the vertical edge of the pool and did not reply because his teeth were already clenched. He felt her fingers pressing gently around the wound in his buttock, then the sting of two short, deep cuts on opposite sides of the arrowhead, then it being moved gently from side to side and drawn out. She transferred her attention to the hip wound and he tensed, knowing now what pain to expect. Her voice was brisk, confident, and reassuring as she went on talking, but there was an undertone of concern in it that made him wonder if she thought she was working on a body that was expected soon to die.

". . . I shall allow the wounds to bleed themselves clean for a few moments before I stitch, cover, and bind them," she said, tossing the bloody arrowheads onto the ground close to his face. "Do you want to keep those in memory of your battle?"

"No," said Declan firmly, "I hate the sight of blood . . ." he tried to laugh but instead the body movement made him gasp in pain, ". . . especially my own."

"I hate the sight of your blood, too," she said, and added

quickly, "or anyone else's. We owe a lot to Padriag of Cashel; his leather tunic stopped the arrows from penetrating deeply. Now for the shoulder. Your muscles are like rocks. It will come out easier if you let the arm go limp. But to return to your earlier questions, after Ma'el's djinn frightened off the raiders, he moved you into his wagon and put you into what he called hibernation anaesthesia . . ."

"What's that?"

". . . I asked the same question," she went on, "and he said cold sleep. I haven't seen inside his wagon. What's it like?"

"I don't know," said Declan. "I was sleeping, remember."

"You sarcastic son of a . . ." Sinead began angrily, then she shook her head and went on in voice filled with growing wonder, "Indeed you were. For nearly four months you were sleeping while Ma'el used the large and two of the smaller djinns, he calls them soft-landed sensors, to seek out the medical knowledge that was needed. The big djinn is the one that usually remains very high and sends down the pictures to the magic chart. It found the libraries in Athens, Rome, Alexandria, and one in Xian in Far Cathay, and another in a vast country that nobody knows about where they make human sacrifices to a god called Huitzilopochtl so that he will allow the sun to rise each morning, but they have great knowledge about the internal arrangement of bones and organs and the workings of our bodies.

"The two small djinn that live in the big one's belly," she rushed on, "came down at night to look at the scrolls and pictures and send all they saw to Ma'el's chart for us to study. Sometimes it was difficult for their long, iron fingers to find and open the books at the right place, and scrolls were knocked from the shelves, but the disturbance was usually blamed on robbers. Once Ma'el had to find and question a scholar through a small djinn which he used to make the other believe was the manifestation of a strange god. But he gave us the knowledge I needed. . . ."

"Wait," said Declan weakly, shaking his head and immediately regretting it because his shoulder muscle also moved. "What are you talking about? Where is this place, what has happened apart from djinns coming and going, what knowledge are you talking about, and why do you need it?"

She continued answering him quietly while she eased the arrowhead out of his shoulder and threw it away so violently that it might have been a disgusting reptile. She left the wound to bleed for a few moments while she returned her attention to the other two, pressing them closed with gentle fingers before stitching their edges together and covering them with pads, soaked in something that smelled strongly, that were held in position with firm bindings.

They were not very far from the scene of the battle, she told him, and when Ma'el had told Bashir that the wagon would remain behind for a while he had told the truth without being accurate about the exact duration. With the help of the chart their master had found a suitable ravine, moved the wagon into it, and performed a spell to ensure that nobody would ever stumble across it, or even see it or the comings and goings of the djinn that visited them regularly with charms that Ma'el said he needed. One of them had been a strange, glowing staff that he had pushed into the sand saying that it was drilling an opening into a stream that was flowing deep underground. When he removed the staff a few moments later, a spring of clear water had bubbled up to form the pool he could see beside them. Time and the dried-out but still-living seeds in the ground had produced the young grass and desert flowers that were growing all around them.

"Are you sure it's been that long since . . . ?" Declan began.

"You were cold sleeping," she answered shortly. "Weren't you listening to me? Now roll over a little onto your stomach, but without hurting your side. I have to work on the leg, now. The arrowhead went in behind and above the knee. There is an important vein there and I mustn't cut it when the barb is coming out. . . ."

"Why not?"

"Because you might bleed to death," she replied, "or end up with a wooden stump like Tomas the helmsman. Unfortunately there is none of Brian's wine to ease your hurting so I will understand if you make noises or use unseemly language. I would do both in your place. Just be sure to hold the leg steady while I'm working on it. . . ."

He began by biting his lower lip until he tasted his own blood and changed to clenching his teeth instead, but he did not make a sound. It seemed that she was spending a much longer time on the back of his leg than she had on the other wounds. He felt her fingers moving the barb back and forth by tiny amounts and sometimes twisting it before it was drawn out and he felt the gentler, regular pricking of the stitches that pulled the edges of the wound together. But at last he felt the firm binding being wound on and heard her sigh of relief.

"Good," she said. "Now for the side wound. Roll slowly back onto your other side and . . . Your mouth is bleeding. Surely you're losing enough blood from other places without chewing off bits of your lip?"

"I was hungry," said Declan, forcing a smile. "I still am."

"And that's how your going to stay," she said firmly. "How long is it since you ate anything, not counting the time you spent cold sleeping in the wagon?"

Declan thought for a moment. "At the caravanserai I was too tired to eat," he said, "and I overslept and had to leave quickly to catch up on Bashir's men and so missed breaking my fast. Since then there wasn't a chance to . . . Please, I'm starving to death."

"That's good," she said looking relieved.

"That's cruel, heartless," he replied. "I tell you, my stomach thinks my throat's been cut. . . . What's *is* that thing?"

"Another device of Ma'el's," she replied. "It resembles the chart except that instead of showing where we are it lets me to see what is happening inside your body. Lift yourself, gently now, onto your elbow and look into it. Isn't it wonderful? My father would have sold his soul for a device like this. I may want you to hold it in position if I have to use both hands."

It was a flat, square box more than a hand's length on the side and no thicker than a man's index finger. Instead of a motionless picture the upper surface of the box showed a landscape that seemed to be in regular, twitching motion. Bright and clear at its center was the short length of arrow and barb penetrating his flesh while around and behind it there were many thick and thin lines, which from the operation of Tomas's leg he recognized as veins, and even thicker masses that curled about each other in a wet, slippery tangle.

"It's horrible, disgusting," he said, easing his good side back onto the litter. "My belly looks like it's full of serpents."

"Hopefully they are empty serpents," said Sinead, "and ensuring that they remain that way is what may keep you alive. If the subject doesn't disgust you too much, would you like to know why?"

"Yes," he said. "You talking about it is better than me having to watch it. But why are you always angry with me? I haven't done anything to deserve it, especially not to you."

She hesitated for a moment while looking at him with a strange and very serious expression, and Declan had the feeling that when she spoke the words were not those she had originally intended to say. "You make me angry because you give me so many wounds to treat, and because most of them are yours.

"The snakes inside your belly are in fact a long, continuous tube," she went on before he could reply, "which takes out the good part of the food you eat and allows the poisonous waste that remains to be passed out of your back passage as excrement. The arrowhead made a small cut in this tube and it may have allowed a quantity of the fecal matter to leak and gradually find its way into the rest of your body. If that happened you would die, just the way that young boy shot with a poisoned arrow died on the ship. The fact that you haven't eaten for a long time, and will not be allowed to eat until the cut in the tube is healed, is good because the amount of poison in there should be small.

"Now I'll need both hands for the next part," she added, "so hold the seeing box over the wound, just here. That's it."

Again he gritted his teeth as the arrowhead moved from side to side and was coaxed. The pain eased as he felt but did not see a warm trickle run down and onto his stomach.

"And now," he said through dry lips, "you're letting it bleed clean?"

"No," she said, bending low over him. "This one will need more than that."

Declan felt her fingers pressing and pulling the wound open, then her lips being placed around it and the painful but strange sensation of the blood and he knew not what other poisons being sucked out. After a moment she raised her head, spat onto the ground and bent over the wound again.

"Wait!" he said urgently. "That is stupid. If the blood is poisoned you shouldn't be . . ."

"Stupid yourself," she said angrily, "I'm not stupid enough to *swallow* it!" She continued the process for what seemed to Declan to be a long time even though the tiny movement of the sun's shadow indicated otherwise, before she straightened up and said, "That should do it. Any more of that and I'll end up sucking you inside out. I'm going to close and cover the wound now. After what has gone before it won't hurt you much. This has gone well, Declan, but now you must try to ease your mind, cover your body again, and let yourself sleep."

"I don't want to sleep," he said. "I want to talk."

"What about?" she said.

He remained silent until she had finished binding the wound and returned from the pool where she had rinsed out her mouth with cupped handfuls of clear water, washed the blood off her lips, and splashed some of it onto the back of her neck. From the sight of her perspiring face he realized that the sun must be hot even though he himself was just beginning to feel warm.

"About you," he said, "and why, after all you've just done, you're angry with me? You would be nicer to the horse if it had been wounded by arrows."

"Yes," she said, "because the horse wouldn't talk back to me. Please change the subject. . . ."

She broke off suddenly to bend over him again, one hand going to his forehead and the other resting lightly on his chest. Muttering to herself she moved to the opposite end of the litter and lifted it from the ground, unfolding a support that kept it in that position. Declan chose his words carefully and was surprised by his teeth chattering when he spoke.

"I'm not c-calling you stupid," he said, "but what h-healer's reason had you for t-tilting my feet up?"

"Because you're growing cold," she said, "and sweating, and your heart is beating fast but weakly. I was afraid of this happening. Despite your physical strength, the pain and duration of the surgery is sending you into shock. The treatment for shock, which is agreed by stupid healers from Hibernia to Cathay is to elevate the feet so that the blood your heart is able to pump goes to your chest and brain where it is most needed. You must also be kept warm. . . ."

She fell silent because Ma'el, whose hearing must have been very good, arrived beside her carrying another one of his strange, thin, but very warm blankets. She took it from him and draped it over Declan, tucking it around him as if he had been a child close to slumber while being careful not to press it against the underlying wounds. Ma'el spoke as soon as she was finished.

"Will he live?"

Sinead's face was angry, Declan saw, and her eyes were opening and closing rapidly. If he hadn't known her better he would have thought that she was blinking back tears.

"I don't know," she said.

TWENTY-FIVE

...My earlier fears about the effect of revealing Taelon science to the female Sinead have proved groundless. She is both mentally flexible and pragmatic to a high degree, and shows no fear of what she still calls Taelon magic and, even though she cannot understand its workings, she insists that if she is properly instructed in its use there should be nothing for her to fear. Declan is still uneasy about what they refer to as the smaller djinns that land from time to time with information and supplies, but he will not allow himself to show fear when Sinead is so obviously not afraid. The magic Sinead most desires and persistently requests is that which I cannot provide, a means that will enable Declan to recover from his wounds and continue living.

"Following her confused forecast of the arrival of the first djinn which ended the ambush of the caravan in our favor, I had hopes that she was at last developing the precognitive faculty, but since then she has shown no other indications of possessing the time sense in spite of me questioning her closely regarding her dreams and the suppressed memories from her childhood. She co-operated fully in this interrogation even though the process was emotionally painful for her, but suggests respectfully that I am wasting my time.

"It now seems certain that the concealed and protected environment that I provided here was a wasted effort. My behavior toward them and the emotional attachment I have developed for these two members of a planetary population under investigation is lax and unprofessional in the extreme, and the fact that there was a possibility of the female developing timesight is no excuse, and neither is the increasing feelings of loneliness and lack of support engendered by my self-imposed withdrawal from the Commonality.

"When my male servant, the brave and resourceful Declan, expires as it seems he must, I shall reluctantly dispense with Sinead and install her comfortably in a place and among people of her own choosing, after which I shall seek out another female who with treatment will be able to see into this world's future.

"That has become a matter of great urgency."

With the sheet pushed down to his waist, Declan was half-lying, half-sitting on the litter that had been angled in the middle to form a legless chair. The tent awning shaded him from the sun and the gentle morning breeze, cooled slightly by its passage across the intervening water of the pool, fanned his hot, sweating face and upper body. Sinead placed her palm briefly on his forehead and it, too, was hot by the time she took it away.

"I don't understand this," she said, frowning. "Your shoulder and leg wounds, even the one in your side, have healed cleanly. All are being covered with healthy scar tissue. By rights you should be up and trying to walk."

"I did try to walk . . ." Declan began.

". . . Without me half carrying you," she went on. "Instead you are much weaker than you were after the battle, thinner in spite of the food I force into you, and with every few days a recurrent fever . . ." she looked at the perspiration beading her palm,

". . . that is increasing in severity. The potions you have been given and the roots you chewed that are used in many countries to reduce such a fever do not affect you, or perhaps are affecting you too slowly. You are burning up. We must cool you down or you will die."

He stared at her serious, concerned face for a moment, trying to make it remain steady among all the distorted, feverish images that were dancing around the inside of the tent. It surprised him that he was still able to speak clearly.

"I'll drink more cold water."

"You couldn't drink enough," she replied, pulling off his sheet and pressing the indentations on the litter that returned it to its customary flat shape as well as making it float in the air. "Instead of putting the water into you I'm going to put you into the pool."

"Wait!" he cried, the very thought of it shocking him into sensibility. "That's a horrible idea. I'm not a Druid like you, I've never bathed in a mountain pool. . . ."

"Try to be brave," she said scornfully. "You can survive it for a few moments. In we go."

"But you're going to bathe me," he said, "with all your clothes on. You'll catch an ague in wet garments and who will heal you? Or do you think . . . ? No, Sinead, even if I was fit and well again I would never be roused to a frenzy by a scrawny, flat-chested child, nor would I try to take advantage of . . ."

"Enough," she broke in. "Look the other way."

He did not look directly at her as she pulled off her boots and began to disrobe, but out of the corner of his eye he saw her end by removing a broad, tight binding from around her upper back and chest. No wonder, he thought surprised, she had looked like a young boy. She would not meet his eyes when she turned to face him again, but instead busied herself with lowering the litter until it floated on the surface before wading with it down the steeply sloping sides of the pool until they were at its center where the water was up to her waist. She did not speak but it seemed that her face was red from more than the heat.

"You're not all that young," he said, trying very hard to look only at her face. "You're old, but small. And without those chest bindings you are . . ."

"Such compliments," she said in a derogatory voice. "Scrawny and flat-chested, you said, and now old. Declan, have you ever won a woman with words, or first do you need to stun her with your long-axe?"

"Without them," he persisted, "you are slim and well-formed and pleasing to the eye and, and beautiful."

She inclined her head and was silent for a moment before she said thoughtfully, "That sounded better. There may be hope for you yet. Now hold your breath."

Her hands grasped the sides of the litter and pressed it under the surface. Heated by the desert sun as it was, the pool water was not cold, but against his burning skin it felt as though his body had been suddenly encased in a block of ice. Afraid of sinking deeper into it, his arms reached up instinctively and wrapped themselves around Sinead's neck. But she must have bent forward because he remained under for a long moment before she again raised the litter to the surface where he caught his breath and released his hold on her. Without mentioning the arms that had come close to strangling her, she placed a hand on his forehead.

"Better," she said, "but you're still too warm. I'm going to leave you alone for a while to try cooling yourself, by putting your hands and arms underwater or by sprinkling your body with it whenever you feel it necessary."

"Where are you going?" he asked, suddenly afraid of being abandoned. "I didn't mean to hurt you."

"To enjoy myself," she replied, smiling, "and you didn't."

In the event Declan did not have to sprinkle himself because Sinead was doing it for him as she swam in tight circles around the litter, sometimes diving under it and then surfacing with a great splash, or beating at the water enthusiastically with hands and feet. She was indeed enjoying herself to such an extent, that Declan wondered if there was still a lot of the child's mind inside that young woman's body. He was sorry when the watery disturbance settled and she swam over to feel his forehead again.

"Much better, but still too warm," she said, and dragged the litter to the sandy edge of the pool and across to the shade of the tent awning. "Here the breeze will dry off your wet body and cool you even more by evaporation. If you become too cold, use the blanket, and if the fever comes back we'll try the pool again." She moved a few paces beyond the tent and turned her back. "I must dress myself now."

Declan knew that he should have turned his attention to the wagon or the tent awning or his own dripping and unsightly body, but he would have felt both dishonest and stupid if he refused himself the chance to look at the only object of true beauty in the ravine.

"You have no need of that wrapping around you," he said. "It will make your breast flat again, but I will know what it hides and you will feel only its heat and discomfort."

"It is irksome," she said in grudging agreement, letting the binding fall to the ground and pulling on her burnoose.

"Your hair is long," he said, "and beautiful. There is the darkness of a starless night on it. You should not crush such hair into a ball to hide it under your helmet. We have no need of helmets in this place."

She didn't reply, but instead ran her opened fingers through the damp hair, spreading it out over her back and shoulders for quicker drying in the sun before she turned to face him. Her expression was thoughtful, and wary.

"Declan," she said, "the cold bathing seems to have worked wonders for your manners as well as reducing the fever, for suddenly your compliments are worthy of the silver tongue of Brian O'Rahailley himself. But his were usually bestowed with a selfish end in view and, well, I think I preferred it when your words were unmannerly but more honest.

"I must speak with Ma'el, now," she ended, "and light the cooking fire. Keep the blanket around you, lie still, and try to rest."

A few moments after she left him he did as he was told, but not before he sat up, rolled onto his hands and knees, and tried to climb to his feet with only partial success, and he came close to fainting while he was half crawling the short distance along the the ravine to where they relieved themselves. It took all of his strength to cover his results with sand. He could not believe how weak he had become during the past few days and he was glad to roll back onto the litter and pull the blanket around him.

It was dusk when he wakened with his shoulder being shaken and Sinead demanding that he eat and drink some of the water with her foul-tasting herbs in it. He did try but she insisted that a hungry lark would have eaten more and that he should go back to sleep.

It was still night when next he wakened, shivering and with his limbs shaking so much that the sheet threatened to slip from his body. The lamp was turned down and the dividing screen had been partially removed in case he needed attention. He could barely see the muffled form of Sinead, who was sleeping with head, hands, and feet drawn inside her burnoose. He pulled the sheet tightly around himself and clenched his teeth to stop their chattering because he did not want to waken her or bear the brunt of her tongue if he did.

"I'm not sleeping," she said quietly as if reading his mind. "What's wrong with you? Has the fever returned?"

"N-no," he replied. "I c-cold."

In a moment Sinead had the lamp turned up and she was kneeling beside him; her hand went to his forehead before slipping under the sheet to rest briefly on his chest and the upper muscle of his arm. Then she stood up quickly, turned and upended the bag that contained his clothing and emptied it onto the ground. Choosing his own burnoose and the blood-stained cloak, she spread them over him and waited for what seemed like a long time before speaking again.

"You are indeed cold," she said, again laying a hand on his chest. "In fact, your muscles were tightening and threatening to go into a rigor. Do you feel any warmer now?"

"I-I don't th-think so," he said through chattering teeth even though her palm felt like a hot poultice pressing on his icy skin. "I-I'm colder."

"There is no time to build a fire," she said in a quiet, serious voice, "and you could not get close enough to it without scorching yourself. I have to make you warm again or you will die. . . ."

For the second time in a day he saw her pull off her burnoose, but this time instead of dropping it to the sand she spread it over him.

". . . Turn onto your side," she went on briskly, "so I can lie close against your back. And Declan, behave yourself."

For an instant there was a blast of cold air as she opened the covers, then he felt the wonderfully hot contours of her body pressing against his back and leg while a warm arm tightly encircled his waist. He did not try to say anything because his teeth were chattering and he did behave himself because, difficult as it was for him to believe, he was sharing the blankets with a comely young woman and all he wanted from her was her body's warmth. He did not tell her that because to a young woman the words might not have been complimentary.

Dawn was showing through the fabric of the tent and bleaching out the lamplight by the time he stopped shivering and began to feel really warm, so much so that he was perspiring again. He felt Sinead waken and her hand slide briefly across his wet chest, then heard her say something very unladylike before she rose, pulled on her burnoose and left the tent. A moment later she was back with Ma'el's inner-body–seeing charm and a pitcher of cold water.

"What's *wrong* with you?" she said in a worried, exasperated voice. "Last night you were freezing to death and now you're burning with fever again. Drink as much of this as you can and sprinkle yourself with the rest until I can douse you in the pool again. But first let me look at your wounds. Turn onto your good side."

She talked quietly to herself while she was examining the places where arrows had pierced his leg and shoulder, pronouncing them healing cleanly and well. But the one just above his hip, while it had closed over and knitted to her satisfaction, was surrounded by an area of deep pink inflammation. The cause, according to the deep picture that Ma'el's charm was showing her, was a large, pus-filled abscess growing on the wall of the bowel where the arrowhead had nicked it. If it were to burst, which it might do soon, and flood through his body, her patient would quickly die.

"I'm sorry, Declan," she continued speaking to him rather than to herself, "I must cut into you again. Deeply."

TWENTY-SIX

The sun was still low in the sky by the time Sinead had immersed him several times in the pool and pulled his litter back to the sandy bank where her instruments, bowls, boiled cloths, and several short lengths of rope lay spread out on a sheet ready for use. Declan felt cooled by the bathing but it was not the icy, breath-stopping cold that had gripped him during the previous night. Sinead shivered in the cool, morning breeze, then dressed herself quickly and knelt beside the litter and raised it a short distance above the sand before speaking.

"Please lie on your good side," she said, selecting a length of rope and passing it around his body and the underside of the litter as she spoke. "I am going to tie down your chest, waist, thighs, and lower legs so that, in the event that you have another rigor, you won't be able to move and perhaps cause me inadvertently to cut you in the wrong place. I will leave your arm free so that you may assist me by holding the deep-body–seer in position, but in case you have a serious tremor and lose control of it, I will place a noose around your wrist so that I can pull down the arm and secure it to the litter and proceed unaided unless . . ." she raised her voice slightly, ". . . Ma'el decides to help me."

The old man had left the wagon and was walking toward them. They both knew that Ma'el had keen ears and would have heard her, but when he stopped beside them he made no mention of her words. Sinead tried again.

"With respect, Ma'el," she said, "surely you have it in your power to help Declan. Some magical device or potion, perhaps, that will remove this sac of poison and . . ."

"You have mentioned this matter to me earlier this day," the old man broke in gently, "and my answer then as now is no. Believe me, there is a strong reason why I will not provide medication for one of your people's bodies. I have given away many of the secrets of my own people and done things to yours in the hope of providing you, and myself, with a timesight into your world's future. I thought that your forecast of the arrival of the djinn was an early demonstration of the faculty, but continuing timesight you could not give me."

"I'm sorry that I disappointed you," she said, "because I owe you much. . . ."

"Do not be sorry," he broke in. "You are not responsible for the physical and emotional damage that was done to you, or for the sexual negativity that resulted over which you have no control. So clear your mind, and allow mine to aid yours in the only way it can, by wishing you sharp eyes and steady hands.

"If Declan is not to die this day," he ended quietly, "it is your skill alone that will make him live."

In the short but seemingly endless time that followed Declan thought that he suffered twice, once because he had already undergone this cutting and knew what to expect, and again when it was happening but taking much longer. But his muscles did not lock in a rigor as he held Ma'el's device steady above Sinead's gentle, precise hands, and his body remained still and unflinching without help from the ropes. Deliberately he did not look at her in case that would be a distraction and instead looked into the eyes of the watching Ma'el, which were so dark and deep that he did not know whether they were empty of feeling or showing too much of it for him to read. While he did not watch Sinead he knew exactly what she was doing from moment to moment because she talked about it continuously in a quiet, competent voice.

He thought this might have been the teaching method of her dead healer father while demonstrating to his young apprentice daughter, and perhaps she was hoping that he might be watching her from somewhere and approving.

A triangular incision had been made and below it she had cut out a cone-shaped hollow that revealed and gave access to the abscess at its point. It was large, bulging, and covered by a thick skin that would have ruptured and spread poison throughout his body very soon. The skin was pierced, but only enough to introduce the cleaned quill that enabled most of the poison to be sucked out, then it was widened to remove the rest of it until her eye and Ma'el's device showed that no more remained. As much of the emptied abscess shell as it was safe to remove—part of it was adhering to the bowel wall—was cut away. For several moments the wound was allowed to bleed clean before it was packed with herbs that would promote healing and a flamwort to reduce inflammation before she inserted a drain, closed up, and finally looked at his face.

"Declan," she said, "you are a strong, stubborn, and brave man. You did not move and neither did you cry out, even though I would have thought none the less of you if you had done both, many times. But now you can be at ease, it is over and it went well. Close your eyes and let sleep take you."

His eyes were already closing so that he felt only a tired surprise when she bent forward and touched her lips lightly to his forehead.

It took many weeks before a steadily increasing appetite caused the thin, knobbled sticks that were his arms and legs to thicken again with firm, healthy flesh and muscle. Gradually he became able to walk unaided about the ravine and even climb its rocky walls and, best of all, to splash daily in the pool. When he watched her it was evident that Sinead, too, enjoyed using the pool, but he doubted that she derived as much pleasure from

watching him, and there was some invisible and unspoken con-
straint that kept them from swimming in it together. Their
words to each other were more polite than they had ever been,
but neither of them seemed to say anything of importance and he
could not find the words he wanted to speak. Without making
any mention of the situation between his servants, Ma'el said that
he was pleased that Declan was returning to full health, and the
hints that he dropped about them soon continuing their journey
to Cathay became less gentle with each passing day.

At night Sinead continued her recent habit of leaving the
tent's dividing curtain open but only by enough, she said, for her
to know at once if he was having a feverish relapse. Declan felt so
well that he did not think that would happen and he could not
understand why she did not think so, too. Yet every night when
his eyes were closed and he was pretending to sleep, he could feel
her eyes watching him until he opened his whereupon she would
close hers. It was like some stupid, childish game that increasingly angered and disturbed him until one night he could stand it
no longer.

"Sinead," he said quietly, raising himself onto one elbow, "I
know you are not asleep."

"I'm not," she agreed. "Have you a fever, a chill? What ails
you?"

"I have no fever," he said, "nor am I cold. But I would like
your body warm beside me again."

She sighed and seemed to pull herself more tightly into her
burnoose as she said, "I have seen the way you look at me, not
only when I'm bathing, and knew that soon you would ask that of
me." She regarded him in silence for what seemed like a long
time, then said, "The answer is no."

"I do not like or want that answer," Declan said. He took a
deep breath and went on, "Perhaps my manners are unsubtle and
my words too direct. But even though they feel strange to me my
feelings for you are true and strong, stronger than any that I
have ever known in my past violent and unruly life, and much
too strong for me to want to risk hiding them behind pretty and,

you might think, dishonest words meant only to sway you to my will. That is what I want to do, but there is much more that I want to do."

She looked at him, her expression serious but not angry, and did not speak.

"You are a woman and a gifted healer," he went on, speaking slowly and clearly as if he was instructing a child. "You are a woman who is graceful, comely of face, and with the beauty of form and person that all men desire but so few live to attain. You are a woman well taught in the healing arts in spite of your tender years, who is soft and gentle when gentleness is needed, and firm and direct in your encouragement when it is not. You are a woman with a lively wit and a mind that can accept, and even use, strange and fearful wonders that would drive another into gibbering madness. You are a . . ."

A small hand appeared from her burnoose, palm held outward. There was an impatient edge to her tone as she said, "A woman. If I had not already known that I would of a certainty know it by now. Please, is there a point to these endless statements of fact that you are trying to make? And if your next weighty pronouncement is to be that you are a man, I know that, too."

"I am a man," he went on doggedly, "who has traveled with you, and shared many strange and dangerous adventures with you over the course of half a year. When a man and woman are forced to be in each other's company for a lengthy period, I have been told, they grow either to hate or to love each other very much, and we have . . ."

"Who told you this," she broke in, "your wise old father?"

"My father did not ever speak to me about such matters," he replied. "It was Brian who told me during the voyage to Alexandria, while we were sharing a night watch and he had grown tired of asking me about Ma'el's secrets and was being serious and philosophical rather than amusing. He also said that when women had the choice they rarely chose as their intended mates men who were charming or skilled with words. Instead they

sought out husbands who would be strong and constant and
capable of providing for and defending the home they would
build and the children they would beget, rather than some
charming weakling with winning ways and an endless store of
pretty compliments.

"But I was saying," he went on, "that we began by hating
each other from the first moment we met, until in time the
hatred faded and, on my part at least, has changed to love. It is a
love that disturbs and delights my sleep and, when I awaken
unfulfilled, it puts an ache in my chest and a hunger in me that no
herbs or food will ease, and whenever I look at you it makes the
muscles of my hands and arms cramp with the effort of not
reaching out to grasp you and hold your lovely body close and . . .
We have been near to each other and yet apart for a long time.
On the ship when we worked on the leg of Tomas, and at other
times, I thought that your hatred of me and what I am was fading,
and surely your treatment of my wounds was not the act of a person who hated me. Have you none of these softer feelings for me,
no smallest spark that with time and patience and continued
pleading might be made to burn as fiercely as the fire that rages
in me for you?"

She had closed her eyes while he was speaking. A moment
passed before she opened them and said, "I am a small, weak,
beautiful woman and you, you are what you are. What is to stop
you taking me?"

"No!" said Declan fiercely. "I could take you, now and for
many nights to come. You would bite and scratch and doubtless
add more scars to this already scarred body, and the pleasure
would far outweigh the pain. But I do not want to take you like
that, not against your will, for that way you would really come to
hate and despise me.

"Hatred is not what I want from you for the rest of my life."

Her eyes were closed again, tightly. She did not speak.

"I do not want to make you my property," he went on softly,
"like a cloak or a pair of boots or something else of use or value
that I have come to own. No, I am a man who would have died

and who you made well and strong and vigorous again, so I and the rest of the life you have given me are your property, not mine."

Her eyes were open again, very wide, but still she did not speak.

"If you do not want this property," he went on, "if your answer is still no, then I must leave you, and quickly, lest my resolution and self-control fail me and my behavior becomes that of a rutting animal rather than a thinking man. When we reach the caravanserai and you and Ma'el continue the journey to Cathay, I shall ask to be released from his service and take employment as a guard on the next caravan returning to Alexandria, or wherever else fortune takes me. And if other women should come into my life, none of them will be the one I truly love. . . ."

Declan broke off. It was difficult to tell in the light of the dimmed lamp, but it seemed to him that her eyes were wet. He felt a small stirring of hope because he thought he might know the reason.

"I have never seen you show fear," he continued in a reassuring voice, "but you are very young and virginal and, as is natural, afraid of what I would do to you. . . ."

"You are well experienced," she interrupted, "in deflowering virgins?"

The words were a stinging criticism but somehow her tone sounded sad and disappointed rather than angry. He shook his head firmly.

"I have not had that experience," he said. "But all women begin as virgins, and when I was much younger and a virgin myself, one of the nicer, motherly ones told me that it had been far from pleasant when it happened to her. Even though I would be as gentle as I am able, if you were to allow this to happen between us, I would hurt you, but only for the first time. After that . . ."

"It hurt for the first, second, and third time," she broke in, her face dark with remembered pain and terror. "I was scarcely eleven summers when those three brave warriors came to loot our home and kill my family. They took their pleasure of me, thrice within the hour, and left laughing." Suddenly her voice was thick with shame and anger as she ended, "So you see, Declan, you must search farther for your first virgin."

He took a deep breath and exhaled slowly through his nose before he would trust himself to speak. "If ever I find your three brave warriors," he said, "the rest of their lives would be numbered in moments. But the gross dishonor that befell you is in the past and it is your future, hopefully our future years together that concerns me now. My feelings for you are . . . But you know my feelings for you. Please come to me, or at least give me hope. Give me an answer other than no."

"Declan," she said, and the sheen of tears in her eyes was plain even in the dim lamplight, "you are a brave and resourceful warrior, noble and uncomplaining under pain, and in many other ways you have proved to be the gentlest of men. I have grown to admire you more and more over the past months and I too, have harbored feelings so fierce and strong that a young woman like myself should not dare to speak them aloud. But I keep trying to tease you, and test you for weaknesses where no weakness exists. But . . ." suddenly she smiled "the answer is still no. . . ."

Slowly her slender arm reached reached upward to pull aside the curtain and Declan saw that she was lying under the burnoose but not wearing it, or anything else. The petals of many, sweet-smelling desert flowers lay under and around her.

". . . But I ask with love that you should come to me."

Four the next four nights they slept closely together in the tent and wakened in the morning to bathe together in the pool, and during the daylight hours they were never far from each other. Ma'el, who had tact and a gentle understanding, remained in the wagon so that they had nothing to do but be with each other. Then early on the morning of the fifth day Declan was awakened by Sinead who was trembling violently, bathed in sweat and with her arms locked so tightly around him that he could scarcely breathe. Before he could speak she was almost screaming at him. "Declan!" she cried out before he could speak. "Please help me. Protect me from these horrible visions. They are of creatures of iron and smoke and great, screaming metal birds that take hundreds of people into their bellies before flying away with them. Save me Declan, I am losing my mind. . . !"

TWENTY-SEVEN

...**A** physical and emotional coupling between my servants Sinead and Declan has taken place, but completely unexpected was her sudden acquisition of the timesight. The images that she foresees are terrifying her—they are so forward-reaching and clear in their implications that they frighten me as well—so that I must work with the assistance of her mate to save her mind from becoming dysfunctional. If this is successfully accomplished there will, of course, be no need to replace them as servants, a fact which on a personal level pleases me very much.

"It has become apparent that if I am to make the maximum possible utilization of her new faculty, the remainder of the Taelon surface and orbiting technology, as well as a little about my purpose in coming to Earth, must now be revealed to them without further delay."

As Ma'el sat down cross-legged under the tent awning Declan thought, not for the first time, that for a man so ancient in years the other's thin body had a flexibility and ease of movement that rivaled his own. At his right Sinead could not have been sitting closer to him, with an arm around his waist and hanging on so tightly that the sand under them might have been water in which she was afraid of drowning. She released her grip when Ma'el inclined his head and looked at her.

"That is not necessary," he said gently. "During the words that I must say to you, a close physical as well as the emotional contact that exists between Declan and yourself will be a reassurance for both of you. Now, please believe me when I say that there is nothing in your mind that can harm you because the things that you have seen are far away and have not happened yet, nor will they happen in your lifetime. Mentally it will be very uncomfortable for you, but when you are ready, please describe to me, in as much detail as you can recall, the sights, sounds, and words, if you heard any, that made up your recent timesighting."

"My timesighting?" said Sinead, replacing her arm even more tightly around Declan's waist and trying to delay the discomfort to come with a question. "Did not you say, after many unsuccessful attempts to awaken the faculty in mc, that I was an unsuitable subject who would never be able to see into the future?"

"I was mistaken," said Ma'el. "I had assumed that when a young woman given the faculty proved to be deaf and blind to the unfolding of times to come, the reason is that she cannot or will not bear the child or children that will extend her line into that future. Plainly that situation no longer applies here. The physical and emotional factors that . . ."

"Wait," she broke in, turning to look at Declan with an expression of surprise and wonder. "Does that mean . . . Am I already with child?"

"Perhaps," Ma'el replied, "and perhaps not. But sometime there will be progeny who will provide the time channel through which you now see so clearly. They will not be as gifted as you, because the degree of excellence of the faculty is dependent on the intensity of the physical and emotional bond between the original progenitors, which in this case is uniquely strong because never before has it been known for a timesight to see across two millennia.

"I say again," he ended, "the visions that you see, strange and terrifying though they will be, cannot harm you. Close your eyes to the present if it helps you concentrate, and tell me in your own words what you have already seen, and what else you are seeing now."

She looked at Declan and he gave her an encouraging smile. He was unable to say anything because the thought that sooner or later they would be parents had paralyzed his tongue. Sinead smiled back at him, closed her eyes, and began to speak.

"The first image," she said, "had been of a great, screaming, landed bird. It had stiff wings, with four huge, open-ended caskets hanging sideways from them, and it was these that seemed to be screaming. It was bigger than the largest ship I have ever seen, larger even than a Roman trireme. Hundreds of people climbed into its belly without being chained or even driven inside with whips before it screamed louder, ran along a great, wide road and flew away with them across a city with buildings like enormous fingers of glass and stone that poked almost into the clouds. Between the buildings, carriages that moved without horses or slaves pulling them ran at great speed and make high, hooting noises. People dressed in bright raiment, more people than it was possible to count, walked the streets almost shoulder to shoulder, and . . ."

"What else did you see?" said Ma'el quickly when Sinead hesitated. Declan could feel her trembling and her eyes remained tightly shut when she replied.

"I—I did not see this the first time," she stammered, "but I can now. An enormous building shaped like a strange, transparent flower, or maybe a vegetable. Tiny people move about inside it and on the trimmed, green field on which it stands. There is a djinn dropping from the sky. None of the people seem afraid of it and one of them, no, I can see three of them now, wearing close-fitting, plush garments instead of cloaks, and, and they all look like *you!*"

Ma'el's body stiffened and for the first time since they had met Declan saw the other's calm, unlined face show emotion. "You are sure?" he asked in a low, angry voice. "Could it be a waking confusion of memory caused, perhaps, by your familiarity with me and the recent appearance of my djinn? My people should not be there."

"Whether or not they be confusions of my memory," Sinead replied firmly as she opened her eyes to look directly into his face, "I am certain of what I saw and still see. Now I hear voices talking. The subject sounds important. Who is Ha'gel? What is the Shaqarava . . . ?"

She broke off, gave a small, involuntary scream of surprise then said sharply, "Ma'el! What's wrong with you? What is happening to your *face?*"

The old man's features, which had been partly shaded by his cowl, were going through a fearful change. A latticework of fine lines had appeared and was spreading over his face, making it look like a picture executed by a craftsman in mosaic tiles. As they stared horrified the change continued; the tiny pieces of face dissolved one by one until the features reflected the sunlight as if they were made from clear, motionless water through which they could see to the inside surface of Ma'el's cowl. Sinead had transferred her hold to Declan's arm, and was gripping it so tightly that his fingers tingled because they were not getting their supply of blood.

"My apologies," said Ma'el gently, his features returning to what they had been. "For a moment I lost control so that without warning you saw me as other Taelons see me, and each other. You are both surprised but not, I believe, terrified by the sight. This pleases me greatly because it means that, in spite of me revealing my true appearance, you realize that I am still the person you have known. Is this so?"

Declan's mouth was too dry for it to form words, so he nodded. Sinead said, "Yes, Ma'el, it is. B—but the Taelons I saw wore faces like yours. . . ."

"Because," he broke in to answer the question before she

could ask it, "I have discovered after many mistakes that your people find it more comfortable to look into eyes and at lips in a familiar, skin-covered face when they speak with me. Unless you request otherwise I shall continue with this practice."

Sinead relaxed her grip on his arm and joined him in silence. Ma'el looked briefly at the sky, produced the chart, and spread it on the ground between them while he resumed speaking.

"Many of my secrets I have revealed to you," he said, tapping the chart, "beginning with this small and simple one. There was my hand light which lit the encampment on the first night we met, and later when Sinead used it to conjure a monster onto the *Orla*'s mainsail and frighten off the Roman attackers. That, like the seamless joining of wood in the dead robber's cross, and the way in which I lightened my wagon so that it made the ship ride high in the water to escape the pirates in the Mediterranean. Each of you saw that happen and wondered about it, but made no mention of it to me or, indeed, anyone else.

"But now there are greater secrets," he went on. "You may call them magic or charms but I know them only as Taelon technology, which must be revealed to you. Not only that, you will be required to become skilled in their use as I am or, because of your youth and the fast-acting precision of movement in your muscles, much better than I am. The lessons will be difficult in the extreme, their teaching will at times terrify you and open your minds in directions they may not want to go, and you will want to run screaming from what you see and the things I will ask you to do. But if that should occur, we will return to the old and slower ways of travel."

"We won't be frightened . . ." Declan began, when Sinead gripped his arm tightly again.

"We might be frightened by your teachings," she said in a serious voice, "but we want to learn from you and we will not run away."

Ma'el inclined his head. "Good," he said, "but it is a possibility that should be considered."

They exchanged looks which said that neither of them were

considering that possibility, then Declan said, "Ma'el, what do you want us to do first?"

"First," he replied, looking at Sinead, "I want you to move your possessions and those of Declan well clear of the wagon, after which I shall cause it and the pool to be buried under sand in case we should need it again soon, which we will not if you are apt pupils."

He indicated the chart, glanced toward their horse and went on, "That is a friendly and hardworking being who, although nonsapient, I have come to admire. I do not want it to starve here alone or to suffer in any other way. There is a camel train close by that is bound for the caravanserai. Please feed and untether the horse at once, then ride it to the caravan where you will arrange for it to be taken to your friend Bashir so that it can be cared for until the time comes when we might need it again. Sufficient gold will be provided to take care of its needs for the rest of its lifetime. Once these arrangements have been made through the caravan master, you will leave him without further explanation. . . ."

"It will be a long, hot walk back here," Declan protested, but it was as if Ma'el had not heard him.

". . . You will conceal yourself from the sight of surface eyes," he ended, "until Sinead and I come for you. It will please me if you were to perform this task as a matter or urgency and without further delay or discussion. . . ."

Without another word, Declan did exactly as he had been told. He had no trouble leaving the horse and making the arrangements for its future needs with the surprised caravan master, who had heard of Declan and had believed him long since dead. Apparently word of the epic battle fought by the men of the caravanserai and himself against overwhelming odds, albeit with the help of a fearsome djinn, had spread up and down the camel trails while losing nothing in the telling. But he had the greatest difficulty in making the man believe that he wanted the caravan to proceed without him and that he was to be left alone and on foot in the desert.

It was close to sunset when he heard a familiar high-pitched, hissing scream and looked up to see the large djinn dropping toward him like a stone. As it neared the ground, the blue fires that he had thought at first were blazing eyes brightened, the sound like the hissing of a thousand angry serpents increased and it slowed to alight gently on the ground. When the cloud of sand stirred up by its landing had subsided, through the partly transparent body of the djinn he could see the shapes of two seated figures, one of which stood up and turned toward him. An opening appeared suddenly in its flank and he saw that it was Sinead.

She had the pallor of one who has recently undergone a frightening experience, but he face was split by a great smile of wonder as she waved him inside.

TWENTY-EIGHT

Instead of looking at it in Ma'el's chart they were seeing a similar picture of the land surface through the large square of transparent material under their feet. When first they had begun rising into the heavens, Declan had tried to grip the edges of the smooth, deeply cushioned stool on which he sat lest he fall out of it and tumble to the distant ground, but by some act of the magic that Ma'el insisted was merely Taelon technology, the seat grew five soft, strong arms that encircled his waist and thighs and gave close support to the curve of his back to hold him steady. He watched the caravan he had met earlier shrink to a thin, dusty worm and then begin to slide to the edge of the transparent substance and out of his sight. In front of Ma'el's position there was another and much larger area of clarity that faced forward. The old man's hands were resting lightly on its surface while he moved them about in a succession of strange, arcane gestures.

"... We are now making the transition from high altitude to orbital flight," Ma'el was saying, "and will overfly the path we traveled from Hibernia to our recent location. I am sorry if a few of the words I use are strange, but soon their meaning and the actions and events to which they apply will become clear to you. Are either of you feeling mental distress?"

Sinead, who was staring at the unfolding surface in open-mouthed wonder, shook her head. Declan made a croaking sound the exact meaning of which was unclear even to himself. To hide the apprehension that must have been showing on his face, he turned his head to look inside the djinn which Ma'el called his short-range shuttle craft.

Like the one in the floor at his feet and that facing the old man, there were large, clear openings in the djinn's shell which made it possible to see outside in all directions except one which was shielded automatically no matter what their change of heading, Ma'el had explained, to keep their eyes and skin from being damaged by the sun. Curving beams supported the interior of the hull which seemed to be much larger on the inside than out. It was divided into three globular rooms whose outlines and dimensions were difficult to judge because their walls were also transparent. Grouped around their walls, ceilings, and floors were strange devices of unknown purpose that resembled glass and metal flowers, and larger objects that had the look of furniture. Trying to focus his eyes on some of them gave Declan an aching head so he returned his attention to the distant and more familiar ground that was hurrying past his feet.

He saw the fan of tiny rivers that was the delta of the Nile before the eastern Mediterranean opened out to reveal both the north coast of Africa and southern Italy. By bending forward and craning his head from side to side—the padded arms encircling his waist would allow him to do that provided he moved slowly— he was able to see the great sweep of land and ocean from the Pillars of Hercules up to Finisterre in Iberia. Objects and land outlines on the ground were growing smaller, which meant that djinn was climbing higher, and he could see scattered over the Ocean of Atlantis the fat, white worms that Ma'el called low-pressure systems. In a clear area where, again in the words of the old man, high pressure dominated, he could make out the islands

of Britain and Hibernia and, hazy with distance through a clear
area of sky beyond it, another stretch of coastline that ran north
to south as far as the eye could see. He became aware that the sky
above them was shading from pale blue to black and the horizon
was no longer a straight line but seemed to be curving into a bow
shape. He was about to mention these inexplicable occurrences
when Sinead spoke first.

"There is land, there, west of Hibernia!" she said pointing,
her voice high with excitement. "Is that the fabled Westland, Tir
Na n'Og, the land of the forever young? Ma'el, if that is where
you come from, you are far from home."

"That land holds many people . . ." said the old man quietly.
He made a series of complicated, fluid gestures with both hands
and suddenly the land below them was shrinking rapidly, the
curve of the horizon increased until it met itself and suddenly
they were looking down at a great brown and blue globe flecked
with white clouds and, tiny with distance, the lands and seas that
they knew as well as many that they did not. ". . . But I do not
come from there."

Sinead gripped Declan's hand tightly as they stared at the
bright, tiny globe that had been the vast and, until now, limitless
world that they thought had contained all things that were and
ever would be. For a moment he wondered if he was dreaming, if
Ma'el had put a marvellous enchantment on Sinead and himself,
but he hoped not because he did not want this wondrous thing
that was happening to him to be a dream.

"Then where *do* you come from?" asked Sinead.

Ma'el waved a hand, their world slipped to the side and they
were looking into an area of sky filled with stars, some bright and
seemingly close, other so distant that they were a glowing haze
too fine for the individual points of light to be resolved.

"Before I answer," said the old man, "you must first be given
instruction so that you will understand the answer I give. Clear
your minds and attend closely to my words. . . ."

Speaking slowly and clearly he told them that the first and
most important fact that they should learn was that all objects

attracted each other, and the larger the object the greater the attraction. This was what the Taelons called, as well as the future learned of Earth would call, the force of gravity. It was the attraction that held them and all living things to the surface of their world. Any object high above the surface would fall toward it unless it had motion at right angles to the direction of fall. If the sideways motion was precisely calculated, the object would continue to fall toward an object that was constantly moving aside so that the falling object would never reach the larger body but would continue to fall endlessly around it, just as now their vessel was falling around the world below them. This was called being in orbit, just as at a greater distance their moon was circling in a stable orbit around their world, and their world and the other planets were circling the sun. All of the stars that they could see were distant suns many of which had worlds circling them on which lived thinking beings like, but more often totally unlike, themselves. . . .

He pointed toward one of the glowing star clouds and went on, "The place from whence I came, the parent sun and world of the Taelon, lies there. I am far indeed from home."

They looked at each other in astonishment but not disbelief, then back to the old man with an expression that reflected sympathy as well as wonder. Declan was too surprised to think of anything to say that would fit the situation but Sinead was not.

"You have been with us a long time," she said softly. "We are sorry. You must sorely miss your family and friends."

Ma'el inclined his head and looked at them for a long moment, then said, "A few of them. But the sympathy from you is unexpected and deeply appreciated. You have been exposed to sights and knowledge that could well have sent your minds into gibbering madness. Instead, my more than servants, you are thinking of me."

He paused while his hands gestured briefly and on the clear surface of the canopy before him appeared the gray outlines of circles, squares, and long curving shapes so strange that they had no names for them.

"At first I thought of introducing this knowledge to you one item at a time. Instead I was unkind, perhaps even harsh, and confronted you with all of it at once. This was because, having come to know both of you well, I decided that facing you with many shocks at once would keep your minds from being affected too seriously by any one of them. It seems that I was right and later, while your minds and bodies are at rest, you will be able to assimilate this material without mental dysfunction. But one more shock, although later you will look back on it as just another learning experience, awaits you."

He rose from his seat, stood aside and nodded toward the symbols that had appeared on the forward canopy. Looking at Sinead he said calmly, "Your hands, like my own, are small and precise in their movements, so you will be first. The markings you see have been placed there as a visual reminder of their shapes, positions, and control functions. Later, when you become more experienced, they can be removed so as not to interfere with forward visibility. You will be given verbal guidance at every stage. Take the control position, now, and prepare to fly my ship. . . ."

Declan had no way of judging the passage of time except for the dawn to dusk alteration in daylight and the changing positions of the sun, moon, or stars. But out here there was only night and the heavenly bodies gyrated wildly in random directions as Sinead sought, with an early lack of success, to make the djinn go where she wanted it to go. And so it was that for what seemed to be a very long time Declan sat gripping the sides of his chair while it gripped him just as tightly. Then it was slowly borne in on him that the movements of the Earth and stars had become smoother and more precise and that Sinead's features, although still beaded with moisture, were showing pleasure and excitement through their concentration. Beyond the canopy one of the smaller orbiting djinns, looking like an alien, square-winged butterfly with what Ma'el called its power receptors extended, was coming to a halt close by.

"Enough," said Ma'el. "Your ability to think and move in the three dimensions of normal space is excellent. Later you will be shown how to navigate through the interdimensional folds of space, and to travel great distances in an instant. But for now you must return to your place and rest both your body and over-worked mind."

She nodded gratefully and moved back to the chair beside him, but the old man remained standing.

"Now, Declan," he said, "it is your turn. . . ."

Keeping the vessel on the heading indicated by Ma'el, he thought as the perspiration trickled down his face and soaked his body, was like trying to balance with a single pole on an ice-covered pond. The slightest misjudgment sent the vessel sliding and spinning in every direction but the one he wanted it to follow. While sitting in a comfortable chair he was working harder than he had ever done in his life while the muscles of his arms ached with the effort of not forming his hands into the wrong gesture or moving them in the wrong direction or at the incorrect speed. He knew that his great, awkward, weapon-wielding hands had not the same delicacy and precision of movement as those of Sinead, but he felt that slowly he was learning how to make the Earth and sky hold steady and to guide the vessel in the direction it was supposed to go. But suddenly he had to place his sweating hands on his lap and stare through the unobscured side of the canopy and do nothing.

Ma'el made a worried, interrogatory sound.

Carefully so as not to change the control settings, Declan indicated the scene outside where the surface below was in a night lit only by a half moon that made the whole world look like a tenuous ghost of itself. The darkness of the past few hours had so sharpened his eyesight that stars, large and bright and others so faint that he had never been able to see them from the surface, crowded the sky so thickly that it seemed that he could reach out and touch them. He felt no hurt but suddenly his eyes stung with tears.

"That," he said, clearing his throat, "is the most tremendous and beautiful sight I have seen or ever will see. It makes me almost forget to breathe."

Ma'el inclined his head and regarded him for a long moment, then he pointed with an arm outstretched and said gently, "Position the vessel along this line of travel, then you will engage the main thrusters as you have been shown and fly us to your moon for low-level flight, approach, and landing practice."

Once the course was set there was nothing for Declan to do and Ma'el suggested that Sinead and he might like to rest. Before he could voice exactly the same sentiments, she said that they were too excited to think of sleeping amid all this splendor. So they watched the moon grow slowly larger and change from the silvery orb they had known to a dead and grossly pock-marked world that looked as if it had been visited by some gargantuan plague but still, withal, retaining its own terrible beauty.

They watched and listened to Ma'el as he talked about his plans for them, and filled their minds with answers to questions they knew not how to ask, which were even more exciting and wondrous than the scene outside. He told them that he was the only member of his race to visit Earth. He had been sent there by the Synod, which was the ruling group of the Taelon people, to investigate Earth for as long as he deemed it necessary and to report on his findings. . . .

". . . The completion of my report has become an urgent necessity for several reasons," he went on. "Time is not a problem for me, but it is for you and the short-lived race to which you belong. That was why I have decided to disobey the Synod's specific instructions and reveal this and lesser secrets to you. . . .

"That is also why," he continued, "I shall take you to Cathay, and to many other lands, by a faster and more direct means than hazardous sailing ships and camel caravans that are prey to robbers. Such methods of travel, while attracting less attention to myself, would waste years of traveling time as well as placing your already short lives in jeopardy.

"You have been given this knowledge because you two, more

than any other members of your race previously employed by me, are capable of performing a unique service for myself and ultimately for my people."

"But who are we," said Sinead, "that we should be singled out for this revelation? A young woman damaged in mind and body as a child, but now recovering . . ." she squeezed Declan's hand, ". . . and a hulking great warrior with so many muscles that the sharpness of his mind is often hidden by them. I ask again, why us?"

"I am trying to tell you," said Ma'el gently, "but you must have the patience to wait until you receive the whole answer. Voluntarily separated as I am from the Commonality and the immaterial mental force that holds the thinking of all our people together, my own ability to foretell my future has been diminishing to a frightening extent. The timesight is a vital necessity to the continuance and completion of my work here, but I am fast losing it. That is why I have ignored another Taelon prime directive and given timesight to your people so that, through yourself among others, I would be able to see into this world's future. Initially you were a disappointment to me, not through any fault of your own but because of the mind-damaging incident in your past which, I thought wrongly, had rendered you physically and emotionally sterile and, as a result, without a genetic extension into the future. I was considering letting both of you go. That would have been the greatest mistake of my life because you, Sinead, have acquired a timesight that is unique in its power, accuracy, and temporal range. . . ."

"But why?" Sinead broke in. She squeezed Declan's hand again and went on, "I know that I had a change of feeling and that now I will have descendants that will form the organic pathway that gives me timesight into the far future. But why am I so good at it?"

The old man looked slowly from Sinead to Declan and back again before replying.

"What I tell you now is partly speculative rather than entirely factual," he said, "because, regrettably, we Taelons do not have

the intense levels of physical attraction and emotional involve-
ment that are possessed by your short-lived species. It is possible
that, even though you disliked each other intensely in the beginning, when continued close proximity and shared dangers forced
you into recognizing each other's better qualities and depths of
character, the emotional potential that built up between you was
so intense that when the change of feeling came and you joined,
the stimulation of your future time sense was unique in its
strength. On Taelon such an intensity of emotional bonding is
unknown, and on your own world it must be rare. That is the
best answer I can give you."

Sinead looked uncomfortable and said, "Ma'el, are you
telling us that we are the greatest lovers there have ever been?"

Declan gave a small laugh to hide his embarrassment. "I
would think that all lovers feel like this about each other," he
said, then added thoughtfully, "but in this case it is probably
true."

Before Sinead could reply, Ma'el raised a hand to point and
said, "Your moon is less than two of its diameters distant and you
have work to do. Declan, position the vessel for a landing in that
large crater with the low, central peak."

"Someday," Sinead said in a quiet voice, "somebody is going
to name it Tycho."

At last the lessons were over for the day in a place where
there was neither day nor night, Ma'el had urged them to rest
and placed them in a small room whose walls had been made
opaque except for the one that looked out on the beautiful blue
and white Earth that was hanging low above the crater's rim and
dimming the background stars only slightly. Sinead was trying to
do the impossible, which was to move her body closer than it
already was to his.

"Earlier," she said softly, "you told Ma'el that the most beautiful and wonderful thing you had ever seen was the Earth and
the stars in space. You also said that we were the world's greatest
lovers, probably. Probably?"

Declan raised a hand to caress the back of her neck at the hairline, then moved his fingers slowly and lightly down the length of her spine, hearing her soft, ragged intake of breath.

"The Earth and stars don't wrap themselves as tightly around me as you do," he said, "and as for being the world's greatest lovers, we need more practice. . . ."

TWENTY-NINE

Ma'el Report, Day 112,178 . . .

. . . The advanced instruction in ship handling was completed within the period it took for their moon to circle twice around its parent planet, a learning time that I consider not only satisfactory but impressive. The operating principle governing instantaneous navigation through the dimensional layers of quasireality, while they learned to perform the required hand movements with precision, were difficult for them to grasp. In a gross oversimplification I finally explained it by spreading out Sinead's white linen burnoose, marking it with a spot of dark liquid and them folding it so that the stain was copied onto a different part of the garment before spreading it flat again to show the distance that could be traveled instantaneously between the two marked places. The demonstration enabled them to understand how if not why interdimensional travel worked.

"This illustrates once again the essential difference between intelligence and education. These people of Earth are uncivilized, technologically backward, and woefully ignorant, but they are highly adaptable and intelligent. With the possession of intelligence, especially where these two are concerned, ignorance is a temporary condition.

"With this purely organic life-form, a prolonged stay in the light gravity of their moon means that muscular deterioration with a consequent loss of physical coordination will gradually take place. This could prove embarrassing and even dangerous for them in the Earth environment, so their return should not be long delayed.

"The lack of a breathable atmosphere on this world means that they have been unable to leave the ship, but this close confinement together does not seem to worry them. . . ."

They had come out of orbit over the Mediterranean and were descending toward Alexandria to overfly the course they had been following in the wagon at an altitude at which the vessel's physical shape would be mistaken for that of a high-flying bird, but low enough for them to see clearly the remembered contours until they passed over the caravanserai and new territory began to unroll like an endless carpet below them.

They continued to follow the well-used camel trail that some poetically minded merchant had named the Golden Road to Samarkand and on to the famed Dzungarian Gate in the mountains above Lake Ebi Nor, and thence across central India with its green jungles, lush grassland, deserts, and richly decorated palaces to the Jade Gate that was set in the spectacular and recently completed Great Wall which guarded the eastern flank of the world's most ancient civilization and empire of Cathay. They were staring in awe and wonder at the structure that followed the contours of the mountains and valleys like an endless square worm of stone when Ma'el broke a lengthy silence.

"This is the surface route I originally intended to follow," he said, looking at Sinead in the control position but addressing both of them, "when it seemed desirable to conceal from you my true nature and that of the work I came to do on this world. You can estimate for yourselves the proportion of your short lives that would have been wasted merely in traveling to visit the far-flung places and people in order to update my report. That wastage, and the secrecy that would have caused it, is no longer necessary because your limited life spans and abilities, especially your time-sight, and those of Declan as a protector and emissary, must be put to more effective use. When we pass over the Imperial City of Xian, bear south and cross the coast to the islands of Nippon and thence across the ocean until you pass over the eastern seaboard of a vast, rich, and beautiful land that is as yet unknown to you except in legend. It is a land of great mountain ranges, rich forests, and vast plains teeming with animal life beyond number as well as the life of its hunting tribes that is far above the animal level. There are the beginnings of empires, too, and civilizations built on human sacrifice and unthinking cruelty. We will return to visit all these places, but for now it is only necessary to prove to you that they exist. You will find a desolate and deserted place in this land and alight there. . . ."

"These animals that you say are numerous beyond count-ing," said Sinead sadly, her eyes seeming to look far into space and time, "so that the thunder of their hooves makes the very land tremble. They are like monstrous, hairy cattle with heavy shoulders, enormous heads, and wide-spreading horns. I see them extinct."

Ma'el was silent for a moment, then he went on as if she had not spoken, ". . . So that you can both learn how to make this ves-sel obey you while you are at a distance from it. You will also exercise and strengthen muscles grown weak during your stay on the moon when you are not listening to me explaining more of my magic."

Apart from it having air to breathe, the place where they landed was as lifeless and arid as the Moon they had left. Instead of being surrounded by crater walls there was a strange, flat-topped mountain and several enormous, rocky pinnacles that poked out of the surrounding desert like black, mis-shapen fin-gers. They would provide ideal navigational obstacles, Ma'el insisted, while he was showing them how to remotely control their ship.

On the ground outside their tents Ma'el unfolded and spread

before them a new chart. Instead of showing pictures of the land
relayed from orbit, this one reproduced in half of the original
dimensions all of the control symbols from the surface of the vessel's forward canopy. He explained that the smaller size would
require their hand and finger movements across it to be even
more precise than those they had learned on the moon, that this
was the means by which he had called down the so-called djinn
which had ended the attack on the caravans, and that he had
every confidence in their ability to perform the task.

Soon they were both able to move the vessel accurately and
make it perform complicated maneuvers within their line of
sight, and then to send it into orbit and bring it down again.
With the other chart to guide them, they learned how to position
the vessel during the night at various ground locations specified
by their instructor and, in daylight, above different seaports and
cities where they were able to remain invisible by interposing it
between the sun and would-be observers on the ground. When
they were able to do that consistently with a placement error of
less than twenty paces, they were very pleased with themselves
until Ma'el told them gently that they had passed the first and
easiest examination.

". . . When we were in the clear and open space around your
moon," Ma'el went on to explain, "I introduced you briefly to
interdimensional travel. This is a rapid and safe form of travel
provided you ensure that you do not materialize the ship inside a
planetary body or a sun. In future, however, you will be called on
to move through the hyper dimension, not over a distance of
thousands of miles but by a few paces. You must learn how to
move the vessel with precision into an enclosed space, the inside
of a building, for example, or into a buried cavern without having
to demolish the intervening walls. This would be necessary if you
wished to conceal the vehicle from the local inhabitants or, if
they proved to be unfriendly, to call it to your assistance for the
purpose of rescue and evacuation.

"When you are ready we will begin. . . ."

They began in the late spring, alternating the lessons

between them day by day, but late summer had given way to mid-winter and the desert was cold in the daylight hours and frigid at night before the old man pronounced them ready for their final examination for precision of control. Sinead took hers first.

Declan had lost count of the times they had each sent the vessel through the solid masses of the tall, rock pinnacles and the strange, flat-topped mountain that dominated their landscape. Each time the operation had been accompanied by a sharp detonation and an expanding circle of blue light as the vessel entered its self-created fold in space beyond one face of the obstruction and emerged on the other, with a comfortable margin for error on either side. During the final stages of the examination, however, the allowed clearances were gradually reduced to no more than a small fraction of the vessel's overall length, no more than a few paces, beyond the entry and exit positions.

Sinead, her hands and arms moving with such smooth and beautiful precision that her bones might have been made of water, was able to do it. Declan was not.

Avoiding Sinead's eyes and feeling his face hot with shame, Declan said, "Ma'el, I don't think I can do this. I'm afraid of rematerializing the ship inside the rock and damaging it." He held up his hands and then indicated the chart on the ground. "The full-size control screen on the ship is difficult enough for me, but I'm too ham-fisted to operate a half-sized one like this, at least, not with the precision you require, and I do not want to try. I'm sorry, in this matter I am craven."

Ma'el inclined his had. "The effect of one solid body materializing inside another would not only destroy both objects," he said gently, "it would cause a detonation which would remove a large proportion of the crust of your world, allow the core magma to overflow onto the surface and convert the atmosphere and oceans into superheated steam and destroy all forms of life on the planet. . . ."

He heard Sinead join him in a quick intake of breath, but before they could say anything, Ma'el went on calmly, ". . . The vessel's systems include a fail-with-safety device that is designed to prevent such a catastrophe from happening, but by its very nature it is as yet untried. And you are in no sense craven. There is a difference between cowardice and caution, which is the recognition and acceptance of your personal limitations. Caution saves many of the lives that unthinking bravery wastes. You are excused this test without blame or reproach, so you should ease your mind.

"Sinead," he added, "return the vessel to us here, then both of you rest and tomorrow you will break camp and prepare for departure. . . ."

They flew eastward over the storm-tossed ocean, without seeing any sign of the fabled Atlantis after which it had been named, and crossed the west coast of Hibernia to come to a stable hover above the city of Sligo. They had positioned themselves between the late afternoon sun and the gaze of any curious city dwellers and so had been rendered invisible, but they themselves could see far and wide through air washed clear by a recent rain squall. Declan's eyes roved inland and eastward across the gray expanse of Loch Gill to the Lachagh Hills, north to the long ocean rollers that broke white against the base of Roskeragh Point, southward to the Slieve Gamphs, shivering in wonder that he was able to view the land in this godlike fashion. To the west he could clearly see An Leathros, the hill above the strand that the Saxon visitors called Strand Hill, whose gentle, seaward facing slopes bore the tombs of the past kings of Connaught, and above them on the dark mountain of Knocknareagh, the burial chamber of the famed and infamous Queen Maeve herself, whose exploits in war were surpassed only on the scented battleground of her bed. Looking at the burial markers, their westward facing stone surfaces orange gray in the setting sun, Declan shivered again without knowing why.

"What reason," he said to Ma'el, "have you for coming to this place of the heroic dead?"

"I have already said that it is a place of power for me," the old man replied in his usual inscrutable fashion, "where I will be able to renew myself and my magic before we set off on again on the journeys that will enable me to complete my work. My buried laboratory is here."

"What is a laboratory?"

"Tonight you will enter one," Ma'el replied, "so that a description in words would be wasteful of our time." He pointed suddenly. "Sinead, your target is a circle thirty paces in diameter that is centered at the intersection of the lines joining those two, pale-colored grave markers, there and there, and a perpendicular line raised to that dark, square rock, just there. . . ."

"It looks like an ordinary stretch of grassy hillside," Sinead said.

". . . Our vessel's dock and servicing mechanisms," he continued, "as well as my laboratory are under that intersection point. We will land at night using our dark light system. If anyone should chance to see us, well, this area has witnessed many strange sights over the years. Horseless flying chariots, screaming and hissing banshees crossing the night sky, the flight of the Fairy King to name but a few. The witness would remain silent because his words would not be believed.

"Compared with yesterday's examination in piloting," he ended reassuringly, "your three-dimensional space for maneuver is generous."

Sinead nodded and Declan looked down again at the standing stones, thinking about his unhappy past and of the things that might have been had his father not disowned him, then he shrugged angrily and said, "It is not a place where I shall ever lie."

Sinead turned to look at him for a long moment, her eyes blinking rapidly as if she was feeling a sudden sadness. But before she could speak, Ma'el raised a hand to point through the control canopy and she returned her attention to the scene below.

THIRTY

■ ■ ■ The technical aspects of the
training are reaching comple-
tion so that their further instruction has become a process of
general education and discussion which, inevitably, leads to questions that I am unwilling to answer.

"The extent of my underground laboratory awed and amazed
them, but not enough to affect their ability to mentate in any sig-
nificant way. Sinead and Declan are adaptable, resourceful and,
considering the less-than-civilized culture to which they belong,
ethical people who are forced to survive among others of their
kind who have much in common with many life-forms who infest
the farther reaches of the Galaxy and are nothing but thinking
and predatory animals lusting after power. These two are even
more unusual for the reason that they have accepted and are
comfortable with the knowledge that they live on a world rather
than *the* world. For the members of any intelligent culture, whatever its planet of origin, this is a major step on the way to inter-
stellar civilization.

"Once they asked if it would be possible for me to fly them to
Taelon. I told them that it was not, but the thought of the Commonality's response to such an event came close to making me

lose control of my outwardly human form. Among the Earth people this emotional reaction is known as intense amusement.

"It is natural in their new surroundings that they persist in asking about the laboratory's origin, and my continuing avoidance of giving the answer must in time lead to feelings of suspicion and distrust on their part. Strange as it seems even to me, I am afraid of losing their respect and, in spite of them belonging to a species of a lower level of physical and cognitive evolution, their friendship.

"It would aid my decision as to whether or not I should give a truthful answer to this question if Sinead would furnish me with a timesight in which I had done so, as well as the emotional repercussions that would result. But no. Although erratic, her ability to see into the future is impressive in the detail of the images and incidents it reveals, but the only timesightings she has mentioned are short-range events of a personal nature concerning Declan and herself of which she is understandably reluctant to speak.

"I remain undecided. . . ."

A fall of rock and earth had long since blocked the direct passage to the open hillside, but that did not mean that Sinead and Declan were unable to take their daily walk.

The space-vessel dock formed only a small part of the interlinked system of caverns and side caves that Ma'el called his laboratory. Wide, stone steps joined the caverns whose floors were on different levels and the same accurately chiseled stonework had been used in the making of large and small workbenches that were positioned in orderly groups inside every chamber, all of which became illuminated as soon as Sinead or himself entered them. The lighting revealed ceilings and walls that glittered as if they were streaming with water, but like the cavern in the Roman catacombs, the whole laboratory was so completely dry that it was plain that here, too, the glassy substance was protecting it from invading damp.

The stone benches, which were topped with flat sheets of the same substance, held racks filled with large and small tools, some of which were made partly of glass, as well as large and more dangerous devices that made warning noises and flashed lights if they tried to lay a hand on one of them. But it was the system of caves leading off the larger chambers that most interested and puzzled them.

"There is no sign of Taelon technology here," Sinead said, waving the hand light that Ma'el had given them for exploring in the smaller, unlit areas. It showed the remains of smashed and age-bleached wooden furniture including a low bed heaped with the desiccated remains of its covering blanket, pieces of broken platters and eating utensils thick with dust, and even what might have been the remains of food so ancient that even the maggots had died of old age. She went on, "These caves were used by people like ourselves. It is likely that they were the builders of this laboratory. But every time I ask about them, Ma'el changes the subject. It is a simple question so why won't he answer it? Are there other secrets he is still hiding from us?"

Declan was silent for a moment, then he said thoughtfully, "I believe that he has grown to like and trust us. If a secret there is, he must have a strong reason for concealing it, whether it is for our benefit or his. We might be more easy in our minds if we do not know everything about him, and we should forebear to ask."

"But Declan," she said, "I'm *curious.*"

He knew then that she would ask the question anyway and that it would probably be during their next meal together. He was right.

"Giving the answer to your question," said Ma'el, "is forbidden by both the Synod and the Commonality of Taelon, as was the revelation of my other secrets. This one I concealed for personal reasons because speaking of it would cause pain to myself as well as both of you. Before I reveal it, have you had a timesight involving the past or future of this laboratory?"

"I tried," Sinead replied, "but I could see neither into the past or future."

"There could be two reasons for that," Ma'el said. "One is that you are not descended from any of the persons concerned because they did not have offspring and the second, I am hoping, is that the events that transpire here when you have full information are not so emotionally traumatic that they will affect our present relationship."

"I—I don't understand you," said Sinead.

"You will," Ma'el replied, rising to his feet. "Please follow me."

He led them to a cavern that they had passed through every day but without spending time there because it held nothing but a low, stone platform surrounded by devices which had warned them away. Ma'el made a slow gesticulation with one hand and two chairs rose from the floor. He indicated that they should be seated.

"Your collars and earpieces will enable you to understand the words that are spoken," he said, "and your eyes will tell you the rest. You will hear my voice as it was recorded in the past, but in the present I shall not speak unless you wish clarification, which you will indicate by raising a hand. We will begin."

Above the stone platform there appeared a wide, vertical cylinder of light that showed bands of color that writhed within themselves as if someone was stirring a liquid rainbow until it settled into an image that was familiar to them, that of An Leathros, the Hill Above the Strand, in the brownish-green colors of winter as if it was being viewed from a descending space vessel. But it was not the same picture that they had seen days earlier. Although Ma'el's lips remained closed they heard his voice.

"This is an excerpt of the report of Investigator Ma'el, made on the 12,775th day of the cultural evaluation of the peoples of Earth, and covering the events while my laboratory was under construction. . . ."

"Wait, wait, this can't be right," Declan broke in. His mind struggled with the numbers for a long moment because in his youth mathematics had been his least-favored subject. "Twelve thousand, seven hundred days is, is thirty-five years, and add to that the age of this place. Judging by the condition of furniture in the caves, it could be centuries old. . . ."

"On Taelon we live longer than you do," Ma'el said. "Shall I continue . . . ?"

Declan wanted to ask how much longer, but the answer had shocked Sinead as well as himself into silence and the recorded voice of the old man, of the very old man it now seemed, resumed.

The image of An Leathros expanded to show groups of young men, over two hundred of them in all, who were stripped to the waist and with their breaths and their sweat steaming about them in the cold air as they pulled sleds containing finished stone blocks up the slopes toward the mouth of a tunnel that was fringed with an apron of dark, freshly turned earth. They heard the young mens' voices as the picture closed on one of the groups and followed them through the tunnel into the caverns of the laboratory while it was still a building. Without exception the men worked willingly, cheerfully, and hard for they had been promised a great reward for both their sweat and their secrecy, and the recorded words of the older Ma'el explained why.

". . . So that there would not be too many unexplained disappearances from one locality, the workforce was recruited and transported from all over Hibernia. My intention at the time was to reward each of them with the gold that would buy them land for farms and cattle, if that was their desire, and thus attract to them the most comely of women for their wives. But at the conclusion of their work, the quality of which pleased me greatly, I decided to give them an additional reward.

"I decided to administer single doses of the Bliss drug.

"It was a substance that I encountered during the early years of the investigation which, according to the records of the sea explorer and adventurer, Jason, gave great pleasure and forgetfulness to those who consumed it. I acquired and tested this drug, and used Taelon science to modify its effects so that it would no longer be addictive.

"Primarily I was acting out of gratitude, but I also expected to benefit in that its administration would further reduce the possibility of them accidentally revealing the position of my laboratory. The substance stimulates the mind into an extended period of pleasure while, on awakening, it wipes all related events and surroundings from the memory so that the experience is remembered only as a pleasant, confused, and fading dream. As well as rewarding them with gold for their faithful service, I wanted to give them a period of ecstasy during which they would forget the reason why they had been given the reward in the first place. . . ."

They watched the images as, at Ma'el's direction, the workers swallowed the tiny capsules and shortly after collapsed onto their beds or the nearest clear area of floor. They saw the wide smiles, the eyes that stared fixedly at some unseen object of pleasure or were tightly closed and with every muscle in their bodies locked in a paroxysm of ecstasy. Time passed and they remained thus, neither eating, drinking, sleeping, nor even moving while periodically their faces were suffused with a strangely colored blush. But when they at last returned to their real world, they had not forgotten their ecstatic dreams.

Instead they sought out Ma'el, at first pleading desperately with him, then demanding and finally threatening him with death if he did not give them more Bliss. Unwilling to do so because of its totally unexpected and mind-damaging aftereffects, Ma'el was forced to seal himself inside a force field while he worked desperately to produce an antidote.

At intervals they had glimpses of the older Ma'el striving endlessly over devices that flashed lights and made low, humming noises, or among delicate, strangely shaped transparent goblets large and small containing liquids of many colors, but mostly it was the actions of the Bliss victims that they were being shown. Many of the formally pleasant and well-behaved young men they had seen were now throwing themselves against the invisible wall with which Ma'el had surrounded his workplace, screaming and fighting each other, damaging their faces, fists, and frequently breaking limbs in their frenzy to get closer to Ma'el and the Bliss that only he could give them. But they were shown the others, too.

In every cave large or small there was more screaming and fighting and cursing. Ma'el had been carelessly generous in his distribution of of the Bliss, and from overheard scraps of angry, shouted conversation it seemed that there were those who suspected that their work mates had received more than one of them and were hiding the others for future use. The result was that they fought each other, viciously and without mercy like wild animals rather than the thinking, hardworking, and friendly beings that Ma'el had come to like well enough to want to reward them with pleasure. The broken furniture and smashed crockery in their living quarters were explained because they had been used to bludgeon or stab or cut each other to death with the sharp edges. Those who fought in the main caverns were using loose rocks, their teeth, or fingers to club and blind and tear each other to pieces.

By the time Ma'el had the antidote ready, the floors and connecting steps of the laboratory caverns ran red with blood and none of his workers remained alive.

There followed a rapid series of images showing Ma'el using one of his floating litters to transfer the bodies one by one to a small, unused cavern which he filled with them to its roof before collapsing and sealing its entrance, ending with the original view of the tunnel leading from the hillside into the laboratory, which was also collapsed and sealed with fallen rock. This scene remained, flickering with the rapid passage of years until the wound in the earth was covered over with greenery and all trace of the entrance tunnel was gone.

The image dissolved with a burst of color to leave only empty air above the stone platform. Declan looked at Sinead, thinking that her features were as pale and still as those of a corpse, and feeling that his own must have been the match of hers. It was Ma'el who spoke first.

"The responsibility for killing all of those human workers is mine," he said. His voice had never revealed any emotion and it did not do so now. "I await your judgment, and punishment."

Declan closed his eyes tightly, unable to speak. The bloody images were being thrown with all their horror onto the black screens of his eyelids, a sight hundreds of times worse than the aftermath of the bloodiest battle he had ever experienced. But Sinead was saying the words that he wanted to speak.

"That, that was horrible, ghastly," she said, and shuddered. "All those young men turning upon each other and . . . But, but you were only trying to reward them out of kindness, not to kill them. From my own knowledge I know how kind you can be, whether it was to myself, that woman whose fortune you told in Cobh market, or even in your treatment of the beasts of burden we've used. You did not intend to do this terrible thing."

Ma'el inclined his head slowly then turned it to look at Declan, who had opened his eyes again but was still trying to calm his mind. It seemed a long time even to himself before he could speak.

"The perpetrator of such a horrendous crime deserves the ultimate punishment," he said thoughtfully, "the forfeit of his own life for the lives he has taken no matter how few or many that may be. You admit to having two reasons for acting as you did, the first one laudable and the second selfish. You wished to reward them for their services, and to make sure that the knowledge of you and the work done here would not be passed on to others. You achieved the second by causing all of them to die.

"Old man," he went on gravely, "and I think of you as that even though we both know that you are not a man, or even a human being, and are old indeed. Rightly has Sinead said, now and many times in the past, that you are a gentle and kindly man who had no intention of perpetrating this evil deed, and it is plain that it was your kindliness that caused you to commit it. For my part, I believe for both our parts, the judgment must also be tempered with kindness and the punishment is not for us to administer. From what we know of you, it is and has been administered over many centuries of time by yourself, for the memory of the terrible thing that a kind and thoughtful man has done will always be in your mind and, for you, that is the worst of all punishments.

"But this punishment has lasted for far too long.

"Ma'el, you have said that there is a great task to complete," he ended. "I think we should return to it, and that you should begin this work by trying to forgive yourself."

The old man continued to stare at him in silence for what seemed a long time, his large, soft eyes blinking rapidly in a way that made Declan wonder if the other was capable of shedding tears. Finally he spoke.

"It seems that I have two healers now," he said, "for on Taelon you, Declan, would be called a Healer of the Mind. My thanks to you both. Tomorrow we will leave for the capital city of the Incas. . . ."

THIRTY-ONE

Since their empathic reaction to ... my confession regarding the fate of the laboratory workforce, my feelings toward Sinead and Declan are changing from simple affection to complete trust. The reason is that for members of a backward species they continue to display intelligence and a degree of understanding in their dealings with the members of other cultures, including my own, that is rare on this world and on many others that I know. During the recent visitations their presence has been a positive asset.

"I have revealed much but not all, about my true purpose in investigating their world. The imparting of full information is forbidden not only by the Synod but by the entire Taelon Commonality which includes myself.

"Sinead's episodes of timesight are rare, but startling in the detail they reveal. It is well that neither she nor Declan understand the significance of what she is seeing. . . ."

In the growing Empire of the Incas, the fabulous Land of the Sun Kings that was closely confined by a great ocean on one side and high mountains on the other so that it could only expand north and south, Ma'el had left such a lasting impression during his centuries-earlier visitations that he was treated as a deity. He was seeking the most recent knowledge of their affairs, but instead of answers he was heaped with costly presents of finely-worked golden ornaments, weapons, and armor. As a god he was expected to already know the answers to everything and it was felt that no lesser being could relieve his pretended ignorance without offering him the gravest of insults. It fell to Sinead and Declan, who as his servants were not considered to be omniscient, to find the answers to Ma'el's questions and relay them back to him.

They, too, were heaped with presents and favors of every kind although not on the same lavish scale. But Sinead, who had to bind herself into becoming a boy again because the Inca females were considered something less than human, was becoming increasingly dissatisfied with the situation and said so.

"I'm not," said Declan, steadying his heavy, golden helmet with one hand while he spun on his heel so that his cloak flared out in spectacular fashion. "They dress us like royalty."

"Yes," she said, "and their High-Inca discards even the richest of cloaks after only one wearing. That is taking conspicuous waste to extremes."

Declan glanced at the nearest passersby, none of whom were as richly arrayed as they were, and said, "Keep your voice down."

"My translator collar is off," she said impatiently. "Look at them. They match the engineering feats of the Romans with their bridges and royal roads, their agricultural projects, their temples, and their art. And they are trying to join their empire together by teaching their people a common language. But the people themselves, a few are too rich and the rest too poor. And the way they treat their womenfolk is . . ."

She broke off to glare at him. "Speaking of which," she went on, "I as a boy have been offered the facilities of the High-Inca's harem by the head of his household, heaven help the man's foolish wit, as I know you also have been. If you even look as though you are tempted, or if you ever call me "boy" in public again. . . ."

"I would never dream of calling you a boy in private," said Declan, smiling. "But this is not like you. Why are you so argumentative today?"

". . . I shall instantly and on the spot," she ended furiously, "render you incapable of fathering any more children."

"More children . . . ?" Declan began. Then suddenly the meaning of what she had said dawned on him and he stopped in his tracks to sweep her very gently into his arms, not caring what the onlookers would think about him embracing and kissing what appeared to be a boy.

"Are you sure?" he said. "Have you had a timesight?"

"I have had a timesight," she replied when he had loosened his arms enough for her to breathe. "It was about this empire. It will grow rich and top-heavy and, many years in the future, a little over one hundred men, soldiers from our Europe, will bring it down and loot it of all its treasures. But no, there are ways other than the timesight that let a woman know when she is with child.

"I said nothing until I was certain," she ended, smiling. "But now let us return to Ma'el and tell him, among other things, that he is to be a godparent. . . ."

Ma'el reacted to the news, as he did to everything else, with no visible change of expression.

"Your information regarding the social organization and work activities among the lower orders of Inca, and in particular your timesight covering their eventual fate, is enough for me to complete my report on this culture. Later tonight, when the occurrence will cause minimum disruption to the local population, you will bring our vessel down from orbit on remote control and prepare to leave for the Aztec Empire on the north continent. Do not overload the vessel with the rich apparel you have been given here, because it would attract unwelcome attention in Hibernia, and take instead the goblets, ornaments, and coins made from precious metals which may be exchange for services in any part of the world.

"The news that you are expecting to produce one or more of

your kind," he went on, fixing his attention on Sinead, "is not a surprise since your recent emotional bonding and continuing regular episodes of physical interpenetration has made such a consequence inevitable. Are there any precautions to be taken, do you expect a deterioration in your physical capabilities and, if so, how soon is that likely to take effect? Should our planned visits to the Aztecs and Cathay be advanced or postponed until after the birthing time? In the absence of sufficiently advanced infant life-sustaining mechanisms on this world, will Declan and yourself share this work and if so, how much time will be available for your duties as my only technically trained advisor and protector? You must already know that a space vehicle of limited size is not a suitable environment for very young progeny, so have you thought about where you should live?"

By the time he had finished speaking, Sinead's face had darkened to a deep pink except for the white lines around the mouth where her lips were pressed tightly together.

"For some time," Ma'el went on in his gentle voice, "I have observed that your features and conversational tone has been reflecting increasing excitement and pleasure, and now that I know the reason I am pleased for you. But I have asked questions which require serious consideration, and answers must be found for them."

The angry color suffusing her face began to fade as Sinead replied, "I have considered some of the answers, but the decisions taken on the others require the joint agreement of Declan and myself, or even all three of us. Subject to your consent, your laboratory would be spacious and safe enough to raise . . ."

She broke off, shook her head in puzzlement before going on, "I'm most grateful, Ma'el, that you do not intend to dismiss us from your service because of this. But you do not show any strong feelings about something which to us is of surpassing importance. Coming from another world as you do, you are perhaps in the position of a farmer who cares for and cherishes certain animals among his stock, but not to the same extent that he would if it was happening in his own family. If this was happening on Taelon, how would you feel?"

Ma'el inclined his head. "The situation would not be the same," he said. "There are natural limits to procreation. Short-lived species like yours breed freely and often in order to compensate for the natural losses from old age, accident, and disease. By comparison the Taelon are immensely long-lived. That being so, there is an evolutionary imperative which limits reproduction so that the resources of the planet and its population will remain in balance. Consequently the incidence of birthing is very low, in fact, rare, and the arrival of a newborn Taelon is a cause for planet-wide celebration.

"As you will already have observed," he went on, "this shell of flesh and organic sensors that I hold about myself in human company has features that do not register subtle changes of emotion. However, as I have said earlier, I am truly pleased for you, Sinead, and I offer my congratulations to you both."

Sinead was smiling again. Declan tried to control his feelings and the facial expression that would have revealed his growing discontent with the situation and the problem that was developing. He needed time to think it through.

Ten days later he still had not found an answer that satisfied him completely, and it was not a time to think about anything but his immediate surroundings while he forced his aching mind to remember all that Ma'el had told Sinead and himself about the principal local gods—including the strange fact that they were constantly at war with each other so that their worshippers had to walk a careful spiritual path between them—lest an unguarded word cost the visitors their lives.

There was Quetzalcoatl, the Winged Serpent, of whom it was said that he had journeyed to the underworld to collect the bones from which he had fashioned mankind after sprinkling them with his own blood. His sacrificial offerings of human meat were distributed among his worshippers and in particular to barren women. His rival, Tezcatlipoca, the ever young and virile Creator of the Universe, was god of the night sky, sorcery, and all warriors. Considering the long-axe he carried at all times, it was assumed that Declan might be of his worshippers. And then there was Huitzilopochtl, the manifestation of the Sun who continually battled against the forces of night and darkness. He required, as he did today, the regular sacrifice of human hearts and blood that gave him strength.

Declan did not like being present at living human sacrifices, and Sinead certainly did not approve of the practice although it did enable her to observe the precise and wholly admirable surgical skill used to remove the still-beating human heart for consumption by the high priest, and later to acquire some of the instruments employed during the operation for her own use in future curative procedures when, she hoped, the patient would stand a greater chance of survival.

Neither of them could understand why the sacrificial victims were so happy to die in this fashion.

Moving in stately and unhurried fashion a few paces behind and below Ma'el, and surrounded by an escort whose priestly robes almost put the sun to shame, Sinead and he climbed the broad, stone stairway toward the sacrificial altar atop the great Temple of the Sun whose massive pyramid dominated the Aztec capital city of Teotihuacan.

They had been traversing one of the broad terraces that broke their long ascent to the top, and Sinead's attention had been on the view of the city and jungle all around them, when an uneven section of paving caused her to stumble. Immediately Declan's hand reached out to steady her.

Sinead turned off her collar translator so that the others around them would not comprehend the words, then said irritably, "Stop that. I'm with child, not a cripple, and I'm supposed to be a boy." She smiled suddenly. "As yet I'm not even a fat boy."

She was silent while they continued their stately climb to the level of the darkly stained altar stone with its array of shining bronze cutting tools and the three sacrificial victims, smiling happily and with eyes dulled by the potent native drugs, then she said in a voice whose softness could not conceal its anger, "I wish this bloody foolishness was over."

Three days later they left Teotihuacan to travel in a wide curve to the northeast that would bring them ultimately to the hills, lakes, and forests of the Algonquin whose nation spread over the north continent's eastern seaboard. At Ma'el's direction they maintained a low altitude and a speed that would enable them properly to view the beauties of the intervening mountain ranges, deserts, forests, and rolling grasslands and the vast herds of buffalo that covered them with uneven blankets of moving fur. He did not say it in so many words but the implication was that he wanted Sinead to see as much of her own beautiful world as possible before the circumstances following the impending birth confined her to Hibernia.

That had been the matter uppermost in Declan's mind since he had learned of her condition. Now he had finally come to a decision which might displease both Sinead and Ma'el, and which he would have to make known to them as soon as possible and in a fashion that would cause the least hurt to both. Not for the first time he wished that he possessed the silver-tongued diplomacy of Brian, but he knew that a few simple words would have to suffice if he could only force them through the cowardly barricade of his teeth.

They were seated cross-legged by the dying cooking fire in the manner of the tribe, Ma'el said, whom they would be meeting on the morrow. It was important that they know and understand the beliefs and customs of the Algonquin who as persons were friendly and warm-hearted but as a nation warlike. In a voice that came as close to being enthusiastic as the old man was capable, he went on to tell them of the Kitci Manitou, the Great Spirit and most powerful of all the Manitous, the Father of Life who was never created, and the source of all good things. The Great Spirit dwelt in Heaven and was above all other powers. He was master of light and was manifest in the sun. He was the breath of life and, as the wind, moved everywhere. The Algonquin believed that there was another great spirit, Michabo called the Great Hare, who was the father of the race and he created water, fish, and the great deer. . . .

There was much more.

Sinead sat close beside Declan in the darkness, not speaking but holding his hand and often squeezing it in their shared impatience to be out of the night breeze and under the blankets where there was a very pleasant way to keep each other warm. That was the other reason why Declan decided to interrupt.

"Ma'el," he said, "you have said that when our visit to the Algonquin is completed, we will return to Hibernia for a time. For how long a time? What other visits do you plan, and when?"

There must have been something in his tone that worried Sinead because she gripped his hand again. He also felt the old man's eyes on him in spite of not being able to see them in the darkness.

"After Hibernia," Ma'el replied, "I have to pay a final visit to Cathay, and then retrieve the wagon we buried in the sand by the camel track. It contains devices that are necessary for the completion of my work. But these matters are not of great urgency and they will not require the presence of both of you. . . ."

"Wherever you take him," Sinead broke in firmly, her grip on his hand tightening, "it will be with me."

". . . And they can wait for an opportune time," he went on. "But there is concern in your voice. What is the reason?"

Declan took a deep breath. "We will do as you bid us gladly," he said, "and with grateful hearts. But we will do it together, and sooner rather than later. As a father to be, it is my responsibility to provide sustenance and a safe home for my family. But that home . . ." his voice became very serious, ". . . should not be a deep and sunless hole in the ground, a tomb shared with the bodies of hundreds of slain, even though their deaths were not intended. That is why I shall make proper provision for my wife and child, and if I am fortunate our children and, in the fullness of time, their children as well.

"I am sorry," he ended quietly but firmly, "this is a decision that is not susceptible to argument."

THIRTY-TWO

During the short stay in the laboratory which followed the visit to the Paramount Chief of the Algonquin Nation, and in spite of some nonsubtle questioning on my part, Declan did not elaborate on the plans for the future provision for his family and descendants. So far as I can detect he has not made further mention of it to Sinead, either. Normally he is not a secretive person, and I hope that he is formulating a plan and was not merely expressing a wish.

"Since neither of them require further training in ship handling or in the use of my other mechanisms, more time is being spent on discussions of this world's religious beliefs and philosophies. Both of them have keen and above all flexible minds that I enjoy seeing at work even though I do not always win the argument. But Declan's great bodily size and the monstrous long-axe he carries look strangely at odds with his growing aptitude as a debater.

"Except for the present visit to Cathay, I have decided that the constant revisiting of cities and cultures that are long familiar to me is no longer necessary for the conclusion of my report and may, in fact, be a psychological stratagem aimed at delaying its completion and the unwelcome recommendations to the Synod that it will contain.

"The present visit to the oldest and relatively most stable of this world's civilizations will be the last before the wagon is retrieved and I return to the Hibernian laboratory to complete the work that I was sent here to do."

They had long become accustomed to walking on each side and a few paces behind Ma'el, and it seemed to Declan that only the costumes of those around them were different. As the foreign servants of their master, the rough and unembellished clothing of Sinead and himself aroused no comment and had changed not at all apart from her having to return to the pretense of being a boy, but this was because no mere female, much less a foreign servant woman, would have been allowed within the richly draped and decorated resplendence of the inner audience chamber of His Celestial Majesty the Emperor of Cathay.

Ma'el's dress was not as elaborate or costly as that of the Emperor, and had he been guilty of committing such a blatant act of impoliteness as to compete with the other in the matter of finery, the remainder of his life would have been short indeed. Nevertheless, while he appeared as dowdy as everyone else in comparison to the godlike presence into which he had come, the old man made an impressive figure.

From his cylindrical, richly embroidered skullcap and full, silken robes to the jewelled slippers encasing his feet, he was arrayed in the quietly resplendent apparel of a Mandarin of the Osprey Rank. His hands, held loosely at waist level, were encased in metal-stiffened gloves whose fingers extended beyond the elbows on both sides. This was an indication that a highborn personage like himself would not allow his fingernails to be cut and was therefore incapable of performing any task with his hands and, in fact, required servants to feed, clothe, clean, and perform all of the necessary actions of a personal or intimate nature that his lofty rank forbade him doing for himself. Suspended from his neck and held in position on his breast by silken cords tied around the waist was the most important part of his apparel, a small brassard of gold.

Yellow was the color of the Imperial House. The brassard of precious yellow metal signified that its wearer was an important and trusted servant engaged on the personal and urgent work of the Emperor, that he should be offered no let or hindrance, and that he should be given all possible assistance in men, time, or material resources in his performance of that duty.

That brassard would have taken them in perfect safety from the eastern face of the Great Wall, across the mountains, rivers, forests, deserts, and the often-unruly people that lay between, to the Imperial Palace in Xian where they now stood. But Ma'el had decided, in the interests of saving time, to avoid those natural hazards by flying over them.

They walked slowly to within five paces of the high dais which bore the Imperial throne before Ma'el stopped, went down on his knees and then prostrated himself, arms outstretched on the processional carpet while Sinead and Declan did likewise. The Emperor made a small, permissive gesture signifying that the old man should rise and come forward to speak, but not so his two servants. They remained motionless and face down, for any movement might have been considered a threat to the Emperor, and the six massive and heavily armed statues ranged on each side of the Imperial throne, whose watchful eyes were the only parts of their bodies that seemed to move, would have come violently to life and killed them instantly.

Speaking in a soft voice which nevertheless seemed to reach every part of the audience chamber, Ma'el began to relate a fable which began and ended with a lie while the remainder contained the truth.

"Your Celestial Majesty," he said, "I am Ma'el. My father's father was given a task to perform by the former Emperor in the uncivilized lands beyond your western border. It was a mission of great political delicacy about which I would not wish to commit the impropriety of speaking in public, for at the time only the then Emperor and his principal advisor knew of it. Regrettably, circumstances including his untimely death prevented my grandfather from returning in person. He did, however, entrust his eldest son with the secret and through him his eldest son, my unworthy self, to report to you that the mission was successfully accomplished. I am also bound to return the symbol of Imperial trust and to renounce the high rank conferred on my grandfather, for I have no right to either."

There was silence for a moment, then the prostrate Declan heard the soft sound of slippers approaching and stopping beside Ma'el, a polite exchange of words as the brassard was removed and then the light clink and scrape of metal as it was placed on the lowest step of the Imperial dais. Only then did the Emperor speak.

"The personal loyalty to my illustrious predecessor," he said in a voice that was surprisingly strong to be coming from such a frail and ancient source, "that has been passed down to you in all its original strength is commendable. The symbol of office I shall reclaim but, in recognition and gratitude for your progenitor's services as well as your own exercise of discretion while returning it, the Order of a Mandarin of the Osprey Rank you shall retain for the remainder of your days. If there is anything else that you desire as a reward, be it riches, servants, a dwelling place commensurate with your position, or some other requirement, perhaps of a personal nature, you have but to name it. Rise. You have done well, Ma'el. You may speak."

Declan heard the soft rustle of the old man's silken robes as Ma'el rose to his feet and bowed low. "Your Celestial Majesty is most generous," he said, "but I neither need nor deserve material rewards for these poor services that have been done in the past. I am a man of learning, however, a philosopher and some say a magician, who finds himself in your court, an establishment where knowledge of the natural sciences has been unsurpassed for thrice a thousand years and where true magic abounds. I would welcome a chance to spend some time among your great philosophers, and to speak with and learn from them. This, Great Emperor, is the only favor I ask."

There was a short silence, and when he replied the Emperor's voice sounded disinterested to the point of boredom. "It is yours."

Thereafter Sinead and Declan were allowed to accompany Ma'el when his investigations took him into the hilly countryside outside the palace or during the night when, as palace custom dictated, his personal servant and his guardian were expected to sleep on the floor outside his chamber. At all other times, and provided they remained in the servants' area, they were free to go where they pleased because the self-acknowledged greatest minds in the world who occupied the Imperial College of Xian Palace would have found their presence a distraction during the weighty deliberations that were taking place there, and the old man had assured them that the assassination of a foreign visitor so soon after arrival, particularly when he had yet to reveal any useful information regarding the nations beyond the western wall, would have been considered a great waste as well as a grave impoliteness.

Forbidden the company of the great thinkers, they explored the rabbit warren of low-ceilinged service tunnels reeking of lamp oil and the even more smelly and horrendously over-crowded quarters of the thousands of slaves who were forbidden to show themselves unless something was required of them, and there they learned much. They did it by turning off their transla-tor collars, pretending that they could speak only in their native Gaelic and proving it by making many ridiculous and often humorous mistakes. But they used their earpieces to listen to the conversations of senior slaves that the speakers thought were pri-vate, and in this fashion they were able to learn more than Ma'el. But the old man had recently taken to inviting the learned and venerable Hsung Hwa, who had the finest intellect as well as being the most entertaining of his Xianese mentors, to his quar-ters every evening. As a result the first chance Declan had to tell him of what Sinead and himself had learned was when they were outside the palace in the late afternoon of the next day, where

Ma'el was to be entertained to a demonstration of kite flying and, after dark, a display of pyrotechnics.

Hsung Hwa's silk-tented chair carried by six of his servants was about twenty paces ahead, and Declan had to make a great effort of will not to arouse the suspicions of Ma'el bearers by dropping his voice when he spoke.

"Please listen carefully, Ma'el," he said. "I have no factual information, merely the overheard gossip of highly placed servants, but the talk is that you have aroused the suspicions of the Emperor. It is said that you appeared suddenly at night outside the palace gates, and try as they will, his countrywide army of Imperial spies is unable to uncover any evidence of your journey here. To him this means that your journey was undertaken in secret, that your progress was concealed by enemies wishing to overthrow the Emperor, and that your sudden appearance means that a uprising is imminent. It is rumored that you are shortly to be taken, tortured for whatever seditious information you possess, and killed. Sinead and I are unlikely to be spared. I strongly advise that we leave here without delay."

With a thoughtful inclination of his head, the old man said, "I expected that something like this was being planned for me, but not so soon. My work here is complete and there is no excuse for extending my stay other than intellectual pleasure, so I shall take your advice. The display of pyrotechnics is something you will not see elsewhere on your world, and I would not want either of you to miss it. I do not believe that I am in any immediate danger because the Emperor thinks it would be impossible for me to escape him. But if it will ease your minds, during our return to the palace this evening, I shall make an excuse to detach myself from Hsung Hwa, and Declan can stand guard while Sinead brings our vessel down from orbit."

Declan was glad that Ma'el had insisted on delaying their departure until after nightfall because the kite flying was a truly wondrous sight. Many of them were box kites whose silken sides bore brightly painted designs which, according to the old man, had a religious significance. Others took the form of outsized birds with wings permanently outspread, or giant bats or flying dragons. One of them looked like the shadow monster that Sinead had made with her hands to frighten off the sea raiders off Finisterre at what now seemed to be a long time ago. They looked particularly beautiful when the last rays of the setting sun lit them against the darkening sky. As the highest of them were overtaken by the deepening twilight, a series of sharp, closely spaced detonations dragged their eyes groundward to the lower slopes of their hill where fountains of stars in a dazzling variety of colors were bursting upward into the heavens. A thunderclap accompanied every star burst.

Declan found it difficult to take his eyes off them, but fortunately, not impossible.

"Look there," he said urgently, pointing behind them. "Men with swords, eight, no nine of them, coming out of the darkness above the shoulder of the hill. They probably expect us to be dazzled by the fireworks and unable to see them. Ma'el, we need the space vehicle, now!"

Hsung Hwa, who had been standing beside Ma'el, turned his head to follow the direction of Declan's pointing finger. The sight of the approaching men did not seem to surprise him, for he turned away without a word and, quickly for one of his advanced years, hobbled back to his carriage shouting orders to his slaves as he came. In a moment they were running down the slope. Ma'el's bearers, who had already abandoned their vehicle, were racing after them.

Sinead looked at the men advancing toward them, the light from the fireworks reflecting like stars off their swords. "Ma'el," she said quickly, "we need your vessel to make a transdimensional jump, there's no time to bring it down through normal space. Do you want to do it?"

Ma'el replied by withdrawing the chart and the remote-control screen from his cloak and tossing them to the ground where they were already unfolding for use. He said, "Your digits are smaller and faster than mine."

Slowly and with the confidence of their greater numbers the men advanced in line abreast, swords carried across their chests. It was too dark to see their feet, but Declan felt sure that they were marching in step. Each end of the line was curving forward into a crescent formation, the obvious intention being to encircle their victims. Knowing that was not a tactically desirable situation when there was only one defender trying to protect three, he sprinted toward the center of the line with his long-axe swinging in wide circles around his head.

They heard him coming, but now it was their eyes that were being dazzled by the fireworks display behind him while his had grown accustomed to the darkness. His first blow knocked away his opponent's weapon and, judging by the sound he made, smashed the other's sword arm as well. He continued the swing toward the next man in line, who tried to turn away and received the axe blade in the small of the back. That one dropped to the ground, immobilized by legs that would no longer work. Of the six that were left, four moved out of range of his weapon intending to encircle him while the other two began running toward Sinead and Ma'el.

Those two had to be stopped.

It took a moment and several prodigious swings of his axe to to break away from the four, and Declan was still several paces behind them when one of the two men grasped Ma'el by the cowl, baring his head and bringing the sword point to his throat, obviously intent on a capture and the extraction of information rather than a quick killing. Sinead was on her knees and looking down intently with both hands moving over the remote-control screen. The other man was closing on her with his weapon raised high to bring it down on the back of her neck.

For an instant a terrible fear took Declan as he thought of that small, beautiful body he loved being converted into bloody dead meat, with her bright, agile mind and healing skills that together had labored and coaxed and nagged and finally loved him back to life gone forever, and with them their unborn child. Unable to control his feelings, he filled his lungs and emptied

them with a sound, part scream of anger and pain at her expected
loss and part bellow of sheer rage so loud and terrible that it
frightened even himself. The men attacking Sinead and Ma'el
froze at the sound, giving him a chance to get close before both
turned to look at him. It was the last thing that they would ever
do because by then his axe was already sweeping toward them in
a wide, transverse swing that made a bloody end to both of them.

"This is difficult enough as it is," said Sinead irritably, her
attention still on her rapidly moving hands, "without you getting
blood all over my control screen. Can't you move the fight
away?"

"Thank you, Declan," said Ma'el quietly, and went on,
"Sinead, nullify the sound attenuators. When you bring the craft
in, it must make much more noise than the fireworks."

Declan moved clear of them and the four remaining soldiers
followed him, knowing that they would have to bring him down
before they could risk attacking the other two. They circled him
cautiously beyond the radius of his rapidly swinging weapon,
occasionally jumping forward to try to stab him in the side or
back as the axe head whistled past. He countered that by leaping
forward, too, and shortening the distance to the attackers in front
who retreated. Then one of then, plainly impatient with a game
that nobody was going to win, moved back several paces. Grasping his blade at the weapon's center of balance, he hurled it
spearlike at Declan's. The Hibernian dropped to his knees
quickly and the blade glanced off his shoulder, opening a long cut
in his forehead, eyebrow, and cheek as it spun away. Blood was
running into one eye, partially blinding him, but he was able to
see the thrown sword lying nearby. Still swinging the axe he rose
to stand over it, knowing that while it was at his feet there were
only three men with swords to contend with.

He swore as he saw the fourth man with what looked like a
short knife in his hand moving toward Sinead and Ma'el, but he
was too far away and too busy with the other three to do anything
about it.

Suddenly the hillside was lit by an intense blue light and

deafening, hissing scream as the space vessel emerged from its dimensional jump almost on top of them, bleaching out the light of the fireworks and reducing their thunder to a low grumble. For a moment the four remaining attackers stood paralyzed by fear so that he could have slain them easily, but instead he watched them run screaming down the hill while Sinead brought the vessel into a gentle but incredibly noisy landing. Carefully, she folded and put away the chart and remote-control screen and followed Ma'el into the vessel with Declan close on her heels. The soundproof seal hissed shut behind them and they could hear themselves think again.

"Declan, you're wounded," Sinead said in an angry, concerned voice. "That eye . . . Let me look at that eye before we lift off. . . ."

"Not yet," he said, and pointed through the forward screen into the valley where the fireworks display had ceased and the only lights visible were a few bobbing torches that were being carried by members of the fleeing crowd. Reassuringly, he went on, "My eye isn't damaged, just bloody, the cuts are above and below it. So first I want you to take us down there so that I can steal some of their abandoned fireworks. I might have a use for them. . . ."

THIRTY-THREE

. . . **D**eclan emains secretive regarding the setting up of a family home in Hibernia other than that it will not be in my laboratory, and his secrecy includes Sinead. His explanation for this is that if his plan proves not to be successful, only he will know the full measure of his disappointment. Both of them remain intensely loyal to me. Over the past year they have become much more than friends and protectors. But I know that if either of them had to make the choice between myself and the other one, the decision would not go my way.

"I could implant each of them with a CVI, which would bind them emotionally to me rather than each other, but that would only make of them willing but unhappy servants, and they are already willing and happy to serve me while loving each other. I am in great need of their assistance, but I will not do such a cruel thing to them.

"Instead I will break the most important precept in the canons of both the Commonality of Taelon and its Synod by revealing to a lower order of intelligent life the truth.

"Although not all of it . . ."

. . .

Sinead had sewn closed the wound, and covered half of Declan's face with what he thought was an unnecessarily large and foul-smelling pad, when she sat close beside him and lifted one of his arms to wrap it tightly around her waist. They had returned to orbit; both the sun and the moon were hiding somewhere behind the darkened world below them so that the stars that filled the sky were bright and beautiful and seemed closer than they had ever been before. She put her head on his shoulder and sighed.

"Ma'el," she said, "when will we be finished with all this traveling, and the killing even when we only have to watch it rather than being forced, as in Cathay, to take part in it? The way I feel these days, the constant fighting and needless cruelty down there on our world seems so stupidly wrong. With your Taelon knowledge, cannot you teach us to make our world a place where a child can grow and learn in health and safety?" She gestured at the crowded sky beyond the forward screen. "Look at the stars where you live, they are so lovely and serene and, and most of all, peaceful."

When Ma'el replied there was more pain and anger in his usually quiet voice than they had ever heard in it before.

"Believe me," he said, "the stars are not peaceful."

They were silent knowing that to ask questions would only delay the answers that were coming.

"You inhabit one small and at present unimportant world among many hundreds," he went on quietly, but with the angry edge remaining in his voice. "The peoples of some of them are less intelligent than yours and some, including the Taelon, are more. Most of these species have no idea of the fate that lies before them and a few, again including the Taelon, do. You know of the wanton cruelty and indiscriminate slaughter that many of your kings and emperors have meted out to their own people as well as those of neighboring countries to bring themselves to power, and the even greater crimes committed by them to maintain it. But those excesses are as nothing compared to the actions on a planetwide scale by the Jarridians, who begin by . . ."

"Wh—what does a Jarridian look like?" Sinead broke in. In the dim lighting of the control canopy her face had gone a sickly shade of gray and suddenly her body felt as stiff and unyielding as a statue.

"It is plain from the language of your body muscles," said Ma'el, gentleness returning to his voice, "that you already know. You had a timesight that you did not tell me about?"

"No." Sinead shook her head in agitation, then immediately contradicted herself. "I mean, yes. I was sleeping at the time and thought it was a nightmare, not real and therefore not worthy of mentioning. It was in a city of the far future, with tall buildings whose walls had more glass in them than bricks and smoothly paved streets crowded with people and shiny, brightly colored horseless coaches, and I could see and hear one of the metal birds flying high overhead. The thing, whatever it was, rampaged through the streets sending out thin bolts of lightning that burned and cut down the people even as they fled and made the vehicles explode into flames. The screaming was terrible to hear."

Her hold on Declan tightened as she went on, "It was like a squat, metal beast, or perhaps a beast encased in metal armor, but a beast it certainly was. Despite the entreaties of the men and women around it, it burned and killed and destroyed completely without mercy and nobody could stop it. I, I could not believe that it was real. Are you saying that it is?"

"The Jarridians," said Ma'el, "are real."

Declan felt the stiffness in her body begin to ease. Now that Sinead's worst fear was confirmed, some perverse streak in her nature was enabling her to regain control of herself.

She said calmly, "In the dream, I mean the timesighting, nobody there could stop the Jarridians. Can you?"

"No," said Ma'el, "not without help."

Declan said, "Sinead did not mention this to me, either, so I know nothing about the strengths or weaknesses of this seemingly unbeatable enemy. Will it come here?"

"Yes," Ma'el replied. "Sooner or later they will find your world."

"Terrible they may be," said Declan in a quietly furious voice, "but they will not find it an easy conquest."

"I know," said Ma'el, "and that is what gives me hope."

For a long, silent moment Declan and Sinead looked at each other, then she detached his arm from around her waist before she spoke.

"You say that you need our help and you must already know that you will have it," she said and, smiling, patted her waist, "at least until the expected event is imminent and, naturally, after I am safely delivered and the child is well. What do you want us to do for you? And you said that we gave you, or perhaps you were including your people, hope. Can you clarify that?"

It was Ma'el turn to be silent as he looked from one of them to the other. Finally he said, "Over the past year you have become my protectors and trusted friends. You are not my slaves nor are you bound to me in any way other than by your self-imposed bonds of gratitude and duty. In the light of the event to come, the duty of parents to care for their offspring becomes the prime consideration and is, in fact, an evolutionary imperative that supersedes any duty that you may think you owe to me. Both of you are free to leave my service, with my gratitude and what some people on this world would be called my blessings, at anytime you choose."

"Thank you, Ma'el," said Sinead. "But you haven't answered my question. We ask again, what help do you need from us?"

"And there is another question," Declan said before Ma'el could reply. "Why do we, a lowly and ignorant race by Taelon standards, give you hope?"

"I need help," Ma'el replied, looking at Sinead, "to recover my wagon, which contains treasure, devices, and records necessary for the completion of my report on your world. It must be brought back from the desert on what should be its final journey to Hibernia. This task can be accomplished within the physiological time limit imposed by the birthing and, as will shortly be explained, without risk to either of you. The second question . . ." he turned his eyes on Declan, ". . . will require time and in all probability a lengthy debate between us if it to be answered fully. I do not have the time to answer it now.

"Please attend to my words . . ."

. . . To return the wagon to Hibernia with the fewest possible risks, he explained, would mean employing the same ship and trusted crew as they had used on the way out. Unknown to Captain Nolan, Ma'el had placed a combination tracer and listening device in the other's cabin and he was aware, therefore, of both the ship's position and its reason for being there. At present it was three days from Alexandria where, after leaving Brian for nearly half a year in Egypt for reasons the diplomat had not mentioned to anyone, ti was returning to bring him home. Declan would land at night as close as possible to the ship's berth, make contact with the captain and enlist his help in recovering the wagon which would be cleared of its sandy protection to await him driving it back to the *Orla* for its return to Hibernia. There was no need for Sinead to take part in this routine matter since she and Ma'el would be watching over the entire operation from orbit. Ma'el showed him how to make his ear ornament and translation collar act as a long-range communications systems so that the three of them could speak to each other when necessary.

And so it was that Declan, flanked by Captain Nolan and Black Seamus presented themselves at the gates of the caravanserai. For sailors they looked strangely at ease on their mounts, but he supposed that the transition from the heaving deck of a ship to the saddle of a galloping horse was an easy one. He identified himself, unnecessarily since the guard detail seemed already to know him, as Declan the Hibernian and friends who wished words with their officer Bashir was with them in moments.

"Declan!" he cried. "I did not expect to see you alive, much less looking so well. Any friends of yours are friends of mine and are welcome here . . ." he looked at the fierce countenance of Black Seamus, and smiled, ". . . and this one I wouldn't want as an enemy. What can I do for you . . . ? But I forget my manners. Dismount and refresh yourselves and tonight we shall talk of that glorious battle and . . ."

"Thank you, Bashir," said Declan, "but again I am pressed for time. My master and the other servant are, elsewhere, so we will not be assisted by his magic or a screaming djinn. . . ."

"Relieved I am to hear it," said Bashir.

". . . But I must retrieve his wagon and the valuables it contains from their place of concealment in the desert. For that I need one of your officers and a mounted escort to convey them to Alexandria. That is if you can spare the men and we can agree a price."

"The escort would be happy to be led by you," Bashir said, and laughed, "whether or not you call down another djinn. Since that battle and rescue of the caravan, our warlike local sheik has left us in peace. So I can spare the men and you, Declan, my fierce and fair-minded friend, can set the price. But it will take a little time for the escort to be readied and provisioned for the journey. Please friends, dismount and take refreshment. . . ."

It was eight days later, *Orla* was three hours out of Alexandria, the sun was dying a spectacular death off their starboard bow, Ma'el's wagon was again tightly secured in its former position amidships, and Declan was looking forward to the evening meal in the captain's cabin. He had spoken to the orbiting vessel many times—the collar enabled this to be done in an undertone and it did not matter if some of the crew thought he was talking to himself—and mostly in soft and private words to Sinead.

Brian had gained several inches around his waist and looked to be his usual cheerful self but, Declan thought, there was a look in his eyes which suggested that he had matters on his mind that were making it difficult to hold his smile in place.

"Declan, it is good to see you again," he said, when they had finished the meal and more of Brian's wine had been poured, "even though your face is showing a few more scars. Perhaps you can pass the time amusingly for us by telling how you came by them, always bearing in mind that a certain amount of exaggeration for dramatic effect is expected. Drink up, friend, and tell us of your adventures."

Without returning the other's smile, Declan shook his head.

"Come, now," said Brian, "shyness sits oddly on such a large and heavily scarred man. The captain, Seamus, and I already know all about each other, your magician master and the young woman healer aren't here to entertain us although, since there is no female company to offend, we might talk about the women we have known. Were we to do that, however, Seamus would use it as an excuse to talk endlessly about the young woman in Cobh to whom he has lately become betrothed, perhaps the one foretold by Ma'el. We all wish him joy, but I do not want to listen to any more of his lovelorn conversations. You, at least, will spare me that fate."

Again Declan shook his head. "With respect," he said, "I will not."

They were all staring at him, surprised not as much by his reply as by the serious tone of his voice.

"You are trusted friends," he went on, looking from the captain to Black Seamus and ending with Brian, "and ones whose unique experience and advice will be of great value to me. For I, too, love a young woman. I will not list her abilities and attributes and strength of character because you know them and have already met her, and the gentle intensity of our love is something that we feel but will never speak of to others.

"She bears our child."

They continued to look at him so intently that it seemed that they had forgotten to breathe, and the lengthening silence made the sounds of the ship's timbers, the wind in the rigging, and the gentle, irregular tapping of the helmsman Tomas's wooden leg seem loud.

"This being so," he went on, feeling the warmth of embarrassment spreading over his face but ignoring it, "I must provide a safe and comfortable home for my wife and child, and the others that may come, so that they will not go hungry or in fear. Once I had such a home and the lands to support it, but in my headstrong youth I left, or rather I was forced out of the inheritance that was rightfully mine. Now I am mature and, I think, more thoughtful and aware of my responsibilities, so I want to return to my people and reclaim my home.

"That," he ended simply, "is why I need your advice and help."

It was Brian who broke the silence. He said, "Declan, I speak for all of us when I say that we will help you in whatever way we can. The way Ma'el and your young wife and yourself defended this ship and treated its wounded demands no less. But with respect, to me you always seemed uncomfortable in the role of a servant. If you feel yourself free to do so, will you tell us your family name and the position of the land that you wish to reclaim?"

Declan did so.

Brian slapped his hand so hard on the table that wine spilled over the rims of their goblets. "I *know* of these lands. I remember the sad and dishonorable story told about them. There was a great wrong done by a stupid, petty-minded, and cruel father to his only son who was driven to . . ."

He broke off, his eyes beginning to shine with the excitement of a challenge. "Oh, Declan, my friend, you have given us a puzzle whose solution will make this voyage pass quickly indeed. It is prime meat for the platter of a devious-minded person like myself, and it is a matter with which I can and will help you although I will, of course, disclaim all knowledge of it. But righting this particular and long-standing wrong will involve more than the settling of a longstanding family dispute over the ownership of a few paltry acres of land.

"Declan, you are, no, we will be plotting high treason!"

THIRTY-FOUR

   . . . **C**ontact is being maintained between the vessel in orbit and the sailing craft bearing my wagon, where Declan has ostensibly developed the habit of muttering to himself at odd times of the day or night. Since the revelation of his origins, the majority of the conversations have been between him and Sinead, who was irritated at him for not first telling her of his intentions regarding setting up a home for them. His response was that, to avoid disappointing her, he had not wanted to reveal his hopes and plans until they had a reasonably good chance of coming to fruition, which they now have. She said that if he got into trouble he would need a healer and she wanted to return to the surface and accompany him on the venture. I advised against this because of her physiological condition, and Declan agreed with me and expressly forbade her to do so.

"On a surface voyage as well as in orbital flight there is little for such short-lived, impatient people to do except look at the sea or, in her case, the stars, so that they have begun to discuss my problems, although often it felt to me like an interrogation in depth rather than a discussion. It is becoming increasingly difficult to conceal information from them and they are learning more about my work than subjects of an investigation should be allowed to know.

"They are engaging my mind with the empathy and persistence of Companions, and with the counsel of my fellow Taelons no longer available to me by my own choice, I find their concern strangely warming.

"Sinead had another timesighting. The episodes are spectacular in their detail but irregular in the intervals of manifestation. It frightened her badly, as it frightens me, because if my planned recommendations to the Synod are to be followed, she should not be able to foresee these future events because they should not happen.

"With advancing age and the diminishing faculties that isolation from the Commonality brings, I am becoming increasingly dependent on them, and again considered investing each of them with a Scrill weapon and the cyberviral implant which together would greatly increase their physical and mental powers as well as binding them emotionally to me to the exclusion of their present feelings for each other. But this would not have been fair to them because, as well as the strong emotional bond they have formed for each other, they remain faithful to me and their minds are already of admirable quality. I have finally decided to let them follow their own inclinations and not to interfere in any way.

"By Earthly good fortune rather than through the intervention of Taelon technology, the surface vessel *Orla* carrying my equipment made a fast and uneventful journey to Cobh."

Once again Declan strode through the wide, cloth and garment-hung entrance of the tailoring establishment and bath house of Padriag of Cashel to stop before the long garment cutting table. The old tailor and his seamstress wife looked as though they had not changed position since the time of his first visit. Padriag moved his work aside, climbed stiffly to the floor.

"A good day to you," he said, smiling, "and pleased we are to see you again. You show a few more scars, and that helmet has seen serious use, but otherwise you look well. Is the young servant who was with you also in good health?"

Declan nodded his appreciating of the other's careful choice of words because at that time he had thought Sinead was a boy and the old tailor had known she was not.

"She fares well," he said, returning the other's smile, "in spite of now being my wife." He tapped the side of his helmet. "She sends her sincere thanks for your contribution to keeping my head intact. I regret my haste and seeming discourtesy, but there is an urgent service that I would ask of you. That is if you and perhaps your many relatives are capable of performing it."

Padriag inclined his head and waited for him to go on.

Lifting his heavy satchel onto the table, Declan opened it and withdrew a scroll which he unrolled and held flat while the other read it with a face that grew paler by the moment.

"I can provide all that you need," Padriag said finally, "but it will take time. I will have to employ many of my female relatives as seamstresses, and my brother will need more help at the smithy to beat out all these weapons. The horses and other equipment are less difficult to obtain, but expensive. Have you considered the cost?"

"Yes," said Declan, reaching into his satchel again.

"And you must realize," Padriag went on quickly as if ashamed of having mentioned the subject of payment, "that with the best will in the world these arrangements cannot be kept secret. There will be talk and it is sure to reach the high and powerful of this land." He tapped the list with a bony index finger. "Declan, are you preparing to fight a war?"

"You have been honest and even kindly in your previous dealings with me," said Declan, temporarily avoiding the question, "which is why I am asking for an additional favor. I know there will be talk, but I would like you to do most of the talking and to guide any wild rumors there may be back onto the paths of good sense. You might point out that I am not a threat to this province since I will be equipping and training my men outside Cashel and in full view of the King of Munster so that my warlike intentions must therefore lie elsewhere, and in the meantime the traders of this town will be benefiting from the gold I shall spend.

If asked I would be pleased to explain my plans to your king, but not the position of their objective.

"The answer to your question is that I am preparing to fight a small war," he went on. "I will prepare for it so well, with cavalry and foot soldiers dressed and equipped uniformly and trained so highly that their very appearance and bearing will instill fear in an enemy, that it might not be necessary to fight it. At least, that is my hope.

"And to answer your unspoken question," he ended, "I have no purse of gold for you this time, but I hope that these, when melted down, with the gems and precious metals they contain, will cover the cost. If it should be necessary, more of them will be provided."

From his bag he took the golden shield, helmet, and wide, ornamental cuffs that had been given to him by the Aztecs and laid them on the workbench. Padriag's wife rose from her seat and hobbled forward for a closer look. For a long moment they neither breathed nor spoke.

"They, they are beautiful," Padriag said when he had again found his voice. "The craftsmanship, the delicacy of the embellishments . . . I have never before seen or heard of their like. It would be a crime beyond crimes to melt them down. If I may ask, how and where did you come by them?"

"They are gifts," said Declan in a voice that politely discouraged further questions, "from the rulers of a far country."

"My apologies, I did not mean to pry," said Padraig, and suddenly he smiled. "But you will not be surprised to discover that I have another cousin, a distant one who moves in high places, too high for us to have need of him, until now, that is. He is a usurer, a money lender among other things, and a provider of services to those in the highest places. In these islands and in Gaul he will know of rich Roman governors and kings who would welcome these as unique additions for display in their treasure vaults. Even with the exorbitant fee my cousin will charge for making the arrangements, the sale of this strange helmet and accessories undamaged and whole as they are will bring you a goodly sum that should will be enough for your purposes.

"It will, however, take a little time."

It took more than a little time. On his return, Brian and Captain Nolan said that it might take anything up to a year, and agreed with him that he should not begin choosing and training his force until he was able to pay and equip them. Black Seamus would not have been averse to a long stay in Cork, since it would have allowed him more time with his Maeve. But Brian, regrettably, would shortly have to separate from them because he had to report back to his principals without further delay. So they sailed east and then northward past the ragged western edges of the kingdoms of Munster and Connaught to the harbor of Sligo. There Declan and Ma'el's wagon were disembarked in pouring rain within a short drive from the Strand Hill, their final destination, before *Orla* continued to its home port of Donegal town in the Kingdom of Tirconnel.

The night was wet, heavily overcast, and Ma'el's sensors reported nobody within visual distance but themselves when he drove the wagon into a narrow, steep-sided ravine and released the horse to find its own way home just as the space vehicle dropped to a silent landing beside him. Sinead ran to him and wrapped her arms so tightly around him that she seemed intent on squeezing the life out of his body while complaining that listening to him in her earpiece was not the same as having him there. Declan had no argument for that. But they had to prise themselves apart to help the old man transfer most of the wagon's contents to the space vehicle, after which it was concealed as it had been earlier in the desert by collapsing the walls of the ravine and covering it. Sinead made the dimensional jump into the laboratory where as soon as possible they resumed trying to squeeze each other to death, among other delightful things.

The days and nights, which were the same inside Ma'el's caverns, passed happily through the late summer into the autumn and winter with Sinead seeming to grow larger by the day. In a poor attempt at humor he had once called her "fat boy," but she had cried sorely and he did not do so again. She was afraid, or at least deeply concerned, and he thought he knew why. But in the intensity of his own concern his manner in broaching the subject that night was direct and not as gentle as he would have wished.

"I am a very large man," he said, "and you are a small woman. My own mother was small and perfectly formed and, I was told, very beautiful as are you. She died bringing me into the world. I have felt the movements, the kicking in your belly, and they are very strong. I—I am fearful that it will happen again."

Sinead blinked and looked away for a moment, and when she turned her eyes on him again they were wet.

"So that is what has been eating at you for these past weeks," she said gently. "I, too, am concerned but not afraid. Ma'el says that it seems to be a law of nature on this world that small women are attracted to large and even ugly men, look at Seamus the Black and his Maeve . . ." she smiled impishly, ". . . although you are not quite as ugly as he is. They mate with men who will give them big and healthy children, they have been giving birth to such children since time began, and as a rule they do not die while doing so. The deaths that occur have other causes. Besides, you forget that I am a healer, that Ma'el scanner enables me to look inside myself, and that so far all is well."

"You are sure?"

"As sure as I can be," she said, moving closer to him, "so ease your mind because there are other matters to concern it. And speaking of which, are you not being overambitious? I would be happy with you on a small farm or a . . ."

"No," said Declan firmly. "I want a secure home for my family to be, not one that can be threatened by robber bands or wars between neighboring tuaths. Besides, I do not see myself as a farmer. . . ." He broke off, then went on in an excited voice, ". . . You said that Ma'el's scanner showed you that everything was all right. Could you see if . . . Is it a boy? Or a girl?"

"Yes," she said.

"I meant," said Declan, "if you could see which it was?"

"Yes," she said again. "It is, or rather they are, one of each."

On Declan's next interdimensional visit to Cashel—Padriag no longer remarked on the fact that he appeared suddenly out of the darkness on foot and departed in the same fashion—Sinead warned him that she was nearing her time and would not be able to fly him there again until it was all over. But it transpired that Padriag's cousin, after an initial lack of success throughout Roman Britain, was reporting serious interest in the Aztec treasures from their own Hibernian Kingdom of Dalriada that was being led by an unobtrusive court advisor and diplomat called Brian O'Rahailley, but that the transaction was not expected to be completed until the late spring. Padriag, who seemed unusually knowledgeable about such matters for a tailor, listed the strategic and tactical advantages of fighting a war in the summer. Declan received the news with happiness and relief because it meant that he would be close to Sinead when she needed his reassurance most.

But when the time came, he was terrified rather than happy because she wanted more from him than spoken reassurances.

"Listen closely to me, Declan," she said in a voice that was firm and impatient between her increasingly frequent gasps of pain, "and stop shaking as if you had an ague. We cannot bring another woman in here even if I would trust myself to a local midwife, which I would not. But you are level-headed, have steady hands, and are not afraid of the sight of blood, all of which you proved when we took off the leg of Tomas the helmsman. This will be much easier for you, so stop shaking your head." A grimace of pain tightened her mouth for a moment before she turned it into a smile and said, "After all, you are only helping to take out what you already put in, so just follow my directions and we will both be all right. . . ."

She continued to give directions, not only during the double birth itself but for cutting and tying off both umbilical cords and slapping the newborns' bottoms until they cleared the fluid from their lungs with thin wails of protest, and for removing the afterbirth. Again at her direction, Declan and the old man gently washed the blood from the infants' bodies, and the boy, who was in Ma'el's arms, began crying again until a thin, Taelon fingertip was placed gently in his mouth and he sucked at it and was quiet.

Declan placed the girl on Sinead's breast, and Ma'el, his eyes seeming to be larger and softer than usual, did the same with the boy before they tucked a warm blanket around all three of them.

Declan looked down at Sinead, unable to find any words that would convey what he was feeling while she looked up at him. Never before had he seen a woman look so pleased and proud of herself.

"They're very hungry," she said finally. "I'm fortunate that there weren't more than two of them."

THIRTY-FIVE

It was a strange force that Declan led, too small to be considered an army that would worry the tuaths and small kingdoms through which it passed, and a little too large and well-disciplined for them to be mistaken for a band of marauding robbers. Even stranger, but more reassuring, was the fact that while his men were more than capable of living off the land by going out and taking what they needed in the way of food or reluctant female company, they did neither of these things. Instead they remained close to their tents, spent the daylight hours engaged in fighting drills and kept no company but their own while Declan replenished the supplies for men and animals by paying the local farmers and town merchants a fair price for them.

After one look at his size, weapons, and scarred face, they thought better of trying to ask an unfair price.

The traders were happy as were the local clan chiefs and minor kings who exacted their tithes for these transactions. When anyone asked about his intentions he would reply that he was on the way to settle a land dispute involving a small kingdom, which he would prefer not to name, in the far west of Connaught.

And now he was here.

The territory stretched from the lower slopes of the Nephan Beg mountain to the eastern shore of Loch Conn and enclosed three large towns, many farms, a lake fishery, fields well populated with cattle, and all dominated by a sprawling, uneven castle of stone and wood that covered the top of a low hill. It was a land that was fertile but with too many rocky outcropping to make its cultivation easy, and it was doubly beautiful in that he had not expected ever to see it again and because it was his home.

He halted his men within clear sight of watchers in the castle but far enough from the line of defenders placed across his path to make it clear to them that, even though his force was better equipped and outnumbered theirs by two to one, he did not intend to attack at once. Instead he led his horsemen forward until they faced the other line at a little more than speaking distance, then he dismounted and walked forward in the prescribed manner to show that he wanted talk before fighting.

The defending line ranged from the old to the very young. A little over half of them carried swords and shields; the rest looked as if they had been called from the fields in haste and bore only their farming implements, and only ten of them were mounted. One of these, a huge, white-haired man of enormous girth who carried a long-axe that was the twin of his own, dismounted and came forward to stop within two paces of him. Declan put out his hand and spoke first.

"Your hair is white, Liam Mor," he said, "and your horse must dearly love you when you are not on its back, but I see that you still favor the long-axe."

Big Liam moved closer to stare intently at Declan's face, the old eyes under the thick, white brows lighting up with recognition. "The face is badly marked," he said, laughing, "and I hope you seriously chastised your barber for it, but . . . young Declan, is it you?"

The question was unnecessary because their handshakes changed suddenly to bear hugs that lasted for several moments before they broke apart with reluctance and Big Liam spoke very seriously.

"Good it is to see you well, young Declan," he said, "but now we know that we must do battle."

"But not this day," said Declan, smiling, "perhaps not ever. I have something to show you." He nodded toward the castle. "Does he still live, and is he watching?"

"He lives but not, I think, for long," said the other, glancing at Declan's weapon, "whether it is your long-axe or his slow, wasting illness that takes him. He is in a pitiable state, if there is any pity in your heart after what he did to you. His wife and her two sons—she gave him no other children—have been running the kingdom as best as they are able. They will be watching."

Declan nodded and pointed to the watch tower on top of a nearby hill. "As I remember," he said, "the stone and woodwork of that structure was unsafe and it was abandoned to the weather. Have you a use for it now?"

"No," said Big Liam, looking puzzled, "we await a large enough storm to tumble it."

"Good," said Declan, and turned briefly to give a pre-arranged signal to one of his wagon drivers who, moments later, began walking carefully toward the tower carrying a heavy urn. Smiling, he went on, "I'm going to meet my man there, place the device, and return at once, so there's no need for that overlarge body of yours to follow me up and down the hill."

Big Liam gave a huge sigh of relief and said, "Bless you, Declan."

When he returned he spoke to his men, but loudly enough for the mounted defenders to hear him as well. "Listen well to me. A device has been placed inside the tower which will make a very loud noise. Everyone, move well clear, then the horsemen will dismount and be ready to pacify their animals when it happens." To Liam, he added, "I filled that jar with fireworks powder from Cathay. I hope there was enough to . . ."

A tremendous thunderclap rent the heavens and shook the ground under their feet. The roof and wood interior of the tower rose high in the sky like pieces of a burning fountain and its stonework burst open into bright red cracks and tumbled onto the hillside. Smaller pieces of rock and dust fell around them like a stony rainstorm.

". . . There was enough," Declan said to Liam when the dust and smoke had cleared and they could hear each other again, then he added, "You have seen what I can do. Know that my force will take no hostile action against your people here unless they first offer violence to me, or if I do not return unharmed to them before sunset. I apologize for making these unnecessary threats to you, for I know you to be neither witless nor suicidal." He nodded toward the castle. "Now I would like to speak with himself."

"Alone?" said Liam in surprise. "Without your personal guards?"

Declan clapped the other on one massive shoulder. "When serious talking has to be done," he said, "I prefer the company of a sensible and honorable enemy rather than a too-loyal and perhaps excitable friend."

They remounted their horses and walked them slowly through the line of defenders towards the castle and into its courtyard where a groom, too aged and infirm by far to join the other servants in the defense of their king, took their mounts. Except for the empty echoing of their feet on the stone-flagged corridors they walked in silence to the audience chamber and almost to the throne itself before Declan stopped and gave a small bow. Liam Mor opened his mouth, but the king held up one skeletal hand for silence.

"I know who it is," he said in a voice that was even more fragile. "What does he want, or do I know that, too?"

Declan cleared his throat, silencing Liam once again. Firmly, he said, "I can speak for myself, Father, and I will begin by telling you what I do not want."

He paused to look at the woman in the chair beside the old king and her two sons standing on each side of them. The queen, who had hated Declan as a child and worked constantly to drive him away so that one of her then very young sons would inherit, was still a handsome woman, but her features were almost disfigured by the fear she was trying vainly to hide. Her two sons, who were scarcely into their twenties now, were armed and plainly not afraid. The dark-haired one was staring at him, his lips pressed into a thin, bloodless line and arms folded tightly across his chest. The redhead was gripping the hilt of his still-sheathed weapon with knuckles white and looking as if he was about to do something brave and stupid. Declan did not want that.

If the redhead attacked him then so would his brother and, out of loyalty to his king, so would Big Liam. He did not want to be forced into killing anyone here, especially not the aging weapons master, Liam. It was time to use the subtler weapons of words.

"I have returned home," Declan went on, "But I do not want it to be a home freshly splashed with the blood of my father and his family and friends. You know of my forces and have seen what devastation I am capable of inflicting on this castle and the buildings in the nearby towns. . . ." He was not telling the entire truth, but this was not the time to tell all of it, that he had used more than half of his store of Cathay black powder in demolishing the watch tower. ". . . You must already have realized that if any harm was to be done to me here, a terrible and merciless fate would befall everyone serving this house and the kingdom it rules. My men are well-trained and disciplined, they obey my every word, and they would be frightful in their anger if any harm should come to me here. You should know also that they are being well rewarded for their work in helping me win this dispute and, if it can be accomplished without loss of life on either side, they will be doubly rewarded and I shall be very well pleased."

The dark-haired son was looking thoughtful, the redhead's grip on his weapon had eased and he was frowning in perplexity while their mother's face was showing suspicion rather than fear. Her eyes moved from Declan to her two sons and the king before she turned them on him again.

"But what," she said, speaking for the first time, "is to happen to us?"

"I am reliably informed," said Declan, without saying that the information had come from the very knowledgeable diplomat and spy, his friend Brian of Tirconnel, "that your kingdom has seen difficult times over the years since I was last here, with cattle raids along the southern border and incursions by neighboring tuaths seeking expansion and who thought that a king too ailing to take up arms against them would offer little resistance. But there was resistance, from you and your sons, who with great effort and difficulty and at times subtle statecraft, were able to maintain the kingdom within its original borders. Those difficulties would be reduced, and I would be grateful, if you were to remain here to advise and assist me in the future ordering and defense of this land of ours. However . . ."

The woman and her sons were watching him intently as he raised a cautionary finger toward her and went on, ". . . You may remain as queen but neither of your sons will inherit the throne. If at any time you should think otherwise, and plot against me, you will be banished and your sons will not live long to regret their error. Is this clearly understood by all of you?"

They did not reply but their expressions said that it was. It was his father who broke the silence.

"I, too, regret an error," he said in a voice so weak and close to a whisper that it sounded like the wind rustling through long grass.

A once powerful, broadly built, and fearless warrior king shaven down to a near-skeleton by age and wasting illness was a pitiable sight, Declan thought, and he felt the last of his anger and hatred drain from his mind. He moved closer, seeing out of the corner of his eye the redheaded son's hand tighten on his sword hilt and then loosen again.

Before Declan could speak, his father went on, "I regretted it soon after you left us, no, were driven to leave by me. A child cannot be held responsible for the death of his mother in childbirth. Perhaps the midwife shared some of the fault, but none of it was yours. But in the madness of my grief and stupidity I would not see this until long after you were gone." His voice strengthened a little. "I hereby forbid my queen, her sons and you, Liam Mor, or any of my people to raise a hand to defend me, for I know what I have done and the fate I deserve.

"Tell me, Declan, am I to die?"

"Yes . . ." said Declan.

He took a long step forward and going down on one knee he grasped his father's hand, but carefully because the fingers were as fragile as the bones in a bird's wing.

". . . But not before you have seen my wife, Sinead," he went on, "and held on your knees the boy and girl who bear our name. And not before you yourself as the reigning king are ready to die surrounded by your family and friends.

"With your permission I will leave you now," he went on quickly, because emotion in grown men, especially in himself, made him uncomfortable. "Liam Mor will want to stand down his men and I must withdraw mine and set up camp. You have many matters to discuss among yourselves. Take time to consider them well and then send word of the result to me."

He bowed again, looked into his father's shining eyes, then turned quickly to leave.

They were approaching the courtyard when a sudden, flat-handed blow struck his back, sending him staggering almost to his knees.

"Young Declan," said Big Liam, "that was well done. You will be a good king."

In his ear ornament he heard the voice of Sinead saying softly, "He is wrong, Declan. I have had a timesight. You will be a great king."

And so it came to pass that Declan returned to his home and his father to the position of Ionadacht, the first lieutenant of the clan and heir to the kingdom. With him came Sinead and the two children, who increased in number to five—another boy and two more girls, all of whom grew up to be as strong and tall as himself or small and slender and comely like their mother. After a period of initial distrust and polite hostility, the queen and her two sons accepted the situation and worked hard and well for the kingdom. When his father succumbed to his illness, the old queen followed him to the grave within a few days. She had been a hard, ambitious, and gifted woman and healthy for her years, but it seemed that she had not the will to go on living without his father and there was nothing that Sinead's healing arts could do about that. Her two sons married well into the reigning families of neighboring tuaths, for love, Declan suspected, as well as statecraft, because the two princesses were beauteous and the two small kingdoms concerned joined with his and made it one of the strongest in all Connaught.

But strangely and in spite of many urgings, Declan made no attempt to use his power to expand further. His specially trained and fiercely able soldiers had either married locally or been rewarded and gone their own ways while his own young people were trained to replace them if or when the need should arise. Although he had learned the ways of war in many foreign countries as well as from orbital observations of great generals at work, Declan was an exceptionally gifted commander in the field who seemed more concerned with the maintenance of peace and the prosperity that went with it than the waging of war, and he became respected more than he was feared throughout the great provincial Kingdoms of Hibernia.

Twice he was invited by his peers to the Hill of Tara, there to submit himself for election to the position of Ard-Ri, the High King, a station open only to those of proven courage and exemplary character. But graciously he refused the ultimate honor saying that he had matters requiring attention at home which involved him in enough responsibility.

The matters included secret visits to and by Ma'el. There was a small, natural cavern under the castle that had been used as a store in times of siege. Declan had caused it to be deepened and enlarged and had then sealed off its only known entrance with a massively thick wall of stone and by tumbling the roof of its access tunnel. It was thought that the chamber housed Declan's treasure and that there was a secret entrance, but if so its position had never been revealed to anyone, not even to the children or his most trusted advisors. This was because the most used way in and out was by the operation of the dimension-folding mechanisms on Ma'el's spacecraft.

Declan and his queen, Sinead, grew old; their children, with the exception of their first-born boy twin and heir called Mal after his godparent, left them to prosper or otherwise to be happy in other parts of Hibernia or far beyond, and the kingdom was stable and its people as content as they could hope to be in a still violent and uncertain land.

But there were other matters of importance for the present as well as the far future for them to discuss and settle with the person they still regarded as their friend and master in his laboratory under the Hill above the Strand.

THIRTY-SIX

From the final comments and entry in the report on sapient Earth peoples, cultures, levels of technology and
future philosophical development by Investigator Ma'el on
the concluding Day 131,278 . . .

I have already forwarded my strong
recommendation to the Synod that
Earth and its people not be approached or exploited in any fashion by the Taelons until they have achieved their full intellectual
and philosophical maturity, and my reasons for advocating that
they then be given the status of our first non-Taelon Companions were given in detail. But my recommendations are being
and will be ignored. I know this because I have given the timesight to the human species and one of them, the being Sinead,
who sees far into the future with remarkable detail and clarity,
has seen the presence of the Taelons on Earth nearly two millennia hence, as well as some evidence of smaller, clandestine
visits in the interim.

"For this reason I intend to conceal the full report lest it
reveals present weaknesses which would enable you to take
advantage of these people. Two copies will be hidden elsewhere
awaiting the arrival on the future scene of a Taelon or a local
Protector with, I trust, more philosophical insight and social
responsibility than the Synod is currently displaying.

"It remains only for me to bid farewell to my short-lived

Earth friends and protectors without revealing too much of what their race's future is to be.

"The report of Ma'el the Investigator is concluded."

It was a small but strongly built crypt with walls and arching roof of well-fitted stone that would survive, Sinead said, until its discovery two millennia hence by the future protectors Marquette and Boone. By then it would be covered by a drinking house in a small town called, by the people of the time, Strandhill. Its exact location would be given, in the Taelon language, by a message inscribed on a mosaic close to but not in the tomb of Declan. . . .

"I hate talking about your tomb like this," she said, looking from Ma'el to Declan with tears close to her eyes. "You should not be walking on the hillside and climbing about in this hole in the ground. Your legs aren't what they were and, and I don't want even to think about you dying."

"It will happen sometime," Declan said, smiling. He rested his hand briefly on her head which, in spite of her advancing years, was still thickly covered by long hair that remained the color of a starless night. He felt the aching in his chest, the constant thumping of the veins in his head, and the even more intense pain of the inevitable separation from her, and silently he added, "It will be sometime soon."

When she remained silent he went on softly, "It seems wrong to me that my memories, our memories, and the thoughts and dangers, and most of all the love of the past and present that we share, should die with us. That would be wasteful on somebody's part. Do you remember that Algonquin medicine man telling us about the body of his newly dead chief? He said that the body was but an empty tent whose former occupant had gone somewhere to do something else." He laughed gently. "I would not like to spend all my time in his happy hunting grounds chasing buffalo, but wherever I do go, I would like you to follow me there."

"I will," she said. For a moment she blinked her eyes rapidly, then she laughed and said, "Declan, you're beginning to sound like a follower of the Christus. Master, where do the Taelons go when they die?"

Ma'el inclined his head in the way that meant he was not going to answer the question, but this time he surprised them.

"My race is long-lived," he replied, "and, except in rare and usually calamitous circumstances, our lives end only when we consider that they have been lived to their full intellectual and emotional capacity and we choose to end them. We have, therefore, no great desire to live another even longer and possibly eternal life. For us this remains a subject for philosophical debate and speculation but we have, however, no direct proof that an afterlife does not exist. The Kimera are said to have gone somewhere, but . . . Perhaps I will be surprised."

"But if you don't have to die, Ma'el," said Sinead, "please stay with us. We don't want to lose you, not yet."

"And I do not want to part from you," said Ma'el, looking into the heavy casket with its stone lid that awaited him, "who are my protectors, trusted assistants, and only true friends. But it is better that we part now for two reasons. By the Taelon measure of longevity, you have not long to go, and you should live the remainder of your lives knowing that you will be free of my interference and, more importantly, that the two of you may have accomplished more for the ultimate survival of both our species than any other human beings in your past and future history. There remains only the one service that you can do for me."

"You know," said Sinead quietly, "that it will be done."

"I know," said Ma'el, "but in the time left to you I must know that you fully understand my instructions and that they will be carried out."

Sinead nodded calmly. She had not taken offense at Ma'el's words because she knew that he was deeply troubled and no criticism had been intended.

"It is plain from your timesightings," Ma'el went on, "that the Synod has and will ignore my recommendations, as they would my report if I were to transmit it. Instead there is one copy of it left in the spacecraft hidden under your castle and another concealed in a location unknown to you. Sometime in the far future they will be discovered by someone who will study my report and, I hope, fully understand its implications."

Ma'el paused for a moment, stepping into the casket and sitting rather than lying down in it before he continued, "They must understand the significance of the mosaic, and of the faces and symbols surrounding mine. This planet's sapient species is a particularly savage and cruel one, although not by the standards of some of those found among the stars. There are wars fought, viciously and utterly without mercy, in which thousands lose their lives for ridiculous or trivial reasons. There are totally unnecessary and incredibly painful human sacrifices, and torturing and bloody violence performed for a few moments of gratification such as those perpetrated by many of the Caesars, although they were not the only offenders by far. Countless lives of members of an already short-lived species are being shortened further, all too often without mercy, without reason or even without thought. To a civilized entity this planet is horrendous, a cultural nightmare which is, regrettably, only one world among many. But it is not entirely bad, and that is what gives me hope.

"For even amid the worst of the carnage and suffering," he went on, "there is increasingly being displayed a high order of bravery, of self-sacrifice and of compassion allied to an indomitable will to survive and surmount the worst that man or nature can throw against you. The behavior of the Followers of the Christus in the Roman arena is only one example. There is a small but growing awareness that showing mercy is not a weakness but a philosophical strength, and that might is not necessarily right.

"I have observed this in you, Declan," he continued, "and seen its increasing presence in others. The cause stems from the influences of the small but growing number of thinkers and philosophers and lawgivers who have arisen among you, but mostly it is due to the prophets and teachers who are awakening in you the racial conscience of what is truly right by spreading the words of your various gods who, for the most part, teach love and respect rather than blind hatred of a neighbor regardless of their strength, weakness, opposing beliefs, or skin pigmentation. . . ."

Without interrupting his measured flow of words, Ma'el slowly lay back and folded his hands across his chest. The high sides of the casket gave his voice an added resonance as he went on, "If this trend continues, and if you are given enough time to benefit from it, your people will reach a degree of philosophical maturity and civilization unparalleled among the cultures of the explored galaxy, and will remain strong with these qualities intact so that we will be able to withstand any threat from the Jarridians or anyone else. That is the reason for the background subjects of the mosaic. They are there for those who will later have the ability to see and understand the implicit philosophical message that the people of Earth and the Taelon should be joined as equals.

"Together we would be unbeatable. But if we fight each other, all hope for the survival of this world and the countless others that fill the night sky will be lost. Farewell, my friends, and please go now."

"But, but we can still talk," Sinead protested, tears coming to her eyes. "About the old times, the things we did together and, we've time to say a proper goodbye. You aren't dead yet."

"No," Ma'el replied gently, "nor do I intend to die for some time." He tapped the back of one hand with the fingers of the other. "You have seen what lies under this shell, the seemingly insubstantial patterns and structures of force that are my true body. Know, then, that all the physical work that you can do for me is completed. In the fullness of time and if our plans reach fruition, you will have the thanks of the entire Taelon species, and you already have mine. But from now onward I must work without this physical body covering, and alone.

"Please, close me in."

As the heavy cover was sliding into place, Ma'el looked up at them with his large, soft eyes and lifted one hand in a gesture that was more like a benediction than a farewell.

.   .   .

After the death of King Declan the years passed quickly for Sinead. She grew old and feeble and even her long, night black hair was showing the gray streaks of dawn although her mind, she told herself, remained young. Deliberately she took little part in the affairs of the kingdom, because her son the king and his queen loved her but were sure that she was too old and frail to be burdened with the affairs of state. So she pleased herself greatly by playing with her grandchildren until they, too, became young men and women with children of their own, and she was left with the timesightings and her memories that were so clear in sight and sound and touch that she was almost reliving them.

Some of the timesightings were so strange that she could not understand what she was seeing and others, especially those concerning the almost magical devices and abilities of the healers of that future time, made her gasp with excitement and wonder. Some were so terrifying that she was glad they were of a distant time and could not affect her as a person. Others were happy because in them she saw another and younger Declan, although that was not his name, who was a Protector of a Taelon Companion called Da'an. She felt pride in his daring adventures and almost jealous because he loved a comely young woman of the future who was not herself.

She remembered the first meeting with her Declan, and her early hatred of him that had slowly changed to a depth of love so great that she could still not fully understand how it had happened, and the incredible gentleness of that great, strong body when it enfolded her and the passion of their lovemaking. Inevitably that led to the more recent memory of the time when she had held his dying body in her arms and he had smiled at her for the last time.

Then there were the memories of his entombment, of him being laid to rest among the other great warrior kings and queens of history, in the time and tradition-hallowed place where he had never expected to lie.

But he did not lie there.

Instead he sat on a stone chair in a burial passage parallel with the one where a thin wall of clay concealed the mosaic of Ma'el. It depicted Ma'el surrounded by representations of some of the Earth gods, prophets, philosophers, and lawgivers—Buddha, Confucius, the great Amun-Ra of the Egyptians, and Quetzalcoatl, the Aztec god of death, resurrection and civilization, and the Christus—all of whom in greater or lesser degree had influenced Ma'el's investigation and who would, he had hoped, likewise influence the thinking of the Taelons so that they would realize that the people of Earth were not merely a resource for exploitation but worthy of becoming their first other world Companions. The mosaic gave directions in Taelon script for finding Ma'el's tomb when the time came for its discovery close on two millennia in the future.

Declan was dressed in royal robes, a simple crown rested on his head and at an unusual and awkward angle across his lap he held a sword whose blade pointed in the direction of his castle and the location of Ma'el's buried space vehicle. On its hilt there was an inscription in Taelon that proclaimed to those who would later come to see, and to understand what they were seeing, that here was not only a great king but the First Protector of the Taelons on Earth.

But she was becoming selfish in her old age, Sinead thought, and her druidic beliefs were being influenced by other teachings. Her work here was done and her timesights into the far future, although confusing, suggested that ultimately all would be well on Earth and in among the stars. All that there was left for her to do was to wait until she could be with her beloved Declan again.

And, if a place could be found for a Taelon in the human hereafter, the gentle Ma'el.

ABOUT THE AUTHOR

JAMES WHITE was the author of the Sector General novels
and lived in Portstewart, Ireland.